D0051510

FULL CURL

CALGARY PUBLIC LIBRARY

MAR _ 2018

CALGARY PUBLIC LIBRARY

MAR _ 2018

FULL CURL

A Jenny Willson Mystery

DAVE BUTLER

DUNDURN
TORONTO

Copyright © Dave Butler, 2017

All rights reserved. No part of this publication may be reproduced, stored in a retrieval system, or transmitted in any form or by any means, electronic, mechanical, photocopying, recording, or otherwise (except for brief passages for purpose of review) without the prior permission of Dundurn Press. Permission to photocopy should be requested from Access Copyright.

All characters in this work are fictitious. Any resemblance to real persons, living or dead, is purely coincidental.

Cover image: ©Alastair Wallace/shutterstock.com
Printer: Webcom

Library and Archives Canada Cataloguing in Publication

Butler, Dave, 1958-, author
    Full curl / Dave Butler.

(A Jenny Willson mystery)
Issued in print and electronic formats.
ISBN 978-1-4597-3903-1 (softcover).--ISBN 978-1-4597-3904-8 (PDF).--
ISBN 978-1-4597-3905-5 (EPUB)

I. Title.

PS8603.U838F85 2017   C813'.6   C2017-900100-0
                                      C2017-900101-9

1 2 3 4 5   21 20 19 18 17

We acknowledge the support of the **Canada Council for the Arts,** which last year invested $153 million to bring the arts to Canadians throughout the country, and the **Ontario Arts Council** for our publishing program. We also acknowledge the financial support of the **Government of Ontario,** through the **Ontario Book Publishing Tax Credit** and the **Ontario Media Development Corporation,** and the **Government of Canada.**

Nous remercions le **Conseil des arts du Canada** de son soutien. L'an dernier, le Conseil a investi 153 millions de dollars pour mettre de l'art dans la vie des Canadiennes et des Canadiens de tout le pays.

Care has been taken to trace the ownership of copyright material used in this book. The author and the publisher welcome any information enabling them to rectify any references or credits in subsequent editions.

— *J. Kirk Howard, President*

The publisher is not responsible for websites or their content unless they are owned by the publisher.

Printed and bound in Canada.

VISIT US AT

 dundurn.com | @dundurnpress | dundurnpress | dundurnpress

Dundurn
3 Church Street, Suite 500
Toronto, Ontario, Canada
M5E 1M2

CHAPTER 1

OCTOBER 31

The high beams of two vehicles pushed a lonely tunnel of light through the black night of Banff National Park. With snow blowing from the top of the propane tanker in front of him, obliterating his view of the nearly deserted Trans-Canada Highway, Bernie Eastman felt as if he were driving his battered pickup truck in the vapour trail of a comet.

Leaving Calgary earlier in the day, he'd already passed through an early storm, a black wall of cloud that had, after devouring the Rockies, boiled from the mountains onto the prairies. It filled the valleys ahead of his truck, rolling and rumbling, erasing forests, peaks, and sky. Facing the dark void ahead, he'd imagined driving off the edge of the world.

Just as quickly, the violent storm had skidded eastward, leaving clear skies behind. That meant cold, and cold it was. Since noon, the temperature had tumbled from 4 degrees Celsius to -6 and was still dropping.

The two vehicles now continued west, ferocious winds threatening to toss them off the highway. Eastman felt their frightening power deep in his forearms as he wrestled with the steering wheel. He sympathized with the other driver when he saw the tanker shift left and then right. He could see his own headlights reflected in the tanker's driver-side mirror.

In the dark of the cab, Eastman heard the voice of one of his two passengers. "Why are we following this guy?" the man asked. "Go around him and quit wasting time."

"Hold yer fuckin' horses," said Eastman. "I don't wanna miss our turnoff."

As he spoke, the exit sign appeared out of the blowing snow. "Jesus Christ!" he yelled, cranking the steering wheel to the right, hard, hoping for the best. His blue crew cab fishtailed down the exit ramp and finally came to a jolting halt against a concrete guardrail, facing up the ramp, headlights still on, engine still running. Eastman let out his breath in a rush. He could see the Bow River, a menacing black ribbon, flowing only metres below the truck.

Eastman, a bearded bear of a man, still gripped the wheel in both hands, his meaty knuckles white. His two passengers sat in stunned silence. He heard their breathing, hard and fast. The passenger who'd snarled at him to pass muttered something in Spanish. Eastman couldn't tell if he was praying or cursing.

After a moment, Eastman pulled his hands from the wheel, flexed them once to get the blood moving again, then pushed his well-worn cowboy hat back on his head. "Whew," he said, breaking the silence. "That was a hell of a ride, eh, boys?"

Hearing no answer, Eastman reversed the pickup, steering it clear of the concrete barrier, and then simultaneously punched the gas pedal and turned the steering wheel, spinning the truck around until it faced the right direction. "Enough of this screwin' around," he said decisively. "We got work to do."

Eastman looked in the rear-view mirror to see Charlie Clark staring back, eyes wide in his thin, angular face. The lights of the truck's dash were reflected from the strips of duct tape that held Clark's old down jacket together. "Charlie, grab the goddamn light," he said, "and let's see what we got out here tonight." As he turned to watch the road ahead, he heard Clark rummaging through the litter at his feet for the hand-held spotlight, a million candles of light powered by the truck's cigarette lighter. He felt the blast of cold air on his neck when Clark wound down the back window. He saw the forest to their left dance in sudden illumination, so he dimmed the headlights and slowed the truck to a crawl. The search had begun.

Eastman watched the front passenger out of the corner of his eye. The black-haired Hispanic was still and silent. He saw his gaze following the spotlight that probed the darkness. The man had spoken little since they'd picked him up at the Calgary airport that afternoon.

In their first phone conversation a month earlier, the man's answers to Eastman's questions had been curt, almost rude. But Eastman didn't give a shit about manners. From that one call, he'd understood that the passenger was impatient, a man who thought highly of himself and little of others. In fact, no client had, in all the time he'd worked in the business, ever boasted about his IQ. So this was a man with a big ego and big money. For Eastman, who ran a business guiding and outfitting hunters, it was the money that mattered. If that kept flowing, he'd ignore the rest.

The passenger turned to stare at Eastman as though reading his thoughts. "Are you certain they're out here?" he said, obviously edgy. "I am not paying to be disappointed."

"Yeah," Eastman replied, perhaps too quickly. "They're here. I know what you want and I'll get it for you."

The passenger still stared at him, unblinking. His thick, black moustache paralleled the thin line of his mouth. Eastman felt the urge to drive his fist into the man's arrogant nose. He imagined the crunch of bone, the rush of blood, the warm satisfaction he'd feel when tears came to those dark eyes, if only for a moment. But he also sensed that crossing the man would be good for a bullet in the back of the head, sometime when he least expected it. Eastman fixed his gaze on the road.

They drove for an hour, crawling along the road, peering into blackness illuminated only by the spotlight. A light wind blew snow from the trees. Eastman saw the flakes flashing toward the windshield like tracers, streaks of brilliant white, hypnotizing. To the side, the spotlight reached far out into an open meadow. Then, abrupt and fragmented, it shone against the islands of pine and trembling aspen lining the road.

Eastman held the wheel with his right hand, the fingers of his left impatiently tapping the window as if he were transmitting Morse code into the forest around them. Behind him, he could hear Clark's nervous fidgeting. The beam bounced up and down, left and right, as if the road were filled with potholes or lined with speed bumps.

An hour later, Eastman, exhausted, glanced at the clock on the dash — 12:20 a.m. His tired eyes played tricks on him — shapes appearing and disappearing at the edge of the darkness. Despite the increasingly strident voice in his head urging him to call it a night, to abandon the search, he willed himself to keep going. He knew that his passenger expected to fly home late the next day with his objective met. And Eastman knew that by accepting the man's money, he'd committed himself to succeeding. He felt the keen edge of pressure. He desperately needed the money, though, and knew that if he succeeded on this trip, the man would be hooked. He would come back for more. In that first phone call, Eastman had offered a unique guarantee, and there was no question the man would hold him to it, one way or another. And so he must do everything he could to make this work. Giving up was not an option.

"Well, son of a bitch," he said with a sigh, his voice revealing his growing exhaustion. "We'll keep goin' a bit further and then we'll double back."

No sooner had he spoken than the spotlight picked up the glow of a pair of eyes at the far edge of a meadow. Eastman heard his passenger speak in a voice that was surprisingly calm.

"There," the man said. "Stop the truck ... *now!*"

From the height of the eyes above the snow-covered ground, Eastman knew the creature in the meadow was large, very large. In the darkness, he had no idea what it was. At this point, it no longer mattered.

"Keep the light on it," the passenger said softly and menacingly to Clark. "Do not let me down."

Eastman twisted left to see Clark grip the light as tightly as his two scrawny hands could muster. By the look in Clark's eyes, Eastman could tell that his assistant understood the consequences of failure. They'd be unpleasant, if not painful.

Eastman brought the truck to a slow stop on the shoulder of the road. The passenger beside him jumped out of the truck quickly and quietly, then slid a long, canvas-wrapped package from behind the seat and pushed the door shut with a soft click.

In the darkness, Eastman watched the passenger lean across the hood of the truck. His left arm supported a high-calibre rifle, elbow down. His right eye peered through the crosshairs of a 10X scope pointing into the meadow. Eastman focused on the man's right finger. It moved against the trigger, slowly yet firmly. The windshield exploded with sound and light.

At the far side of the meadow from the idling truck, the bullet found its target. Eastman turned his head to see, in the circle of the spotlight, a massive bull elk first drop to its knees and then topple onto its side, a dark hole in its right shoulder. A cloud of white flew up from the snow-covered grass when the antlers — seven thick points on each side — hit the ground. The fleeting shadows of a quartet of startled cow elk galloped into the darkness, eyes wide and glinting, heads held high. They did not look back. Eastman saw the bull's final exhalation drift upward in gauze-like steam that, for a moment, obscured his view of the thick band of the Milky Way. He smiled a tired smile. Mission accomplished.

CHAPTER 2

Early the next morning, the rising sun kissed the summit of Mount Bourgeau in a band of brilliant orange. Directly below, National Park Warden Jenny Willson turned off the Trans-Canada Highway west of Banff on an early patrol of the 1A Highway. Tucked tight against the Sawback Range of the Rockies, the 1A was a winding route that paralleled the Trans-Canada to the east of the Bow River and the Canadian Pacific Railway. During the summer, cars, RVs, and tour buses poked along the road, eager faces within scanning for elk and moose, bear and bighorn sheep. But now, Willson knew, she could drive from Banff to Lake Louise without passing another vehicle.

As a law-enforcement specialist and the first out of the parks compound that morning, Willson drove the newest truck in the fleet: a green-and-white, three-quarter-ton Chevrolet pickup topped with light bar and whip antennas, the doors bearing Parks Canada's crest — a crest that Willson had decided was either a beaver or a geriatric beagle. It was hunting season outside the park, so she'd bolted a shotgun beside the radio that kept her in contact with the park dispatcher, her warden colleagues, and the RCMP. She'd filled the locked metal box behind her with rescue and first-aid gear, fire extinguishers, and an investigation kit.

As she made her way north, she didn't concern herself with the campgrounds scattered along the 1A; they were gated for the winter. Passing stands of aspen now leafless and bare, she hummed the melody of the Tragically Hip's "At the Hundredth Meridian." Like a slide show on a clunky old projector or a black-and-white music video, flashbacks popped into her head as she drove. Summer nights wrestling and evicting drunken young campers. Finding lost children. Dealing with grizzlies and black bears that had destroyed coolers and barbecues foolishly left on picnic tables. In anticipation of those bruin encounters, she'd always carried a tranquilizer rifle rather than the 12-gauge beside her now. Because she'd seen so many park visitors do so many crazy things around bears, it had become an unspoken fantasy of hers to dart a camper and not a bear, who didn't know any better. Many times during the summer she'd found herself wondering — probably more than she should — what it would be like to sight in on a big human butt cheek and pull the trigger. She recognized that her own ass would be toast if she ever pulled a stunt like that, so she'd have to wait until her last day as a warden to fulfill the fantasy. Because it *would* be her last day. Still, the image of a clueless tourist waking up in a foul-smelling bear trap, kilometres from nowhere with a sore buttock and a drug-induced hangover, brought the first smile of the morning to her face.

Sipping the last of her coffee, Willson listened to chatter on the park radio, a sure sign that the park and its workers were coming alive for the day. She passed the Johnston Canyon Cabins, also closed for the winter. She saw no sign of recent activity in the new snow in the driveway, so she continued northward, taking the long right-hand curve leading to Moose Meadow. Despite the name, Willson hadn't seen a moose there in all her years in the park. She always reminded the sign-crew boss that he could call it Moose Meadow all he wanted, but it wasn't worth shit if he didn't tell the moose. The meadow was open, bordered on all sides by a thick forest of spruce, fir, and pine, likely a remnant of a forest fire many years ago. Now, it was a tangle of knee-high shrub willow and birch interspersed with patches of grass and islands of regenerating coniferous trees.

Through the forest, Willson saw the red blur of a CP Rail engine dragging freight cars eastward to Calgary. Her eyes were drawn to a congress of ravens busying themselves with something at the north edge of the meadow. Normally, avian activity like this was her clue that a wild animal had been on the short end of a collision with either a vehicle or a train. But here, eighty metres away from the quiet 1A Highway and at least twice as far from the railway tracks, she realized that it was something out of the ordinary, something worth checking out.

Willson radioed her office. "Banff Warden Office, three-five-eight."

In response, Willson heard the gravelly voice of Marilyn Bateman. "Warden Office, go, five-eight." Bateman had been the warden's chief dispatcher and paperwork queen for many years and had taken a shine to Willson when she'd arrived. On her first day on the job, Willson learned that if she wanted to know what was happening in the park, she should ask Bateman. With experience, Willson also knew not to piss the woman off — ever — or her life would be hell. Like a magician, Bateman could make holiday requests, uniform requisitions, and expense reports move faster … or disappear into thin air.

"Morning, Marilyn," said Willson, "I'll be ten-seven at the Moose Meadow pullout on the 1A. I want to check what might be a dead animal. I'll have my portable radio with me."

"Ten-four, five-eight," replied Bateman briskly. "I'll check in with you in fifteen." Like all Banff wardens, Willson appreciated that Bateman would mobilize help if the need arose.

She steered her truck to the shoulder, hearing the tires crunch on a thin layer of frozen snow. She grabbed her Stetson from the seat beside her, pushing her curly, shoulder-length, dark-brown hair behind her ears before pulling the felt hat smartly onto her head. She stepped outside and shrugged on her orange Gore-Tex jacket, then clipped a portable radio to her belt. At thirty-two years old, five foot seven, and 120 pounds, Willson liked that she was one of the few women on whom the warden uniform looked good. Before shutting and locking her door, she remembered the shotgun. She unlocked it from its bracket, racked a shell into the breech, and pushed the safety to the "on" position.

Even in winter, Willson always carried a shotgun along with her 9-mm side arm whenever she responded to reports of dead animals. Most other wardens did the same. It had become common practice only after a now legendary incident involving two Yoho Park wardens a year earlier. Both rookies, they'd stumbled across a male grizzly protecting a late-season elk carcass beside the highway. After reading the incident report, Willson knew that it was shithouse luck that neither of the wardens had been hurt. Along with their pride, both had lost their hats in the ensuing sprint to their truck, the bear in close pursuit.

Before leaving her pickup, Willson studied the ravens flitting back and forth from the ground to a nearby snag. They were scolding each other, laying blame for inviting too many to the party, this human most of all. Willson saw their attention focused on something on the ground, unmoving against a copse of spruce. At the sound of the closing truck door, a coyote loped into the trees. Willson could swear it gave her a resentful look over its shoulder.

As she was trained to do, Willson let her eyes and mind wander over the scene. She had no way of knowing what had happened and there was no hurry. Instead of tearing in like an excited rookie, it was easier and more productive to first observe from a distance. She took her time, looking, smelling, listening. After satisfying herself that she wasn't going to destroy evidence, she crossed the field of crunchy, snow-covered grasses, weaving her way through tangles of low birches. With each slow step, she shifted her eyes from the motionless object on the ground to the edge of the meadow and back again, anxious that a pissed-off grizzly might be lying in wait, ready to protect its meal. Willson searched for bear tracks, but saw none. Regardless, she kept her shotgun at port arms, ready, her arms tense and shaking. She pushed the safety to the "off" position.

When she reached the meadow's edge, Willson forgot — at least for the moment — her fear of a bear. What she saw shocked her. Coyotes and ravens had trampled the snow in a circle around the carcass of a massive elk. Splashes of red stained the snow, while pieces of hide were scattered in a wider circle. She assumed it was the coyote that had opened the body cavity — the contents now spilled on the ground in a messy pile. Her eyes filled with tears of rage and sadness when she saw that the top of the elk's head was a bloodied mess of splintered bone.

"Son of a bitch," she whispered, "someone chopped the friggin' antlers off him."

She continued to stand there, staring at the bloodied carcass. There was no doubt in her mind that this was Old 737, a veteran bull elk that she and her warden colleagues had named and watched gather and successfully defend a large harem of cow elk in successive ruts. Through September and early October, she'd seen him aggressively chase off rivals, at the same time adding new females to his group. On evening patrols, Willson heard his bugles fill the valley, the high-pitched whistles bouncing off the cliffs. All wardens recognized and respected the big bull because his rack was so large and impressive, his will to dominate and procreate so strong and inspiring. And now his time as king of the meadow was done.

Emotions pushed aside, Willson again let her eyes wander, searching for evidence. She noticed an obvious trail in the snow leading away from the elk to the Moose Meadow pullout up the road from where she'd parked. She walked forward a few steps to examine the trail, seeing three distinct sets of human footprints. Certain that this was her first case of wildlife poaching in Banff, her mind boiled again with anger.

"Banff Warden Office, three-five-eight," said Willson, after keying her shoulder-mounted microphone.

She was relieved to hear Bateman respond quickly. "Go ahead, three-five-eight, Warden Office."

Willson retraced her steps across the meadow toward her truck. She occasionally looked over her shoulder, wary that a bear might still see her as a rival for the carcass.

"Uh ... Banff Warden Office, three-five-eight, is two kilometres north of Johnston Canyon at Moose Meadow," said Willson in as calm a voice as she could muster. "I have a ten-ninety-one at this location and need you to call Bill Forsyth to assist. I'll stand by until he arrives." In the ten-code system used since Parks Canada began to take law enforcement seriously, Willson used the ten-ninety-one code to tell Bateman that she'd discovered a possible poaching. "I may also need Larry Westerly's assistance. Can you please ask him to head over to the park abattoir? I may have something for him to look at."

"Roger that, three-five-eight," said Bateman crisply, "Three-six-one, do you copy three-five-eight's message?"

Willson heard Forsyth's voice over the radio, crackly as if coming through an old cross-oceanic phone line. "Banff, this is three-six-one. Yeah, I heard you. On my way."

To confirm that she'd heard Forsyth's response, Bateman called Willson again. "Three-five-eight, Warden Office. I have three-six-one responding to your location as requested."

Willson imagined Bateman on the edge of her seat, waiting for a response. "Warden Office, three-five-eight. Ten-four on that. I'm back at my vehicle and standing by. And, Marilyn ... thanks."

While she waited for Forsyth, Willson tried to put herself in the mind of the person, or persons, who'd done this, who'd murdered one of the park's biggest bull elk. Was it a sudden, last-minute decision with no planning or forethought? A hasty impulse? Was it a carload of guys who did it for a lark, on a dare? No.

Everything she saw pointed to premeditation, to calculation, to knowing where to find a big elk in late October, to assuming the chances were slim that a warden would be out in this remote place, in the middle of the night. And with blood still fresh in the snow and most of the carcass still at the scene, she knew that this had happened the night before or early that morning. Whoever was responsible, Willson was certain they had come into the park with a rifle and tools to remove the rack, knowing what they were going to do before they did it. She understood that this was no spur-of-the-moment choice by someone passing by. It was far more sinister than that. It was planned. Whoever did this had done so with purpose. And that meant that other animals in the park weren't safe.

Leaning against the truck, legs crossed, eyes on the distant carcass, Willson thought about the why. Why would someone take only the rack? She knew that elk antlers, when still covered by the hairy, blood-vessel-filled skin known as velvet, were sold as medicine by commercial elk ranchers in the United Stated and Canada. It was pain relief for people with osteoarthritis. Pets received it for the same reason. But she also knew that the antlers on this bull would've been past the velvet stage and so would have had no medicinal value. Aside from someone taking them to make furniture or a gaudy chandelier, only one obvious motive remained. The antlers had been taken by a trophy hunter. Coming from an elk of this size and age, they'd be mounted on their own or added to an already mounted elk head to make it look bigger, more impressive. In a moment of clarity, Willson understood that the perpetrators knew what they were doing and why they were doing it, and that they had purposefully come here, to her park, to do it.

Now that she fully comprehended what she was dealing with, she felt the hairs rise on her arms. Her heart beat faster. It was at times like this that she heard her father's voice reminding her that a Willson never backed down from a challenge. Her resolve strengthened. She was at the start of something very serious, and she was ready for it. In fact, this was why she was here: to protect the park.

CHAPTER 3

The red and blue lights on Bill Forsyth's truck were flashing needlessly when he arrived at the scene twenty minutes later. Willson saw the lanky seasonal warden step down to the pavement after wrestling with his seat belt. As always, he had his cellphone in his hand and he was in motion. She took a deep breath, girding herself for what was to come, knowing that her young associate talked more than listened.

Forsyth hadn't been her first choice, but he'd been hired, anyway. Now she was stuck with him for the next nine months. From his first day, Willson recognized him as a classic example of a recent college graduate. He was tech savvy, more sure of himself than he had a right to be, and wanted to be the chief warden by the end of his first week. Willson knew that he was a work in progress, but she also recognized that when it came to people's feelings, her capacity for empathy and patience was limited.

Before Forsyth could tell her what he thought they should do, before he marched over to the carcass, Willson took control. She stood in his path and put her left hand on his chest to stop him.

"Okay, Bill," she said. "This is serious. I know you've never handled a poaching investigation. I want you to listen carefully and do exactly — and only — what I say. You're *assisting* me. Got that?"

"We talked lots about poaching in college," he said, "so I've got a good idea what we need to do here. Let's get started." He moved to go around Willson, but she kept her hand on his chest.

"Bill," she said, more firmly this time, "stop and listen to me."

Forsyth looked down at his phone as though some piece of wisdom would magically appear there. "What?" he said.

"When you first come upon a scene like this, there are *two* things you should do." Willson held up two fingers on her right hand to make her point, nearly poking him in the eyes. "The first is to slow down. Spend time looking and listening and even smelling. Build a mental picture of the place. What are the key pieces to the scene? What's out of place? You need to get an initial sense of what's happened and why *before* you blunder in."

Willson saw Forsyth again shift his eyes down to his phone, so she grabbed it from his hand. With a quick underhand motion, she tossed it into the bed of his truck. "Listen to me."

"Hey! You don't have to go psycho on me."

"I need you to pay attention and forget the fucking phone. This is one of the most serious things you're ever going to deal with as a law-enforcement warden. Now, how many things did I say you needed to do when you get to a crime scene like this?"

Willson saw Forsyth look at her like she was asking a trick question.

"Three?" he asked, obviously confused and embarrassed.

Willson jabbed him in the chest twice. "Two. The first is to stop, look, listen, and smell. The second is to ask me what I already know because I arrived on the scene before you did."

"That makes sense."

"Good. Now we're getting somewhere." She handed Forsyth a clipboard and pen. "You're the official note-taker today. I want you to record everything. And I mean *everything*."

She went on to explain what she'd discovered and then the two of them processed the site where she'd found the elk. As a highly trained investigator, she treated the case no differently than a homicide detective in a major city would a murder. She forced them to move slowly, to pay attention to the smallest of details. She continually reminded Forsyth to keep detailed notes of each step, each observation, each piece of evidence.

They first draped yellow crime-scene tape around the meadow and out to the highway pullout. They marked entries to and exits from the meadow to keep the evidence undisturbed. They photographed the elk carcass, blood patterns, footprints, and tire tracks frozen in the snow. They searched for hairs, fibres, cartridges. They measured, sketched, and mapped. And they bagged samples of the elk's flesh for DNA analysis.

When they were almost done, Willson pulled the clipboard from Forsyth's hands, checked his notes, and then pointed to the bloody internal organs that lay in a messy pile beside the elk.

"We need to bag those," she said.

"Why the hell do we need to do that?" Forsyth asked, looking both incredulous and disgusted.

"Because they might contain evidence … a bullet … a bullet fragment … something like that." Willson knew this was unlikely, but it was a unique opportunity to teach both investigative diligence and humility to the youngster.

While Forsyth pulled on rubber gloves and began piling the organs into a plastic evidence bag, gagging repeatedly, Willson kept her eyes on the edge of the trees, her pistol's holster open. She still wasn't sure if a bear was lurking out there, waiting to take possession of the carcass. She took no chances.

Once the pair of them had gathered all the information they could, Willson showed Forsyth how to use a cable extension on his truck winch to drag the elk carcass across the field, the cable end looped around its back legs and the carcass leaving a red-striped furrow in the meadow. As they worked, the ravens, obviously displeased about losing their smorgasbord, sat in an old snag, nagging like black-draped grandmothers.

After lifting the carcass into Forsyth's truck using the bed-mounted crane, inadvertently crushing his phone in the process, Willson and Forsyth faced each other on the side of the highway.

"Sucks about your phone," said Willson, "but at least I've got your full attention. So … based on what you saw so far, what have we got?"

"It seems clear to me," said Forsyth, "that we had a truck stop along the 1A there." He pointed to the interpretive pullout.

"Why do you say a truck?" Willson asked, even though she'd already worked out the most obvious scenario.

Forsyth was sure of his answer, too sure for Willson's liking. "Looking at the size of the wheelbase and the size and nature of marks made by the tire treads," he said, "I'm sure it was a pickup truck."

"Could it be a larger sport utility like a full-size Blazer, Yukon, Expedition, or Durango?"

"Uh … well, yes … I guess it could be."

"Good. It's okay to have a mental picture, but don't make the picture too specific until you're certain. Now, when did it happen?"

She saw Forsyth pause for a moment. "Maybe within the last twenty-four hours," he said. "The tire tracks were frozen in the snow, which meant the shooters drove here after it stopped snowing, just as the temperature was dropping. The tracks haven't melted at all. So I'm guessing between ten o'clock last night and four to six this morning."

Willson saw him search her face for signs of disagreement. Seeing none, Forsyth continued. "I'm thinking that one of the people shot the elk, probably from the road. While it's hard to tell, it looks like a single bullet, which means he was a decent shot, especially if it was in the dark."

"Why do you say 'people'?"

"Because there are three distinct sets of footprints," Forsyth replied. "It looks like two were wearing cowboy boots ... or something like that ... with smooth soles. One was large, probably a size twelve or more, while the other was small. I guess it could've been a woman. The third person was wearing a boot with an aggressive tread, maybe a mountaineering boot or a serious winter boot of some kind."

"You said *he* was a decent shot. Could the shooter be a woman?"

"I guess so. I never thought of that."

Willson sighed. Now she could add male chauvinist to Forsyth's list of character flaws. Edgy, anxious to move things along, she finished the sequence for him, even though he was making progress. "After the shooting, the trio walked to the body across the meadow," she said, "and they chopped the rack off the animal."

Forsyth nodded in agreement.

"How do you think they got the rack off the elk?" she asked.

Forsyth was again quick to respond. "They used both a saw and an axe. I could see the tool marks in the skull."

Willson would confirm his assessment with the crime lab later, but she had no doubt that Forsyth was right. She paused, watching the young warden. She saw his eyes meet hers, only for an instant, and then shift to the bed of his truck. She was sure he was thinking about his mutilated phone. "What steps do you take next?" she asked.

"I ... I don't know."

"*Now* the correct answer is three." Willson held three fingers in front of his face, like a Boy Scout salute, even though the technique hadn't worked the last time.

"First, I need you to drive the elk to the park abattoir. You and Larry Westerly are going to do an autopsy on the carcass. He'll be waiting there for you. He's an experienced hunter who will show you how to do it properly. If you find a bullet or bullet fragments, I want you to immediately take them to the RCMP crime lab in Calgary. I need to know make and calibre." She pointed to the clipboard. "Write that down."

"But I'm supposed to be finished work at four o'clock today. If I have to go in to Calgary and back, I'm won't get home until late tonight."

"Welcome to the world of criminal investigations, Bill, where time doesn't matter."

"Do I get extra time off?"

"We'll worry about that later. And then tomorrow, after you're back from Calgary, what are you going to do first thing in the morning?"

"I don't know. Maybe talk to the RCMP in Banff, Lake Louise, and Canmore and see if they stopped any suspicious vehicles in or near the park in the last couple of days? If they did, maybe get licence numbers and any other information they have available?"

"Excellent," said Willson. Maybe there was a glimmer of potential here, after all. "And what else?"

"I have no idea," he said, erasing the glimmer. Willson sighed.

"I want you to contact all park wardens," she said, "to see if any of them shot pictures of bull elk in this area this fall. Or maybe they talked to wildlife photographers who were here doing the same. Because if anyone has clear images of this particular bull, we can use those to show other wardens, the Mounties, and conservation officers on both sides of the border what the rack of the murdered bull looks like." She raised her eyebrows. "And why?" She paused, then, "Because if we get lucky and find the rack, the pictures will be useful in court."

Willson paused again. Forsyth took the hint and again wrote notes on the clipboard. "So that's your three things," she said. "And what do you think *I'm* going to do first while you're doing that?"

She watched him look at his notes and then look up. "I don't know ..."

"The first and most important task for *me* is to contact conservation officers on both sides of the park — in British Columbia and Alberta — to ask them to watch for the Banff elk rack. I'll do that as soon as I get back to the office. Because we're still in hunting season in both provinces, those officers regularly speak to dozens of hunters each day. If they run into someone with a big rack that's suspicious or out of place, such as one that's not attached to the rest of the animal, they can let us know. As I said, that's where a picture will be of huge value. Make sense?"

"I was going to suggest that," said Forsyth, in an apparent attempt to reclaim lost dignity and confidence.

Willson gave him a sharp jab in the shoulder. "You were? Well, then, good job, rookie."

She saw that Forsyth was eager to get moving, perhaps to buy a new phone before he drove to Calgary. "I think we've got enough to work with for now. Let's get moving. And don't forget your plastic bag of Halloween goodies," she said, pointing to the bag of internal organs.

Willson watched Forsyth walk to his truck and cast a longing glance in the back before driving away.

Willson waited for the sound of Forsyth's truck to fade into the distance. She turned, staring back at the scene where the bull elk had been killed and robbed of its massive set of antlers, its source of power and prestige during the rut. For a moment, her rage and sadness returned. She vowed to personally put someone's nuts in the wringer over the crime. She would make sure the experience was slow and painful and that they understood it was National Park Warden Jenny Willson who was responsible for their discomfort.

She studied the irritated ravens as they swooped down from their perches, looking for meager leftovers in the bloody, trampled snow.

"Slim pickings, eh, boys? Just like my case."

In her truck again, she grabbed the dash microphone. "Banff Warden Office, three-five-eight. I'm ten-eight and clear of Moose Meadow, heading to the office."

"Roger that, three-five-eight," Bateman said in response.

Willson's mind was a blur of evidence, of emotion, of anticipation. She'd missed the poachers by only seven or eight hours. But in a park this big, with highways heading east to Alberta, west to British Columbia, and north to Jasper National Park and beyond, they could be anywhere. She had nothing more to go on than tire tracks, footprints, and, she hoped, a bullet buried somewhere in the elk's chest. And while she'd dealt with poaching in other parks, those had been minor situations compared to this one — the loss of an iconic bull elk in Canada's most iconic national park. She wondered if in future her investigation would be used as a case study in law-enforcement courses. Or would it be remembered as pathetic, worthy of scorn and derision, forgotten? She blew out a breath through pursed lips. No pressure.

But ultimately, she knew that her biggest challenge was presenting the case to her superiors so they'd let her move forward professionally, thoroughly, and systematically. That meant spending money and time on an investigation. She was painfully aware that such a commitment was foreign to them because none had any training — or interest — in law enforcement, and few felt as she did about the park. And based on her experience to date, she knew that no one in the system liked surprises that rocked the boat or put them in the crosshairs of higher-ups in the food chain. She considered most of them to be ass-kissing, risk-avoiding pencil-pushers who cared more about moving upward than they did about the park.

Again, she released a breath noisily as she thought of the internal battles to come. And then her father's voice came to her, as it often did when she was faced with the greatest challenges life threw at her: *"Remember, Jenny, where there's a Willson, there's a way."*

As she drove along the snowy highway, Willson's mind centred on the stark image of the slaughtered elk, the coppery smell of blood splashed on snow, the lonely whisper of wind in the grasses. This was personal, very personal. Against a background of radio chatter, Willson promised herself to follow the case to the end, even if her bosses didn't approve. "You don't know it yet, but I'm coming for you, you bastards," she said. She would make her father proud.

CHAPTER 4

NOVEMBER 22

The parking lot was empty when Jim Canon swung his truck off the Banff-Jasper Highway, two kilometres south of the stone, glass, and steel edifice of the Columbia Icefield Interpretive Centre. In this third week of November, he'd passed few other vehicles travelling either south or north. It was as if he had the entire national park to himself.

He sat on the tailgate of his truck and pulled on his hiking boots, lacing them tightly. Even though he'd left the Waterfowl Lakes campground in the cold of pre-dawn, he'd been sufficiently awake to tape his heels with moleskin before pulling on socks, his only light the glow of a lantern.

With boots tight, he inhaled the smell of the mountain autumn, smiling at the wisdom of his crack-of-dawn start. The only sounds he could hear were the whispers of the wind and the *kroaks* and *tonks* of ravens as they played in the cool currents of air sliding down the glacier to the west. Canon sipped the last mouthfuls of a special Kicking Horse Coffee blend he'd brewed on the gas stove that morning.

Canon stood, turned, and dragged out his battered Lowe camera pack from under the truck canopy. He called it "the grey monster" because of its ability to carry large amounts of gear. Today, the monster was filled with camera bodies, lenses, memory cards, filters, his lunch, a thermos of coffee, an extra pile sweater, gloves, a toque, and rainwear. He lashed a water bottle and a sturdy ball head tripod to the pack, then shrugged into the shoulder straps and buckled the waist-belt, hefting the weight with an audible grunt.

"Holy shit," he said to a curious whisky-jack that studied him, head cocked, from a nearby Engelmann spruce, "this son of a bitch is heavy."

Finally, Canon locked and shut the driver's door with a bang that echoed off the far slopes. He tucked his truck keys into the toe of one of his worn shoes and dropped the shoes under the canopy before pulling down and latching the door. No matter what happened to him or his pack during the day, the keys would be there, waiting for him. Not like the time they'd fallen from his pack into a crevasse, forcing him to walk ten kilometres to find a ride. He wouldn't make *that* mistake again.

Satisfied that all was secure, Canon strode across the parking lot and immediately cursed the sadistic park planner who had designed the trail from the parking lot to Wilcox Pass. It started uphill and left little warm-up time for a photographer trying to adjust to eighteen kilograms of gear on his back. It wasn't long before his breathing was a chorus of heavy panting. But as he warmed up, Canon used the slow, steady cadence of his bootsteps on the trail to bring his heartbeat and breathing into a pattern he could maintain all day.

After the first kilometre, he broke free from a thick, fir-spruce forest and got his first view across the valley to the Athabasca Glacier. He looked westward to Mounts Snow Dome, Athabasca, and Andromeda. All three were well over three thousand metres high and dusted with the season's first snow. He loved this time of year because the thin layer of white produced dramatic definition of the steep rock faces, nooks and crannies that were otherwise invisible in the flat light of summer. He continued uphill, using short pauses to conserve energy for the long day ahead. The uppermost ridges and snowfields around him were now brushed with the first rays of the sun, and despite his rough start, Canon felt good. He smiled and pulled the crisp mountain air deep into his lungs like a tonic. He thought of the millions of people in places like Toronto or New York who fought traffic and each other in the shadows of tall, sterile buildings. He knew he was where he needed to be, and he felt sorry for them all.

An hour later, he reached the edge of Wilcox Pass and sat on a dark boulder beside the trail. "Let's see what's here today," he said, raising binoculars to his eyes, scanning the slopes around him. It was a spectacular place, and for the moment, all his to savour and appreciate.

Even though the sun was still below Nigel Peak to his right, Canon saw the basin ahead of him as a tapestry of oranges, reds, and yellows. The stunted alpine plants that carpeted Wilcox Pass — the willows, mountain avens, fireweeds, and heathers — were in their annual transition to a long winter, throwing out a final burst of colour, a burst muted by early frosts. For a moment, he wondered whether he had enough memory cards. But then he thought back to the years he'd shot transparencies, remembering the plastic bags he always carried, filled with exposed and unexposed rolls of Kodachrome and Fujichrome film. Things had changed for the better.

Canon sat marvelling at his surroundings, chewing on half of a Spam, pickle, and cheese sandwich. For Canon, Spam was a weakness and a source of friendly debates with his long-time girlfriend, Sue Browning. In his opinion, she was a serious food snob. When he pulled a can of Spam from the cupboard, he'd see Sue stick her finger in her mouth, gag, and leave the room. So Spam made a slurping noise when it plopped from the can. So it glistened with a gelatinous coating, part mucus and part slime. So what?

Canon finished the sandwich, wrapped the remainder in wax paper, and sipped coffee from his thermos. He continued scanning the basin to locate the Rocky Mountain bighorn sheep rams that hung out in the pass during the fall mating season. The main events of the season, usually occurring in November and December, were a violent series of head-banging fights often put to music on TV, contests that offered willing ewes as a grand prize and migraine headaches to the losers.

After a few sweeps of the basin, Canon located a group of fifteen rams at the base of a rocky ridge in the northwest corner of the pass. "There you are," he said, smiling. They were out in the open, each animal facing in a slightly different direction, watching for the few predators they feared — grizzly bears, cougars, wolves, and the occasional wolverine.

Canon again hefted the heavy pack and climbed toward the sheep slowly, methodically. When he passed what he guessed was the halfway point, he lowered the pack to the ground, unstrapped his tripod, and pulled his camera from the depths of the pack, where it was wrapped in a fleece jacket. With a long zoom lens on the front, he ensured the exposure settings were right for the conditions and then clipped the camera to the tripod. He re-shouldered his pack and threw the padded legs of the tripod over one shoulder, the camera lens pointing downward.

By mid-afternoon, Canon had filled two memory cards with images. He'd found and followed the rams for more than four hours and was pleased. Because it was just before the main part of the mating season, the rams had already sorted out who was dominant and who was left to stand on the edge of the party when they finally met up with females in estrus. As if winning the head-to-head fights wasn't enough, the dominant rams continued to chase and threaten the smaller and now deferential rams, occasionally mounting them from behind to add to their humiliation. There were a few half-hearted attempts to butt heads, but Canon knew that he'd missed the best displays.

Sometimes he was so close to the animals that he couldn't focus on them in his viewfinder. "Could you move back a few steps, please?" he would ask. The sheep ignored him. None of this behaviour was a surprise;

Canon had been to Wilcox Pass and always found that the more time he spent with the sheep, the more comfortable they became with him. He was slow and quiet, respectful, and always ensured that the sheep could move wherever they wanted to go. He knew they would never see him as one of them, but if they didn't consider him a threat, that was all he needed.

Canon sat amongst the rams when they rested and chewed their cud. He listened to their breathing. He heard the subtle squeaks as they pulled at tufts of grasses with their teeth. It was relaxing, almost hypnotic.

Canon knew that his best images of the day would come from the hour he spent with a massive ram that lay on its own, away from the group, legs tucked under its body like a cat. The animal appeared unconcerned with his presence, so much so that he moved within five metres of it. He spread the tripod's legs low to the ground and then lay on his belly in the meadow, his eye to the viewfinder, capturing stunning images of the animal with the rock ridges and icefields on the summit of Mount Kitchener as an impressive backdrop. In both horizontal and vertical shots, the ridges of the ram's horns popped in the dramatic sidelight of the morning. Each horn, a triangle-shaped combination of bone core and horn sheath that grew over the core each year, showed the transverse ridges that marked the passing of time. Not unlike the rings of a tree, these ridges allowed biologists and hunters to calculate an animal's age. The two horns curled down and backward from the top of the skull, and then upward and forward again, encircling its ears in a complete circle. It was full curl.

Canon switched to a wide-angle lens so he could capture more of the meadow in which the ram was lying, contentedly chewing his cud. As the shutter purred, the images showed the whole world of the ram in its alpine splendour.

As the sun dropped behind Snow Dome, Canon spoke to the rams one last time. "Thanks, guys, for letting me hang out with you today." Then he slowly gathered his gear.

His photographer friends often asked him why he did this, why he said thank you to his photographic subjects. Maybe it was because he believed it was an honour to be in their presence. Or maybe today he was relieved that none of the rams mistook him for a ewe in heat.

Canon walked down the pass, his boots whispering in the low groundcover, his thoughts still on the sheep. Raising his eyes to the horizon, he saw a storm on its way from the west, the dark clouds boiling, moving quickly. From experience, he knew he would soon be in the middle of a violent tango between weather and darkness. He chose to make a beeline back to the truck rather than continue shooting.

As he reached the distinct line between alpine and forest before heading down to the parking lot, he was surprised to hear voices. He wondered why someone would be walking uphill at the very time they should be racing for their vehicle. *But hey,* he thought, *you can always count on park visitors to make bad decisions.* He moved a few paces above the trail, sat to one side of a small clump of wind-shaped firs, and waited.

In a moment, Canon saw two men trudge up the trail, both breathing too hard to speak. They staggered out of the trees and stopped at a viewpoint immediately below him. Neither looked in his direction.

The first man, big and bearded and wearing a cowboy hat, knee-length raincoat, and heavy mountaineering boots, seemed to be in the better shape of the two. Canon saw him catch his breath fairly quickly and look back at the other man with what appeared to be contempt.

Shorter than his companion, the second man was a sweating, heaving mess of a human. He had pointy, unattractive features and wore the ugliest down coat Canon had ever seen. A battered Kootenay Ice baseball cap, wet with perspiration, sat back on his narrow skull. His thick eyeglasses were clouded. Canon watched sweat run off the man's nose, dripping onto his scuffed cowboy boots.

Who're these dumb-asses? Canon wondered. They were two of the strangest hikers he'd ever seen. Neither carried a pack, but both wore binoculars around their necks. They seemed unaware of their immediate surroundings, only focusing on the open pass ahead of them.

Canon couldn't contain himself. "Hey, guys," he called, "where you headed this time of day?"

Both men whirled in surprise, the smaller of the two tripping over a rock in doing so. He fell with a thud and a grunt. Canon watched his sweat-encrusted hat sail over the edge of the viewpoint.

The bearded man's body language — eyes glaring, fists coiled — made it clear to Canon that he didn't like surprises.

"What'n hell are you doing hidin' up there?" the man said, scowling.

"Sorry to startle you." Canon chuckled, trying to disarm the man. "I was taking a rest before tackling the hill. Where are you guys heading? It looks like a storm's coming in from the icefields."

The smaller man, after dusting himself off and casting a forlorn glance after his hat, answered first. "We weren't doin' nothin' wrong, we were just —"

The big man cut him off. "Shut the hell up!" he barked. He turned back to Canon. "Not that it's any of your goddamn business," he growled, "but we're up here just takin' a walk."

Canon had no doubt the man was bullshitting him. "Hey, no big deal," he said. "I was taking pictures of the rams and decided to call it a day. There's serious weather rolling in."

At the mention of sheep, the two men's faces visibly changed. A look passed between them so quickly that Canon would have missed it if the two men hadn't already put him on edge.

"Sheep?" the big man said. "We didn't know there were sheep up here. What did you see and where were they?"

Canon became increasingly uncomfortable with the men. He considered their clothing, their lack of packs, and the fact that they were heading into the pass when chances were good they would be alone. None of it suggested just two guys out for a stroll. He didn't buy their story for a second.

At this point, the smaller man dropped out of sight below the trail, apparently in search of his hat. Canon heard grunts and falling rocks.

"I saw a few smaller rams," Canon said, intentionally downplaying what he'd seen, "but if there are any big ones, they're probably already off somewhere else."

Canon saw the bearded man fill his barrel chest with air and take a step toward him. Leaving his pack on the ground, Canon pushed himself upright to his full six-foot-three frame, his shoulders broad and his legs solid from years of university rowing. If the man was trying to intimidate him, Canon was willing to show he wasn't in the mood to take any crap. With elevation, gravity, and a lack of fear on his side, he knew he had the advantage, and he stared back at the man, unblinking. They were no different than two bighorn rams, ready to rise on their hind legs and then hurl themselves at each other with speed and force, each trying to dominate the other. Canon saw the man's fire cool when he realized that his adversary wasn't about to back down.

"C'mon, give me a fuckin' break," said the big man, his hands wide in fake surrender. "If there are small rams up there, then the big ones have to be there, too. Maybe you didn't know where to look."

Canon was too smart to rise to the bait. "Why?" he asked. "Have you been up here before?"

"Yeah," said the man, "I've been up here before. Probably more times'n you. And every time, I seen big rams, lots of full curls, many over ten years old."

Out of the corner of his eye, Canon saw the smaller man crawl over the edge of the trail, filthy and breathing hard. The baseball cap was back on his head.

"I thought you said you didn't know there were sheep here," Canon said.

"Don't be a fuckin' smartass," said the man. "I know these mountains like the back of my hand."

"Well, good for you," Canon replied. "If you guys want to get your asses soaked and stumble around in the cold and dark, have at it. Smart folks would head out of this weather, not into it."

"You call 'em smart folks," said the man. "I call 'em pussies."

The first waves of a misty rain began to fall on the three men. A gust of wind blew the baseball hat off the smaller man's head, sending it over the edge of the trail again. "Son of a bitch!" the man cursed.

The larger man apparently realized that he'd get nothing from Canon. "Whatever," he said. "Thanks for bein' fuckin' useless." He spun and stomped up the trail.

Canon turned to the smaller man to see his beady eyes peering and blinking through his thick eyeglasses. He looked frightened by the encounter between the two bigger men. He opened his mouth as if to say something to Canon. But then he clearly thought better of it and stumbled up the trail after his partner.

Canon watched them go, the smaller man tripping awkwardly as he came into view a hundred metres along the trail. "Now *that* was bizarre," Canon said to himself, shaking his head. "Those two dummies are going to be cold and wet by the time they're done for the day."

When he reached the parking lot ten minutes later, the wind was blowing heavy, wet snow horizontally through the air. It stuck to everything like a plaster cast. He laid the pack in the back of the truck, grabbed his shoes and keys, and dropped the canopy door — the hinges squealing in protest. He started the engine and let the defroster clear the foggy windshield while he peeled off layers of clothes and wrestled with his wet boots.

As he drove out of the parking lot, he glanced in his rear-view mirror at a battered blue pickup truck parked at an angle. He was disappointed to see British Columbia licence plates. "I hate it when assholes come from my home province," he muttered.

Canon steered the truck onto Highway 93, pointing it south toward home. As the truck dropped out of Sunwapta Pass into the valley of the North Saskatchewan River, Ian Tyson's voice poured out of the CD player, telling him, "Summer's Gone."

"No kidding, Ian," he said, "no kidding." With his last mug of lukewarm coffee in hand, Canon toasted the worsening weather outside the truck. He gave no more thought to the two men on the trail.

CHAPTER 5

NOVEMBER 24

Bernie Eastman again hiked up the trail into Wilcox Pass, his stained cowboy hat tilted back on his head. It was late afternoon, the day cloudy and cool. An icy breeze blew intermittently from the south, chilled by the glacier on the north side of Mount Columbia. Behind him, Eastman could hear the bootsteps of the black-haired man, the same one who'd shot the elk in Banff three weeks earlier.

Stopping on the trail as it emerged from a small copse of subalpine fir, one of the few stands of trees remaining at this elevation, Eastman raised binoculars to his eyes. He tipped his hat further back, took a few seconds to slow his breathing, and then began a surveillance of the surrounding terrain. His field of view, framed by dark, overlapping circles, changed as he swung his head slowly from right to left. When he'd traversed the entire meadow, he raised the glasses a few degrees and then began another traverse, this time from left to right. Occasionally he paused, studying specific places with care, ensuring he missed nothing. In ten minutes of searching, he covered the whole pass. He then let the glasses drop to his chest.

"We got three different bands of sheep," Eastman, pointing with a finger the size of a small animal. "The rams are there and at least two of 'em are big sons of bitches you'll want to get a closer look at before you choose."

He saw the black-haired man smile, a thin smile that was more sneer than expression of pleasure. "*Vamonos,*" he said.

"What?" Eastman's face was scrunched in confusion.

"Let's go," the man said.

The two men continued the trek upward, Eastman leading. He knew they should stay in the open and make noise, but not too much. He wanted the sheep to see and hear them but not be startled or surprised.

Twenty minutes later, Eastman paused a dozen metres from a band of bighorn sheep rams scattered along on the edge of a rock rib. Like many sheep in Canada's national parks, these animals had seen humans many times and were unfazed by their close proximity. Both men stared in awe. The ram's chests were thick and powerful, their coats a deep brown. The patches of white on their rumps, inside their ears, and on their muzzles were a dramatic counterpoint to the dark fur. But most impressive were the massive horns.

As Eastman had observed earlier, two of the rams were bigger than the others. By counting the rings on the horns, he could tell that the largest was around twelve years old. He estimated its weight at about a hundred kilograms.

The tips of its horns were broken and tattered, like the end of a worn toothbrush, a sign that it had been an active combatant for many seasons, earning the right to pass its DNA on to future generations. The other ram was slightly smaller, and Eastman guessed he was a year younger.

"Those are remarkable," said his companion, pointing at its horns. "Thick, well beyond full curl, and very little brooming on the tips."

Eastman studied the spread, length, and circumference of the horns, the lack of wear or breakage on the tips, knowing that the other man cared about how the animal would score in the Boone and Crockett trophy system. "I'm guessin' he'll go over two hundred points," said Eastman. "That's a nice ram."

The black-haired man stared at the younger ram for a moment longer and then said to Eastman, "He is the one." Then he pulled a compact digital camera from his pack's shoulder strap and handed it to Eastman.

The outfitter watched him move up beside the younger of the two rams, remove his pack and drop it to his right, then lower himself to the ground only two metres from the ram. Eastman snapped three images of the scene, the ram unaware of the men's intentions.

Eastman watched the man turn to his right and open his pack, slowly, carefully, with no sudden movement. With his right hand, the man slid a Magnum .44 pistol from inside a fleece jacket. Holding the large gun in both hands, he cocked the hammer with his right thumb and took aim at the point on the ram's chest where the heart was. Eastman noticed the ram's ears perk forward at the sound of the click. The man slowly squeezed the trigger.

Eastman, an experienced hunter, had expected the clap of thunder from the gun. It echoed around the basin in which they stood. But what he hadn't planned for was the stampede of bighorn rams terrified by the sound. They scattered in all directions at a full gallop, their eyes wide with fear. The largest ram raced by him, nearly catching his pack straps with its massive horns.

The younger of the two rams followed the others for about five metres. But the bullet had done its work, tearing a bloody path through the ram's chest and heart. Eastman saw the animal drop to its four knees, heard it bark out a racking cough, and then topple on its side.

The two men stood over the animal for a few moments. The shooter stooped to stroke the ridges of one thick horn, pleased the trophy was intact.

Eastman heard the man humming as though he were enjoying a good meal. The sound stuck a chord with him, and it was off-key. For the first time in many years, a sliver of doubt worked its way into Eastman's brain. For a man so sure of himself, it was an uncomfortable feeling. His father had taught him to hunt and had always impressed on his son the need to act ethically. Hunting, he'd said, was a source of food for the family table, nothing more. Eastman's move into the guide outfitting business at a young age had created a wedge between father and son, a divide that lasted until his father's death. Standing where he stood now, looking down at a magnificent animal whose death he'd facilitated for the sake of a trophy, Eastman knew that his father would be angry, ashamed, disgusted at how far his son had strayed from the path he'd tried to set. But Eastman pushed those uncomfortable thoughts to the corner of his brain where they'd hidden for decades, forced there by constant money problems and his wife's relentless badgering.

Eastman cleared his throat and shook his head as though to focus his thinking. "Let me get started before someone wanders up here," he said.

Thirty minutes later, Eastman had carved and sawn the head and hide off the dead sheep in one piece. He rolled the hide under the head and, using white parachute cord, lashed the entire package to an aluminium pack frame.

It was nearly dark when the two men moved down the trail toward their vehicle, Eastman again in the lead. Their earlier footprints were melted dark and large on the snowy trail. About halfway down, when the trail reached a thick stand of spruce, Eastman slipped a headlamp from his pack. The bright LED light illuminated their path through the trees, casting shadows to each side as they moved downhill.

When Eastman reached the edge of the parking lot, he paused in the trees for a few moments, ensuring their truck was the only one there. Then they walked quickly across the lot, stowed their packs and the ram head and hide under a blue nylon tarp in the bed of the truck, and climbed into the cab.

When they were seated, with the engine started and the heater on, Eastman watched his passenger reach into the glove compartment for a silver flask. The man unscrewed the tiny lid, took a long swig, and then sighed. Eastman reached for the offered flask in the darkened cab. He took the same long swig, pausing for a few seconds as the smooth warmth of single-malt scotch slid down his throat and into his stomach.

"Thank you," the black-haired man said. "*Un buen día.* That was a good day."

CHAPTER 6

JANUARY 27

Jenny Willson parked her Subaru Outback with two wheels in the gravel driveway and two on snow-covered grass. As she climbed out and stretched, her arms high in the air, she gazed up at the Rocky Mountains. Only the summits were lit by a late-January sun, which was quickly dropping behind the more subdued Purcell Mountains to the west. After a half day in the office in Banff and then a three-hour drive to Jim Canon's house at Fort Steele, in the south end of the Rocky Mountain Trench near Cranbrook, Willson was weary. But coming here for the weekend was like coming home. After growing up two and a half hours to the north in Golden, she found comfort in this wide valley, a sense of welcome that was as powerful as it was inexplicable. With her right hand, she ensured that her fat-tired mountain bike was still secure on the roof rack.

Willson raised a hand when she saw Jim Canon sitting within view at the front picture window of his log house. Each time Willson came here, she not only marvelled at the incredible views east and west, but also envied the solitude that Canon and Sue Browning had found here. It was clear why he'd picked the property, not only as a place to live, but also as a home for his photography business. Willson reached into the passenger seat for the bottle of Talisker single-malt scotch that she'd brought from Banff, a housewarming gift that was as much for her as for her friends.

By the time she climbed the front steps, Canon was outside to meet her with a hearty hug. "So glad you're here, Jenny," he said, a warm hand on her shoulder. "Come in and have a cold one. Sue's in the shower so I'll let her know you're here. How was the drive?"

"It was good," Willson replied. "As always, I had to avoid a couple of bighorn rams south of Radium ... and then I had a near miss with an elk crossing the highway near Skookumchuk. Other than that, all good!" She understood the horrible irony that would have come from a national park warden taking out large mammals with her vehicle and silently thanked the goddess of luck.

With Canon following and then closing the door behind her, Willson entered a large room that was kitchen, dining room, and living room in one. She leaned her hip against a wooden island, accepting a cold beer from her host. They toasted with a clink of the long-neck bottles and both took a satisfying first sip. She sighed. It was good to be away from the office, off the highway, and with close friends again. It truly felt like home here.

"Make yourself comfortable, Jenny, while I tell Sue you're here." Canon placed his beer on the island and grabbed another from the stainless-steel fridge.

Willson watched him disappear down a hallway, and then she wandered aimlessly around the room. A massive wooden table, its shiny top reflecting the setting sun, sat near the front window. The warm pine walls were a gallery for Canon's wildlife photographs, many enlarged to near life-size. Where the walls were free of pictures, bookshelves were abundant. She ran her finger along the spines of first-edition novels, tall volumes of photography, histories of western mountain ranges. Leather furniture, heavy coffee tables, and thick rugs were scattered around the room.

As she took another sip of her beer, she heard a shriek from the bathroom and then pounding feet as Canon ran down the hallway.

Willson heard Browning's voice from the back of the house. "Asshole!" she yelled.

Canon was laughing as he picked up his beer from the island. "Geez, I bring her a nice frosty beer and that's the thanks I get?" he said. "The fact that it touched her bare ass as she bent over to dry her hair is no reason to be ungrateful."

Looking at Canon's mischievous grin, Willson joined in the laughter. Whenever she was with her two friends, she saw a relationship that made her emotions flip between happiness and envy. Willson had shared a house with Canon and two others while they were studying resource conservation at the University of British Columbia. They became close friends but nothing more than that. The year after she graduated, Willson met Browning at her first warden climbing school. Browning was an instructor, Willson a rookie warden. It was on a cold night, jammed in a cramped tent high on a rocky ledge between Mounts Edith and Louis near Banff, when Willson told Browning about her photographer friend. While her heart swelled with pride to see that the two had formed a bond that was deep and strong, Willson felt a parallel ache for something she didn't have.

But Browning gave her no time for melancholy as she swept into the room in a plush terry robe, her feet bare, her hair twisted in a thick towel. "Jenny," she said as she wrapped her strong arms around Willson, "I've come to save you from this incredible jerk of a man."

They all laughed as they raised their bottles in a toast.

"Jim, what time are the others coming?" said Browning.

"Uh, I think I said six … but I might have said seven," Canon replied. "But you know those guys — if they arrived here at the time we asked them to, it would be pure coincidence."

"I better get dressed," said Browning, finishing her beer with a flourish and a loud burp. "While I'm gone, Jim, try to be less of a jerk to Jenny than you are to me."

Just as she left the room, the front door opened with a bang. Willson turned to see the evening's other invitees — Brad Jenkins and his fiancée, Kim Davidson — barge into the living room in the midst of a hockey debate.

"They shouldn't have pulled the goalie so early in the game," said Jenkins.

"Don't be such a conservative candy-ass," Davidson replied. "The coach had to do *some*thing. His job was on the line if they didn't win."

This wasn't the first time Willson had met Brad Jenkins. She knew him to be a twenty-eight-year-old conservation officer and a former student in a photography course Canon taught at the local College of the Rockies. Canon called him his keenest student and the only one to show talent. Jenkins was a tall, trim man with a blond, military-style crewcut. He attempted, like many young conservation officers and wardens, Willson included, to maintain his idealism about the world around him, despite the politics and bureaucracies in which he worked. She liked to tell herself it was that common ground that drew her to him. But when she looked at his soft brown eyes and sincere smile, she knew it was more than his idealism that raised her heartbeat.

Willson had never met Kim Davidson before, but Browning had filled her in on the woman's background. She was a physical education teacher at a Cranbrook high school, with broad shoulders that hinted at a history in competitive swimming. Davidson and Jenkins had apparently built a relationship based as much on competition as anything else. They'd met at a triathlon and still argued about who'd finished first that day. Willson's eyes dropped to the engagement ring on Davidson's left hand. Her heart sank as she realized that Jenkins was truly off the market.

When she looked up, she knew — by the sly smile on the woman's face — that Davidson understood what she was thinking. For a moment, Willson locked eyes with the woman's penetrating blue ones, and then saw Davidson raise her beer in a kind of toast, perhaps signifying a truce ... or a warning.

"So, Jenny," said Davidson, "Brad tells me you're a park warden in Banff. How did a woman like you get into that line of work?"

Willson wondered what Davidson meant by "a woman like you," but considering she was surrounded by friends, chose not to pursue it.

"My dad passed away in a railway accident when I was ten years old," she replied. "My uncle Roy, my father's brother, was in the RCMP and became a de facto father. He tried hard to persuade me to join the force. But I really love the mountains and couldn't risk being posted to Moose Crotch, Saskatchewan, or Out-of-the-Way, Newfoundland. So I went to UBC and got a degree in natural resource conservation. That's where I met Jim."

"And now you're a warden in Banff? Geez, what a cool job. It looks like you made the right decision."

Willson looked at Davidson and couldn't help but smile. She realized that it was going to be tough not to like this woman. And that pissed her off.

Half an hour later, the five friends sat down to a feast of barbecued steaks, home-baked buns, and broccoli coleslaw. When Willson helped Canon bring the steaks to the table on a large platter, she saw the glint in his eye. "Tonight, I wanted to show you how good this marinade would be with barbecued Spam," he said with mock sincerity. "Spam's just as good as steak. But Sue wouldn't let me. So you can blame her." Buns flew at him across the table.

During the meal, Willson lost track of the number of times that either Canon or Browning filled her ceramic wine goblet with a dark merlot, its dry, oaky flavour an ideal complement to the spicy beef.

The banter during dinner was irreverent and, like the wine, free-flowing. Browning regaled them with stories of the heli-ski lodges where she worked as a guide. "Some of them are calm and relaxing," she said, "where the guests ski hard all day and then sleep hard all night. Others, yeah, not so much ..." She told them about an Austrian mountain guide who was infamous for the number of women he'd bedded in his career. To achieve his objective, he'd impersonated a ski instructor with a broken leg, a foreign airline pilot, and a German investment banker. By the time Browning ran out of stories an hour later, tears of laughter streaked their cheeks.

"Speaking of love lives," said Canon, "how's yours coming along, Jenny?"

Willson didn't hesitate. Her wineglass was again full, her inhibitions long gone. She no longer cared if Davidson knew her romantic challenges. "It's like a friggin' string of car-crash videos," she said, shaking her head. "I've signed up on three online dating sites. You'll laugh when you hear that my first date ended up being our dispatcher's son. He's a tobacco-chewing, bow-legged, failed rodeo cowboy who answered 'yup' or 'nope' to every question I asked him. We were barely past the pre-dinner drinks and I was already bored out of my mind. As my thoughts wandered, I couldn't decide if I was going to end my misery by shooting him or shooting myself. I finally walked out when he pulled a big, brown, disgusting wad of chew out of his cheek when our meals arrived."

"You walked out and left him sitting there?" Browning was incredulous.

"Oh, yeah," said Willson in a slow, Southern drawl. "His momma ain't gonna be happy with me."

When the hosts cleared the plates and brought in dessert and coffee, the wine-fuelled conversation shifted from trophy women and less-than-trophy men to wildlife. It was like chaos theory in action, with the discussion bouncing and changing, shifting and evolving, difficult to track and far from linear. Canon and Jenkins first talked about a recent trip in search of mountain caribou images. They had stomped around in deep snow for an afternoon but come back with nothing but wet feet and empty memory cards.

When Davidson asked what they thought about chasing cougars with hounds, the noise level in the room increased dramatically. Some around the table thought it was acceptable if the cats weren't shot while treed, while others found the concept despicable, no matter who did it or why.

"Speaking of hunting, what do you guys think about trophy hunting?" asked Willson. "I'll explain why in a second."

As expected, she heard Canon jump in first. "It's goddamn criminal is what it is!" he said, slamming his palm on the table. "It's one thing to hunt for food. I get that. Seems like most people around here do that, and it's well managed. But how can someone be so arrogant and selfish that they feel it's okay to shoot an animal in its prime so they can stick it on their wall? I can take pictures of the same animals over and over again, and others can enjoy the same experience. That's the definition of a renewable resource. But killing an animal for a trophy, and the only person who enjoys it is the sad guy who lives in his parents' basement and stares at it on the rec room wall …"

"Geez, Jim," said Browning, "that's a massive generalization, isn't it? Is that the wine talking?

"Fuck, no," said Canon. "They probably do it because they can't get a girlfriend. It's their pathetic way of proving their manhood. They're the kind of guys who buy big trucks to make up for their small …" He stopped talking when Browning punched him in the arm.

"What about shooting a trophy animal in a national park?" asked Willson. Anxious to share her recent experience with the poached elk in Banff, she took them through the incident step-by-step. The room was quiet and tense, the suspense building to her final discovery of the missing rack. A single lamp hung low over the table, illuminating the faces of the five friends as they sat in a tight circle, the rest of the cabin dark around them.

Willson's earlier tears of laughter over the Austrian guide's exploits changed to tears of anger as she spoke about finding the elk dead, mutilated, the day after Halloween. It had been almost three months and she still shook when she described the experience. Browning, sitting next to her at the table, put a consoling arm across her shoulders.

"But what's even worse," Willson continued, "is the call we got from the Jasper wardens three weeks after that. It appears we also lost a bighorn sheep ram at the Columbia Icefield."

"What the hell happened?" Davidson asked from across the table, her face a mask of concern. Willson heard an explosion of voices, all directed at her. When did it happen? What did she know? Did anyone see a vehicle? Did she have any other evidence? Were there any witnesses? Did she think it was the same guy did both animals?

"I don't know much yet," said Willson. "All I know is that a hiker found the ram's body in Wilcox Pass about three weeks after we lost the elk, about a hundred metres from the main trail."

She paused, purposefully taking three deep breaths to calm herself. She saw her friends watching as she made a conscious effort to place her hands palms down on the table. They were shaking, her knuckles white.

"The head was gone," she said quietly, "along with some of the hide. There was one bullet wound to the body with powder burns around it. The Jasper wardens are assuming that whoever did it shot the animal at close range. They sent the slug to the crime lab, so it'll be a while before they know what kind of weapon was used. They think the ram's head was taken off with a saw."

Willson sat in silence for a moment and saw the stunned looks on her friends' faces. "Based on what we've got so far," she said at last, "it appears we have a trophy hunter at work in our parks. Maybe it's only one guy … maybe it's more." She then told them about discovering the writings of the outspoken American author and environmental activist Edward Abbey while she was at UBC. "I love what Abbey said about trophy hunters," she said. "He thought that humans who smiled over their kills were morally and esthetically inferior to the animals they killed."

Abbey's quote kick-started a new round of discussion, with increasingly strident and aggressive opinions about shooting animals so body parts could become wall ornaments. Amidst the tumult, Willson saw Canon push his chair back and disappear into the dark room beyond the table. The others, busy with their debate, appeared not to see him go.

When Canon took his seat again a few moments later, Willson's eyes opened wide as he dropped a pile of eight-by-ten images on the table.

"I may have the last photos of that ram," he said solemnly.

The room exploded with questions. "What the hell, Jim?" Willson asked.

While Canon answered, the pictures were passed around the circle, from one hand to the next. Willson stared at images of a massive bighorn sheep ram sitting in a heather meadow, its eyes partially closed. Its horns, more than full curl, were thick and ridged with growth rings. Nicely lit with a touch of fill flash, the ram's head and thick shoulders were a dramatic silhouette against the rock and snow of distant peaks.

"I was up in Wilcox Pass around the twentieth of November," he said, "and I spent most of a day with a band of rams up there. I do that almost every year about this time."

He pointed to the ram in the photograph. "This one in particular had such peaceful, dark eyes," he said. "I still remember the sounds of its breathing and the way it dominated its colleagues in the basin. It constantly tested the wind for danger … but at the same time, it also radiated a sense of calm."

"Did you see anyone else?" asked Willson.

"Yeah, that was the strangest part of the day," Canon said. "I was on my way back to the truck and I ran into these two guys who seemed totally out of place. They weren't dressed for the weather or the mountains. One was a scrawny little guy, the other guy much bigger. At first, the big guy tried to tell me they were out for a hike, but he was full of shit. And he could tell that's what I thought. So he tried to bully me into telling him where the big rams were."

Willson knew that Canon rarely backed down from anything, and she knew, from experience, about his hair-trigger temper. "How'd that go for him?" she asked with a smile.

"Well," said Canon, "we didn't go toe-to-toe or anything, although at one point I thought we might. But let's say he didn't get what he wanted from me."

"So when were you there again?" she asked. Her heart began to race.

"It might've been the twenty-second," he replied. "It'll be in my computer, on the digital data for the images I took that day."

Willson paused to consider the new information. "Well, I have no way of knowing if it's the same ram or not, but the time works," she said. "The Jasper wardens think it must've happened around the second or third week of November. With the cool weather, there was little in the way of decomposition. The ravens had discovered the carcass, but despite that, it was in good shape." She paused again, then asked, "When can I get copies of these prints?"

"Take them when you go home on Sunday," said Canon.

Willson felt the adrenaline in her system beginning to override the effects of the alcohol. She asked Canon questions about the two men, prodding him at key points. In response, Canon described details of their clothes, their mannerisms, and their speech patterns.

"You know," Willson said, "you got a decent look at those guys and there's a chance they're the ones who took the ram. You've got a good memory, Jim. Why don't I schedule an interview with an Identification Section member in the Cranbrook RCMP detachment? Maybe he can use the Identi-kit to develop a likeness of one or both of these jerks. I'll set it up for Monday morning. If it works, we can circulate the sketches to see if any wardens, conservation officers, or even Mounties recognize them. That will give us somewhere to start." She saw Canon nod in numb agreement.

"Did you see what kind of car they were driving?" asked Willson. "Or even better, the licence plate number?"

"I'm kicking myself," said Canon, "but no. All I remember is a beat-up blue pickup truck with B.C. plates."

Willson could tell that Canon was embarrassed and angry, now that he understood the importance of his short interaction with the two men in Wilcox Pass. Before she could let him off the hook, Brad Jenkins spoke up.

"Jenny," he asked, "why the hell didn't we in the Conservation Officer Service hear about the elk or the bighorn ram? We might have seen or talked to these guys if they came through British Columbia." He looked around the table for support. "Christ," he shouted, his voice amplified by five glasses of merlot, "we could've grabbed the head and the guys on the spot if we'd known! Shit!"

Willson saw Davidson put a hand on his arm to calm him. When he didn't relax, she watched the gentle hand became a judo hold. The two were soon on the hardwood floor beside the table, trying to wrestle each other into submission.

For a moment, Willson was speechless, not because of the spontaneous sparring match occurring in front of her but because of the accusation Jenkins had made.

"Bullshit, Brad," she said, when he and Davidson had dusted themselves off and rejoined the group at the table. "I personally sent a detailed email to all regional wildlife offices in B.C. and Alberta the same day I found the elk. I asked that it be forwarded it to all field officers. Another message about the sheep was supposed to go from the Jasper wardens to the same offices."

"Son of a bitch, there's the problem," said Jenkins. "We didn't get anything like that, or at least, I didn't see it. And I thought the federal government was incompetent." He paused and then lowered and shook his head. "Shit," he muttered again.

Apparently Davidson kicked him under the table, because Jenkins then apologized to Willson. "Sorry, Jenny. That was out of line. It's not your fault. How about I get you the phone and fax number for my office?" he said. "Then you can send the information directly to me. I'll make sure our guys in Cranbrook see it and I'll copy it to the guys in Invermere, Fernie, and Golden, as well. With a sketch from Jim, we might get a name."

It was two o'clock in the morning when the party broke up. After Willson and Davidson shared a hug on the front porch, Willson watched the woman — as the pair's designated driver — pour Jenkins into her car and drive off into the cold night. As hard as she'd tried, she realized that she couldn't hate that woman. Damn. Closing the front door, Willson saw Canon, still fully clothed, asleep on an overstuffed couch. His snores filled the room.

Willson and Browning bundled up in thick fleece jackets and moved out to wooden chairs on the porch. They each sipped a few final fingers of scotch from heavy crystal glasses, which was tough to do while wearing gloves. They gazed at the night sky filled with a blizzard of stars. As their eyes grew accustomed to the darkness, they saw the season's first display of northern lights. Bands of light pulsed and swirled above them in a spectrum of colours. Despite expert claims to the contrary, they both heard the lights crackle and sizzle.

Willson turned to Browning. Her friend's head was tilted back. "What are you thinking about?" she asked.

"Oh," said Browning, "I'm trying to make a list of the gear I need to pack for our guide-training sessions — they start tomorrow night. But I think I've had too much to drink. I keep losing the list."

"We're still doing that ride tomorrow that you promised, right?" asked Willson. "I brought my bike."

"Abso-fuckin'-lutely," said Browning, "although I offer no guarantees of any Olympic-calibre performance. Not after what we consumed tonight. But I'll still kick your butt on the trail."

Willson smiled and looked again at the night sky. Despite talk of the next day's bike ride, her thoughts remained firmly on the dead animals and on Canon's story. She pictured the two men in Wilcox Pass, shooting the bighorn sheep at close range. It was, she thought, an incredibly sick thing to do. What kind of people were these? Did they have something to do with her murdered elk, or was it a coincidence? Was she chasing two groups of poachers or just one? Were the same people so bold as to execute two animals within weeks of each other, both within the boundaries of national parks, places where animals were supposed to be safe — at least from humans?

She began to fantasize about suitable penalties for the horrendous crimes once the perpetrators were caught. They would appear in Willson Supreme Court, where she was the judge and jury. They would wait to hear their sentences, sweat pouring from their cowardly brows. Would she choose castration with the same bloody knives they'd used to carve up the animals? Would they be staked, in an alpine meadow, naked and face down over rocks with their butts in the air during bighorn mating season? Or would it be a life sentence in a culvert trap with a drugged grizzly bear — a sentence that would be short and painful? She didn't realize she was speaking out loud until Browning put a hand on her arm.

"All good ideas," her friend said with a lopsided smile, "but you have to catch them first. And I believe you will. Based on what we heard tonight, I'll bet those two guys Jim saw *did* shoot the ram. And if that's the case, there's a good chance they did the elk, too."

"You really think so?"

"Yeah," Browning replied, "and it looks like you've finally got something to go on … or on which to go. Shit. I was never good with grammar. Or is it 'well with grammar'? Whatever …"

CHAPTER 7

MARCH 24

Through the front window, the man watched an old woman shuffle along Park Drive, a quiet street on the south hill of Spokane, Washington. She paused, a dark, bent shape with stick legs and winter boots under the illuminated cone of a streetlight. The collar of her coat was turned up high against the cold air that gripped the city. A black dog strained at the end of a retractable leash, digging its weasel-like face under bushes. Beside her, the streetlights reflected on the glass and chrome of the Mercedes, BMWs, and expensive sport utility vehicles parallel to the curb.

Beyond the woman was Manito Park. During the day it was a calming mix of rose and lilac gardens, a lush conservatory, ponds, playing fields, and picnic areas. At night, it was a dark and mysterious place, very different from its welcoming daytime presence.

The man was surprised to see the old woman out so late at night, but wisely, she'd chosen the west side of Park Drive, where the curved street was lined with historic homes perhaps giving her a sense of comfort that the nighttime park could not. The houses, whispering of wealth, presided over the park as if guarding it from the sprawling subdivisions and shopping malls that pushed the city's boundary eastward, toward Idaho.

When the woman looked up at the house where the man stood watching her, he knew that she saw him just as he saw her, a vague silhouette. He wondered who she was and what she was thinking as she returned his gaze. Was she part of this world of wealth and status, a former focus of Spokane society pages? Or was she living in someone's basement or grannie suite as a family burden? As if refusing to answer his unspoken question, he saw she trundled into the darkness, dragging her dog behind her.

The man turned his back to the window. Inside the house, the party was well under way. Martinis, daiquiris, champagnes, and vintage wines flowed freely. Noise levels soared, inhibitions fell. He watched tuxedoed waiters discreetly roam the main floor, filling glasses, distributing waves of appetizers. Guests moved back and forth between rooms, forming and re-forming conversations. They chatted, laughed, and flirted. Quiet and subtle in the background, a Latin beat moved many to sway unconsciously.

From the outside, the house was no different than others on the block. But the inside offered subtle clues to its owner's nationality. It showed the casual simplicity of a southern clime, a stark counterpoint to the freezing temperatures outside. It was a look that didn't come cheap. Heavy Douglas fir beams framed the ceilings and walls; the spaces between the beams were a creamy white. Throughout the house, floors were covered with a brown terracotta tile that seemed warm and cool at the same time.

Earlier, the man had wandered amongst guests who filled every room on the main floor, from a solarium with stuffed white furniture covered in colourful wool blankets to a gleaming tan-coloured kitchen. There he'd watched a chef prepare hors d'oeuvres under the attentive eyes of three women perched on leather-topped stools. Those eyes had showed hunger, not only for the fresh food but for the muscular, ponytailed chef.

The man now stood in the corner of the living room, aware that he looked as out of place as he felt. While others were clearly comfortable in tailored suits, his off-the-rack bargain felt and fit like a burlap sack. He attended few parties like this, and when he did, the gulf between him and the people around him was almost painful. Their backgrounds were different, their lives were different, and their economic situations were certainly different. It was as if he were an alien in their midst. He sipped a glass of cold beer. At least *it* was comforting.

Watching his fellow guests swirl around him with irritating insincerity, the man leaned against a massive half-circle fireplace. Along the mantel he saw a line of lilies, their green leaves and bright white flowers paying homage to Easter.

Across the room, he watched the hostess move between groups of guests, chatting and smiling, her delicate hand always on someone's forearm. The man was enchanted by her, by the spell she wove on the room. She was beautiful, overtly confident, radiantly alluring. Her dark hair was long and luxurious and matched her coal-black eyes. It shimmered down her bare shoulders, continuing to her perfect buttocks. She wore a floor-length gown that flowed on her voluptuous body like a mountain stream. She paused to chat with a quartet of guests who stood to the right of a large ceramic figure on a wooden cross that was incredibly realistic, as if it were a visitor to the party, desperate for attention but ignored. The man saw the woman laugh, and then he gulped when her nipples visibly hardened under the diaphanous material of her dress.

"She is *muy bonita,* no?"

Startled by the quiet voice at his right shoulder, the man slopped his beer down the front of his pants. He turned his head and saw his host's dark eyes burning into him, the perfect white teeth forming a smile that a wolf would envy, a smile about which nightmares were made.

"Ah, Mr. Castillo," he said with a croak, "I was admiring your art on the wall there." He gestured clumsily at a painting across the room, again spilling his drink, this time on the tile floor.

Luis José Castillo's gaze was one of open contempt, though his smile did not waver. "Please … acquaintances such as you may call me Señor Castillo." With a subtle flick of his hand, Castillo pulled a white linen handkerchief from his breast pocket and bent down to dab at the wet spots on the tile. He threw the cloth into the fire.

"When I invite a man to my home," Castillo said calmly, moving closer to the man's right ear, "I expect he will enjoy himself." He paused, his gaze sending a shiver of fear up the man's spine. "But I also expect he will treat my possessions with respect."

The man leaning against the fireplace knew that his host was not talking about the painting, the spilled drink, or the floor. Before he could respond or apologize, Castillo was gone.

The man hated how Castillo made him feel, and yet, every time they met, he was unable to find a way to turn the tables, to make Castillo feel as useless and bumbling. He felt his cheeks flush with anger and shame and then looked around guiltily as if Castillo might reappear or read his mind. *It's going to be a long night,* he thought as he moved toward the kitchen to find another beer. He wished he were anywhere but in Castillo's home.

He grabbed another glass from a passing tray and then heard the bass tones of a bell sounding from the end of a long hallway. This was his second time at a Castillo party and he knew the signal. His host was about to make a pronouncement.

The man trailed his fellow male guests down the hall. Somehow the women knew this was not for them. For some guests, this was their first time in Castillo's home. But even for the others, it was unusual to be summoned in such a mysterious and presumptuous manner.

The man joined others as they moved into the house's main entrance area. It was a massive open space soaring up to the second floor. A long stairway led up into darkness on their left; on their right were closed double doors carved in dark wood. The man watched Castillo open the doors with a flourish. The room beyond was instantly illuminated. Filing in with the others, the man stood in a dark corner with his back against a bookcase. He leaned there in relative anonymity, sipped his beer, and peered at the men around him. He saw prominent lawyers, wealthy realtors, two federal court judges, a United States senator, and two older gentlemen whom he knew were Castillo's partners in one of the most successful construction firms in the inland northwest. As a mid-level government bureaucrat himself, the man felt like a scruffy alley cat in a pack of preening panthers.

He nodded at a local construction architect with whom he'd met a week ago. While they'd reviewed a set of drawings for a multi-storey parking garage, he hadn't missed the smell of alcohol on the architect's breath. He remembered pointing to the numerous building code violations he observed in the drawings, advising the man that a permit could not be issued. "You and I both know," the architect had said, his red eyes resigned, "that when Mr. Castillo wants something by a specific date, those minor details are irrelevant."

The man watched Castillo pause beside a massive mahogany desk and then turn to face the group. He held a champagne flute in his right hand, gripping the edge of the desk with his left. He waited until all conversation ceased.

"*Mis amigos* ... my friends," Castillo began, "I am honoured that you have graced me with your company this evening." His smile swept through the room, alighting on each and every guest in turn. "I wish each of you a *feliz semana santa*. Happy Easter to you and your families." When Castillo's dark eyes met his, the man felt like he'd been strip-searched by airport security.

"I consider each of you to be a special associate," the host said after his eyes had circled the room, taking possession of everyone in it. "I am pleased you have joined me for this celebration. Our company had a very successful year, and that is in large part due to the unique services each of you has offered to me and my partners. And I hope you all brought your cheque books tonight. If my wife hasn't approached you yet to donate to her charity, she soon will." Many in the room chuckled and nodded their heads.

The man knew why he was in Castillo's house on this night. He was an assistant chief inspector in the Spokane County Building and Code Enforcement division, and he was expected to ensure that Castillo's Spokane-area construction projects received building permits, swiftly, efficiently, and without question. He'd done this many times over the past five years, too many times to count, despite the fact that few of them met building codes. He was aware of the risk he faced. But Castillo compensated him handsomely for that risk. And ever since the first time he'd taken it, he'd had no choice but to act when asked. And he knew that Castillo would keep asking and keep expecting him to deliver. Each time, the risk grew like rows of bricks in a wall. He wondered what others had done to receive their invitations to this party.

Castillo continued with his speech, breaking the inspector's train of thought. "Thirty-two years ago, I left the Mexican mountain town of San Cristóbal de las Casas to come to America, with only a suitcase of clothes and, like all new immigrants, the hope that I could find the American dream. My parents sacrificed their own dreams so I could come to Gonzaga University here in Spokane to study engineering. When I stepped off the airplane in late August that first year, I had no idea where my education would take me. I worked evenings in my uncle's restaurant while studying and attending class during the day. Today, I am proud to have a beautiful wife and two amazing daughters, and proud to lead a growing and successful corporation that employs hundreds of people." Castillo smiled.

"To you, my friends, each of whom has helped me on this journey, I raise a toast. *Salud*." He raised his glass and his greeting echoed across the room.

"Now, I have something special to share," said Castillo. He paused for dramatic effect, the silence its own power in the room. "As many of you know, I love the hunt with a passion equal to my passion for my family and my company."

The inspector saw Castillo touch a panel on the side of the desk, and the upper reaches of the room grew brighter. When he looked up, he saw trophies of wild animals arranged on the walls. This was no redneck hunter's den. He saw species from around the globe, clearly prepared by a taxidermist with world-class skills. They appeared almost alive. Almost. A black rhino, its ears perked forward, its tiny eyes shining. A gemsbok, the face a mask of black and white, the horns long and sharp. A mule deer with thick branched antlers. A massive cape buffalo with curved horns and black beard, menacing even in death. A grizzly bear, its toothy mouth open, snarling as if ready to charge. But between the trophies, there were empty spaces.

"I am about to devote myself to a quest to obtain a trophy from every major game species in the world," said Castillo. "I have already begun pursuing my goal and I will invite many of you to accompany me on parts of that journey. Over the next few years, I will be travelling to Alaska, Canada, Africa, and Russia."

The inspector knew of Castillo's love of hunting and his desire to fill the room with mounted heads. He remembered a day in late fall of the previous year when he'd joined Castillo for an antelope hunt in south-central Montana. The trip was in appreciation for his efforts in expediting building permits for a large downtown office complex. But the thanks were tainted by Castillo's reminder that the man's career and reputation were at stake. "You and I will be in serious trouble if we have problems with that building," Castillo had said. "So, we will have no problems, correct?" The man had squeaked out an affirmative response, even though the quality of the construction was not of his doing.

The hunting season for antelope had closed weeks before their trip, but Castillo shot three bucks that day. He took only the biggest of the three, leaving the other two corpses to the turkey buzzards circling above them. The man saw the antelope's head on the wall above Castillo now and thought back to the speed with which the animal had moved across the short-grass prairie, slowing only to crawl awkwardly under a barbed-wire fence. That was when the big buck was felled by the shot from Castillo's gun.

The inspector also recalled the look on Castillo's face when he had turned, rifle in hand, and said, "I have honoured you with the chance to hunt with me today, and you will repay me by not breathing a word of this … to anyone. Do you understand?" They had been in the middle of a windblown prairie, miles from the nearest town. The man knew that the wrong answer to Castillo's question could make for a very bad day.

"Thank you," he had responded, feeling his face redden and his Adam's apple bob up and down. "You don't have to worry about me. My … my lips are sealed."

He thought about the many ways in which Castillo could destroy his career and his already sad life. He could lose his pension and he'd probably end up in jail for fraud. It was something he tried not to think about during the day, but it haunted his dreams. His day-to-day existence was already so illusory, so fleeting, and yet he'd let Castillo take control. Each time Castillo introduced him to a friend or colleague, Castillo gave the inspector's full job title, as though reminding him, over and over again, of the professional risks he faced. And he did the same with the others. So, like it or not, they were all tied together in a web of deceit and risk. A web woven by a master manipulator. But it was not like he could stand up to Castillo, demand Castillo stop pulling the strings that controlled his life. He remembered how he'd felt out on that windblown prairie in Montana, with Castillo's dark, glowering eyes piercing his. He'd sweated and shivered at the same time, his heart banging like a drum. The Mexican was capable of anything. Of that he had no doubt.

As the inspector drove home from the party later that night, his disgust at himself and his situation grew like a malignancy, consuming him from the inside. He was angry because he'd allowed himself to be trapped in a classic no-win situation. He was sick at the power Castillo held over him. He despised Castillo for his possessions, for his ego, and for his success. And for the way he made him feel: weak, sad, powerless. He was a puppet, with Castillo the mad puppeteer, forcing him to dance, to do his bidding. He knew that Castillo took pride in his accomplishments and cared deeply about what people — at least those he considered his equals — thought of him. But the inspector understood that he was nothing more than a stepping stone to Castillo's success, trampled by his handmade leather shoes, to be immediately forgotten when he was no longer needed.

By the time he unlocked the door to his rundown townhouse located in a very different part of Spokane than where Castillo lived, he'd decided that he wanted to do something, needed to do something, in order to take back the control he'd unwittingly lost along the way. What would it take, he wondered, to wipe the stupid smirk off that asshole's face? Castillo clearly loved his family, his business, and hunting, not necessarily in that order. The inspector couldn't touch Castillo's family. That's wasn't who he was. He couldn't expose Castillo's illicit business dealings without implicating himself and destroying everything he'd worked for, as meager and pitiful as it was. It came down to Castillo's hunting. He had to find a way to expose his illegal pursuit of trophies that could not be traced back to him.

The man sat in the dark, brooding, a plastic tumbler of cheap bourbon clutched in his hand. Small circles, tremors of energy, bounced across the surface of the liquid, colliding with each other and with the sides of the tumbler.

CHAPTER 8

MARCH 28

Comfortable in the dark leather seat, Luis Castillo peered through the oval window of his private jet. The sleek wing was a dark silhouette against the setting sun. His eyes were unfocused, his mind lingering on that morning's tearful departure of his two daughters — one nineteen years old, the other twenty-one — for the last few months of their year at Stanford University. His heart swelled with pride at the thought of them, at their beauty and potential, at the futures that lay ahead of them. But his gut clenched with worry. They were again far from home, and he could not protect them as he had in the first two decades of their lives.

The bump of a gentle landing interrupted his thoughts. His eyes now focused, he saw the buildings of the Canadian Rockies International Airport flash by in streaks of light. The reverse thrusters roared as the pilots slowed the jet down the runway. They rolled to a stop near the terminal. As the only passenger, Castillo waited for the engines to wind down, and then — a few moments after one of his company pilots cracked open the door — he saw the silhouette of a lone Canadian Border Services agent stride across the tarmac, his black uniform and bulletproof vest making him almost invisible in the darkness. He waited while the officer boarded the aircraft up a short flight of door-mounted stairs. Without a word, he handed the officer his U.S. passport.

Castillo watched the officer open the blue cover, peer at the main page, compare him to the photograph, once, twice, and then flip through other pages, apparently looking to see where in the world he'd travelled. Castillo knew the man was watching his eyes and his body language for signs of nervousness or deceit. He showed him none of that. But he made no effort to hide his impatience.

"Welcome to Cranbrook, British Columbia. Where are you from, Mr. Castillo?"

"Spokane … Washington," he replied.

"What's the purpose of your visit?"

"I've come up here to hunt."

"I see. Who are you hunting with?"

"A local guide-outfitter."

"What's the outfitter's name?"

"Bernie Eastman," said Castillo, passing over a letter from the outfitter that confirmed he was in Canada for a guided hunt.

"And how long will you be up here?"

"No more than ten days," said Castillo. "Perhaps less than that."

"Where are you staying?"

"As far as I know, we're staying at Eastman's guide camp in the Purcell Mountains."

"Are you bringing firearms into Canada?"

"Yes, I have a rifle in that case stowed against the wall. It's not loaded and I have no ammunition with me."

The officer opened the aluminum case. Castillo watched as he checked and recorded the model and calibre of the weapon in his notebook.

"Do you have anything else to declare? Tobacco? Alcohol? Currency over $10,000?"

"I have nothing else to declare."

Seemingly satisfied with Castillo's answers, the agent handed back his passport. "Enjoy your stay … and good luck."

Castillo stepped down to the tarmac, pausing to take a deep breath of icy Rocky Mountain air. He saw the Steeples Range to the east, its rocky ridgeline silhouetted against a brilliant rising moon.

Following the directions of a bored-looking security guard, Castillo entered the airport's arrivals area. It was empty. He took his leather bag and rifle case from the pilot and then heard the mechanical doors behind him open with a hiss. Bernie Eastman and Charlie Clark, looking rushed, hurried from the early-spring darkness into the bright space. Clark, with the nervous eyes of a hunted animal, jumped as he rounded the corner, surprised by a full-scale bronze sculpture of a grizzly bear sow and cubs.

"I hope like hell he isn't here already," Castillo heard Eastman muttering. "Oh, shit."

"Gentlemen," said Castillo, handing the bag and case to Clark, "you are late but finally here. Let's get moving."

Eastman led Castillo to his crew cab truck in the snowy parking lot as Clark struggled behind. After watching Clark load his bags into the back, Castillo climbed into the passenger seat. He watched the passing ponderosa pines, rough and rugged, flicker in the headlights as they drove into the St. Mary's Indian Reserve and crossed the St. Mary River, the truck dancing on the washboarded gravel road.

"Where the hell are we going?" asked Castillo.

"Don't worry," said Eastman, "it's a shortcut for headin' up the valley. Saves us some drivin' time."

It was a quiet trip north up the Rocky Mountain Trench. Castillo had little in common with Eastman and Clark, so he was content to let the scratchy sounds of country music fill the cab. He had low expectations of conversation with the two men, and they never failed to deliver.

Passing the small community of Skookumchuk, Castillo glimpsed the blinking lights and eerie plumes of steam coming from a pulp mill. He found it surreal, so different from Spokane or Mexico, as though a massive spaceship had landed in the middle of the dark valley. The multicoloured lights illuminated the ice fog lying along the Kootenay River — a common condition this late in March.

Out of the corner of his eye, Castillo sensed Eastman's uneasiness with the silence. The man fidgeted, shifted in his seat, his eyes bouncing from road to speedometer and back again. Castillo purposefully did nothing to ease the discomfort. In the dark, he heard the man try to engage him in discussion about the weather for the next two days. "Looks like we'll have low cloud and some snow," Eastman said.

"The weather makes no difference to me," said Castillo curtly. He was pleased when Eastman said no more.

After ninety minutes on Highway 93/95, Castillo stayed in the truck while Eastman checked them into the Alpen Motel in Radium Hot Springs. Castillo had one room, Eastman and Clark shared a second. Castillo opened the door to his room, turned to the two men, and said slowly: "We will leave here at 5:00 a.m. Please have everything ready."

By six o'clock the next morning, the three men were climbing the south-facing slopes of Mount Wardle in Kootenay National Park. They'd left the truck parked in an abandoned gravel pit a few kilometres west of the Simpson River monument. The route was not easy, the ground steep and snow-covered. Castillo took the lead; the other two were labouring under packs, Clark falling farther and farther behind. All three were dressed in white insulated coveralls with white toques and gloves covering their faces and hands, partly for the cold, but mostly as camouflage. After two hours, they reached an elevation of 1,750 metres, 500 vertical metres above the truck.

The men sat for a moment, sipping hot coffee poured from a beaten steel thermos and chewing partly frozen energy bars dug out from Eastman's pack. They shared a dramatic view across the Simpson River valley to north-facing slopes carpeted in forest. Castillo continued to set the tone by saying nothing.

After a short break, the three men were climbing again. They cut across two sets of fresh tracks in the snow. It was a meandering trail uphill and to the northeast.

"Is that what we're looking for?" asked Castillo, pointing to the tracks.

He watched Eastman kneel and move his hands to check size and direction, then look up to where the trail disappeared behind a small ridge scattered with stunted subalpine fir.

"Yes, it is," Eastman said with conviction. "Two animals, one much bigger than the other."

This was the news for which Castillo was waiting. Rather than blindly following the animals on their haphazard route, he took a rifle from Clark when the man finally caught up with them. He verified that it was loaded and began to climb. He was slow and quiet. He kept his breathing under control with by pausing after every few steps.

Thirty minutes later, Castillo was on his hands and knees, peering around a rock outcropping. At first, he saw nothing. The sky was overcast and there was little to help him differentiate between snow-covered ground and off-white clouds. After scanning the slopes, Castillo finally saw movement; a subtle shift of black against white. It was two mountain goats, both billies, to the east and slightly below him, no more than thirty metres away. Immediately, the smaller of the two goats moved uphill and away from him. The larger of the two stood still. As Castillo had hoped, his two companions were still below him and making enough noise to distract the animal, but not enough to make it flee. It was perched on a rock rib, nervously peering at the sounds below. Castillo knew he had little time before the animal scrambled further up the slope, following the other.

Castillo pulled behind the rock, swung the rifle off his shoulder, and checked the safety. At the same time, he took deep, calming breaths. Inch by inch, he moved forward on his knees and elbows, ignoring the rocks and the frozen ground, until he could again see the big billy. The animal's winter coat was as long as it would be all year. The hair was thick and only a slight shade yellower than the surrounding snow.

Castillo studied the goat through the rifle scope. The razor-tipped horns were black and gleaming. He smiled, liking what he saw. He estimated the goat to be about 130 kilograms in weight, in the prime of its existence. As on most hunts, Castillo felt his entire biological system come to life. It was the same feeling he got when he saw a beautiful woman for the first time. Despite the cold creeping into his body from the snow on which he lay, his pulse quickened, his palms went damp, and he had an erection. *Like foreplay,* he thought, *only better.* He willed the animal to come closer to him. But it was alert, still, peering down the slope. The crosshairs of his scope wavered slightly on the goat's chest. It was time.

Three more deep breaths. In and out, in and out, in and out. On the outtake of the third, Castillo squeezed the trigger slowly and smoothly. By the time a loud crack reverberated across the valley, the goat was already down on its left side as though hit with a hammer. With an impressive effort of will, it climbed to its feet again and took two stumbling steps before falling off the ridge, disappearing from Castillo's view. To the south, he watched a small avalanche slide into the trees on the north-facing slope of a smaller peak, a cloud of snow dissipating into the air above it. All was quiet.

Castillo climbed noisily down the slope where the goat had disappeared. When he reached Eastman and Clark, he saw that they'd found the animal lying at the bottom of a small cliff. They stood waiting for Castillo to claim his prize.

"Is it damaged?" Castillo asked the men as he slid down the final metres to where the goat lay against a pile of rocks.

"The body's kinda beaten up," said Eastman, "but the head's in good shape. The horns ain't broke, and the hide looks good."

Castillo nodded in agreement and relief. He pulled a digital camera from the pocket of his jacket and, as in previous hunts, told Eastman to take his picture with the goat. With rifle in one hand and his other hand resting on one of the two horns, a black stiletto at least thirty centimetres long, Castillo stared directly into the camera. Despite his accomplishment, he did not smile.

"Okay," Castillo said. "Get started on it."

Charlie Clark had the job of using a large knife and a handsaw to remove the head of the animal, along with the entire hide down to the black hooves. It was messy, bloody work. Castillo watched him closely, ensuring he made no mistakes. Soon, Clark's hands and white coveralls were coated in dark stains. The snow around him was red. Two ravens waited in a nearby spruce, clearly hoping that the men's actions would lead to a meal.

Forty-five minutes later, Clark finished the job. Snow began to fall in big, lazy flakes from a greying sky. He rolled up the hide and lashed it and the head to a wooden pack-board, covering the bundle with a canvas tarp. Two black horns poked out like thick radio antennae pointing to the sky. It was late afternoon. The men began the steep, slippery climb down the south side of Mount Wardle. Their morning's uphill route was obliterated with new snow and the sky had closed in around them.

"Let's go down this gulley," said Castillo, "I think it's a direct line to the truck."

"No," said Eastman, "we need to angle more to the east."

"You'd better have it right," said Castillo as he followed Eastman.

They reached the highway twenty minutes later only to discover they were a kilometre east of their parked truck, forcing them to walk along the edge of the snow-covered pavement, exposed and vulnerable.

"This is completely unacceptable," Castillo hissed, his eyes dark with rage as he stared at Eastman. "If this causes us a problem, I will hold you personally responsible."

Walter Krawczyk had worked for the Parks Canada highways crew for over thirty years. He'd seen it all and little surprised him. Cars buried in avalanches. Overturned tour buses. Summer bear-jams and long lineups behind paving crews. No matter what was thrown at him, his job was to keep traffic moving through the park. Today, his biggest worry was the recent snowfall. The highway through Kootenay National Park was already icy from a previous storm, and this latest had turned the road into a treacherous ribbon from one end of the park to the other.

As Krawczyk drove his green-and-white Ford pickup east on the highway, it was reaching that time of day when it was dark enough for headlights but not so much that they made a difference. After he passed a mineral lick that was an excellent place to see wild animals, he saw three men walking into an abandoned gravel pit on the north side of the highway. Krawczyk turned his head to the left and noted a dark truck tucked against the trees. One of the men held what looked to be a rifle, while another, who appeared to be coated in blood, carried a large pack.

Krawczyk was travelling at the posted speed limit of ninety kilometres an hour, so he passed the three men quickly. "What the hell was that?" he asked himself out loud. He grabbed his microphone from its clip on the dash, ready to contact the duty warden he knew was near the north boundary of the park. Krawczyk paused, realizing the warden would be pissed off with him if he didn't at least get a licence plate number. So he continued to the Simpson River monument, reversed direction, and headed west on the highway, back toward the spot where he'd seen the three men.

When he came around the last corner, slowing to turn into the gravel pit, he saw that the pit was empty. "Fuck!" he said to the sky.

But tire tracks were fresh in the new snow on the access road, showing skid marks out to the highway. It was clear to the park veteran that the vehicle had left the rest area in a hurry, heading southwest toward Radium.

His mind raced. While bloody men carrying rifles and loaded packs were a common occurrence in hunting season *outside* the park, they shouldn't be *in* the park. He needed to catch up to the truck, get a plate number, and then contact dispatch to call out the RCMP. He could follow the truck into Radium.

As he came over a rise, Krawczyk glimpsed the truck as it raced along the highway beside the Simpson River below him. In the darkening sky of late afternoon, the truck's headlights illuminated the path ahead, a trail of snow blowing like a churning wake behind a ship. He pounded on the gas pedal, roaring down the hill. He was leery of the icy road but confident that he had the weight of eight sandbags in his truck, the best studded snow tires the government could afford, and all four wheels powering in the same direction.

Krawczyk closed the gap between himself and the other truck and again grabbed his radio mic, ready to call in the licence plate. He wasn't surprised, however, to see the back of the truck obliterated by caked snow. Not only could he not read the plate, he couldn't even tell the truck's colour. It looked like a Dodge. In the swirling snow, he wasn't even sure of that.

Now Krawczyk was uncertain. He knew that getting a licence-plate number would be helpful, especially if he lost the truck on the highway to Radium. If he tried to pass the vehicle, there was no guarantee he could see the front plate. The caked snow could be as bad there, or the truck could be from Alberta, where only rear plates were required by law.

"Screw it," he said. "I better call it in. Maybe they can set up a roadblock and I can tell them which vehicle it is when we reach it." Krawczyk looked down to his lap for the microphone, grabbed it, and began a call to dispatch in Radium.

"Warden Office, this is Maintenance two-seven-one. I'm following a suspicious vehicle with three occupants that was parked when I first saw it. I saw one of the men holding a rifle. We're heading —"

At that moment, the truck in front of him slammed on its brakes. Even if Krawczyk had been more attentive, he wouldn't have seen the red brake lights through the caked snow. His eyes widened and he sucked in his breath with a hiss as the rear of the truck came at him fast. His radio transmission ended. He dropped the mic into his lap and grabbed the steering wheel with both hands. Without thinking, he turned the wheel hard to the right to avoid a collision. In the space of a heartbeat, he knew it was a mistake.

The right front wheel of his truck rose up on a patch of thick ice along the concrete guard rail. It was enough to send the vehicle off the travelled portion of the road. The forty-five-centimetre-high concrete barrier, its top slightly rounded, launched the truck into the dark sky beyond the highway. It began a slow rotation to the left. A few seconds later, the truck hit the steep slope below the barrier. The full force of the crash came through the driver-side door. Krawczyk's head snapped against the window, the impact breaking his neck. He died instantly. The truck cartwheeled down the slope, end over end in a storm of snow and flashing headlights. It came to a stop, lying on its roof, on a layer of ice covering a small pond. For a moment, there was silence.

The weak ice cracked loudly and then Krawczyk's truck dropped into the water, with only its wheels visible above the surface. One wheel continued to spin, with nowhere to go.

The dark truck carrying three men and the remains of a mountain goat billy continued down the highway toward Radium.

CHAPTER 9

MARCH 29

Jenny Willson and Jim Canon leaned outside Giorgio's Restaurant in Banff, their hands in their pockets, each with one leg bent against the wall of rounded river rocks. They knew they looked like two gunslingers waiting for the bad guys to appear at the other end of the avenue.

Willson's chin was tucked into the collar of her thick down jacket, a blue wool beanie pulled low on her forehead. She watched an RCMP cruiser pass slowly on the opposite side of the street, heading north. The car's tires threw up a dusting of the snow that had fallen that afternoon. The lone Mountie inside gave her a quick glance and then, in a momentary salute of recognition from one colleague to another, touched his forehead with his hand. She watched him turn away, seeing nothing more of interest.

She understood what a Banff posting must be like for that young constable. As it was with her job, in the summer he'd see everything and anything, all from people who left common sense at home when they went on vacation. He'd see dumb stunts pulled by drunken teens with more bravado than brains, and the reactions of families when Mother Nature created a sudden gap in their family tree. She also knew that the young officer would yearn for action at this time of year, faced as he was with mind-numbing shifts of nothing.

Willson saw Canon pull up his puffy left sleeve to consult his watch. After spending the day in snowy meadows north of town shooting images of bull elk and bighorn rams, he'd invited her to join him and a friend for dinner. After a day in the office, she was ready for food and drink — and lots of them.

Five stomach-rumbling minutes later, she saw a stout man approaching them from around the corner of the local fudge shop.

"Hey, Jim," said the man. "Sorry I'm late."

"No problem," said Canon. "We were just watching the world go by. Bob, this is my friend Jenny Willson. Jenny, this is Bob King, my photo agent."

The man thrust his hand at Willson after pausing to remove a thick leather glove. "Hi, Jenny," he said with a smile. "Pleased to meet you."

King was almost as wide as he was tall and he had an unfortunate nose that would be the envy of many Banff elk. Willson knew that he was one of the best photo reps in Canada and that his Halifax-based stock agency had sold Canon's photographs for nearly ten years. Willson was no photographer, but she understood that the man did well by representing Canon, and that book publishers, advertising agencies, and websites all gravitated toward her friend's work, even when given the choice of images from higher-profile shooters, because he had a photographic style that was unique and compelling.

Willson, not one for social conventions, opened the restaurant door and stood aside to let the two men pass. She grinned at Canon. He was used to her antics and slapped her on the shoulder. "Thanks, buddy," he said.

But King paused, clearly uncomfortable.

"Go," said Willson. "We're never going to eat if you stand out here."

As the three entered the dark entryway of the restaurant, Canon said, "This worked out well, Bob. You don't get out to Calgary much, so I'm glad you phoned me."

"Uh …" said King, clearly still wondering about Willson, "I had to meet with a book publisher there, so I'm glad, too. It was easy to rent a car and come out here."

In a few moments, they were met by a raven-haired hostess with a big white smile and dark-framed glasses. Willson shook her head. She knew that hiring attractive staff — female and male — was a conscious (and normally very successful) business decision made by many restaurateurs, but it still pissed her off as being blatantly sexist.

Willson, Canon, and King followed the hostess through the restaurant and up the carpeted stairs to the second floor. She showed them to a sturdy table overlooking Banff Avenue, then opened the menus and listed the house specials in a sensuous voice that was clearly designed to appeal to the men at the table.

"Too bad your wife couldn't join us tonight, Jim," said Willson, jumping into the role of shit disturber to show the hostess she knew this was a shallow attempt to increase her tip at the end of the meal. "She'd really like this."

She returned the hostess's look with an innocent smile, knowing Canon was the last guy to fall for something so obvious.

"This place is nice, Jim," said King. "You come here often?"

"Not a lot. It's called a trattoria. To be honest, I have no idea what that means, but I do know two things: one, it's a lot better than a pizzeria, and two, it has, in my humble opinion, the best food and wine in town."

At the urging of the hostess, Willson agreed to share a bottle of Argentinian Malbec with the two men. Her first sip was a long one, and she sat back in her chair, content to listen to King and Canon talk about commercial photography. Based on many hours of listening to her friend, she knew it was a rapidly evolving field, and with millions of people around the world taking millions of pictures every day, the competition was fierce. Despite that, Canon's work was in constant demand.

"I received an intriguing request for you, Jim," King said. "The client wants you to shoot new Ferraris with captive cheetahs at a safari lodge in Namibia. I expect you'll like it because the car company is in partnership with a local conservancy. Interested?"

Willson saw Canon's face light up. "Count me in," he said.

Their server, a much pierced and tattooed young woman, approached their table to take their order.

"Hi, I'm Melissa. What can I get you for folks?"

"Well, what do you recommend?" replied Canon.

"If I had to choose one thing on the menu, I'd order the bison stroganoff. It's strips of slow-cooked, range-fed bison, in a rich red wine and mushroom sauce, on a bed of fettuccine noodles. And it would go well with your Malbec."

Willson, Canon, and King simultaneously nodded in agreement. They'd all get the stroganoff.

"Are you a local, Melissa?" Willson asked curiously, intrigued by the tattoos.

"Nope," she said. "I graduated with a degree in mechanical engineering from the University of Waterloo and came here to ski for the winter before I head to the University of Calgary to start my master's."

The three gaped at her.

"I know," she said with a grin. "I get that reaction a lot. People don't expect it when they see my tats and piercings. Hey, let me get that order in for you."

The evening wore on, and between mouthfuls, Willson watched Canon fill many pages of his ever-present moleskin notebook with suggestions from King. She understood Canon well enough to know that his creative mind was already planning how to tackle the challenges King laid out for him, even as King was still talking. Willson occasionally envied Canon's life of travel and diverse projects. While it was standard commercial work that paid his bills, she'd heard him talk of shooting locations on assignment for travel publications, normally to accompany articles prepared by contract writers. But at other times, he worked with finicky ad agency art directors, capturing images of models or products in exotic places. It was his stories of those exotic places that most fascinated Willson; he brought out the travel bug in her.

They again chatted with their server as she handed the dessert menus to each of them. "If you want something light," the young woman said, "try the spumoni ice cream." She continued with a sales pitch she'd obviously perfected on other diners. "But I really suggest the wild huckleberry cheesecake." She drew out the word *really,* making it sound like something illegal or immoral, or both.

In the end, the three ordered the ice cream. As Willson shifted in her seat, she was bumped in the shoulder by a man passing behind her. When she saw Canon's eyes widen, she turned in time to see the man, clearly unsteady on his feet, heading toward the stairs behind her.

"Jenny," whispered Canon across the table, "*that's* the guy!"

"What guy?"

"One of the two guys I saw in Wilcox Pass."

"What? Are you sure?"

"I am. And there's the other guy who was with him that day, at that table there." Canon gestured to a far corner of the room where a large man sat at a table for two. They saw him wipe his face with a linen napkin, stand, and then stumble toward the stairs, joining the other man.

"Jesus," said Willson, twisting in her seat to grab her coat. "You stay with Bob, Jim. I'm going to follow these guys, see if I can get their names."

"Not likely," said Canon. "There's no way I'm letting you go out there on your own, no matter what you do for a living."

Willson realized that chasing after two men in the dark, both of them apparently drunk, wasn't a great idea, at least not without backup. And her friend did deserve to be a part of this. "Maybe you'd better," said Willson. "Stay here, Bob. We'll be right back. Let Melissa know that we're not skipping out on paying. And don't eat my dessert."

Willson and Canon sprinted down the stairs, skirted a fallen plant that the two men must have bumped into and knocked over in the entryway, and then caught sight of them crossing Banff Avenue toward the Visitor Centre. A taxi travelling slowly southbound swerved around the men, the driver hammering his horn in protest.

They caught up to the two men as they exited a brick walkway into the parking lot adjacent to the Bow Valley Credit Union.

"Hey, guys," called Willson, "hold up a minute." She saw the big man turn toward her, while the smaller man stumbled into the side of a car.

"What the fuck do *you* want?" said the big man.

Willson flashed her badge at the man. "I'm a national park warden. Can I see identification for both you guys?"

"I'm not showin' you and your boyfriend nothin."

"You're required by law to show me identification on my request."

The man took a shaky step toward Willson. She shifted one step back to stay out of the reach of his big arms and his even bigger fists, fists that were clenched at his side like two hams.

"Fuck you, lady ranger," the man said. "Are you and your friend gonna make me ... or what?"

Willson could see that this was going south in a hurry, and she didn't want Canon to get into a fight. Her friend could take the big man, she had no doubt of that, but he might get hurt in the process. Egos and testosterone were never a good combination. With some karate training under her belt, she could do her part, but battling it out with a giant in a dark parking lot was stupid. And she had no handcuffs, no radio or cellphone to call for reinforcements. As well, her car was parked blocks away, so she couldn't follow them, and at this point she had little to arrest them on other than a refusal to identify themselves … and an oblique link to poached park animals.

"Jim," she whispered out of the corner of her mouth, "have you got a cellphone on you?"

"Nope," he said quietly, while they watched the big man weave in the darkness like a punch-drunk boxer. "I left it on the table in the restaurant."

"Shit," she said. "We're going to have to back off here, or one or both of us are going to get hurt."

"C'mon, Jenny," said Canon, "I can take this guy."

"Nope, I'm not going to risk it. You're a civilian and this guy is bigger than I am. We're going to stand down here."

Willson raised her hands, palms open. "Okay, guys, why don't you go on your way." She focused her attention on the big man. "You look like you had a fun evening. Is your friend good to drive?"

The smaller man responded to Willson's question while moving forward to grab the big man's elbow. "I'm good. I don't drink no more, although I know it don't look like it. C'mon, Bernie, let's get outta here."

Willson watched the big man shake off his friend's hand and then stagger away. "Fuckin' wardens," he muttered.

Willson and Canon watched the two men climb into a blue pickup truck, the small man in the driver's seat, the larger wedging himself into the passenger seat. The engine started as though in pain, and then the truck careered down the alley paralleling Banff's main street. Willson heard a crash and assumed they'd demolished either a garbage can or a fence.

Standing in the now quiet parking lot, Willson turned and smiled at Canon.

"Why the hell are you smiling, Jenny?" he asked. "You let them go. Those were the two guys we were looking for."

"I'm smiling for two reasons. One, because it was the smartest thing to do — it could have ended badly. And the second reason? Because I got a name for one of them and the licence plate of their vehicle. There's no way that shit-box of a truck's a rental. It belongs to one of those guys, and I'll soon have more information to work with, information that I didn't have a few moments ago."

She wrote the licence plate number on the palm of her left hand and looked back to where the pickup had disappeared down the dark alley. She heard a dog bark under the sky filled with stars, an exclamation mark to what she'd just witnessed.

"Time to celebrate with a scotch, Jim."

CHAPTER 10

MARCH 30

Jenny Willson had nothing good to say about the park warden office in Banff National Park. It was an ugly building located in an equally ugly industrial compound east of town, a part of Banff that most tourists never saw. Unlike the park's administration building, which presided over Banff like an imperial castle at the south end of the main street, the dumpy warden office shared its space with gas pumps, a warehouse, and a fenced compound filled with machinery and maintenance vehicles. To the north was a helipad and hangar where the red-and-white rescue helicopter, supplied by Alpine Helicopters from nearby Canmore, sat at the ready during the summer months.

Down the hallway from the spartan reception area, Willson sat at a grey metal desk in her equally spartan office, peering at a computer. Piles of files, notebooks, and a well-thumbed copy of the Criminal Code of Canada surrounded her. As she did every Monday morning, Willson had already reviewed a stack of reports prepared by seasonal wardens for the weekend shifts. She'd paused and sighed when she read the description of a double fatality the night before — a carload of local teenagers driving well over the speed limit had skidded into a copse of pine trees on the road to the old hot springs. It was all tragedy and no opportunity for learning. As court warden, she'd also prepared the paperwork for two court cases coming up later that week; she would drop them off at the Crown counsel's office after lunch while in town.

It was 9:30 a.m. and the weather was cold and blustery. Willson was catching up on email, the morning's second cup of bad coffee in hand. She was no fan of texting, tweeting, Instagramming, or Facebooking, so email was her one surrender to the world of social media. And it was a reluctant surrender at best. Scrolling through her inbox, she saw a message from the RCMP crime lab in Calgary. She opened it, her anticipation rising. It was a brief note from a civilian lab technician. It was the long-awaited report on the bullet they'd carved out of the shoulder of the bull elk she'd found on the 1A Highway nearly five months ago. She clicked on photographs of the slug — both the whole piece of lead as well as close-ups of its markings — and read the conclusion that the projectile was a .308-calibre bullet. Willson swore when she saw that it had no matches in the national database.

Even though she had expected the report to be clinical, Willson was disappointed. She knew that the .308 was a common bullet for North American hunters.

There were hundreds of thousands of them produced each year, and they could be fired from many different rifles. So without something to compare it to, such as the rifle used to shoot it, she had little to go on. But after seeing the two men in Giorgio's the night before, she wondered if either of them owned a gun that would fire a .308 cartridge. Wouldn't *that* be interesting.

She yawned and rolled her shoulders. Since finding the slaughtered elk, she hadn't slept through the night. Each time she was in a new investigation like this, her nights were filled with sheet-twisting, ceiling-staring, pillow-punching periods of consciousness, her mind a blur of possibilities and pathways, with shadowy perpetrators lurking out of her reach. She was tired from the previous night, when she'd repeatedly jerked awake from dreams of chasing shadowy men down shadowy alleys, running but never catching them.

And the long phone conversation with her mother, just before she was headed to bed, hadn't helped her insomnia. The phone had rung when she was sitting in her favourite reading chair, willing her eyes to stay open so she could finish the last chapter of a novel. The chair sat under a lamp in the living room of the old house she rented from Parks Canada. The house was on a quiet part of Cougar Street, near the railway and the strip of forest between it and the Trans-Canada Highway, only a ten-minute walk from her office. She loved the house and had twice saved it from the wrecking ball by surreptitiously siccing the local preservationists on her bosses. She was only a renter, but felt that the house had become hers and that, in turn, she had become part of the house. With the old walls popping and cracking around her in the cooling evening air, she'd simply listened to her mother talk about her father.

It had been twenty-two years since he'd died and it was still painful for both of them. While Willson had come to terms with it, at least on the surface, the loss remained a constant focus for her mother, an unhealthy focus that seemed to have become a barrier between her and the rest of the world. Willson knew it was unhealthy, knew her mother needed help, but just didn't know how to make that happen, particularly at a distance. She felt guilty and frustrated at her inability to fix her mother's challenges.

When she did finally sleep, her father appeared in the background of her troubled dreams, his eyebrows bushy, his eyes a deep blue, his insistent voice telling her to keep trying. "C'mon, Jenny," he said, "you can do it. Where there's a Willson, there's a way."

She wondered what the dream meant, what some new-age shrink would tell her about her childhood, or her relationship with her father, or who she was in a previous life.

A phone rang on the desk beside her, derailing her train of thought.

"Willson, Warden Office," she answered.

"Jenny, it's Brad Jenkins. We haven't spoken in a while, and I wondered if you've got any news on the poaching investigation."

"Hey, Brad," said Willson, her heart momentarily fluttering. She clenched her fists, frustrated with her inability to control her emotions. "I was going to call you this morning once I got through this mound of paperwork. I have a question for you."

"Go for it."

"Do you know a guy from Cranbrook … Charles Clark?"

"Yeah, I know Charlie Clark. Why are you asking?"

"What do you know about him?"

"He's a sad little man who's an assistant guide for an outfitter named Bernie Eastman. What's he got to do with this?"

For a moment, Willson pondered this latest news. An assistant guide, working for a guide-outfitter … a hunting guide … a guide by the name of Bernie? Now *this* was interesting.

"Bear with me for a second," said Willson. "Give me a description of Clark and Eastman, would you?"

"Clark is barely five feet tall, no more than a hundred and thirty pounds soaking wet, with brown scraggly hair and a face that looks like one of his parents was a ferret. I've never seen him without a baseball cap. And he's meek, mild, seemingly afraid of his own shadow and wobbly on his feet."

"And Eastman?"

"They're complete opposites," said Jenkins, "like Arnold Schwarzenegger hanging out with a thin Danny DeVito. Eastman's a big man, probably two hundred and seventy-five pounds, nearly six and a half feet tall, with a bushy beard and a bad temper."

"Huh," was all Willson said.

"Are you going to tell me why you're asking about them, Jenny? Or are you going to keep me in the dark? Are they involved in the elk poaching?"

"Sorry, Brad," said Willson. "My mind is racing here. Let me take a step back. I was out for dinner in Banff last night with Jim Canon and his photo agent, and we almost got into it with two guys outside the restaurant, both apparently hammered, but one claiming he didn't drink. Guess what? Jim's certain they were the two guys he saw on the trail in Wilcox Pass shortly before the ram was shot."

"Are you shitting me?"

"I shit you not. Jim was sure of it."

"So did you talk to them?"

"We did. We followed them from the restaurant to the parking lot and tried to get identification from them. That didn't work, and I decided not to push it. But I got the licence number of their truck, the same colour of truck that Jim saw in the parking lot that day. When I ran the licence plate first thing this morning, it came back to Charlie Clark."

"Holy shit," said Jenkins. "Talk about good timing and even better luck."

"And Clark called the other guy Bernie before they left, so it's gotta be them. So tell me more about this Eastman character."

"Eastman lives on a ranch in Ta Ta Creek near Kimberley. I've been to his place a couple of times. He operates north of there in the Purcell Mountains, in a guide territory where he pays the government for the exclusive right to guide non-resident hunters. He's a pain in the ass to deal with. He's a bully, plain and simple. All our guide-outfitters are real characters, but out of all of them, Eastman is the only guy I can think of who might get wrapped up in something like this."

Willson's mind raced with the news from Jenkins. What the hell was a Kootenay-based guide-outfitter with his own licensed territory that was probably full of wildlife doing in the national park? What was going on? Her thoughts leaped ahead. If she could tie Clark and Eastman not only to the poached elk in Banff, but also to the dead ram in Jasper, she'd have the start of one hell of a case, instead of being at what appeared to be a dead end. She remembered that neither the RCMP nor the wardens had stopped any vehicles matching Canon's description on the night the elk was shot, nor even a night or two before. As a good investigator, she automatically jumped to the next obvious step.

"Brad, these guys may have stayed in Banff overnight. Not just last night … but around the time the elk was shot. If they were scouting prior to that, they might have stayed a night or two in town and/or they probably ate in a restaurant somewhere. It's unlikely they stayed here the night *after* they shot the elk because the risk would be too great. I'm going to canvass the local hotels, motels, and restaurants to see if they have any record of them."

"That's a hell of an idea," said Jenkins.

"Can you get me copies of their driver's licences, Brad, so I have pictures of them?"

"I'll get them to you as soon as can."

"This is fantastic!" she said excitedly. "I'm going to start now, gotta go. Thanks for this. I may finally have a good lead."

"Good luck, Jenny. Keep me —"

In her haste to get moving, Willson disconnected too quickly, but no matter. She'd apologize to Jenkins some other time. She immediately jogged down the hall to the maze of seasonal warden cubicles.

"Bill!" she yelled to Forsyth. His head popped up from behind a divider like a prairie dog in a brush fire. "I need you in my office, now."

"I'll just finish what I'm doing," Forsyth said, sitting down again, "and then I'll come down to see you later."

"No, Bill," Willson said, like a pet owner to a disobedient dog, "not later. I need you RFN. Right fucking now."

Forsyth hurried to Willson's office, cellphone in hand and a curious look on his face. "What's up?"

Willson had a map of the town of Banff spread out on her desk and did not look at him as he came through the door. "Whatever else you're working on, Bill, stop. Starting now, you and I are going door-to-door."

"Looking for what?" asked Forsyth.

"Looking for evidence that one or both of these two guys," Willson said, handing him a piece of paper with the two names on it, "ate or stayed in Banff during the few days prior to the shooting of the elk at the end of last October."

"You think these guys are our perps?"

"If they aren't," said Willson, "there's a good chance they know who is."

"How did you identify them?"

"Seems a friend of mine saw them in Wilcox Pass only days before Jasper lost its ram, and then we saw them last night here in town, at Giorgio's. I got one name from running the licence plate and I got confirmation of the other name from a friend who's a conservation officer in B.C. I drove around Banff early this morning to see if I could locate their truck, but no luck."

"B.C.," Forsyth echoed. "Are they from there?"

"Yup," said Willson, pointing one at a time to the names in Forsyth's hand. "Clark is an assistant hunting guide from Cranbrook, and Eastman is the guy he works for. He's a guide-outfitter with a territory in the Purcell Mountains. I've requested copies of their driver's licences. They might be in my inbox now. I'll make copies for us if they are."

"So where do you want me to go?"

Willson pointed to the map on her desk. "I want you to take *all* the hotels on the west side of Banff Avenue, and I'll take the hotels on the east side, including the Banff Springs, the Rimrock, and the others on the south side of the river. I need you to ask at each one of the places about the three or four days leading up to and including the night of October thirty-first. Check to see if either of these guys stayed overnight. Talk to the desk clerks first, then the managers if you can. We can use the driver's licence pictures to jog memories. If either of these guys are in their records, get a copy of a credit card receipt as evidence and find out which employee checked them in or out so we can follow up."

"Geez," said Forsyth. "This is going to take a lot of time. Shouldn't we get others to help us?"

"This one is just you and me, Bill. Welcome to the world of slogging it out in the investigative trenches, where you get muddy and tired and pursue thousands of leads before you uncover something substantial. Let's quit talking and get at it."

He turned to go, but she stopped him with, "By the way, Bill, did you ever find any photographs of the elk taken before it was poached?"

"I did," he replied. "It took some digging but I tracked down a wildlife photographer who took some shots of the bull two days before he was killed. He was happy to share them with us when I told him what it was for. I'm pretty sure it's the elk we lost. I had him sign and date the photographs and put them in the case file."

"Excellent. If we get lucky, we'll need those."

Two days later, Willson leaned against her truck in the parking lot outside the warden office. It was the end of the day and she was exhausted and frustrated, with nothing to prove that either Clark or Eastman had stayed in town prior to the elk's death. She looked up at the face of Cascade Mountain, a cold breeze blowing her hair across her face.

She watched as Forsyth pulled into the lot and parked, then climbed out of his truck. As he approached her, his hands were in his pockets, and he had a smug look on his face.

"What's up?" Willson asked.

"Well," he said, unable, it appeared, to hold back a grin, "I checked all the hotels in my area and found nothing. So when I finished an hour ago, I thought I would drop in to Giorgio's because you told me that was where you saw these guys the other night. It seems we're not dealing with a bunch of geniuses. Would a credit card receipt in the name of Charles Clark for two people for dinner on October 30 of last year, be of interest to you?" He waved a piece of paper in front of Willson, his eyebrows raised, his grin wider. "Isn't that the night before the elk was shot?"

Willson grabbed the receipt and the young warden in a bear hug that was both vigorous and awkward. When she regained her composure, she asked the next obvious question. "If they were here in Banff for dinner that night, they must have stayed somewhere. Jesus, Bill. What are we missing?"

"I have no idea," said Forsyth. "If they were here the night before the elk was shot, they wouldn't have gone all the way back to East Kootenay and then come back again the next day. That makes no sense. They must have stayed *some*where."

Suddenly Willson had a thought. "Did you check the Juniper Hotel?

"No. Where's that?"

"Shit!" she said, and in a flash, she was in her truck and gone, leaving Forsyth to cough and wave in the cloud of dust she left behind.

Willson's mind raced as she drove. The Juniper was the only hotel in Banff on the north side of the Trans-Canada Highway and was, as a result, easy to forget. It was a place people stayed if they had money or wanted privacy. Willson sped through Banff, near-ly clipping a tourist taking pictures of Mount Rundle while standing in the middle of Banff Avenue. She passed the train station, crossed the Trans-Canada highway on an overpass, and turned left into the Juniper's long driveway.

She left her truck running in front of the hotel and burst through the main door, heading directly to the front desk. The big, blond-haired woman behind it looked up as Willson approached.

"I'm Park Warden Officer Jenny Willson and I need to speak with the hotel manager." Willson could barely contain her excitement and sense of urgency.

The woman smiled at Willson. "I'm the on-duty manager for the day. What can I do to help you, Officer?"

"I need to see a few of your guest records from last fall — the nights of October 29, 30, and 31."

The woman looked uncertain. "Uh … I've never had to deal with a request like this before. I might have to talk to our general manager, who is away in Calgary."

Willson had dealt with issues of guest confidentiality before in previous investigations and realized that she had to jump on it quickly before company processes and policies acted as needless speed bumps. She leaned across the counter, looked the woman in the eye, and dropped her voice to a whisper. "With all due respect," Willson said, "it's your decision if you want to give me the information or not." She paused for effect. "But I don't have time to screw around. I bet your boss does not want to have to deal with a bunch of parks people showing up to review your garbage and waste-management systems, your water system, and your fire protection, and to check whether your landscaping matches our wildlife requirements. Who knows what might come out of that …"

The woman visibly gulped. With a nod to show she had decided, she moved over to a computer and worked her way through the hotel's guest records, her fingers flying across the keys with confidence.

"Can you tell me who you're specifically looking for?" the manager asked.

"How about if you let me look at those dates, and I'll see if the folks I'm interested in are there," Willson said, not yet wanting to name names.

The woman flipped the large computer monitor around so Willson could see the list of guests on the three nights. There appeared to be about thirty guests on the twenty-ninth, and fewer on the thirtieth and thirty-first; they all appeared on one screen. Willson's eyes first moved slowly down the list for the thirty-first, the night the elk was killed, and saw neither of the names she was looking for. Her heart sank.

Then just as quickly, her spirits leaped when she saw the name "Clark, C." printed twice on the list for the night *before* the elk died.

"Bingo!" she said softly.

"You find what you want there?" asked the manager.

"I did," Willson said. "Now I need your help. I see the same name twice on the night of the thirtieth. Can you explain that?" She pointed to Clark's name on the screen.

"That means one person paid for two rooms."

"Was there a reservation made for the rooms?"

"No," responded the manager. "They're coded as walk-ins."

"How do I know who actually stayed in the rooms?"

"I'll have to go a separate screen where we'll have the actual guest names."

"Could there have been a third person staying in one of the two rooms?"

"There's no record of it," said the woman, "but someone could have joined them without us seeing them."

"Okay. Can you please print a copy of this screen and then give me a copy of the full records for that night under the name of Clark?"

"I can do that for you."

The manager handed the three pages of records across the counter to Willson, who looked carefully at the list, running her finger down one name at a time. The name Charlie Clark was there, twice, on the first printed page. He had paid for the two rooms. On one of the next pages, she saw that a Bernard Eastman was registered as the guest in the second room. At this point, Willson realized she held another piece of evidence that might crack open her poaching case.

"Can you tell me which desk clerk was on when these guests checked in?" asked Willson, "I need to talk to him or her."

The manager again returned to the computer and then wrote a name and phone number on the back of a hotel business card for Willson.

"The clerk that afternoon was Samantha Haskins," the manager said, handing Willson the card. "She's here from Australia. She's not working today and won't be on again until Saturday night. But give her a call on her cell and maybe you can catch her."

Willson thanked the manager for her assistance and then walked out to her idling truck, much calmer than when she arrived. Sitting in the cab, she punched in Haskins's number on her cell and, when there was no answer, left a message asking the woman to call back as soon as possible. Willson sat for a moment, digesting the importance of the information she'd uncovered at the hotel.

The investigation had suddenly changed. "Those guys were here in town the night before the elk died. It *must* be them," she said to herself. "Now the real fun begins."

It wasn't until a frustrating day later that Willson interviewed the young desk clerk who checked in Clark and Eastman at the Juniper Hotel. She met the woman at the warden office, speaking with her in a small interview room. Willson discovered that Haskins, a twenty-three-year-old with rainbow hair, remembered the two men. She told Willson it was Clark who paid for the rooms, and she remembered the larger man lurking behind him.

"The little guy looked like he was scared of the big guy, and that's why I remember them — the big guy didn't want to give me his name," she said. "I remember telling them they wouldn't get the rooms if I didn't know who was staying in them."

"Do you remember the big man's name?" asked Willson.

She watched Haskins think for a moment, her eyes moving up and to the right, concentrating.

"Sorry," said Haskins. "I really don't. I see and talk to so many people in my job that I can't remember them all." Willson saw her face brighten for a moment. "But his name should be in the hotel's guest records. I always note the names of all guests who stay in the rooms, just in case. It's hotel policy."

"That's okay," said Willson. "I've already got it."

Then she showed Haskins the driver's licence pictures.

"That's them. That's the two guys!"

Willson pushed Haskins about the presence of a third man.

"I don't know," said Haskins after a pause. "There may have been a third guy with them when they came back to the hotel later that night, but I really don't remember. I was helping other guests check in, so I was a bit distracted. Sorry. I wish I could help you more."

After the interview with Haskins, Willson sat in the empty interview room. She now had the identity of two of the key suspects for the elk kill. But she was stymied by the mysterious third man, if in fact there was a third man. She remembered the three distinct sets of footprints the night the elk was shot, so this would not necessarily be inconsistent. Willson also knew she now had enough to pursue search warrants. She walked down the hall to her office and phoned Brad Jenkins in Cranbrook.

"Brad," she said, trying to stay calm, "I think I've finally busted this thing open."

"Don't tease me now," said Jenkins. "What have you got?"

"Evidence that Clark and Eastman rented rooms at the Juniper hotel here in Banff the night before the elk died, and that Clark and one other person — probably Eastman but no way to know — were at dinner in Banff that same night," said Willson. "And Clark and Eastman are the same guys Canon saw in Wilcox Pass the day before the ram was found there. This has got to be more than a coincidence."

"This is good … really good," said Jenkins, his voice rising in excitement.

"It friggin' well is," said Willson. "I'm thinking that two of our suspects — likely Eastman and Clark — were here on October thirtieth, maybe doing some scouting …

and then a third guy somehow joined them the next day. They did the deed that night, left the park right away, and then I found the animal the next morning."

"Makes sense, said Jenkins. "Now we've got to find a judge who'll give us a warrant to search Clark and Eastman's houses here in the valley. If we can find a rifle and then match its ballistics to the slug in the elk … or if we can find the elk's rack and match it to any photographs of the bull, we've got these assholes."

"That's exactly what I was thinking. I've got pictures of the bull on file. And the same goes for the sheep in Jasper. So, Brad, tell me which of your local judges I should call."

CHAPTER 11

The clock on the mantel chimed twice, softly, respectfully, a gentle reminder that it was two o'clock on a quiet Saturday afternoon. Luis Castillo sat in a leather chair in his den, a section of the *Spokesman Review* newspaper open on his lap. He was thinking about the upcoming city elections, about the slate of candidates running for mayor and council.

According to recent polls, the current mayor — with whom Castillo had a long-time understanding — was in second place behind a contender campaigning to clean up City Hall, to make it more transparent and accountable to Spokane taxpayers. Castillo knew that this kind of platform played to the public, a public with a deep distrust of politicians. He also knew that a leadership change would mean a change to the way he ran his business. And not in a good way. He couldn't let it happen.

It was time to take action, to stall the competitor's momentum by investing more money in his favoured candidate and by uncovering dirt on the upstart, dirt that would find its way into the local media.

Castillo heard a knock on the den door. *"Por favor, pase,"* he said.

His housekeeper, a sixty-something woman who'd been with him long enough to have met both his daughters when they were first brought home from the hospital, poked her head around the heavy door.

"Señor Castillo," she said, "the men are here with your animals."

"Ah, *muchas gracias,* Juanita. I will be right there." Castillo smiled, carefully folded the newspaper, and set it on the table to his right. He stood, stretched, and then strode down the hallway, his leather slippers whispering on the polished wood floor.

"Jimmy," he said when he saw the man standing in his front entrance. He shook the man's hand while glancing at the logo on his fleece jacket. Spokane Valley Taxidermy. "I'm excited to see what you've brought me today."

"Hello, Mr. Castillo," said the man, passing him a clipboard and pen. "If you would sign this receipt for me, please, we'll bring them in from the truck. The third one should be ready in a few weeks."

Ten minutes later, Castillo stood in his den, alone, gazing at two mounted trophies that leaned against adjacent sides of his desk.

The first was a massive bull elk's head, the antlers wide and thick and spreading beyond the edge of the desk. He knew the antlers were from the elk he'd shot, but what was really impressive was the skill of the taxidermist, how he'd artfully connected the rack to an equally large skull from another animal. It was a magnificent job, well worth the money, with no sign that the parts had not spent their lives together as one.

His gaze shifted to the other trophy. It was the bighorn ram from the other Canadian park, its horns rugged and ridged, full curl. Castillo stared at the eyes. They seemed alive and bright and curious, as though pondering their new surroundings.

As the clock ticked gently in the background, Castillo stood without moving, his chest swelling with pride. Visions of his childhood in Chiapas flooded back, a time when his father would leave home in early-morning darkness to hunt the red brocket deer, white-tailed deer, collared peccary, and small rodents known as *paca* that lived in the forests and fields adjacent to their neighbourhood. Not only did his father's hunting protect the local crops from the voracious animals, but those animals then became food for the family, and often for other local families in need. And when his father returned home with his quarry over one shoulder, his gun over the other, his steps echoing down the cobblestone street, Castillo recalled their neighbours smiling and nodding in respect and appreciation. Because his father took lives purposefully and skillfully, those looks were often edged with a glimmer of fear.

Because of his ability as a hunter, his father had played a more prominent role in the community than was normally afforded a common shopkeeper. For his father, it was not about the thrill of the hunt, and it wasn't a deep-seated spiritual appreciation for the lives of the wild animals he harvested. Instead, it was about providing for his family and about his position in the community; he was a provider, protector, predator rather than prey, a man not to be taken lightly. Since then, Castillo had always associated a successful hunt with the admiration of friends and family. It was no different now. He wanted to be like his father, a successful hunter respected — and perhaps somewhat feared — by those around him.

Castillo turned when he felt a presence at his right shoulder.

"Are you okay, Luis?" said his wife.

"Ah, Adelina, I did not hear you come in. How did things go today?"

With a sigh, she dropped a leather attaché case on the floor to her right. "The planning meeting went well," she said. "We've almost raised enough money to begin building our first supervised injection site at the edge of downtown. It's not going to stop people from doing drugs … but it should keep them a lot safer when they do."

"That's good," he said, nodding his head slowly. "I hope my contacts helped you obtain the permits. Any chance my company will get the construction contract?"

Adelina smiled and shook her head. "Luis, you and I both know that's not a good idea on so many levels."

"Perhaps you're right, but I had to ask." He saw his wife shift her gaze to the two trophies against the desk. Her eyebrows and mouth moved downward in tandem, a sign of either distaste or — after twenty-four years of marriage — resignation.

"Are those new?" she asked.

"Yes, the taxidermist delivered them this afternoon. They're the ones I got in Canada."

"He *is* an artist, that taxidermist. His skills are remarkable."

"I think the hunter should also be given credit for his skills," said Castillo.

"I'm sure you do. But as you often say, Luis, the hunter is only as good as the guide he hires to accompany him."

Castillo realized that his wife was not in a praising mood, which was a surefire way to dampen his spirits. He stared at her. Since his daughters had left home for university, he had noticed a change in the woman. Whereas before she had been loving and largely obedient, he now found her to be increasingly distant and willful. As long as there was money to spend, her interest in his businesses turned to disinterest. And most difficult of all, her passion for him had turned to indifference, the passion transferred to her charity work.

"After all these years, you still do not understand or approve of my hunting, do you, Adelina?" It was more a statement than a question.

"I certainly understand *why* you hunt and ... at least on the surface, I don't disapprove," she said, meeting his gaze unflinchingly. "I simply wonder how many lines you're willing to cross, how many laws you're willing to break, how much you're willing to put our family at risk, all in the single-minded pursuit of your beloved trophies."

"What do you mean?"

"Please, give me *some* credit," she said, shaking her head. "I've heard you speaking to that Eastman fellow on the phone. I know you pay him more than you've ever paid any other guide. I know you talk to him about parks, about hunting only at certain times, about getting the animals back into the United States. It sounds to me like you are literally crossing some of those lines, Luis, lines that could get you into serious trouble with the law." She paused, then continued. "What do I mean? I mean that none of us can afford such trouble." Suddenly her gaze was full of challenge. She was clearly daring him to disagree with her, to lie to her. "Am I wrong, my dearest husband?"

"I have always put the well-being of this family first," Castillo said. "As long as I do that, and as long as I keep doing that, then how I run my affairs should be of no concern to you."

"You did not answer my question, so I will leave it at that for now. But despite your elusive assurances, Luis, you need to understand that I'm *very* concerned about your actions. *How* you do something is just as important as *what* you do. You must remember that your decisions affect all of us."

Castillo watched his wife pick up her briefcase and walk away from him, with a quick baleful look over her left shoulder as she entered the hallway.

For the third time that afternoon, he was alone in his den, the clock ticking from its place on the mantel. Earlier, it was a subtle sound in the background, marking the pleasant passing of time, the celebration of the arrival of his latest trophies, an opportunity to reflect on his role as a successful hunter. Now, the clock was loud, insistent, obtrusive. It reminded him that his world was shifting under his slippered feet, second by ticking second.

CHAPTER 12

APRIL 11

Jenny Willson understood how Hudson's Bay Company governor Sir George Simpson must have felt when he first passed through Sinclair Canyon in 1841, and why he had written of his impatience to escape "this horrid gorge." While Bill Forsyth drove, Willson was just as impatient about having to follow a trio of transport trucks crawling down the long hill into Radium. The road was snowy and slippery, the trip unbearably slow.

"You're right, Sir George," she said, "this *is* friggin' horrid. C'mon people, c'mon!" She pounded her fist on the dash to make her point. "I could *walk* faster than this."

Forsyth nodded his agreement. But eventually, like popping out of a rocky birth canal, they passed through the final dramatic walls of the canyon and entered the broad valley of the Rocky Mountain Trench. Ahead of them, silhouetted by the setting sun, were the Purcell Mountains and the blocky form of Farnham Tower.

Now they were in the open, freed from the horrid gorge, Willson heard her cellphone chirp to indicate a waiting message. She listened to it as they rolled to a stop at a service station at the corner of Highways 93 and 95 in Radium Hot Springs. Their gas tank was nearly empty.

"Jenny, this is Paul Hunter from the Jasper Warden Office. You left me a message yesterday asking whether we had information on the weapon that killed the big-horn sheep ram in Wilcox Pass. I finally had a moment to get back to you."

As soon as she heard Hunter's annoying, nasal voice, Willson felt skepticism and suspicion rise in her throat like bile. She put the message on speakerphone so Forsyth could hear it. Hunter had a reputation as a com-petitive jerk who looked for every opportunity to put himself and Jasper ahead of everyone else. It was com-mon knowledge that his goal was to be a park super-intendent one day. While few in Parks Canada shared his optimism for achieving it, Willson knew that it made him happy to look good at the expense of the Banff war-dens. She had no time for the ambitious prick.

Hunter's voice droned on. "We don't have anything conclusive yet. The bullet that killed the ram in Wilcox Pass could be from a .357 Magnum revolver. But it could be from something else. We're not sure yet. We heard you might be heading into the Kootenays today to execute search warrants and we thought it best that you not do that until we are sure what we've got and can work with you on it. Give me a call if you need anything else." Hunter left his phone number before the message ended.

Willson and Forsyth looked at each other for a moment, expressionless. Then they both guffawed.

"Does he really think we're that stupid?" said Willson when she caught her breath. "I don't believe a word of what he said. Fuck 'im."

A few moments later, Forsyth steered them to the café at Kicking Horse Coffee on the edge of Invermere. Willson saw an army of windmills rotating slowly on the roof, and with a deep inhale, she smelled the aroma of roasting coffee beans lingering in the air.

"I'll grab you a coffee," said Forsyth. "It's something special here. You're gonna like this."

While she waited, Hunter's message began to crawl in the back of her mind like a reptile searching for prey. She considered him to be an arrogant, uncooperative son of a bitch, the kind of slimy ladder-climber that she hated as much as she did poachers. Infuriated, unable to avoid the impulse, she punched in Hunter's number.

The Jasper warden answered after three rings. "Hunter here."

"Paul, it's Jenny Willson. I got your message."

"Ah, Jenny. I'm glad I caught you before you did something you shouldn't. I hope you are not going ahead with the search warrants. We're just not ready for that yet. It's too soon."

"Look, Paul," said Willson, "I *am* going ahead and it's not your place to tell me if I am or am not ready. I guarantee you that I'm ready, even if you're not. In fact, I'm only moments away from visiting a Justice of the Peace to get the warrants. I discovered the names of our two main suspects only two days ago, and I'm not prepared to waste any more time. So … I need you to tell me what you've got on the weapon that was used for the Wilcox Pass ram. If you tell me what you have, I can use that in my application for the warrants. If you won't, then I can't. We might only get one chance here."

"Which JP are you meeting with?" asked Hunter.

Willson knew better than to tell him anything. She wouldn't put it past Hunter to phone the JP and derail their application before they met with her. "I don't know. The B.C. Conservation officers are taking the lead on that."

"Well, we're disappointed you're jumping the gun on this, and we think you're making a mistake."

"Paul, *you're* making a mistake by assuming I care what you and your multiple personalities think," Willson said, trying but failing to keep her anger in check. "And you're making an even bigger mistake by withholding critical information to our case. Have you got something for me or not? I'd hate to lose the opportunity to grab the gun if I see it. And it would be a real shame for me to have to tell everyone later that Jasper wouldn't co-operate with me on this … or even worse, that Jasper purposefully sidetracked the investigation. That would not look good for you."

Now back in the truck, Forsyth grinned, giving her a fist pump to show his support.

With her free hand, Willson took the cup that Forsyth had placed in the console between them. A warm calm flooded her body when the deep, rich flavour of the coffee hit her taste buds.

"This is not a matter of us not co-operating with you," Hunter said, not taking the bait. "It's an opportunity for us to slow down so we can both go to our bosses in Calgary and show what we've done together ... on what could be a very big case."

"That's where you and I differ, Paul. For me, this is *all* about protecting the park. It's not about trying to impress people higher up the food chain so I can get a promotion."

"That's not what this is about ... and I resent that remark. You're trying to twist my words. Why are you being so uncooperative?"

"Look, Paul," said Willson, her patience exhausted, "I have no time for your bullshit. Tell me what I need to know."

"Sorry, I wish I could help, but I've got nothing for you. I again ask that you not go ahead with this. You're making a mistake, Jenny," he said.

Willson had enough. "Once again, *you're* the one making the fucking mistake," she said, ending the call with a punch of a button. It was at times like this that Willson found cellphones frustrating. It was so much more satisfying to slam a phone into its cradle when dealing with an asshole like Hunter.

Two hours later, Willson, Forsyth, and Conservation Officer Brad Jenkins sat in the living room of a Kimberley home across from a surly Justice of the Peace, a woman who was clearly annoyed at being pulled from a family dinner to deal with their request. When they'd met on the street outside the woman's home, Jenkins had passed on a greeting from Kim Davidson. At that point, Willson had finally given up on there ever being anything between the CO and herself. Jenkins was happy, his fiancée annoyingly likeable. It was time to move on.

Even though she was the JP on evening duty, the wire-haired, middle-aged woman — who seemed afraid to smile — was putting them through the wringer, making them as uncomfortable as she could. Willson let Jenkins start with the introductions because he'd met the woman; he sat on a provincial union committee with her and knew she had a left-leaning environmental bent, perhaps useful in a case like this. But that didn't appear to help, so they quickly switched to Willson in the lead.

"Let me lay out our case for you, if that's okay," said Willson.

"Let me tell *you* something," said the woman, wagging her chubby finger at Willson. "When I get calls like this, after normal business hours, my assumption is that your case is weak and you don't want to appear before a real judge."

Willson had observed this kind of response from other judges and JPs, so she waited out the woman's rant, trying to act calm and compliant so as not to further annoy her. When the woman's momentum finally waned, Willson presented to her the Information to Obtain (ITO) document, where the basics of the warrant request were laid out. She also gave the JP a copy of the warrant they wanted her to sign.

Their application focused on proving that the shooting of the elk in Banff National Park was a *National Park*

Act offence, why the items they were searching for were relevant to that offence, and why they were asking to search the houses, outbuildings, and vehicles of both Charlie Clark and Bernie Eastman that night. It also referred to the shooting of the ram in Jasper. Willson had attached to the ITO a series of background documents, including the crime lab report on the .308-calibre weapon, the sworn statement from Jim Canon indicating when and where he'd seen the two men in both Banff and Jasper parks, and copies of the hotel and restaurant receipts from Banff proving the date they had been there.

After reading the reports, some of them two or three times, the JP peered up over the reading glasses perched low on her sharp nose.

"So, is this about the elk in Banff or the ram in Jasper?" she asked.

Willson responded quickly. "Along with the elk, we believe these suspects were also involved with the bighorn sheep, and we believe they — or someone with them — shot it with a handgun. But we don't at this time have enough evidence to prove that beyond a reasonable doubt, nor can we confirm the calibre of the weapon used. The crime lab report on that should come in any time. As you can see in the ITO, we're asking you, in anticipation of that, to give us the authority to seize any handguns we might find during the search, along with any .308s."

After tense back-and-forth discussion that focused largely on why they had to do the search that night, the JP finally agreed to give them warrants based on what was presented in the documents. She let them know of her lingering reluctance. "The evidence you've presented to me doesn't make me comfortable," she said. "However, because of the concerns you've expressed over the potential for these two individuals to hide or destroy evidence if they get wind of your investigation and because, quite frankly — and I did not say this — I'm personally sickened by people using our national parks as a source of trophies for their walls, I'm prepared to sign the warrants. But I'm going to make them very specific."

After signing, the JP wrote and initialled comments on the bottom of the warrants and then looked at each of the officers in turn, like the teacher of a class of remedial students. "These warrants relate only to the main residences at the two addresses on your application, along with any outbuildings, vehicles, or equipment at those addresses," she said. "I am allowing you to seize any and all .308 calibre weapons you find, elk antlers if you find any, and any other evidence directly related only to the shooting of the elk in Banff National Park on or about October 31 of last year."

The woman dashed Willson's hopes with her final statement: "I'm not prepared to give you the authority to seize any handguns or to go beyond evidence relating to the elk," she said while glaring at Willson, daring her to raise a challenge. "And you cannot seize evidence that is in the personal possession of people other than the two named subjects."

Willson's mind was filled with profanity, all directed at Hunter and his Jasper warden colleagues. But she was smart enough not to poke this woman any further. "I understand," she responded. "Thank you very much for your time tonight. Our apologies for disrupting your dinner."

From the Justice's house in Kimberley, Willson drove Forsyth and Jenkins directly to a Tim Hortons coffee shop at the north end of Cranbrook. By now, she had discovered that not only was Forsyth was a pain in the ass to work with, he was a certified coffee snob. This became more evident when he complained, like a petulant child, about entering a place that he claimed served an inferior brew to that of his beloved Kicking Horse Coffee. On this point, Willson thought him to be a nutcase in need of professional help, but she'd already decided not to tell him — so as not to encourage him — that whatever it was he'd bought for her in Invermere was the best damn coffee she'd ever had. "Suck it up, Princess," she said to him as they entered the coffee shop.

By 7:00 p.m., they were joined at a shiny, round-topped table by three other conservation officers — two women and one man. Willson slurped a black coffee that made her grimace, while across the table from her, Forsyth sipped tea with a smug I-told-you-so look on his face.

With the signed search warrants in one hand and a white porcelain mug in the other, Willson urged the officers to lean in close, so that others in the restaurant could not hear their conversation, and then laid out her plan for executing the warrants on Clark and Eastman.

"Okay," she said. "We know that Clark is a nervous weasel of a man and that Eastman is a big hothead who'd just as soon fight as talk, so I'll lead an all-woman team to hit Clark's place. I'm betting that will make him uncomfortable."

As they'd driven down the valley that afternoon, dodging elk on the highway, Willson had originally wanted to visit Eastman herself. Assuming he was the ringleader, she wanted to see him again in person, to see the look on his face when he realized that she knew what he'd done, to ensure he understood that she would be an irritating burr under his saddle, a burr that would remain until she had him behind bars. But on reflection, she knew the revised plan was the right one. Her gut told her that Clark might be the weak link. She wanted to be the one to push him, to crack him open like a walnut.

She pointed across the table to Jenkins, Forsyth, and the male CO. "That leaves you three to hit Eastman's place at Ta Ta Creek," she said. "If you're okay with that, it's going to take you about thirty minutes to get out there, so let's plan to hit the two places simultaneously." She glanced at her watch. "Let's say 8:00 p.m." She reminded them that the warrant expired at 9:00 p.m.

Willson looked for agreement around the table and saw it in five nodding heads.

"Good," she said. "Bill, I want you to call me when you're in Eastman's yard, ready to bang on his door. I won't knock on Clark's door until I hear from you. When I give you the word, put your phone away and then do it. I don't want there to be any chance that Eastman might phone Clark … or vice versa."

"Got it, boss," said Forsyth.

Willson then gave each team a copy of the appropriate warrant and, one more time, led them through the documents, line by line and clause by clause, to ensure everyone was clear on where they could and could not search and what they could and could not seize. She pointed to maps and copies of Google Earth images to reconfirm the locations of their targets.

"This is a big deal for us," said Willson, wrapping up the conversation. "I sincerely appreciate your help. Stay safe out there, and let's do this." With that, she rose from the table, shook hands with each officer, and then placed her now-empty mug into a plastic bin. She saw the looks of surprise on the faces of other patrons as the six uniformed officers rushed by them.

CHAPTER 13

Charlie Clark lived in a mobile home park on the northwest side of Cranbrook. An older complex, it was a mix of old and new, each home showing varying levels of care. In the shade of some yards, dusty, abandoned toys encircled vehicles up on blocks, awaiting repairs that might never come. In others, solar lights lined neat pathways of gravel and paving bricks. Clark's yard and trailer were the worst on the street, forlorn and derelict. Neglected would be an understatement.

Jenny Willson received the call from Bill Forsyth confirming that his team was in Eastman's driveway. When the illuminated dial of her watch blinked to 8:00 p.m., she banged her fist on the front door of Clark's trailer. One of the female conservation officers stood on the porch on her right, her hand resting on a 9-mm pistol in a worn leather holster on her hip. The other stood a metre behind them on the bottom stair.

Willson knew they made an impressive and intimidating team, particularly in the dark. That was the point.

Willson banged once more, louder this time. In response, they heard rustling inside, and then a woman in a tattered bathrobe opened the door, slowly, cautiously. The light in the room behind her was on, unlike the porch light, so she was a silhouette with a halo of frizzy hair.

Willson gave the woman no time to react, opening the aluminum screen door with her left hand and immediately informing her why they were there. "My name is Jenny Willson. I am a park warden from Banff National Park. I have a warrant to search these premises. Is Charlie Clark here? Are you his wife?"

The woman did not immediately respond, instead using her left hand to turn on the porch light as though its illumination would give her mind time to catch up to what she'd just heard. Her eyes widened when she saw the three female officers on her front porch. "Yes, I'm Wendy Clark," she said, her voice a gravelly croak. She took the copy of the warrant that Willson pushed toward her and turned into the house. "Charlie, you need to come here right away." She turned back to the door, swaying slightly, but by then, Willson and her colleagues were pushing their way inside.

Behind his wife, Charlie Clark had risen from a leather recliner and was taking his first steps toward the door. Also in a bathrobe, he slowed in surprise when he saw the three female officers in his living room. Behind him, Willson saw a television paused in the middle of a black-and-white movie. A table in front of a faded couch was littered with half-empty whiskey bottles and overflowing ashtrays. The room smelled stale and smoky.

Willson saw that Clark was unsteady on his feet and yet was trying to gain any control he could over the situation. She remembered the same instability from the Banff parking lot almost two weeks earlier — and his claim that he didn't drink.

She watched him puff out his scrawny chest, but the effort made him cough. "What the hell's goin' on here?" he asked after catching his breath, his confusion obvious. He obviously hadn't heard Willson announce herself when his wife opened the door. "You got no goddamn right to do this." But his eyes widened when he saw Willson. "You …!"

Willson responded with authority. "Mr. Clark, I see you remember me. Your wife has a copy of a valid search warrant that we have for your house, vehicle, and outbuildings. We do have the right to do this. I want you and your wife to sit here while this officer and I undertake the search. The other officer will ensure you stay in this room while we do what we have to do. If you interfere with us in any way, you will immediately be arrested for obstruction. Do you understand?"

Clark sat back down on the couch, muttering as much to himself as to anyone else in the room. "This is fuckin' bullshit," he said. His bathrobe gaped open as his bony knees splayed, exposing Willson to a view that would haunt her dreams. She quickly turned away, nausea tickling at the bottom of her stomach. Clark's wife stood, frozen in place, with one hand still clutching the open front door, her eyes wide and her mouth opening and closing as though on a mechanical hinge.

After pulling on blue surgical gloves, Willson and her partner searched the trailer, each taking one room at a time. They opened drawers in cabinets and dressers, they looked under tables and beds, they peered under and between worn mattresses. Willson opened the sliding closet doors in a guest bedroom and found a cardboard box brimming with sex toys. She pushed back more nausea and kept searching.

Forty minutes later, the two officers had looked in every corner of the small trailer. They found no elk antlers. The only rifle was an unloaded over/under shotgun leaning in the corner of the closet in the main bedroom — not what they were looking for. They'd found nothing to seize other than a cellphone on the kitchen counter that might hold incriminating photos, emails, or text messages.

Willson was crushed as she walked down the narrow hallway to the smoky living room. She decided to push Clark, to get him talking before he lawyered up. "So, Charlie, what can you tell me about you killing a bull elk in Banff National Park back in late October?"

Willson watched a bulb of comprehension, albeit a dim one, light up in the man's twitching eyes. If he didn't drink, then she wondered if he was sick, perhaps suffering from multiple sclerosis, Parkinson's, or even ALS. Whatever it was that was afflicting him, it didn't prevent him from understanding, at that moment, what this search was about. His face jerked and grimaced as if he'd been hit by a jolt of electricity.

"I don't know nothin' about that," Clark said, his mouth a trembling line across his face, a face that in its wrinkles and abrupt movements showed layers of trouble and pain.

With little physical evidence from the search, Willson refused to walk away from Clark's trailer empty-handed. She pressed the point. "Would you answer me any differently if I told you we have evidence that you and Bernie were in Banff the night before the elk was shot? I know you remember talking me to in Banff a couple of weeks ago. I know you've been there."

At the mention of Eastman's name, Clark's head snapped toward Willson. "I'm tired of talkin," he spat. "You can talk to my lawyer." He turned his head back to stare at the TV, crossing his arms over his chest as though that ended the matter.

"Charlie, are you going to let Bernie get away with this?" asked Willson.

"What in hell are you talkin' about?" said Clark, his brow furrowing.

"He bullies you into taking your truck on hunts in the park. He makes you use *your* credit card for meals and hotels," said Willson, "so the whole trail of evidence leads us to you and only you. And he's out there at his place, right now, telling my colleagues that it was all you, and that he had no part in it."

"That's bullshit ... do you think I'm stupid?" asked Clark. "Bernie wouldn't say nothin."

"No, I don't think you're stupid, Charlie," said Willson. "Not unless you let him keep setting you up like this."

"C'mon, Charlie," said Wendy, "don't let Bernie pin this all on you!"

Sensing an opening, Willson pushed. "Your wife sees what's going on, Charlie. Why can't you?"

"There are too many women talkin'," Clark whined. "It's hurtin' my head. I got nothin' to say to any of you. Leave me alone."

"Think about what your wife is saying, Charlie," Willson said. "In a situation like this, the first one to talk ends up in the least amount of trouble. The last one to talk gets the shaft every time. Every time, Charlie. Looks to me like Bernie is giving you the shaft and you're going to let him keep doing it?"

Willson saw Clark lean back on the couch and close his eyes. "Get the hell outta my house," he said.

"Aren't you at least willing to tell us who the third man is, Charlie? The guy who was with you when you shot the elk?"

"I didn't shoot no elk, and I don't know nothin' about anyone who did. I told you to get outta my house."

"Well, I guess we're done in here," said Willson. "You lost your chance, Charlie." She paused. "We need to search your truck and the shed behind the trailer. Where are your keys?"

Reluctantly, Clark grabbed car keys from the coffee table and threw them at Willson. They dropped well short, hitting a stand stuffed with public-television catalogues.

Willson bent to pick up the wad of keys and then, with the two COs following, crossed the living room, opened the screen door, and headed toward the wooden shed behind the Clarks' trailer. It was tucked against a sagging fence. One CO shone her metal flashlight at the door of the shed and they all saw the shiny padlock that secured it.

Willson tried all of the keys on the ring with no luck. She turned to Clark, who was now leaning against one of the posts on the front porch, watching them. "Which one is it, Charlie?" she asked.

"Go fuck yourself," he said with a smug smile.

Willson asked the CO to remove the lock with a set of bolt cutters retrieved from the back of her truck. Just as the lock hit the ground, Clark surprised them all by flying across the yard. He jumped on Willson's back, screaming and spitting. "You can't go in there!" he wailed.

Clark was not a big man, but he was wiry and surprisingly strong. Nevertheless, in the twenty-second struggle that ensued, Clark ended up face down on the ground. His bathrobe was bunched up against his shoulders, his gaunt white buttocks reflecting the trailer's porch light. Willson's knee was in the middle of his back as she clicked handcuffs closed around his thin wrists. "Well, Charlie," she said, barely breathing hard, "you're going to spend the night with us. You're under arrest for obstruction of a lawful search." She handed Clark over to a CO, who got him into the passenger seat of her truck and then stood watch beside the door. Through the window, Clark's wispy hair was wild and he alternated between mumbling and yelling incoherently.

Willson pulled open the door of the shed and shone her flashlight into the interior. It looked to her like any other garden shed, filled as it was with lawn chairs, faded gnomes, garden tools, and two large garbage cans. As they did in the trailer, she and the same CO went through the shed methodically, finding nothing of relevance — until they opened the second of the two garbage cans. Under a layer of dry lawn clippings, they discovered the probable reason for

Clark's outburst: two bales of marijuana, wrapped in plastic and secured with packing tape. The smell was unmistakable, but Willson cut open a small corner of each package to be sure. It was dark green, pungent, and valuable. With the contents confirmed, the two officers smiled at each other in the dark. Clark could now be charged with a second offence.

As they considered their find, Willson voiced what they were both thinking. "Well, shit. We didn't get what we came for tonight. But we ended up with a hell of a piece of leverage we can use on Clark. Let's hope the guys at Eastman's place found something relevant."

While one of the COs drove away, taking the hand-cuffed, dishevelled, and now quiet Clark off to a cell in the Cranbrook detachment, Willson turned to the other CO. "Have you got any connections in the local RCMP drug squad?" she asked. "We can't seize the drugs without a separate warrant, so we'll have to wait for them to get one and then get out here."

"I sure do," said the CO before stepping away, her cellphone to her ear.

Back in her own truck but still sitting in Clark's driveway, now babysitting two bags of dope in the shed, Willson could no longer contain her curiosity. She punched the number for Bill Forsyth's cell and heard him answer after four rings. She put the call on speakerphone so when she returned the other CO could hear him, as well.

"Bill, it's Jenny. Are you guys done out there?" she asked. "What did you find?"

"By the time we got to his house down a long drive-way," said Forsyth, "Eastman was out on his front porch, waiting with his arms crossed. From a kennel behind the house, we could hear his cougar hounds baying at the disturbance. It was a bit surreal. The first words out of his mouth were 'What the hell do you want?' I told him why we were there and asked him if he would co-operate with us. He flew down the steps toward me without saying a word. I had no idea what he was going to do, but luckily, I didn't get to find out. Brad intercepted him and immediately put him under arrest, sitting him in his truck in handcuffs. As you can imagine, he wasn't a happy camper. But there was nothing he could do. His eyes, peering out at us through the window, would have burned holes in steel."

"Come on, Bill, tell me. What did you find?" asked Willson impatiently. The young man's tendency to drone on and on while circling around the point like an airplane in a holding pattern was going to drive her to drink … more.

"The house is huge, so it took the three of us nearly forty-five minutes to go through it," said Forysth. "I seized three fully-mounted elk heads, all of which were the right size for the elk in Banff. I remember you telling me that a taxidermist could've added the Banff antlers to another skull, so that's why I grabbed them. There were lots of other mounted heads there, too — mountain goats, bighorn sheep, bears, an antelope, and even a huge, black Cape buffalo. I would have loved to take them all. I also got digital cameras, two boxes of business records from his office, a hard drive, and a laptop. It's going to take us a while to go through it. We also went through his garage, a hay barn, and two large sheds, but I found nothing there other than tack for his horses and some of his camp stuff."

Willson could not hold back the obvious question. "Did you find a .308?"

"Oh, sorry, I forgot to mention that," he said. "No, not in the house, but we did find two out in the garage, so we grabbed those."

"Great! And what about handguns?"

Forsyth sighed. "Yeah, I found a floor-mounted gun cabinet in his office that was full. And there was a .357 Magnum in there. It was bloody painful to leave them. I did find permits for all of them, so I recorded the serial and permit numbers. I don't remember the JP saying we couldn't do that."

He finished the story by telling Willson about releasing Eastman from the truck when they finished the search. "He was like a grizzly bear coming out of a culvert trap," he said. "We just stayed the hell out of his way. He stormed across his yard and threw a feint at the other CO as though he was going to punch him. He laughed like a madman, stormed up onto the front porch, turned and told us to get the fuck off his property, and then went into the house, slamming the front door. We didn't get a chance to ask anymore questions. At that point, I'm certain he wouldn't have said a thing. And what about you, Jenny? What did you guys get there?"

"Well, I was goddamn glad we were wearing gloves when we did the search," said Willson, the disgust clear in her voice. The CO joined her in the truck, her thumb up, confirming that RCMP members were on their way.

"Jesus. My skin was crawling when I left there. I'll need a hot shower tonight if I ever want to feel clean again."

Then she proceeded to tell Forsyth that they'd found nothing relevant to the poaching investigation, but had found a few kilos of marijuana in Clark's shed.

The CO interrupted from the passenger seat. "Jenny hasn't told you about the best part of her night," she said. "Clark, half-naked and crazy, jumped her in the yard while we were searching his shed. It was like she was wrestling with a skinned wolverine. He was spitting and cursing and rolling."

"I had to be really careful about what I grabbed and when," Willson said, laughing. "That's the strangest fight yet in my career, and I've had some strange ones. And I can tell you that the two COs with me weren't real quick jumping in to help."

"You looked like you had it under control," the CO replied with a grin, "and we weren't sure you weren't enjoying yourself and wanted it to last longer."

Willson could hear Forsyth's laughter over the speakerphone, with Jenkins chuckling in the background.

"We'll see you two back at the office in a while," said Willson.

"Okay," said Forsyth. "After tonight, I don't see Eastman saying anything to us. There's no reason for him to do so."

"You're probably right," said Willson. "Of the two, I'm guessing Clark will be the one to make a deal because of the drug and obstruction charges he's facing."

"I don't know," replied Forsyth. "From all we've heard, he's scared of Eastman. Do you think he'd roll over on him? The thought of prison time for the drug charge, in particular, might be a big incentive — he's got a lot to lose. But I still don't think he will."

"I'm not going to argue with you, Bill," said Willson. "Once the RCMP get here and sort things out, we'll head back to the CO office. It'll be a while yet, so that will give you lots of time to ensure your notes and the seizure reports are complete. I'll meet you there." She ended the call, not concerned that her partner might have to sit on his ass for a few hours.

Three hours later, Willson climbed back in her truck, exhausted. The RCMP had secured the scene, seized the drugs, and finished their interviews with her, the CO, and Clark's wife. Now they were inside the trailer, doing their own search.

As she backed out of the driveway, Willson saw Clark's wife on the trailer porch. The bare light bulb above the woman allowed Willson to see tears glistening on her cheeks as she held a cellphone to her ear — a phone that the grumpy JP had put out of Willson's reach. Wendy Clark was not moving, not talking, but simply standing there, the phone clutched to the side of her head like a security blanket. Inside the trailer, the shadows of the Mounties moved back and forth across the windows. Willson momentarily tapped the brake and slowed the truck as she wondered what was going through the woman's mind. Wendy Clark must understand the degree to which her husband was in trouble. So was she calling a lawyer? Was she calling Eastman to tell him what happened? Was she calling Clark's drug supplier?

Or was she trying to reach the third member of the trophy hunting triad to warn him that Willson was pursuing him?

CHAPTER 14

MAY 8

Luis Castillo sat in the quiet of his Spokane office. It had been a month since the confrontation with his wife. With the phone against his left ear, he listened to a male voice that was angry and insistent. Castillo's jaw was tight, his face hot with acute discomfort. From the south-facing corner window of his new three-storey building on the edge of downtown, he watched the Spokane River as it carried the cool, clean waters of Lake Coeur d'Alene westward to an eventual meeting with the much larger Columbia. The river gave him no comfort this afternoon.

"Mr. Castillo," said the voice, "the shipment has not arrived. We are concerned, very concerned … and we are not prepared to wait any longer. Our buyers are very angry. I need you to tell me what you are going to do about this problem." The man purposefully used language that would suggest to anyone listening — in case someone *was* listening — that they were discussing a legitimate business matter.

Castillo responded with as much calm as he could muster under the circumstances. "Yes, all is fine and there is no reason for you or your buyers to be concerned. I certainly understand their unease with the delay. I checked with my people before I phoned you; they advised that the truck was stopped by Highway Patrol in Montana this morning. Apparently, there was confusion about the paperwork, but it was sorted out after a few hours. The truck is on its way again and my people have guaranteed me that the shipment will be at your warehouse by dawn tomorrow, if not before."

The voice on the phone made it clear that failure to meet the deadline would not be acceptable. "If it is not here by that time, Mr. Castillo, then you and I will both have a problem on our hands, a big problem. I will contact my buyers now; I'm sure they'll be relieved to hear that we're back on track. Please give my warmest regards to your wife and daughters. Good day."

After disconnecting, Castillo looked down at a pad of paper on his desk, his nervous doodlings filling one corner of the top sheet. But his thoughts were not on the drawing. The mention of his wife and daughters was a clear warning to him and he knew it. A sheen of sweat appeared on his forehead at the thought they might be dragged into this. Alone and in a strange town far from home, he knew that his two girls were easy targets for men not known for understanding or patience. Castillo had hired a private investigator to keep tabs on the girls when they moved from Spokane to California to attend university, but despite that, he understood their day-to-day well-being was beyond his control.

As he replayed the telephone call in his mind, he heard a knock at the heavy wooden door. His executive assistant, a middle-aged Latino woman who had worked for him for nearly twenty years, opened the door and stood with her hand on the handle. "The inspector is here for his two o'clock appointment," she said.

"I will see him in five minutes," Castillo answered without looking up. He put the pad of paper in a desk drawer on his right, sliding it shut. He took three deep breaths to calm himself.

This was the second call of the day to disturb his calm. Castillo was a man who liked to call the shots, to be in control, to understand every aspect of a business empire that stretched across the Pacific Northwest. In fact, he'd set up the businesses so that he was the only one who saw the whole picture, how products moved, how dollars flowed, and who played what role in making the complex enterprise work. When a surprise dropped on his desk, either a small one or a big steaming pile, his temper rose to the surface quickly.

Earlier that morning, Bernie Eastman had called to tell him about the warrants and the searches at his and Charlie Clark's houses three weeks before. It was unusual to hear the big man sound hesitant, subdued, so Castillo knew that the call was made reluctantly. He listened as Eastman told him how B.C. conservation officers and two park wardens had combed through every inch of the buildings on their properties.

"Do we have a problem?" Castillo had asked, subtly reminding Eastman — as the other caller had just done with him — that any problems would be shared problems, with the bigger share falling squarely on the shoulders of the guide-outfitter.

"They seized two rifles, but those won't be a problem," said Eastman in response.

"Is that all they seized?"

"Yes ..."

"Bernie, I get the sense you're not telling me everything. Are you sure that's all they seized?"

"I was in handcuffs and in a police car for a while, so that's all I *saw* them seize at my place," said Eastman.

He then told Castillo that Clark had been arrested for obstruction and drug possession during the search at his trailer. "Charlie attacked a female cop when they were about to discover his dope stash. That was stupid. He spent the night in jail but our lawyer got him out the next morning."

"You will make sure he understands he must keep his mouth shut, won't you? He is your employee and I expect *you* to keep him under control."

Eastman answered quickly, too quickly for Castillo's liking. "Yes, I've already talked to him and he promised me he'll shut up and take his lumps."

"You will make certain there is no problem," said Castillo before ending the call. Castillo did not like loose ends. And despite Eastman's assurances, Charlie Clark had become a loose end.

A soft knock came at the door and, preceded by Castillo's secretary, a Spokane building inspector shuffled into the room, sitting down when Castillo told him to do so. It was the same inspector he'd caught ogling his wife at the Easter celebration a month earlier. While the man fidgeted, his eyes wandering the room nervously, Castillo checked his email on the small laptop to his left.

"I see you have a new photo there," said the man, pointing to the credenza behind Castillo. "Nice ram. Where did you get it?"

Castillo stared at him for a moment, saying nothing. He couldn't help but wonder how the man always looked rumpled, no matter what he was wearing or when in the day he was wearing it. It was disgraceful.

"It *is* a nice one. It was very considerate of the parks folks up in Canada to grow and safeguard that one just for me," said Castillo. "But I didn't ask you here to talk about hunting." Time to get to the point of the meeting. "Tell me where you're at with the approval of the new parking garage on Sprague Avenue," he said, his eyes drilling into the inspector like twin laser beams. "I am tired of the delays. I bought that land three months ago and every day is costing me money. I have subcontractors waiting to start. As you know, the hole for the foundation has been dug. I need to begin building."

The inspector may have tried to appear calm and confident, but his tentative voice betrayed him. "Uh, there were other projects in the work ledger that were submitted before yours, so I had to call in favours in the planning department to get them to move your project to the top of the pile. We're also short-staffed by two people, so there's more work for us to do than there is time in the day."

"You did not answer my question," said Castillo, his impatience showing.

"S-sorry," said the man. "I can tell you that I hope you should have all of your permits in place by the middle of May, end of May at the latest."

"You hope by the middle of May? Another two to four weeks away? That is simply not acceptable." Castillo moved forward in his chair, against the edge of his desk, placing both hands flat on the leather surface, his knuckles white. Even though the desk was large, the inspector shifted his chair back, overtly trying to distance himself from the angry man across the desk.

"Your incompetence is making me extremely angry," Castillo said, again staring at the man without blinking. "I pay you good money and I want results. I need those permits by the end of this week or there will be consequences for you personally."

Castillo paused, ensuring the inspector understood the situation and then continued. "I assumed you're the right man for this job. I don't want to find out I was mistaken. That would be bad for both of us. As you well know, my friend, you have more to lose in this matter than I do. Do you understand me?"

"I do," said the inspector. "But some of this is out of my control."

"That is not my problem," said Castillo. "It is yours."

"All right, all right, I'll do my best."

"Your best must be good enough." Castillo pushed back from the desk and stood up, signalling the end of the meeting. He said nothing more to the man as the inspector left the office, meekly closing the door behind him.

CHAPTER 15

MAY 9

The inspector felt as if his brain was burning with a toxic cancer. Castillo's arrogance and lack of respect for him were like malignant cells, growing, dividing, out of control, affecting his every waking moment.

On the regulatory side of the development industry, he often met people who walked the edge of legitimacy. Or maybe "walking" was too strong a term. Most of them teetered and wobbled as if drunk and on a tightrope, nearly falling but always catching themselves from crashing with awkward last-second movements. However, Castillo was, in his experience, the first to abandon any pretences; he walked boldly on the far side of the line, using his many contacts to keep him out of trouble, to continue to build his empire ... and to grow his revenues.

By late afternoon, with a few glasses of liquid courage under his belt, the inspector decided he'd had enough. He sat in his office, the door closed, brooding, fuming. He resented the fact that Castillo didn't recognize how hard he worked on his behalf. He was tired of being used as a pawn! The developer was making serious money from his many projects and it was on the backs of people like him. Most of all, he was tired of waking up from nightmares where the man was pushing him off a cliff or out of a plane and resistance was futile. Yes, it was true that Castillo was paying him well. But what little self-respect remained was slowly being eroded by the man's conceit and threats, his constant bullying and belittling.

He thought back to his earlier musings on how to take Castillo down, how to make him pay for the way he'd taken control of his life, how to change the balance of power between them without letting him know that it was this low-level inspector who'd done it. Those were his choices. And then he remembered Castillo's passing comment yesterday about taking a ram from a Canadian park. The son of a bitch's previous boasting about working with an outfitter north of the border came back to him, and the inspector's plan of revenge began to fall into place.

A quick Internet search for "Canada national park" gave him the information he needed. Banff National Park came up first on the list of links. He'd heard of the park but had never been there. He scratched the phone number on a notepad, and then, using his cellphone so the call couldn't be traced to his office, he phoned the Banff Warden Office. Always paranoid about Castillo's reach, he turned his back to his door, hunched forward in his chair, and cupped his free hand around the phone to muffle his voice.

He heard a woman answer the phone after two rings. "Banff Warden Office dispatch, this is Marilyn, how may I direct your call?"

"Please put me through to one of your rangers ... or wardens ... or whatever they're called," said the inspector.

"They're wardens," said the woman. "Can I tell the officer what it's about?"

"No," he said. "Quit asking stupid questions and wasting my time. Put me through or I'll hang up. It's about someone taking animals up there they shouldn't be taking. They're going to want to hear what I have to say."

"Stand by," said the woman. "I'll put you through to Warden Willson."

The man heard a series of clicks, twenty seconds of silence, and then a second woman's voice, younger, more abrupt.

"Jenny Willson. What can I do for you?"

"I'm not going to give you my real name," he said. "You can call me Sprague for now."

"Hi, Sprague. Thanks for calling. My dispatcher said that you wanted to talk to me ... something about animals being taken from our park?"

From the tone of her voice, the inspector could tell that the woman was interested ... and was taking his call seriously.

"Do you know that someone poached a bighorn sheep from one of your parks?" he asked.

"I do. In fact, we had a bighorn sheep *and* an elk taken from two of our parks. Do you have information for me on either of these cases?"

"I don't know anything about the elk, but I do know something about the sheep," the inspector said, feeling more confident as the call proceeded. "I'm not ready yet to tell you the guy's name at this end … but I will tell you what I know about what's going on up there." He heard another distinct click on the line. "Are you recording me?" he asked.

"Yes, I am," said Willson. "I don't want to miss anything you say. As you can imagine, this is a major deal for us."

The building inspector hesitated. "I'm not sure I want to be on tape," he said.

"Look, I don't know who you are and I have no way of tracing the call. So … what do you know?" she asked.

The inspector again paused, but his anger drove him forward. "Okay. There's an outfitter up there who offers guaranteed hunts … and the guy I know down here has been taking advantage of that. He has the money to pay for it and I can tell you he doesn't give a shit about rules. He also thinks you guys up there are a bunch of incompetent bozos. That's what he thinks of most people … so welcome to the club."

"Guaranteed hunts?" asked Willson, "What do you mean by that?"

"The outfitter's clients, like the guy down here, pay him for a ten-day hunt," the man said. "He guarantees they'll get a trophy animal of a specific species, and so they pay a significant premium over a regular hunt. If they don't get a trophy in the first five days in his area, or territory, or whatever the hell you call it, then the outfitter takes them into one of your parks and they get the animal there. That's probably why and how the sheep was taken."

"What's the outfitter's name?" asked Willson.

"I honestly don't know," the inspector replied. "But I can tell you the guy at this end boasted to me — just yesterday — that he got the ram in one of your parks. I wouldn't be surprised if the arrogant prick sends you a thank-you card."

"Do you know if he was with the outfitter when he took the ram?"

"I don't know for sure, but he always likes to hunt with someone local. So I would be surprised if he wasn't."

"When was this?" asked Willson.

"He told me yesterday."

"No, sorry," said Willson. "I mean, when did he shoot the sheep up here?"

"I have no idea. It must've been recently, though, because the photo of it wasn't in his office the last time I was there. He loves to boast about his hunts."

"Tell me something," said Willson. "How do *you* know about this guarantee that the outfitter offers?"

The inspector looked over his shoulder toward his office door, just to be sure that Castillo wasn't standing there listening to him. He wouldn't put it past the sneaky fucker. His anger drove him forward again.

"I … I was with the guy from here when he shot a huge black bear in Glacier National Park in Montana a year or so ago," he said. "He told me then about a guide he'd discovered in the Kootenays who'd started offering the guarantee. He loved the idea. At that point, I don't think he'd hunted with the guy yet and he didn't tell me his name. But as I said, the guy from here doesn't care about breaking the law."

"Why are you telling me this?" asked Willson.

The inspector didn't hesitate. "Two reasons. First, because the guy is an arrogant prick who thinks he's better than everyone else and because he's trying to screw me over. I'd love to see him take a serious fall to burst his huge goddamn ego. But I don't want to get directly involved because he scares the crap out of me."

He paused again. "And second, I was with him down here when he shot animals at times and places he wasn't supposed to. I don't want to go down with him. I want immunity from charges if I help you guys."

"It's a bit early to talk about that, Sprague," Willson said, her voice composed. "And you're not willing to give me his name?"

"Nope, not yet. Not until I'm *way* more comfortable with you and what you're going to do with my information. That's all I'm going to say for now."

"Can you at least confirm for me that he's an American?"

Shit. This woman was good. "Why do you think he's American?"

"Aside from the fact that your accent is different from mine," Willson said, chuckling, "you've said 'down here' a few times and you mentioned Glacier National Park. Based on that, I've got to assume that he is, like you, an American."

The inspector recognized that he'd said more than he'd meant to. And that the warden he was dealing with was no dummy.

"That's enough for now," he said. "Maybe I'll call you back again … if and when I know more."

"Wait!" said Willson in an urgent tone.

The man waited, not saying anything but not disconnecting.

"Let me give you my cell number," she said, "so you can reach me whenever you want to call again." She gave him the number.

He wrote it down on a pad of paper and then clicked the phone shut, ending the call before the woman could ask more questions. He again looked over his shoulder. With no Castillo in sight, he breathed out loudly and then smiled, a nervous, lopsided smile. He should be feeling good about this. So why, he wondered, were his guts churning like a stormy ocean?

CHAPTER 16

MAY 15

Through an east-facing office window in the red-brick RCMP detachment in Cranbrook, Jenny Willson watched two men sitting in a black Lexus on the street below. Outside the two-storey building, the Canadian flag hung loosely against a tall aluminum pole, signalling another calm and sunny East Kootenay day. It had been a week since Willson had taken the startling call from the anonymous Sprague, a call that confirmed the existence of a third suspect and narrowed the list to 140 million American males.

She could see Charlie Clark in the passenger seat of the car, and he appeared to be rolling and unrolling a stack of documents in his hand, no doubt anxious about what was to come.

In the driver's seat, Willson could see only the lower half of the man she assumed was his lawyer. The man was waving his arms as though making emphatic points to his client. Clark nodded from time to time, showing that he was hearing, if not agreeing with, what his lawyer was saying. Willson imagined the lawyer giving Clark the same speech that every client got before talking to law enforcement.

"Remember, Charlie," he'd be saying, "you do the listening and I'll do the talking. These guys called you, so it's up to them to tell us what they want. You volunteered to come in today, so all you have to do is listen."

Willson watched the two men get out of the car. They ignored the expired parking meter beside them and climbed the front steps of the detachment. When they were inside, Willson turned to watch the closed-circuit TV on the monitor beside her. The lawyer stepped up to a circular, wall-mounted intercom in the waiting area, while Clark hung back behind him.

"I'm Samuel J. Lindsay, lawyer, and I'm here with my client for an interview," the man said into the microphone.

Willson knew about Lindsay. He was an elderly gentleman, well past his legal prime, infamous for being scattered and disorganized. As a result, he was affordable, which may have been Clark's only criterion for choosing him.

"Who are you here to see?" asked a receptionist, her voice metallic in the tiny speaker.

"What?" said the lawyer, his hearing clearly not as good as it used to be.

Willson saw Clark close his eyes and lower his head.

The receptionist repeated herself slowly, louder. "Who … are … you … here … to … see?"

"Oh," the lawyer said, apparently understanding the question. "We were called by Jenny Willson. I understand she's a park warden? She asked me to bring my client in for an interview this morning."

"Please wait there. Someone will be with you shortly," she said.

"What?" asked the lawyer again.

"Stay there, someone will be right with you," the receptionist shouted.

Jenny Willson waited ten minutes before opening the door to the waiting area. She wanted Clark to be as nervous, uncomfortable, and on edge as possible. From experience, she knew that staring at Wanted posters often did that. She shook hands with both men and introduced herself, twice, to the lawyer.

"Good to see you again, Charlie," she said as she walked them down the hall to an interview room.

"Sorry I don't feel the same," said Clark.

Already seated in the interview room were the RCMP sergeant in charge of the local drug squad and the federal prosecutor, an imposing woman in a dark pantsuit, her red hair perfectly styled. Pens, pads of lined paper, and two bulging file folders, both closed, lay on the table in front of them. As part of her strategy to put Clark on edge, Willson had printed his full name in bold letters on the outside of each file. Most of their imposing thickness came from the many pages of blank paper added that morning. But Clark didn't need to know that. By design, neither the RCMP sergeant nor the prosecutor stood up when Clark and his lawyer entered the room.

Willson waited while Clark seated himself in the small metal chair offered to him, his lawyer beside him. She saw Clark's eyes widen when he saw the files. Then she watched him glance nervously around the room, like a wild animal in a cage.

Formally starting the interview, Willson turned on a digital video recorder mounted on a tripod in the corner of the room. "It's May 15, 2014, 9:20 in the morning, at the RCMP Detachment in Cranbrook, B.C. I'm Banff National Park Warden Jenny Willson. With me today are RCMP Sergeant Stan Millen and Susan Blake, federal Crown counsel. The purpose of this meeting is an interview with Charles Clark. Accompanying Mr. Clark is his lawyer, Samuel J. Lindsay."

"Thanks for coming in to see us, Charlie," said Willson, sitting directly across the table from Clark. She purposefully used his first name, as though she was his only friend in the room.

Clark grunted in response.

"You'll remember when we visited your place a month ago. As a result of the events that night, you've been formally charged with one count of obstruction of a lawful search, one count of assault of a peace officer, and two counts of possession of narcotics for the purposes of trafficking." Willson followed a script created with her colleagues during a tactical session the day before. "These are serious charges. If you are convicted, you're facing serious jail time. You understand that, right?"

She looked at Clark. The man stared back at her, his eyes blinking uncontrollably.

"So, Charlie, what can you tell me about Bernie Eastman," asked Willson, "and his offer of guaranteed hunts in his guide territory in the Purcells?" She saw Clark's eyes snap open in surprise.

Already ignoring his lawyer's advice on the first question in the interview, Clark responded immediately: "I had nothin' to do with —"

Clark's lawyer cut him off before he could say more. "What's going on here?" said the lawyer, looking confused while shuffling papers in front of him. "Why are you asking my client about hunting ... and what has that got to do with the alleged crime for which he's charged?"

"Fair question," said Willson. "Our ongoing investigation has uncovered information that suggests to us that Charlie may be involved in other illegal activities beyond those for which he is charged. We'd like to know more about those. Your client may not have told you, Mr. Lindsay, that we asked him questions the night of the search and his subsequent arrest. Don't worry, he didn't answer them. But I'm sure it became clear to Charlie then why we were there and what we were looking for. We want to give him the opportunity to explain himself. He didn't seem inclined to talk to us that night at his residence."

The elderly lawyer looked at Clark, his continued confusion obvious to everyone in the room. He turned back to the officials. "I ... I ..." he stuttered. "My client and I need time to confer."

With a nod, Willson turned off the video recorder after stating for the record that the interview was paused at

9:35 a.m. She and her colleagues left the room, using the opportunity to pour themselves cups of coffee in the detachment's lunch room. The coffee was hours old and bitter.

"Great start, Jenny," said the prosecutor. "Now they're off balance." She grimaced as she sipped the thick brew. "Jesus. What *is* this shit we're drinking?"

Twenty minutes later, Willson, Millen, and Blake re-entered the interview room at the request of Clark's lawyer. Willson re-started the recorder and continued the discussion.

"So, Charlie, what can you tell us about Bernie and his guaranteed hunts?" she asked.

"Look," said the lawyer, "you're asking my client to talk about something that's obviously of significant interest to you. I don't see how it's relevant to the charges he's facing. I can tell you that he may or may not be prepared to give you information. But you know, and I know, that you need to make it worth his while to talk to you. I have not heard you offer him anything in return for such information. So before my client says a word, we need to know what else, if anything, he might be charged with and what's on the table this morning."

At this point, Willson let the prosecutor take the lead. "As you said, Mr. Lindsay, your client is in possession of information that's of interest to the Crown." Susan Blake clicked her pen as she spoke, like a metronome of impending doom. "As Warden Willson stated earlier, your client has been charged with obstruction of a lawful search under the Criminal Code of Canada, assault of a peace officer, also under the Criminal Code of Canada, and two counts of possession of a controlled substance for the purposes of trafficking, under the Controlled Drugs and Substances Act." Her repetition of the charges was purposeful. Each charge punctuated by the clicking pen.

Blake paused and looked directly at Clark. "I'm sure your client understands that if he's convicted of those charges in a court of law, he will do time in a federal penitentiary. This is not insignificant."

Clark's throat bobbed up and down like a puppet on a string.

Blake continued. "Your client is in an interesting and rather fortunate position this morning. We want to offer him an opportunity to come clean, to get things off his chest, to assist these officers and himself, all at the same time. It's an incredible opportunity for him. There may be other charges laid, but I'm not at liberty to say anything about those at this time."

"That was an excellent speech, Ms. Blake," said Clark's lawyer when she was finished. "Bravo. But I still don't hear anything from you that would be of interest to my client, other than the chance to be a helpful citizen on a matter that I don't yet fully understand."

"Fair enough," said Blake. "I need your client to do a number of things for me. First, I need a written statement giving us all details about Bernie Eastman's offers of guaranteed hunts. We need to know about any and all hunts outside of Eastman's guide territory that Mr. Clark was involved in, or about which he has direct knowledge. As part of that, I need the full names of any and all clients involved in those hunts and anything that Mr. Clark knows about those clients."

At this point, Clark's limbs began to tremble as though he was experiencing a minor seizure.

"In addition," Blake continued, "I need Mr. Clark to tell us from whom he received the marijuana that was seized in his shed. As you've seen from the documents we shared with you, it was, in our minds, a significant amount — clearly not for personal use."

Everyone in the room jumped when Clark shot up from his chair, knocking it onto the floor behind him. "Are you fuckin' kiddin' me?" he yelled, his face a strange shade of purple.

Lindsay put a calming, heavily veined hand on his client's arm. "You realize, I'm sure, how much you are asking of my client," he said. "I assume you have a very generous offer to make to him."

"What I am prepared to do in exchange for all that," said Blake, "is reduce the two trafficking charges to a single, simple charge of possession. I can't drop the obstruction charge, but I'm prepared to drop the charge of assault of a peace officer. I will also offer your client immunity against all charges under the National Parks Act relating to any poaching incidents in which he might have been involved with Eastman while in any of our national parks."

Clark sat with his head in his hands while the two lawyers spent the next half hour negotiating his future. While the lawyers talked, Willson watched Clark. It was clear that he was trying to figure out how to get himself out of the mess he was in, but she knew it was a classic no-win situation. What a pathetic life he must lead, Willson thought. Here was a poor, downtrodden shmuck, obviously not in the best of health, not smart enough or strong enough to keep himself out of these situations. And he must go through life dealing with piles of crap of his own creation.

Finally, Clark sat up straight and said, "Okay, I'll do all of that, 'cept I won't name the guy Bernie took into the parks and I won't tell you where we got the dope."

Clark's lawyer immediately jumped in. "Wait, Charlie. We should talk about this first."

"Nope," said Clark, "I've had enough of this legal bullshit. I hate cops, I hate lawyers, and I want to get the hell out of here."

Willson saw an opening and could no longer stay silent. "Charlie, we already know that Bernie's client, the one who shot the animals in the parks when you were with them, is an American."

Clark turned a paler shade of pale, staring at Willson in disbelief. "How the hell do you know that?" he asked. "I never told you where he came from. You … you can't tell anyone that came from me."

Willson smiled, but it was a grim smile. Clark had confirmed for her what she'd learned from the anonymous caller, the man who called himself Sprague. But at the same time, the confirmation was potentially devastating to her investigation. It meant that the main piece of evidence in her case — the elk rack — had probably gone across the border into the United States. The bighorn sheep head had probably followed it. Now, more than ever, she desperately needed the name of the American hunter who was taking advantage of Eastman's guarantee. That was the missing piece in the puzzle.

Willson opened one of the file folders and slid a list of names across the metal table toward Clark. It was a list that Bill Forsyth had created by working with Brad Jenkins, a list of all of Eastman's American clients from his post-hunt guide-declaration forms during the most recent fall hunting season. Unfortunately, it was a list of twenty-seven names.

"Is one of these names the hunter you saw illegally shooting the animals in the parks, Charlie?" asked Willson, pointing to the list.

All eyes were on Clark as he peered at the names. His reluctance and fear were a palpable presence in the small interview room. Willson watched him run his thin finger down the list, hopeful that she could pick up a pause, a sudden intake of breath, some subtle hint of recognition that one was their third suspect, the man who'd left the third set of footprints in the snowy meadow in Banff. But Clark gave her nothing.

Head up again, Clark stared at Willson, at his lawyer, and back at Willson. He slid the list at her as though trying to distance himself from it. "Shit," he finally said, "I can't do this. I can't tell you if he's on there or not."

Willson was not going to back down. "Are you sure about that, Charlie? Can't or won't? This is your chance to get this off your chest. Your chance to do the right thing."

"Nope," said Clark. "I'm not doin' it. I can't. Bernie or the guy you're lookin' for, or both, will kick my ass somethin' serious if I rat him out. I might as well buy myself a plot in the cemetery."

Willson watched Clark fold his arms over his chest. He was obviously shutting down, the fear of Eastman and the American freezing both his brain and his vocal cords.

"Is there anything more you can tell us about the American hunter, Charlie?" she asked.

"What I can tell you is he thinks his own shit don't stink … and that he looks down on people like me. I hate that fucker. He uses fancy words, but he's, like, Mexican or somethin'. And he's scary as hell, with those dark eyes that never seem to blink when he's lookin' at ya." Clark shook his head as if to erase the memory. "I can also tell you I was there when he shot the elk and when he shot the goat. But I wasn't there when he shot the ram. You can't pin that one on me."

Willson paused, realizing that Clark had given her something new. *What goat?* She tried to hide her surprise with an innocuous question. "Tell me more about the goat, Charlie. That's the one we know the least about."

"We were in Kootenay Park, near Mount Wardle. He shot a huge mountain goat billy. We took the head and cape and left the rest there."

"When did this occur?"

Clark vigorously scratched his head. "Dunno for sure. It was around Easter, maybe just after."

"So it was you and Eastman there with the American, and it was the American who shot the goat?"

"Yup, saw it with my own eyes. It was a nice one."

"And what happened after he shot it?"

"I carved it up," said Clark, with a note of pride in his voice, his thumb pointing to his chest. "I done a good job. And then we hiked down to the truck and got the hell outta there." He told them about missing the truck and walking along the highway. "The client was pissed off at Bernie about that."

"Do you know if anyone saw you?" asked Willson, hoping for a witness.

"Some guy in a truck was behind us for a while, so Bernie was drivin' extra fast. But then the guy disappeared. I don't know if he gave up, or what."

"So you guys didn't stop to talk to this guy who was following you?"

"No way. Bernie slammed the brakes to get him to back off. That's when he disappeared. We just kept goin'."

"And where's the rifle that the American used to shoot the goat?"

"Dunno," said Clark. "Bernie took it and the goat. Like he always does. The American guy brought his own rifle ... but he didn't use that one. He used Bernie's, like always."

"What kind of gun was it?

"It was Bernie's .308. The guy likes it."

Another link made, thought Willson. She could now tie Eastman and the American to *a* .308, but was it the same .308 that was used on the elk? She had to find the rifle to know for sure.

"Where does Bernie keep the gun, Charlie? The .308."

"Probably in the gun cabinet in his garage," said Clark. "That's where he keeps all his good rifles."

Shit, thought Willson. Neither of the guns they'd seized from the garage matched the bullet dug out of the elk. There must be another gun somewhere and Forsyth had missed it. "Are you sure about that, Charlie? We seized two rifles from Bernie but neither matches."

"What can I say? Anytime Bernie asked me to get guns for a hunt, he always gave me the key to that cabinet."

Time to take the questions in a different direction. "So let's go back to the guarantee, Charlie," she said. "What can you tell me about that? How does it work?"

"It's not complicated, far as I know. Bernie guarantees 'em a trophy animal in their ten-day hunt. If he gets it in the territory, great. But if they don't by the fifth day, he goes into one of them parks. He makes 'em pay extra for it, that's for sure."

"How long has he been doing this?"

"Maybe a year? I dunno for sure."

"How many hunters have taken him up on it?"

"There was one other guy when he first started — that's all I know about. But I think they just went into a park once. The American is the only one who took it serious and has been with Bernie a few times. But I guess you already know that. The last few times, they never bothered to go in the territory. They just headed straight for the national parks."

"How many times has the American been with Bernie doing this?"

Clark again scratched his head, like he had lice or bedbugs or something worse. "Maybe four or five? There were the times you already know about, and I think they went to Banff at least once where the guy didn't get anything. Bernie was really pissed off because he had to give the guy his money back."

"So why's Bernie doing this, Charlie? He's got a perfectly good territory in the Purcells, full of animals. Why's he risking that?"

"Same reason we all do things we ain't supposed to. Money."

Willson knew she was circling in on an important part of the investigation. Motive. "So why does Bernie need the extra money, Charlie? He already gets good money for the hunts in his territory."

For the first time in the interview, Clark smiled. But it was a crooked, cynical smile. "Same reason we all need extra money. Wives."

This brought a laugh from everyone in the room, everyone except the prosecutor. Willson glanced at her designer clothes and the huge ring on her finger, and was willing to bet that her husband, whatever he did for a living, would agree with Clark's analysis. But perhaps not in front of his wife.

"Tell me more, Charlie."

"All I know is what Bernie tells me. He says that the woman has a serious online problem — she plays poker on the computer and buys stuff from all sortsa websites. Bernie's up to his eyeballs tryin' to pay off the credit cards. But it was the wife's money, some kinda inheritance, that allowed Bernie to buy the territory. So she's got him by the short and curlies."

"So it's all about money."

"It is," said Clark. "When I first got hired by Bernie, he was pretty strict about followin' the rules. He made sure we all did that. But once he got into money troubles, he didn't seem to worry as much about the rules anymore."

There it is, thought Willson. *There's the reason Eastman's doing what he's doing.* It went right back to her first days in law enforcement school. Serious crimes were always committed for one of three reasons: money, sex, or power. Now she knew what was likely driving Eastman. What she didn't know was why the American was taking him up on his guarantee. To understand that, she first had to figure out who the hell he was.

And then a small light bulb went on. "Charlie, you said Bernie was with the American four or five times," she said. "Would he have to submit any records of those hunts to the B.C. authorities?"

"I don't know nothin' about that — you're askin' the wrong guy. If Bernie wanted to make it look legal, he'd probably do the guide declarations for the government and report that the animals came from his territory. But I'd be surprised if he reported anythin' at all, because some of the animals he took — like the sheep — don't even live in his territory. And he'd have to name the hunter. I know he ain't gonna do that unless he's got no choice."

Willson's mind was flip-flopping with possibilities, with new avenues for questions. "Thanks for clearing that up for me, Charlie. Good point. So, let's go back to the elk and the bighorn sheep again. First, tell me about the elk. What happened there?"

Clark led them through the shooting of the elk, how he and Eastman had scouted the secondary park highway the night before, how they'd picked up the American at the Calgary airport the next day, and then, after they'd gotten the elk, how they'd driven him to Cranbrook where he was getting a ride home to the United States.

"And he didn't have the rifle or the elk rack with him?"

"Nope. Bernie dropped them off at his place before we took the guy into Cranbrook."

"Did you see who picked him up?"

"We didn't. We dropped him off at Denny's restaurant on the main highway through town. He said some other guy was gonna to pick him up there."

"Okay ... so tell me about the sheep in Jasper, Charlie."

"Bernie and I scouted out those sheep in that place near the icefields," said Clark. "I forget what it's called. He told me that ... uh ... the American was comin' up the next day. But I wasn't there for that one. I'm pretty sure it was the client who shot the ram, but I wasn't there, so I didn't see him do it. I swear."

"So you weren't there when the sheep was taken?"

"Right." Clark looked almost relieved. "I wasn't there that day. Bernie said they didn't need me."

"Do you know what kind of gun they used?"

Clark shook his head. "Like I said, I wasn't there."

Willson decided to try again, this time with more emotion. She slammed her open hand on the table to make her point. "Charlie, it's time to quit screwing around with me! I'm losing my patience with you. I need you to tell me the name of the American hunter. If you do, then I can find ways to protect you as a source. But if you don't, and I find him — and I *will* find him — then I can't help you if Bernie ends up thinking it was you who told me."

She watched Clark pause. He looked right at her, his eyes again wide. Her hopes took a jump when his mouth started to open. Maybe he was changing his mind. But then his gaze dropped to the table and he again crossed his arms over his chest.

"Nope," said Clark, "ain't doin' it. You can threaten me all you want, but you're not gonna get the name from me."

Willson knew then that she had all she would get from Clark, at least for now. She turned and nodded to the prosecutor, who rejoined the conversation.

"Mr. Clark," Blake said, "we're willing to make a deal with you. But I'm concerned that you're not being co-operative, that you're not taking advantage of the opportunity in front of you. If you tell my colleague what she wants to know, we'll do all we can to protect you. But you're already into this up to your eyeballs and there's only so much we can do. This isn't TV; it's real life. As you can see, we've got enough evidence on your friend Bernie and the American to charge them both with a number of serious poaching offences."

Clark, looking deflated and beaten, yet at the same time defiant, turned to his lawyer in search of advice.

"I think my client has told you all he's willing to tell you today," said Lindsay, "despite your offer to drop or reduce some of the charges. You've heard that his involvement in the three poaching incidents is secondary at best. I'm sure that a judge will look at it that way, too, and as a result my client might face a small fine at most. He seems to be okay with that. I'm not going to advise him otherwise."

"As we both know," the prosecutor said to him, "that's what the courts are for. But let's shift back to the drug charges for a moment. If we can agree that your client will give up the name of his dope supplier in exchange for a reduction in the trafficking charge, we're probably done here for today. Perhaps that's easier for him to do than name the American hunter. Officers Willson and Millen will sit with you and your client to get his statement. He can then be on his way."

"He can then be paid?" asked the lawyer, his head tilted like a dog hearing a strange noise.

"I said he can then be on his way."

"Ah. Well, I don't think we're there yet on the drug charges, Ms. Blake," said Lindsay, his client shaking his head beside him. "I want to talk more to my client. We will get back to you on your offer."

"Okay, but I will only keep that offer open for seventy-two hours," said the prosecutor, looking back at Clark.

Willson jumped in again. "Oh, and Charlie. If you want to ensure that you have no further trouble from us, that you don't dig yourself in any deeper, we need you to keep us informed about what Bernie is up to from today forward. In particular, we want to know the details, well before they happen, of any hunts planned, inside or outside his territory. We want to know everything about hunts that are booked, or even hunts that are only being talked about. And we want you to tell us as soon as you hear about them."

Clark was again incensed. "What? You're asking me to snitch on these guys for what they already did … and then keep rattin' them out on things that might happen in future?"

"Your life will get a whole lot easier if you do that for us, Charlie," said Willson. "That's *my* guarantee to you."

Two hours later, after Willson and Millen had again taken Clark through his story, step by step, writing everything down for him, Clark's signed statement, many pages long, sat on top of the same file folders he'd seen that morning. During that time, Clark's lawyer had nodded off twice, at one point startling himself awake with a jerk and a snort.

Through the same office window, Willson watched Clark and his lawyer walk out of the Cranbrook detachment into the afternoon sun. Clark shuffled the shuffle of a hungry, empty, and broken man. And perhaps a sick man. She'd thought about asking him if he was suffering from something, but decided that the interview wasn't the time or the place to do that.

While Clark had not given her all she wanted, Willson now understood what had transpired with the elk and the sheep. And in the process, she'd learned about a mountain goat taken in Kootenay Park, a goat that her agency didn't know anything about. So that was something. She now had the *when, where, what,* and *how* ... but not the *who* or the *why.* But she had looked across the table at a man who was the key to the entire investigation, a nervous and frightened man who, given the right line of questioning and some comfort about whether or not he could be seen as a snitch, might be persuaded to give up the name of the American hunter. He wasn't there yet, but maybe a few days to stew about his troubles would help him change his mind. She had to talk to him again, face to face, with no lawyers. Just the two of them. *Maybe,* she thought, *that would be the time to ask him if he was sick.* Maybe she could play the sympathy card to get him to open up to her.

She watched the two men approach the parked car. The lawyer struggled to open the door, at one point staring at his keys as if they belonged to someone else. She saw Clark look up at her, as though looking for relief from the mess he'd got himself into, as though she could release him from a life of mistakes and predicaments that kept piling on him like a slow-moving avalanche.

She nodded her head. A signal to him. "You and I will talk again soon, Charlie," she said into the silence of the empty office, then turned away from the window.

CHAPTER 17

MAY 17

Jenny Willson sat at the kitchen table in her house, a copy of Charlie Clark's file open in front of her on the pitted wood surface. As she pushed down the plunger of her French press coffee maker, she looked out the single-pane window to see the branches of an aspen showing the first sign of green buds. It was a long-overdue day off for Willson, so she was taking advantage of the quiet time to figure out her next moves in the investigation. A long bike ride was on the schedule for the afternoon. In the background, tunes from Spirit of the West, Blue Rodeo, and the Tragically Hip shuffled and soared from her Bose sound system. The ancient wood walls and floors seemed to come to life with the sounds of the music. She knew that, along with her clothing and her bikes, the sound system was the only thing she would take with her if she ever had to move. But she had no plans to do that.

Willson poured coffee into an old ceramic mug, grabbed it with both hands, took her first sip, and then focused on the file. When Clark had left the RCMP detachment two days earlier, moving like a zombie down the front steps, Willson had found herself almost feeling sorry for him. Almost. Clark's life wouldn't be the same after his interrogation, but she knew he was his own worst enemy. Her compassion for the man and her determination to solve the case fought a battle in her mind, a battle that was unfamiliar to her.

She thought about how to approach him next, what strategy to use to get the name of the American hunter. In the long interview, Willson had listened to Clark describing what it was like to work for Bernie Eastman. The big man was a bully, and it was clear that agreeing to assist him was one of the many bad decisions Clark had made in his rough life.

Brad Jenkins confirmed that in a phone call after the interview. "Whenever we deal with Eastman," he'd said, "no matter if it's at his camp or in our office, he's always an asshole. We've had all sorts of complaints against him. Clients have complained, other guide-outfitters have complained, regular hunters and hikers and fishermen have complained. Intimidation is his modus operandi. If we talk to him, we always go with at least two of us."

In her time as a warden, Willson had dealt with many tourism businesses, from hotels and restaurants to tour operators and mountain guides. Most of them understood that treating their guests well increased the chances of a return visit and a successful business. She couldn't help but wonder if Eastman had ever had clients hunt with him more than once. Probably not. But then she thought about the American, and even though she'd never met the man, she assumed from what Clark had said that he was as much a bully as Eastman.

Willson flipped back and forth through the pages of Clark's statement, hearing the man's voice, tired and beaten, as he described the events of the last few months. She had to find a way to offer Clark a release from the mess he was in, to free him from the bullies making his life miserable.

In that one interview, she'd gathered a significant amount of new information. But there were still big holes in the case. After rereading Clark's account of the mountain goat poaching in Kootenay National Park, she decided that her first move was to phone the Kootenay Warden Office to let them know what she'd discovered. And then she had to persuade her bosses to continue to let her run with the investigation and, perhaps, to get her some additional help. She had to have that support *before* having another go at Clark.

Willson used her cellphone to dial the direct line for Peter MacDonald, a Kootenay warden she'd first met on a bear-handling course early in her career. MacDonald's office was in a fenced compound a few kilometres up the highway from the hot springs in Sinclair Canyon, near Radium Hot Springs. Willson had passed it on her way back to Banff after the interview with Clark, but by then, it was well after normal business hours.

"Kootenay Warden Office, MacDonald," answered the familiar voice.

"Hey, Peter," said Willson. "It's Jenny from Banff. How's it going over there?"

"Hi, Jenny," said MacDonald. "I work for the federal government, so I'm living the dream." It was his standard response after twenty-five years with Parks Canada. "What can I do for you?"

"Are you guys missing a mountain goat?" she asked.

"Uh … not that I know of," said MacDonald with a short laugh. "Why? Did you find an extra one?"

"Not exactly. Do you remember when I was talking to you last week about the elk-poaching investigation I was working on?"

"Yeah. When we spoke, you were on to some new leads."

"Well, we interviewed one of the suspects two days ago in Cranbrook," she said. "He confirmed that the guy we're looking for shot the Banff elk. But then, he let slip that the same guy also shot a goat in your park, near Mount Wardle. He did it with a local guide-outfitter."

"Are you kidding me?" MacDonald sounded aghast.

"No. Unfortunately, I still don't have the name of the hunter, but I know he's American."

"That doesn't help much, does it," said MacDonald. "Most of the guys who come up here with outfitters are from the U.S. Who's the outfitter?"

"A guy by the name of Eastman, Bernie Eastman, with a territory in the Purcells west of Fairmont. Based on what our suspect said — and this was confirmed by an anonymous phone call from someone across the border — it looks like Eastman is offering guaranteed hunts. And our American suspect took him up on it."

"I've heard of Eastman. He's supposed to be a real piece of work. What's a guaranteed hunt?"

Willson explained the guarantee, adding, "It's like you and me are protecting private hunting reserves for these fuckers. Nice of us, eh? You'd guess right if you said this American paid a premium. Our guy told us it was an extra ten grand on top of the regular cost of a ten-day hunt. It looks like Eastman is using at least three of the national parks. Clark told us that after they started working together, Eastman and his client rarely bothered going to his territory anymore. They now head to one of the parks as soon as he arrives in the country. From what we got in the interview, we've confirmed that Eastman and the American got the elk in Banff, the bighorn ram in Wilcox Pass in Jasper, and … your goat in Kootenay."

"Unbelievable," said MacDonald. "But wait. I didn't hear anything about a bighorn sheep in Jasper."

"Oh, sorry. The Jasper wardens have been keeping that quiet because they want to solve it themselves — to impress the brass in Ottawa," said Willson.

"You're not talking about our friend and brown-noser Paul Hunter, are you?"

"What a surprise, eh?" As she spoke, she heard the click of computer keys at MacDonald's end of the phone line.

"Wait," said MacDonald. "I do see a report in our system about a goat." He paused for a moment; Willson assumed he was reading.

"One of our new wardens found a goat carcass near Mount Wardle on April second," said MacDonald. More keys clicking. "The report says it was a couple of hundred metres uphill of the highway. I guess he found it because he saw a bunch of ravens on it. Apparently, he checked and it was mostly bones by the time he got there. He mentioned there was no head or cape and the parts were scattered. The report states that either wolves or coyotes had been on the carcass by the look of the tracks around it, so he assumed they dragged the missing pieces off elsewhere. He thought it might have been killed in a fall or an avalanche. Geez, the fact the hide was missing should have been a clue for him that something wasn't right. This goat might be what your suspect was talking about, Jenny."

"Yup, that could be it," she said. "Could you possibly get your guy to go back there with a metal detector and see if he can find a bullet? We seized rifles from the outfitter and it would be huge if we could get a ballistics match. We know from the interview they used a .308. We've got a signed statement from the suspect who says he was there; finding the bullet would be another nail in the coffin. A few photographs of the scene would help. Send me his written report, as well?"

"Absolutely," said MacDonald. "Since he's the only one who knows where the carcass was, I'll send the guy there tomorrow with one of our avalanche techs, just to be safe. There's probably snow still hanging up high, waiting to come down."

"Keep me posted, will you, Peter?" asked Jenkins.

"Hey, hang on a minute," said MacDonald. Willson heard more clicking. "There's another potential connection here. A few days before the goat was found, one of our highway maintenance guys died in a traffic accident in the park. I forgot about that."

"How's that a connection?" asked Willson.

"We didn't find him until the day after he died," said MacDonald. "His truck was upside down in a pond near the Kootenay Crossing Warden Station. The potential connection is this: in his last radio transmission, he said he was following some guys with what he thought was a rifle."

"How did he know they had a rifle?"

"He said something about them being parked, so he must have seen it as he went by."

"Are you kidding me?" asked Willson. "Do you know how he died?"

"He broke his neck," answered MacDonald. "The only evidence the RCMP's accident reconstruction guys have is that he slammed his brakes on and then went over the guardrail into the pond. The truck probably flew a good thirty metres before hitting the ice."

"Were other vehicles involved?"

"They couldn't tell. They found other skid marks but told us that because of the road conditions, they couldn't be sure if they happened at the same time."

"Did the guy say anything more before he died?" she asked.

"We've all listened to the recording many times," said MacDonald, with a catch of emotion in his voice. "All he said was that he was following a suspicious vehicle with three occupants … he didn't say male or female … he'd seen them parked and thought he saw a rifle. The transmission ended just as he was telling us where they were going. It shook us all up. He left a wife, two kids, and five grandchildren."

"Holy shit," said Willson, sitting well back in her chair, the back legs audibly complaining. She remembered what Clark had told her about Eastman slamming on his brakes when they were being followed. Did they cause the park worker's death?

"You got that right," said MacDonald. "With what you've told me, Jenny, I'm thinking we can connect some dots that we hadn't connected until today. As soon as I can, I'm going to get our guys up to the site where the goat was found. If we find something, do you want me to send it to you or direct to the crime lab?"

"Send it direct to the crime lab," said Willson. "I'll give you our file number so they can check the bullet against the rifles we seized. The rifles are already at the lab." She read the number to MacDonald. "I'll also call the RCMP in Invermere about the possible link to the death of your colleague. They'll probably want to talk to Eastman."

"Consider it done, Jenny," said MacDonald. "Thanks again. Until your call, we were completely in the dark about this. As this keeps moving, let me know what I can do to help."

"Absolutely," said Willson. "Thanks, Peter."

Willson put the phone on the table, stood, and then paced the length of the house from the back kitchen to the front living room, back and forth, her hands clasped behind her back, the old floors creaking under her as if offering advice. She stared out the front window onto Cougar Street and saw a middle-aged couple dressed in hiking gear, confused looks on their faces despite the map in the man's hand. Another pair of tourists lost in the town of Banff. "At least you *have* a map," she muttered. "That would be real helpful to figure out where the hell I'm going."

CHAPTER 18

MAY 20

Bernie Eastman watched Wendy Clark steer down the long driveway leading to his house, her beat-up Pontiac splashing through puddles in the gravel. It was the second week of May and spring had the East Kootenay in a warm embrace. Wendy stopped the car. Eastman saw her take a generous mouthful from a bottle hidden under the passenger seat. *Some things never change,* he thought. *The woman is still a drunk.*

Wendy walked to the front door of the log house and pushed the doorbell repeatedly. After getting no response, she turned back toward her car, her eyes widening when she noticed Eastman leaning against it.

He scowled at her, his arms folded across his barrel chest. "What're you doin' here, Wendy?"

"I need to talk to you, Bernie. It's about Charlie. I think he talked to the cops," she said.

Eastman stared at her for an awkward moment. "Come inside," he said. He directed her to his den in the back of the house. They sat across from each other in matching chairs covered in green camouflage. In the background, he heard the sound of his two sons playing video games, their laughter and loud voices abrupt and unpredictable. He knew that his wife was elsewhere in the house, on the goddamned computer, racking up more debt. The bitch held her financing of his territory over him like a hammer. And he was the nail.

"How 'bout a drink?" asked Wendy, her eyes darting around the room.

"Forget the drink," said Eastman. "Tell me what that little shithead has done now. I told him not to say anything to anybody."

"I don't know for sure," she said. "I have no idea where he was one day last week, but when he left, he told me he was meetin' with the lawyer. He came back home late that night, a real mess."

"He hadn't been drinkin', had he?"

"No way," she said. "He doesn't do that anymore because of the drugs he's on. But he was shaking and wobbly and mostly incoherent. It was the worst I'd seen him since he was diagnosed."

"Jesus, Wendy," said Eastman, "what did he say? Get to the fucking point."

When they were younger, before either of them were married, Eastman and Wendy had engaged in a weekend affair. Eastman had been dating Wendy's sister at the time, but that had unravelled when the sister discovered the affair. Regretting that fling more with each passing year, Eastman saw that Wendy was aging as badly as any woman could age. She almost made him physically ill — the sight and sound of her, her frizzy hair, her wrinkled frown, and her cigarette-ravaged voice. That the woman worked for him did nothing to diminish his disgust.

"He staggered into the trailer, fell into his chair, and then ranted about lawyers and cops and goin' to jail," she said. "I'm worried he mighta done somethin' stupid."

Eastman's impatience began to grow. "What specifically did he say, Wendy?"

"Well, he rambled on and on about makin' deals," she said, "and refusin' to tell people where the dope came from. And he kept blamin' it all on the fuckin' Mexican, sayin' over and over again it's his fault we're in this mess."

"Did you ask him any questions?"

"I did," she said, "but I got nothin' outta him. Once he wound down, he fell asleep pretty quick … and then wouldn't talk the next day."

Eastman pondered the implications of what she said. When the park warden and conservation officers had shown up to search his house, Eastman was surprised. He'd thought his trophy guarantees were bomb-proof and that his tracks were covered. As a result, he'd kept his mouth shut when they poked, prodded, and pried into his possessions that evening. And he hadn't talked to any of them since. He wasn't going to lift a goddamn finger for them, but couldn't help wondering how they'd found out what he'd been doing over the last year. When he heard they'd searched Clark's trailer the same night, he knew his potential problems had multiplied.

"Shit, Wendy," he said, his face red, his eyes burning into her. He was trying to stay calm, but failing. "You and I both know there's a lot at stake here — for all three of us. We can't afford to have that husband of yours opening his big mouth. Castillo will go crazy if he finds out that Charlie might've talked to the cops about the animals we took — or about the dope. None of us can afford for any of this to get out."

"I know, I know. Them findin' my stash was bad luck," she said. "When Charlie jumped on that woman warden, they knew somethin' was in that shed. I tried to stop him but …"

"This is not good," said Eastman. "I have to talk to Charlie again. He's gotta understand he has to keep his mouth shut, no matter what. Are you sure you don't know what he said to them?"

"I don't have a fuckin' clue, Bernie."

"I gotta talk to him and I gotta talk to him soon. Castillo's gonna want to know."

"Speakin' of that," she said, "I need more dope, Bernie. The cops took all I had when they hit our place. I need to get some cash comin' in so I can pay the lawyer you sent to bail out Charlie."

"Do you think I'm stupid?" asked Eastman. "You already owe me for what the cops took from you."

"I won't keep the dope at the house," she said. "But you know very well that workin' with the lawyer is the only way we can control what Charlie might do. With the lawyer, we might stop Charlie from doin' somethin' stupid. Without him, who knows what he'll do or say. You and me got no other choice, Bernie."

Eastman paused to collect his thoughts. He was in a no-win situation and getting in deeper by the day.

"All right," he said. "I'll give you more — just enough to cover Lindsay's costs — but I want my goddamn money and I want it soon. You gotta move the stuff quickly *and* you gotta keep your fuckin' head down. The cops are gonna be watching you now."

"Yeah, I know," she said. "I talked to a guy who will take it all off me in one deal."

"Jesus. He's not an undercover cop, is he? That's the last thing we need. Who is this guy?"

"No way," she replied. "He's not a narc. He's part of a new gang from Alberta. I checked him out. He moved here a while back and works at one of the mines near Sparwood. If it works out, we could move a lot of product through these guys."

"They're not going to be competing with us, are they?"

"Nope, he said they were going to be selling it in Alberta. I don't know where."

"Shit, Wendy, I'm not sure that's any better," said Eastman. "This makes me nervous. But we got no choice. No matter what, you can't let these Alberta guys find out what we're doing here." He stood up from the chair and walked outside, Wendy following him.

When they reached the front porch steps, Eastman yelled across the yard, "Stevie, are you over there?"

A man's head popped out of the door of the barn, a large, Quonset-style building with a half-circle aluminum roof. "Yeah, Uncle Bernie, I'm still here. What do you need?"

"Bring me two bundles," said Eastman.

"You got it," said the young man before disappearing back into the barn.

"Is that your nephew?" asked Wendy. "The one who was in Afghanistan?"

"Yeah, that's Steve. He's been back and out of the army for a few months now."

"How's he doin'?"

"Okay, I guess," said Eastman, staring toward the barn. "His doctors say he's got that post-traumatic stress thing, so loud noises startle him. He can't work in my outfitting business, so he helps me here through the winter."

Stevie's last name was Barber rather than Eastman; his mother was Eastman's sister, five years his senior. After a six-year stint in the Canadian Armed Forces, the young Barber had recently accepted a discharge, with a case of PTSD as a parting gift. Eastman knew Stevie was still trying to figure out what to do with his life. It would be a tough slog, trying to make a living while fighting his demons, demons that had jumped on his back while he dodged IEDs and Taliban snipers, demons that followed him home. For now, he was working on a silviculture crew, cutting and burning brush piles, and helping Eastman with odd jobs. It was tough and mindless labour, ideal for his current frame of mind.

A few moments later, Stevie walked across the yard, a bundle tucked under each arm. They looked just like the two seized by the RCMP at Clark's trailer. He handed the parcels to his uncle, nodded at Clark, then walked back across the yard to disappear into the barn.

Eastman again stared at Wendy for a full minute, anger and frustration showing on his face. She squirmed under his gaze.

"Don't screw this up again, Wendy. Neither of us can afford it," he said, his mouth a grim, straight line. "And like I told you, I need to sit down with Charlie soon, before he does anythin' we'll regret. I want you to make that happen. I hope we're not too fuckin' late." He handed her the packages.

She nodded in agreement. "I will," she said.

Eastman watched her put the parcels in the trunk of her car, tucking them into the folds of a horse blanket. She slammed the lid, slid into the driver's seat, and drove down the driveway. When she reached the highway, Eastman saw her pause to take another drink. She then turned left toward Kimberley, and her car disappeared behind a stand of pines.

Eastman stood in his yard after watching Wendy leave, his hands tucked deep in the pockets of his worn pants. He looked skyward and shivered, even though it wasn't cold.

"Jesus Christ," he said out loud. "Now I find out that fuckin' Charlie may have told the cops about Castillo, and they might come after him next. If I tell Castillo, Charlie's as good as dead. And if I don't and Castillo finds out the hard way, he'll come after me." Eastman knew he had to tell his client what was happening, but he didn't know how and he didn't know when.

Eastman jumped when he heard the voice beside him.

"Is everything okay, Uncle Bernie?" asked his nephew, who'd come back across the yard without making a sound.

"No, Stevie," said Eastman. "I don't think it is. I may need your help."

CHAPTER 19

JUNE 3

Jenny Willson placed copies of her investigation report on the massive table that dominated the main boardroom of the Parks Canada administration building in Banff. The late-morning sun streamed in the window to her left, illuminating one of her reports in a perfect square of light.

Black-and-white portraits of past park superintendents stared at her from the wood-panel walls. Willson felt them judging her, so she stared back, fascinated to see how many wore handlebar moustaches. She wondered what the expectation would have been if a woman superintendent had been hired during the park's early days. It was a time when there'd been few women around the park, so it was unlikely. But it was also a time when the park struggled with the same questions it now faced, like how to find a balance between allowing people to use and appreciate the park while protecting its unique resources. She struggled with that dilemma every day.

In preparation for the meeting, she'd spent a half-hour down the hall with her supervisor, Chief Park Warden Frank Speer. Stocky with a buzz-cut of pure white hair, Speer was a wise, thirty-two-year Parks Canada veteran who had the unenviable task of sitting, day after challenging day, on the pointy fence between the big bosses in Calgary and wardens like Willson.

"I don't know what's going to happen today, Jenny," he'd said. "They asked for a briefing and that's all I was told. I know you'll do a great job of filling them in on your investigation. We'll see what happens from there."

"Well," she said, "I gotta tell you that my expectations aren't high. These pencil-necked paper-pushers always find a way to avoid doing anything useful."

The chief park warden smiled. "Try not to let that opinion show, won't you?" He gave Willson one last piece of advice that made her laugh, just what she needed to calm her nerves. "The higher I get up the ladder in this place," he said, "the view is not great. I look up to see fewer assholes on the ladder rungs above me, but they are much, much bigger. So remember that. Do your job, and keep your cool."

Now she stood in the corner of the empty boardroom, waiting, her thoughts shifting to her father. An engineer for the national railway when he died, he'd been a zealous union member, never trusting the company bosses or shareholders to care about his interests. She remembered him telling her to look after herself, to assume that "the man" would never give her a moment's thought in the quest for bigger profits. Over her short career, Willson had come to understand what he meant, although in government, people on the ladder above her weren't driven by profit but by power — holding on to what they had, or grabbing more. Politicians wanted re-election, their horizon of time often only four years into the future. Senior bureaucrats, the ones who really ran the show — and who allowed the politicians the delusion that they were in control — appeared to Willson to be all about maintaining the status quo or preserving and growing their empires, empires filled with armies of assistant deputies, executive directors, directors, and managers. And maintaining their big salaries that were much bigger than hers. Willson often wondered how the government ever accomplished anything, with so many people serving upward and so few actually serving taxpayers. And those who did, did so despite the system, not because of it.

As if to punctuate her thought, the heavy door opened and three men entered the boardroom, twenty minutes late. The first was the chief park warden. Behind him was his boss, the park superintendent. And following in their wake, like a remora on a shark, was the Calgary-based deputy assistant regional director for Western Canada. After shaking Willson's hand, the two senior men sat across from her. She saw the chief park warden choose his seat last; he came around the table to sit beside her. It was a much-needed show of support, that everyone in the room understood, a message that could only come from someone close to retirement.

"Go ahead, Jenny," Speer said with a smile.

She smiled back at him to show that she understood what he'd done.

"I appreciate this opportunity," Willson said. "I understand that you want a briefing on my investigation into wildlife poaching in our mountain parks. You'll see that I've given each of you a written report." She pointed to the documents in front of the three men. As anticipated, the two across from her began to read. "Rather than reading it now," she continued, waiting until their heads came back up again, "let me take you through the key facts. I have some questions for you at the end of my presentation."

Because she knew that these kinds of men were impatient, with short attention spans, Willson ensured that she was concise, well-organized, and compelling.

"My investigation began with the shooting and mutilation of a bull elk in Banff," she said. "Since then, I know we have had a total of three animals taken from our parks: the Banff elk, a bighorn sheep from Jasper, and a mountain goat from Kootenay. The bull's rack was taken, while the heads and hides of the sheep and goat were taken. So I believe I'm dealing with people interested in trophies. The last one, the goat, was just confirmed in the last few days." She knew that the news of the goat was a surprise to the men across from her, so she paused while it sank in.

"Based on evidence that's laid out in the report, I'm fairly certain that the same three men were involved, to one degree or another, in all three shootings. I know who two of them are; the third remains unknown. I know they were here in Banff the night the elk was taken, two of the men were seen in Wilcox Pass the day before I believe the ram was shot, and I have an eyewitness to the shooting of the goat. The same witness was also present at the killing of the elk."

"What's the motive behind this, Jenny?" asked the chief park warden, despite knowing the answer.

"The motive is greed," she replied. "One of my main suspects, a man named Bernie Eastman, is an East Kootenay guide-outfitter who offers a unique guarantee: if a client doesn't get a trophy animal in the first five days of a ten-day hunt in his territory, he'll bring him to one of the parks. Unfortunately for us, he's found an American client who's accepted his offer. It's Eastman and the unnamed American, plus the outfitter's assistant, who are my three primary suspects in this case."

"What are the main outstanding issues with the case to date?" asked Speer, providing her an opening to move forward.

"There are three," said Willson. "The first is that, while ballistics has confirmed that the same rifle was used for the elk and the goat and that a handgun was used for the sheep, I don't have either of the weapons, despite executing search warrants at the residences of the outfitter and his assistant. Our agency seized two rifles of the same calibre, but they didn't match. And we've not been able to find any of the missing trophies … yet."

"The second is that my main suspect, likely the shooter in all three incidents, is American. Unfortunately, the potential charges against him do not allow extradition, even if I knew who he was."

"And the third," she continued, "is that I have possible drug connections with at least one of the suspects:

the assistant guide. That means that the RCMP are involved, but it also means I have leverage on the assistant that I'm utilizing to the fullest. You'll see in the report that he is my main eyewitness. Clearly, this has become about much more than poaching."

Willson saw the chief park warden observing the two men across the table, watching their body language for clues. She'd only met the park superintendent once, days after he was appointed to the job, so she didn't have a good read on the man. As she had laid out her case, he mostly had his head down while he wrote in a coil-bound notebook. His natty clothing and cool mannerisms, along with the position to which he'd risen in the bureaucracy, were proof for Willson of a long life in government. For her, that was not a good thing.

She turned her gaze to the bureaucrat from Calgary. *Speaking of assholes on higher rungs of the ladder*, she thought. He was a small, pompous-looking man peering at his Blackberry. He had the body language of someone much higher up the food chain than he actually was. She was certain that he'd heard very little of what she'd said.

Willson finished her presentation and then waited. In the silence, the park superintendent looked up and seemed to realize that he was expected to speak.

"So, Jenny," he said, looking back down at his notebook, "what I'm hearing you say is that you *think* three guys did this, but you don't have the weapons, and you don't have the trophies they allegedly took from the three parks? Did I get that right?"

Willson took a deep breath before answering. "What I'm saying, sir, is that I'm confident these three guys *are* the perpetrators in the murder and mutilation of three park animals. I'm also saying that I almost have enough evidence — according to Crown counsel — to lay charges against all three. I could probably arrest the outfitter and his assistant now. But I don't want to do that until I have enough for a bomb-proof case … and until I have the name of the American hunter."

"Huh," said the superintendent.

Willson waited. The silence in the room was punctuated by a car alarm, abrupt and shrill, somewhere outside.

In the absence of further questions, she completed her summary by laying out her requests of the men. "So," she said, "it's obvious we have an individual who has used, and is continuing to use, our national parks as his private game reserve. We have an American hunter who is taking full advantage of the scheme. We have clear violations not only of the National Parks Act, but also a number of B.C. statutes. It's likely we also have infractions of U.S. laws."

Willson looked at both men across the table before continuing. "What I'm asking you to do is approve my request to focus solely on this investigation, as part of a team of agencies that will include Parks Canada, the Conservation Officer Service in B.C., the RCMP, and probably — quite soon — the U.S. Fish and Wildlife Service. I don't know how long the investigation will last, but it could be anywhere from a week or two up to a few months. But we need to build that bomb-proof case I spoke of a moment ago. Such a commitment from you will, I assume, mean temporarily filling my position until I'm done. I will provide you with regular reports so you know how the case is proceeding."

She had tried to anticipate all the questions she could be asked by the men. "I will need funds for travel," she said, "which I've outlined in the report in front of you. I may also need funds for experts and witnesses to attend trials, if and when they occur."

She waited while the men flipped through the pages of her written brief.

"Gentlemen, I hope you'll agree that this is a precedential issue, not only for Banff Park, but for the national parks system as a whole," said Willson, trying to use language they would understand. "In fact, I'm not aware of any previous incidents of poaching in the national parks in Canada on this scale, at least not in modern times. I firmly believe we need to bring significant resources to bear to show we're serious about this and to assist our B.C. colleagues, who've already invested significant time and resources on this case. I ask that you give me the authority to proceed."

Finished, Willson folded her hands on the table in front of her and waited for a response. For a moment, the little man from Calgary looked up, but only to glance quickly at the park superintendent. His gaze immediately dropped back to his phone. When Willson saw this, her internal radar went on high alert.

"Thanks for that thorough update, Jenny," said the superintendent. "We appreciate the work you've put into this and we thank you for your dedication to protecting the park and its resources."

Willson had heard speeches like this before. The superintendent was going through the motions, preaching like he was in front of the media or a group of his own bosses. *Get on with it,* she thought. *Give me what I need and let me the hell out of here.*

The superintendent's eyes flicked toward the man from Calgary and then he continued. "While we understand the importance of this from your perspective," he said, "I cannot approve your requests. In fact, the main reason I asked for this meeting today is to direct you to stand down on this investigation, at least for the next while."

Willson felt as if she'd been punched in the stomach. The air in her lungs escaped in a rush. She had assumed the superintendent would tell her to continue the investigation, but not to spend any money on it, and at the same time, keep up with her regular duties. That was a normal government response to anything out of the ordinary. But this was not the outcome she'd anticipated. Willson turned questioningly to Frank Speer and could tell from his facial expression that this was a shock to him, as well.

"I ... I don't understand," she said to the superintendent, her surprise reducing her ability to speak coherently. "What the ...?" She stopped herself before adding a word that might be considered inappropriate in the situation.

"I expect this comes as a surprise to you," said the superintendent. "It seems that the local media attention this matter has already received, both in the *Banff Crag and Canyon* and in the *Cranbrook Daily Townsman,* is of concern to the prime minister's office. I assume they heard about it through local members of Parliament. Some major media outlets are sniffing around to see if there's a story here. The PMO wants this matter shut down, now, so it doesn't look like the federal government is improperly managing our national parks. Delicate negotiations are underway with foreign governments about climate change and pipelines, and they don't want this to be a blemish on their environmental record."

Willson could no longer contain her anger. "Perhaps," she said, talking directly to the little man with his head down, "the folks in Ottawa should get their collective heads out of their fat, desk-bound asses and let us *do* something about this! That would show that the government *is* serious about the environment. If you let this situation continue, we're no better than the tinpot dictators in Africa who stand by while poachers slaughter elephants and rhinos. Surely we're better than that!"

For the first time since he'd sat down in the boardroom, the little man across the table raised his head to look at Willson. "Warden Willson," he said in a disdainful voice that brought a further flush of anger to Willson's cheeks, "I don't expect you, at your level, to understand the big picture here. You've been given clear instructions and we have no responsibility to explain this decision to you, no matter what you might think. You need to do what you are told. This isn't open for discussion or debate."

Willson was seconds away from jumping across the table to strangle the arrogant little man. Anger and adrenalin pumped through her veins like jet fuel. She imagined one of her hands wrapped tightly around his scrawny neck, the other pulling his perfect tie ever tighter until his eyes bulged.

Her fists clenched tight below the desk and her heart pounded in her ears. But a look from the chief park warden, who had dealt with more senior bureaucrats than she ever would, held her back from a making a career-limiting move.

"I can't imagine what our colleagues in the RCMP and in B.C.'s Conservation Officer Service are going to do when they hear about this," said Willson, her mind snapping back to reality.

"Jenny," said the superintendent, "the message you're going to give to people you're working with is that you've been given higher-priority projects to work on, so you've decided not to pursue the investigation. And you are not to put that in writing to anyone, at any time. Is that clear?"

"Sorry, sir," she replied, "but that's not going to happen. There isn't a single person who knows me who will believe for a second it was my choice to stop pursuing this. It's not true and it's certainly wrong, so someone other than me is going to have to take responsibility for *that* message. *I* don't give up."

"I'm very disappointed you're being so difficult about this," said the little man from Calgary.

"From what I've seen today, I'm betting you have many disappointments in your life," said Willson, "and, quite frankly, none of them are my concern."

This was punctuated by a snort from Frank Speer. Willson saw momentary anger in the tiny bureaucrat's face. She stared at him, her eyes like laser beams, trying to burn a hole in his pointy head. His eyebrows rose slightly but he said no more.

"That's enough, Jenny," said the superintendent. "I'm telling you and your assistant, and any other wardens involved, to stand down on this investigation. As of right now, I'm instructing the chief park warden to ensure this happens. If you need a reason, you can tell the folks you're working with that I gave you other priorities. Normally, I would put a letter on your file about your insubordination, but I won't in these unusual circumstances. Do you understand me?"

"I don't like it and I believe it's a very bad decision … but I understand what you've said," said Willson, biting her cheek until she could taste blood. "I'll let my assistant know that he's done at the end of July. He's going to be as impressed as I am. And simply for my own interest, what's happening with the investigation in Jasper about the poached bighorn ram?"

"My counterpart there has agreed that they don't have evidence to proceed, so they have put their investigation on hold," said the superintendent, smiling at Willson condescendingly. "Now that I know about the goat in Kootenay Park, I expect the same thing will happen there, as well."

"Seems like a nasty virus has infected the entire organization and it's spreading like the plague," said Willson, again glaring at the little man across the table. "Ebola seems friendly compared to this."

Before the superintendent had the satisfaction of dismissing her, Willson gathered her files from the table, pulled on her uniform jacket, and left the room. As the door swung closed behind her, she heard the chief park warden's words echoing in the near-empty room. "You guys both know this is bullshit, pure and simple."

Willson was numb as she walked across the parking lot behind the building. She unlocked the door to her truck, climbed in, and just sat. She was angry, surprised, shocked, the emotions boiling in her like a biblical thunderstorm. Her gaze focused on a layer of dust along the edge of the dashboard, light grey against dark brown.

This was the first time that politics had affected Willson so directly and so overtly. She'd heard about it, watched it from afar through some of her colleagues' experiences, but had never been this close to it. It looked bad, smelled bad, and tasted just as bad. The directions from the higher-ups had been very clear, and there appeared to be little to no wiggle room for her.

She reflected back to her first days on the job and the pride she'd felt when she first put on the park warden uniform. She'd joined Parks Canada to protect these special places, she thought, not to sit idly by while nervous bureaucrats allowed assholes like Eastman and the American to violently and brazenly steal from them.

She had, however, enough experience in government to know she had to be smarter than the little man from Calgary. She had to play his game if she was going to be successful in keeping this moving. But she'd never played this game before, didn't know the friggin' rules. Without help, the chances of her winning were, she knew, slim.

Despite the warm spring, Willson shivered, so she turned on the ignition to activate the heater. As the cab warmed, she relaxed a little and realized she needed guidance from someone with experience in political sword-fighting, someone who knew how to parry and thrust, who could teach her how to play offence rather than defence. While she respected Frank Speer, she also knew that asking him for suggestions would put him in a difficult position. His retirement was on the horizon and she didn't want to do anything to jeopardize it.

Angry and confused, Willson thought about her wilderness-loving hero, Edward Abbey, as she often did at times like this. *What would Ed do?* she thought. For times like this, she needed a T-shirt with that question across the chest. And then she recalled one of her favourite Abbey sayings. He had compared society to a pot of something, a stew or a soup. Without regular stirring, thick scum would form on top.

She realized that she'd run smack into that scummy layer. Time to do some stirring. With inspiration from Abbey, Willson then thought of her uncle Roy, of his many years in the RCMP. *He might know what to do in a situation like this*, she thought. He'd recently transferred to the detachment in Cochrane, Alberta, likely his last posting before he retired. She called him using her personal cellphone, just in case. He picked up after three rings.

"Yello," her uncle answered.

"Hi, Uncle Roy, it's Jenny."

"Hey, Jenny, it's great to hear from my favourite park warden," said her uncle. "Stand by one, please." She heard him speak to someone in the background, his voice slightly muffled. "You guys go ahead ... I'll catch up with you."

He came back on the line. "Sorry about that, Jenny. I just met with our corporals about changes to our shift schedules. We were about to head out for lunch, but they'll save me a chair. You know I always like to hear from you, but why in the middle of the day like this? Is everything okay?"

"I'm good," she said. "There's nothing to worry about. But I do need advice from you, Uncle Roy. Can I drive to your place this weekend so I can tell you a story?"

CHAPTER 20

JUNE 5

Kimberley's Centennial Hall sat a few blocks north of the Platzl, the Bavarian-themed downtown famous for its yodelling clock and annual accordion festival. Alone at the north end of Wallinger Avenue, the hall was long, cream-coloured, and tucked in a narrow valley framed by forested hillsides to the north, south, and west not easily seen from neighbouring houses. Baseball diamonds lay empty to the east.

Wendy Clark parked on the east side of the building, headlights off. She looked at her watch: 2:59 a.m. Kimberley, a town of 6,500 people, was quiet, its restaurants and bars closed after a busy Saturday night. Wendy knew there was little chance of traffic at this time of the morning on a road that led only to residences, the hospital, and the Cominco Gardens. Other than a fluorescent security light around the corner, the only illumination here was the red glow of her cigarette as she took a drag. A cool wind blew from the Purcell Mountains.

Wendy sat for no longer than ten minutes before a black Dodge pickup drove up beside her, its headlights off. With massive off-road tires and a black canopy over the bed of the truck, it was large and menacing in the darkness. She took a deep breath, quickly exited her car, and leaned against the hood, trying to appear calm.

The truck's engine was running, its exhaust drifting upward. The driver's door opened and a man stepped down. He moved toward Wendy while a second man, visible only for a second, remained in the passenger seat. The man coming toward her was not tall, but she could tell from his solid frame and swagger that he was muscular. Most of the man's face was hidden beneath a black hoodie.

"Are you here for a delivery?" Wendy asked, trying to see the man's eyes.

"Yeah," the man said. "We talked on the phone. Are you Wendy? Have you got what I ordered?"

"I am and I do," she said. "Have you got the money?"

"Of course I do. But I want to check the stuff first," said the man.

"Okay," she said as she moved toward the trunk of her car. As she did so, she saw the second man getting out of the truck. Her pulse quickened. She knew this was the riskiest part of the transaction. The men's behaviour — cautious, secretive, and intimidating — didn't help. She leaned over to pull a package of dope wrapped in plastic and packing tape from inside the horse blanket, and turned toward the two men.

At that moment, she felt a shock of pain as a fist crashed into the side of her head. She bounced against her car, her cigarette spinning away, and dropped to the gravel. The package did the same. "What the hell?" she cried. "Why'd you do that?" Her ears were ringing, and pinpoints of light flashed in her eyes.

The passenger kicked her in the ribs and another jolt of pain coursed through her body. Her breath left her lungs in a rush. She lay gasping on the ground, trying to catch the lost breath.

"Do I have your attention now?" asked the man in the black hoodie looming over her. She saw that both packages were tucked under his arm.

"Jesus … what do you want from me?" she asked, looking up at the man. "I only came here to sell you dope. I don't want any trouble from you guys." She couldn't see the man's eyes, but the skin on his lower face was pitted with acne scars.

"I don't give a crap what *you* want," said the man. "What's important now is what *I* want. Do you know what that is?"

Wendy, still lying on the ground, shook her head to show she had no idea. She groaned in pain the instant her head moved.

"What I want is to put you, and everyone else in the East Kootenay, out of business," said the man. "And you're going to help me by telling me who your supplier is. Not only that, but we're going to pay him a visit. You got that?"

Wendy's shock turned to fear as she realized that the two guys were serious, very serious, and that this was already beyond a drug deal gone bad. "C'mon. You guys know I can't do that," she said, her eyes pleading. "I'll get seriously hurt."

The passenger again kicked her in the ribs, this time in the same spot. She shrieked in pain and curled into a ball, her arms wrapped tightly around her chest.

"You can be in pain today ... or in pain tomorrow," said the driver. "Your choice."

Wendy croaked out the words she thought the driver wanted to hear. "Okay, okay, I'll take you to where I get my stuff. Please don't hurt me anymore." She exhaled on a wheeze.

She could see the man's teeth gleam as he smiled in the darkness. "Good decision," he said. "You're a smart lady." He turned to the passenger. "Grab her, let's get out of here."

The passenger pulled Wendy up off the ground by her hair and belt and dragged her to the truck. He pushed her into the small space behind the front bench seat. She gasped again as her broken ribs made contact with the transmission hump.

The driver turned to look at her, his right arm across the top of the bench seat. "Which way are we going, Wendy?" he asked.

"Head north to Ta Ta Creek," she said through gritted teeth.

Fifteen minutes later, after Wendy had described who owned the place and where it was, the truck slowly pulled up to the front of Bernie Eastman's house, its headlights off again. The building was dark. Eastman's truck was gone, as was his family's Jeep Cherokee.

The driver again spoke to Wendy, this time without turning around. "You may have gotten lucky," he said. "It looks like your friend ain't here. Too bad, I was looking forward to meeting him."

"I forgot he's away for the weekend," she said as the men dragged her out of the truck. Her legs were wobbly, her breathing laboured. Each intake of air led to a sharp stab of pain in her chest that forced the air out again quickly.

The three of them stood beside the truck. The driver gazed around the property and then turned to Wendy. "So, where's the dope at?" he asked.

"If I tell you, Bernie will kill me," she said, tears pouring down her cheeks. "Please don't make me do this."

The passenger grabbed her by the front of her coat, pushed her hard against the side of the truck, and punched her again. This time, she saw the fist coming at her face and felt and heard her nose break. More pain. She would've fallen, but the passenger held her up like a rag doll.

"You dumb bitch," said the driver. "If you don't talk, this situation is going to get worse for you — in a hurry."

"Oh, my God," Wendy gasped, then spat blood on the ground. She was beyond caring what Eastman would think. She wanted for this to be over and for the men to leave her alone. "I'm gonna show you."

The three of them walked across Eastman's yard, Wendy propped up between the two men, her toes leaving a furrow in the dirt. Her mind and heart racing, she pointed them to the Quonset-style garage, the entrance to which was protected by a steel door and a padlock. A large bolt cutter wielded by the passenger made short work of the lock. The driver flicked a switch to the right of the door and a bank of halogen bulbs popped on, illuminating the inside of the structure. It was empty, except for a steel fuel tank against the far wall.

For the first time, Wendy could see the driver's face. She saw broad features, a wide nose, and a small soul patch below his lower lip. The man had no eyebrows and appeared to be bald, although he still had the hood of his jacket pulled up.

"You stupid bitch," said the driver, "there's nothing here. Now isn't the time to play games." He made a move as if to slap her across the face.

"Wait, wait, wait!" she wailed, desperate to avoid more pain. "Pull on that lever over there." She pointed to a place on the near wall about three metres from where they stood.

The driver walked across the concrete floor and pulled the lever, a steel handle about half a metre in length. He was strong but it took both hands to move it. As he brought it to a full upright position, a metal panel in the floor the size of a door and to the left of the fuel tank swung upward on hydraulic hoists. Light shone up from the hole.

"What the fuck?" said the passenger as he stared in disbelief.

The two men dragged Wendy across the floor of the garage to peer down the hole. They could see stairs descending into a basement. The passenger slid a Beretta pistol from under his jacket and cautiously moved downward, the gun in front of him in a two-handed grip. When he reached the bottom, he disappeared momentarily and then Wendy heard him say, "Ho-ly shit. You gotta see this."

Wendy felt a shove from behind and she stumbled down the steps, barely averting a fall by hanging on to a cable railing on her least painful side. When they reached the bottom, she felt the driver loosen his grip on her when he saw what the passenger had already seen.

The subterranean room in front of them was the same size as the garage above, a massive space with three-metre-high ceilings and concrete structural posts every four metres. Between the posts, row after row after row of tall marijuana plants in large plastic pots under banks of grow lights stretched to the far walls. Plastic pipes supplying water and hydroponic fertilizer to the plants stretched around the room like a massive black spiderweb.

Wendy saw the driver's eyes wander from right to left and back again. By the look of surprise on his face, she could tell that while he may have seen grow ops in his time, this was unlike anything he'd ever witnessed — or expected — when he'd brought her here. It was a wall of green, a forest of money. The place was not only brightly lit, but hot and humid, and the man began to perspire. Across the basement to the left a small diesel generator was humming quietly and powering the lights and the myriad fans that circulated air and humidity. Air intake and exhaust vents for the engine and fans ran up the wall of the garage.

"Un-fucking-believable," said the man, looking at his partner with a smile. "This is a serious jackpot. I got to give your guy credit, Wendy. This is pure god-damn genius. It's completely self-contained. The cops would never find it."

Wendy leaned painfully against the nearest post, sobbing and sniffling. "All right," she said, "you guys got what you came here for. You gotta let me go now."

The driver laughed. "I know you aren't stupid enough to go the cops, but you must be pretty dumb to believe we're simply going to let you walk out of here," he said.

With a jolt, Wendy realized that the assault wasn't over. "C'mon. I won't say a thing to anyone," she pleaded. "I don't even know who you guys are. When Bernie finds out I led you here, he's going to kill me, anyways."

"And how's he going to find that out?" the man said, staring out across the sea of green.

"No, no. I mean when he realizes that someone found his plants, he'll know it was me," said Wendy.

"That really sucks for you," said the man. "You should've thought about consequences before getting involved in such a risky business." He nodded to the passenger, who whipped his pistol across the back of Wendy's head. She dropped like a stone onto the concrete floor.

Wendy Clark came to gradually, trying to figure out where she was and how long she'd been there. Her arms and feet were bound with duct tape, only one eye would open, her face throbbed with pain, and she was on a concrete floor, shivering. She rolled to one side and saw that she'd pissed herself. She lay in a pool of her own urine and blood.

With her one good eye, she looked around the room. A single grow light hung at a crazy angle from the ceiling. It did a poor job of lighting a massive space that had once been filled with plants ready for harvest. The remaining lights were smashed and dark. Now she saw that there was nothing green left in the basement. Every plant, carefully nurtured over the last five months, was gone, the stems cut at soil level. The black pipes lay on the floor in puddles of fertilized water.

Before Wendy's muddled brain could comprehend what she'd done and what it meant to Eastman's business, a shadow crossed in front of her, blocking the remaining light. It was a man, a large man, and his fists were opening and closing at his sides. She assumed it was one of the two men who'd brought her to the hidden basement, ready to hurt her again.

"No," she croaked, "please ... don't." And then she heard Eastman's voice, frighteningly calm and slow.

"Wendy," he said, "what the hell have you done?"

She began to sob. "I'm so sorry," she said. "They made me do it, Bernie. They hurt me bad. I had no choice."

"First your husband talks to the cops about one part of my business," he said, still slow and calm as if in a trance, "and then you do *this* to the other part?"

She tried to respond. "Bernie, I'm sor —"

But that was all she was able to say before Eastman reared back and kicked her with his lug-soled boot. He kept kicking and kicking until the life in her eyes was gone.

CHAPTER 21

JUNE 19

"Where are you heading this morning?" said the stocky U.S. Customs and Border Protection agent, two Canadian passports clutched in his left hand.

"Sandpoint," said Willson. Bill Forsyth sat in the passenger seat beside her, peering at the American officer as he ran through a barrage of questions.

The two wardens had left Banff early that morning, stopping in Invermere for a coffee. This time, Willson had followed Forsyth into the Kicking Horse Café to find out what it was he'd bought for her the last time they were there. When she discovered that it was a blend called Kick Ass, she'd literally whooped with surprise, startling the young girl serving them.

"This is perfect," Willson had said to the wide-eyed barista. "This is *so* friggin' me!" She was so pleased that she'd also bought a black T-shirt with a mule on the front. It was like she'd finally found her spirit animal, even though she didn't really believe in that shit. Obstinate, intelligent, ready to respond to tormentors — or simply people who pissed her off — with a swift kick where it hurt.

But now, they were two hours south, at the Kingsgate border crossing, and the coffee mugs were again empty.

"What will you be doing in Sandpoint?" asked the agent.

"We're going to a meeting with a U.S. Fish and Wildlife agent," said Willson.

She and Forsyth were in uniform, the green and brown of the Parks Canada Warden Service. Seeing Canadian officials heading into the United States in uniform was apparently a rarity for the border agent, so he dug deeper. "What's the meeting about and how long will you be in the U.S.?" he asked.

Willson had nothing to hide, so she explained that they'd be discussing a wildlife-poaching case involving suspects from both sides of the border. "We'll only be down there as long as the meeting takes, probably a couple of hours, and then we'll head back through here again."

"Where were the animals poached?" the agent asked, his curiosity apparently piqued.

"We really have to get to the meeting," said Willson, looking down at her watch to make a point. "I can tell you we're dealing with a guide-outfitter on our side of the border who's not playing by the rules and an American hunter who's taking full advantage of that."

"Well, give 'em hell," said the agent. "I'm an avid hunter and this kind of thing pisses me off." With that, he handed the passports to Willson and waved them on.

The two wardens drove southward through northern Idaho on Highway 93, stopping just north of Bonners Ferry for cheap gas. They drove down a long hill and crossed the Kootenay River as it began its big circle back to the north. Now on the verge of summer, the grasses along the riverbank were green and lush, and the river was still aggressive and full, just past the peak of freshet. They picked up a pair of tall coffees from a Starbucks hidden in a Safeway at the south end of the small town. After the first sip, Willson knew that finding Kick Ass had changed her life forever, at least the part that involved coffee. And that was a big part. But she was disappointed to realize that she'd have to stop ribbing Forsyth about his caffeine snobbery. He had previously called Kicking Horse coffee the "nectar of the East Kootenay," and now she no longer wanted to argue the point.

Before continuing south toward Sandpoint, the two switched places. Forsyth drove while Willson sat in the passenger seat with a thick file balanced on her knees, trying to ignore his inconsistent speeds. She felt her upper body moving back and forth while Forsyth used the gas pedal like bellows on a bagpipe.

"Jesus, Bill," said Willson finally, "can't you just pick one bloody speed and stick with it?"

"Don't worry about me," said Forsyth without looking at her. "I've had few accidents in my driving career."

Willson turned back to the files on her lap, trying to read, knowing she would drive home.

"I guess the fact we're heading south today, back on the case, means your little plan worked?" asked Forsyth a few miles later, one side of his mouth and one eyebrow raised in a question.

Willson smiled knowingly in response to Forsyth's question, ignoring his implication that her plan was insignificant. "We lost almost a month on that debacle. But it's funny how the bigwigs in Calgary and Ottawa decided that this investigation was a good idea when they got letters from politicians and senior bureaucrats in B.C. — and from some key environmental groups in the Kootenays — openly applauding them for trying to bring the poachers to justice. The fact that the letters were copied to and reprinted by major news outlets didn't hurt, either."

Forsyth chuckled. Willson had told him that, after being told to stand down from the investigation, she'd made a late-night call to a deputy environment minister in B.C., a fellow she'd worked with early in his career. A letter from him, and one from the provincial environment minister, had arrived in her boss's inbox a week later. And Jim Canon, a director of the Kootenays' biggest and most influential environmental group, was responsible for the other persuasive letters.

"Are our bosses taking credit for it?" Forsyth asked.

"Of course they are," she said. "If you can stomach hearing the politicians talk, the thing was their idea from the beginning. Little did I know, but it was them who pushed me to work on it. They've got their public relations people working full-time on it. According to the crap coming out of their Ottawa crap factories, they've been concerned about this issue for a while. Who knew?"

"Well, that's what anti-nausea pills are for," said Forsyth.

"Quite frankly, I don't give a shit what they say — as long as I can keep this thing moving," said Willson. "I had no intention of giving up, but it was an RCMP contact who gave me the idea of turning the tables on them by getting the letters sent. I owe him big time."

"What about the Jasper ram?"

"It was a Parks Canada miracle," said Willson. "As soon as the politicians decided this investigation was a good idea, the Jasper boys suddenly disclosed that the handgun used in Wilcox Pass was a .44 calibre."

"Did it match any of the handguns I saw at Eastman's house?" asked Forsyth. "Shit. I was there and could've easily grabbed them."

"It could have matched, but the crime lab says there's no way to know without them getting their hands on the gun that shot the bullet."

"Son of a bitch," said Forsyth, shaking his head in disgust. "And the Kootenay goat?"

"The same thing. That investigation is back on, too. The saddest part of this —" Willson tapped her fingers on the files in her lap to the beat of the song on the radio "— is that the jerks in Ottawa aren't smart enough to realize what happened. And even if they suspect what we did to them, there's not a damn thing they can do about it. There is one little asshole in particular, a pompous little prick from Calgary, whose face I would love to rub in this till he squeals. But I'll just give him a big smile the next time I see him."

"Perfect!" said Forsyth. Then he sobered. "But now, to make it all worthwhile, we have to find a way to throw the friggin' book at Eastman and this mysterious American."

Willson nodded in agreement and then decided it was time to raise the elephant in the truck. "It's unfortunate that you can't stay on beyond your ten months, Bill." She wasn't going to tell Forsyth that he'd done a good job, and she wasn't going to admit that she hadn't tried to keep him on, or that he was an annoyance she could do without. So she kept it neutral.

"It's all right," said Forsyth. "I've got an interview the week after next for a conservation officer position in Manitoba."

"Good luck with that, then," Willson said, her head down in the file.

They drove into Sandpoint, a town of 8,200 people on the shore of Lake Pend Oreille, about forty-five minutes later. Neither of them had been there before, so they did a circle of the downtown core before finding Connie's Café, the agreed-upon locale for the meeting with their U.S. counterpart. The café was lit by a large neon sign, a beacon of red on a cloudy day.

As they walked in the front door, Willson turned to Forsyth. "This is another opportunity to learn, Bill. I want you to stay quiet and listen. Got it?"

Forsyth nodded, but did not look happy with the direction.

With assistance from an aproned waitress straight from the 1960s, her hair in a net and a pencil behind her ear, they found Tracy Brown from the U.S. Fish and Wildlife Service. Based on Willson's Internet search, the Spokane office was the closest to the East Kootenays, and after a phone call, she was told that Brown was the top-ranking special agent there. Brown's dark hair was pulled back in a severe bun, but her smile lit the room when she saw the two Canadian wardens. The patches on the shoulders of her tan uniform shirt depicted a rising trout trying to ingest a startled duck above the words "Department of the Interior." Over her uniform, Brown wore a dark-green bulletproof vest. *No nonsense,* thought Willson.

After ordering lunch, Willson got down to business. "Thanks for this, Tracy," she said, looking across the table at Brown. "I've shared our case files with you and we've talked on the phone, so you know what I've got. You also know I'm close to laying charges against Bernie Eastman, who holds the guide territory around which this entire investigation is circling."

The primary case file was on the table in front of Willson. She patted it as she reviewed the list of potential charges against Eastman and the American under the Canada National Parks Act and B.C.'s Wildlife Act and the evidence they had for each. She told Brown that she was pinning her hopes primarily on the Parks Act, which allowed her to charge the two men with illegal hunting and illegal trafficking for the Banff elk and the Kootenay mountain goat. They talked about the Jasper ram and how she didn't have sufficient evidence to charge the two men with that crime, other than hearsay from Clark and Canon's recollection of seeing Eastman and Clark there the day before she believed it was shot.

"I've got to get my hands on the revolver used for the ram so I can match it with the slug in the carcass," said Willson, "and that's only going to come with another search warrant."

Brown shook her head, agreeing that the Jasper wardens had been selfish and shortsighted. "I'm pleased to help, Jenny," she said. "Looks like you've done a good job on Eastman and you seem to be building a solid case on your American suspect. Except, you know, for the fact that you don't have his name yet. You're sure the guy you're looking for is from down here?"

"I am," said Willson, with a blush of embarrassment in her cheeks. "Not only did our witness tell me that the client is an American, but our anonymous caller said the same thing. But neither will give me his name." She smiled. "At least, not yet. So far, I know he's rich, he has a big ego, he loves trophy hunting, and he doesn't give a shit about wildlife laws on either side of the border."

Brown chuckled. "Sorry, but that doesn't narrow it down much."

"I know," said Willson, now leaning on the table with both forearms. "Ideally, I'd like to lay charges against Eastman early next week, but none of the charges I hope to lay on the American would allow us to extradite him to Canada, even if I *did* know who he was. So, one of the reasons I wanted to meet with you, before I go any further, is to see what you can do to help me out. Maybe you've got some brilliant ideas for me…." She let her words trail off.

At that moment, the waitress brought their lunches, the plates stacked up both arms. She splashed extra coffee in their cups and in the saucers underneath. The trio dug in to huge hamburgers, massive piles of french fries, and glistening scoops of coleslaw, talking between mouthfuls.

"Do you know anything about the Lacey Act?" asked Brown after washing down the last of her fries with a sip of black coffee.

Willson openly expressed her ignorance. "I've heard of it, but I don't know anything about it."

"Thanks to forward-thinking politicians back in 1900," said Brown, "it continues to be our premier weapon in the fight against illegal wildlife trafficking. It might be what we're looking for here." Brown described how it allowed them to lay a charge if a person imported or transported wildlife into the United States that had been taken in violation of a foreign wildlife protection law or regulation.

"It seems to me," she went on, "that because your two suspects killed animals illegally in your parks — and if our guy brought the trophies down here afterward — we could charge him under the Lacey Act."

"What are your penalties if he's convicted?"

"If we can prove a felony rather than a misdemeanour, then we're talking a maximum fine of $250,000 and up to five years in jail," said Brown.

"That might slow the bastard down." Then Willson explained to Brown that B.C.'s Wildlife Act offered a fine up to $250,000 and a maximum of two years in jail, while getting a conviction for an indictable offence under the Canadian National Parks Act could lead to a fine ranging from $30,000 to $2 million, and a maximum time in jail of five years. Brown whistled when she heard the maximum fine, showing she understood why Willson wanted to get convictions under the Parks legislation.

"What do we have to prove to get a felony conviction under your act?" asked Willson.

With her elbow on the table, Brown raised her left hand in a fist, and using her fingers one at a time, listed the requirements. "First, we need to identify him. Then, we must prove that he shot the animals in violation of one of your laws. Looks like we've got that nailed. If it's clear that the American client paid for Eastman's services as a guide-outfitter when he took the animals — and you said your witness stated that he paid $20,000 in total for each hunt — then we've also proved that each animal has a market value greater than $350. And if we can prove, through your witness statements, that the client knew he was illegally hunting in the parks, even better."

"There's no doubt about any of that," said Willson.

With four fingers raised in the air, and with Willson and Forsyth both taking notes as she spoke, Brown continued. "Based on that, we then have to prove that Eastman's client brought the trophies into the U.S. That's the key link between the violations in Canada and making any Lacey charges stick down here." Her hand was now open like she was waving, all fingers upright.

Willson frowned and sighed. "That's where we've got a problem," she said.

"How so?"

"The American only needed his hunting licence and cancelled tags to legally get the animals out of the country," Willson explained. "That is, if Eastman reported any of his hunts at all. Because I don't have the American's name yet, I don't know if he did or didn't do that. And I can't check with the border crossings in B.C. and Alberta to see if there's any record of him bringing the elk rack or the goat head down here. Believe it or not, they might've brought the goat to a B.C. government office for a compulsory inspection. But without a name, I just don't know."

"What about the sheep?" asked Brown.

"I don't know *what* happened with that," said Willson. "Because Eastman's territory is in the Purcell Mountains, where there are no bighorn sheep, I'm guessing he didn't bring it to a B.C. office to get a small numbered aluminum plug inserted in the horn for tracking, like he's required to do. It would have been impossible for him to explain where it came from."

"But your suspect must've crossed somewhere," Brown said, "with or without the animals."

"He must have," agreed Willson. "But again, without a name, I don't know where … and I don't know when."

"Well, son of a bitch," said Brown. "He must have got the trophies across the border somehow. How the hell did he do it?" She stared off into a dark corner of the restaurant. "Without proof of that, there's no way we can get a Lacey conviction," she said with a grimace. "And there's no way we'd get a judge to give us a warrant to search down here — the connection just isn't there yet."

"Shit. I was hoping you weren't going to say that," said Willson. "We thought about this a lot and we figure the American could have brought the elk and the goat across legally. It's possible, but in my opinion unlikely. But he must've had help from someone else to get the sheep head across. From what we've heard about the guy, whoever he is, about his love of hunting big game, his huge ego, and his desire to show off his trophies, there's no way he'd leave any of those trophies in Canada."

Forsyth jumped in. "Yeah," he said. "I checked to see if Eastman brought them across for his client, but there's no record of him crossing the border from B.C. or Alberta for the last twelve months." Willson gave him a dirty look, so, chastened, he returned to making notes.

"Do you have any sense of whether the American knows you're looking for him?" asked Brown.

"I don't," said Willson. "Eastman certainly knows we're looking for something because of the searches we did at his and Clark's residences. But whether or not he told his client what happened, we don't know."

"If you lay those charges on Eastman next week, we have to assume the American will know what's going on for sure," said Brown. She sat back in the booth and stared at the ceiling. "If we want to bring the hammer down on both of these guys," she said, "we need to trace the American from shooting an animal in a park in Canada to bringing it across the border into the United States, with a clear and unbroken chain of evidence." She nodded her head, as though she'd convinced herself that this was the only way forward. "Do you know if he has any more trips planned up your way?"

"I don't," said Willson. "But I've been thinking about that. Once I lay charges against Eastman, I assume he'll tell his client. Then we probably won't see him in Canada again. If I don't catch the American in the act on our side of the border, I've got no way to ever get him in a Canadian court. Based on what you said, I might not get him in a U.S. court, either. And if Eastman is convicted, I'm sure he'll lose his guide territory … and probably his right to hunt in B.C. for a long time. And there goes the client's trophy pipeline."

Forsyth again spoke up, despite Willson's glare. "The only way Eastman wouldn't say anything to his client is if he's scared of him, or if he wants to get him back up here for another animal," he said. "That's another twenty grand in his pocket for what might be his last hunt. Only Eastman knows how much risk he's willing to accept."

"Is there any way to get him to flip on his client?" asked Brown.

"I doubt it," said Willson. "He doesn't appear to be that kind of guy. But I do have a potential informant in Charlie Clark, his assistant guide. If there's another hunt planned, he might know about it."

After waving at the waitress to get their bill, Brown summed up what they were all thinking. "Well, it looks like you have a decision to make, Jenny," she said. "If you're okay with only getting Eastman, then you've got enough to charge him now. That means you'll probably never see the American again. And then there's nothing we can do on our side of the border."

The waitress dropped the bill in front of Brown. "My treat," she said and handed the waitress a government credit card. She also left a healthy tip to express their collective appreciation of the waitress's leaving them alone during lunch.

Then she continued her summary. "If you want the American, you appear to have two choices. If you nab him up there in the act, you may or may not get a conviction under your laws. One thing we know for sure is that, if you do arrest him in Canada, you'll be dealing with an army of lawyers and the U.S. consulate. Most rich guys have top-notch lawyers on speed-dial. Who knows how that'll turn out? But if we catch him *after* crossing the border into the U.S. with an animal taken illegally in Canada, we can throw the book at him down here. Regardless of which of those two options you choose, it means the guy you're chasing needs to go back up to Canada for one more illegal hunt."

Willson and Forsyth both nodded their agreement, and after a few minutes all three made their way out of the café. "Thanks for this," said Willson as they walked to their vehicles. "I enjoyed talking to you, Tracy. You've given me lots of great information and I really appreciate your willingness to assist. I've got decisions to make and I need to make them soon."

After shaking hands with the U.S. agent and promising to let her know what they decided, Willson and Forsyth began the drive back to Canada. Willson was behind the wheel, and as they passed the northern edge of Sandpoint, she glanced over at the young warden.

"Bill, what are you thinking?" she asked.

"Oh," said Forsyth, after a petulant pause, "am I allowed to speak now?"

"Don't be an ass," she said.

"As much as I hate to think about losing another animal in one of our parks," he said, "I'd love to see both these assholes behind bars. Not just Eastman, the American, too."

"I'm with you one hundred percent," said Willson. "I'm confident I've got enough to charge Eastman now and that's not going to change if I delay a while. But if I can get both of them, that's my preference. I would hate to charge one, only to lose the other. Time to roll the dice."

She turned on the windshield wipers as a light rain began to fall. "When we get back to Banff," she said, "I'm going to call Clark, see if I can meet with him, ideally without his lawyer. I've got to find a way to persuade him to name Eastman's client, because there's no way in hell Eastman will roll on him. Everything rests on getting the name. Failing that, maybe the guy is coming up for another hunt and I can squeeze Clark into telling me when and where. That's not a great Plan B and there's a hell of a lot that could go wrong with it. But at this point, it's my *only* Plan B."

"And what am I supposed to do while you're talking to Clark?"

Willson smiled. "You can hang out at Tim Hortons and finish your reports. Sound good?"

Forsyth scowled. "Not bloody likely."

CHAPTER 22

JULY 12

Through a long one-way window in his second-floor office, Luis Castillo gazed down on the three rooms and five hundred gaming machines in his Bonners Ferry operation, a casino overlooking the Kootenay River where it looped south into northern Idaho. Castillo's hands were clasped behind his back as he watched his staff use every tactic he'd taught them, all subtle yet effective, to pull as many dollars as possible out of his guests' pockets. From slots to poker tables, cigarette machines to cocktails, meals to hotel rooms, the pieces were in place for money to flow. Outside, the mid-July sun was brilliant and scorching. But in the casino, air-conditioning kept his guests alert and spending.

Castillo's mind, however, wasn't on the scene below him. With the economy of the Pacific Northwest worsening and the dropping Canadian dollar translating to fewer gamblers coming south, he was concerned about cash flow. Revenues were shrinking throughout his business empire, not only in his legitimate enterprises, but also those operating on the other side of the law. That made it difficult for him to shift money from one side of that line to the other. As a result, he was putting pressure on managers in all his businesses to find new sources of revenue and, at the same time, to cut their operating costs. His partners were pressuring him, as well.

Castillo pondered the mounting challenges that were making him lose sleep and snap at his wife more than he should. In this rapidly changing environment, it was tougher and tougher to stay on top of his suppliers and meet the demands of those to whom he supplied. And that was his biggest concern of all. Every one of his business colleagues had high expectations and a low tolerance for delays or excuses. They were neither patient nor forgiving.

There was a discreet knock on the office door behind him. He turned, vigorously rubbing his hands against his face in an attempt to refocus his thoughts.

"Entras," he said.

The casino security director opened the door and stepped into the room. Billy Whitehead, a muscular, six-foot-five Native American from the local Kootenai tribe, had worked for Castillo for ten years. Dressed in a dark-blue suit and open-collared white shirt, his broad face unsmiling, his nose hawk-like, his hair hanging down his back in a thick, ebony braid, he was a guy you didn't mess with. One glare from Whitehead calmed the unruliest of casino visitors, making it rare for the man to have to put his hands on anyone. When he did, the offender would be removed from the casino quickly and with little commotion.

"A Mr. Eastman says he has an appointment with you, Mr. Castillo," Whitehead said.

"Send him in, Billy," said Castillo, "and please hang around in case I need you."

A man of few words, Whitehead nodded and then stood aside to let Bernie Eastman enter the office. The two men were the same height. Castillo watched Whitehead stare at the visitor, eye to eye and without expression, as the Canadian passed him in the doorway. He saw the brief look of surprise in Eastman's eyes when he realized that Whitehead showed no fear of him. None at all.

"Welcome to my casino, Bernie," said Castillo. "Thanks for coming down."

"Sure," said Eastman gruffly. "I decided that you and I needed to talk ... so I brought my boys down with me."

"I hope they're comfortable."

"They are. They're at the pool. Nothin' personal, but I won't let my wife anywhere near this place. I can't afford it."

Castillo moved toward a sitting area that occupied a corner of his office. "I understand. May I get you a coffee or a beer?"

"Yeah, I'll take a beer," said Eastman.

Leaving the Stella Artois for important guests, Castillo pulled a long-neck Budweiser out of a small fridge hidden in the wall, opened it, and passed the sweating bottle to Eastman. With any other guest, he would've poured the beer into a glass. But he knew that the man would neither care nor notice the difference.

He served himself a sparkling water on ice. They sat in matching armchairs, facing each other.

"I hope your family enjoy themselves while they're here, so please let me know if you need anything," said Castillo. "Now, what is it you wish to talk about?"

"Well, we got some problems ... so I thought we should meet in person," said Eastman. "I didn't want to talk on the phone."

"Does this concern Charlie Clark and your last phone call to me?" asked Castillo, holding the crystal water glass in his left hand.

"Yeah, that's part of it."

"What's happening?"

"About two months ago, I think the little fucker talked to the cops about our huntin' trips."

"Two months ago?" said Castillo. "Why am I hearing about this only now?"

Eastman began to tear at a corner of the label on the bottle. "Because I planned to handle it myself," he said, "and nothin's happened since then."

"I see. What do you think he told them?" asked Castillo.

"I don't know," said Eastman. "He's been doin' his best to avoid me, so we haven't talked face to face yet. But I talked to his wife and she thought he and his lawyer met with cops and some wildlife-and-parks guys about some kinda deal."

"Have any of those officials come back to talk to you after they searched your house the first time?"

"Nope," said Eastman, "so I'm pretty sure they don't have much on us — no evidence or proof or anythin' like that — beyond whatever it was that Charlie might've yapped his gums to 'em about."

"You're *pretty sure*?" asked Castillo. "That does not give me a high degree of comfort, Bernie."

"I'm tellin' ya what I know, and that's all I know," said Eastman, tearing more of the label off the bottle. "He works for me, so I decided to deal with it my way. I'm gonna keep chasin' that piece of shit until I find him … and find out what he told 'em. And if I have to beat it out of him, I will. So you don't need to worry."

"I wouldn't be where I am today if I didn't get concerned when people I rely on screw up," said Castillo, emptying his glass and then placing it on a folded linen napkin on a table to his left. "This is definitely *your* problem, Bernie, and *you're* going to have to make it go away, sooner than later." Castillo held Eastman's gaze, his face devoid of expression. "But let's not be hasty. While those pretend cops up there aren't smart enough to figure out what we've been doing, I don't want you to do anything to get them *more* interested in us. In the interim, I think we've got something Clark can do for us."

"What the hell could he do for *us*?" said Eastman with a scowl. "That skinny prick is so dumb I want nothin' more to do with him."

"You know I've got my eye on one more animal up there," said Castillo, "and I believe your Charlie Clark can help me get it."

"What in hell are you talkin' about?" said Eastman. "The guy coulda talked to the cops about what we've done and you wanna keep workin' with him? That makes no goddamn sense."

"I know why you hired him, Bernie," said Castillo, "and I know how little you pay him. We both know he's a scared little man with no self-confidence. I have no doubt that, as soon as the cops put any pressure on him, he spilled his guts."

The label was off the beer bottle now. Castillo watched Eastman crumple it in his meaty hand and drop it on the table beside him.

"I already told you that there's one trophy still on my list from your part of the world," Castillo said. "I can't get it in Idaho because there are too few animals left and they're very difficult to locate. We've talked about where I can get it in British Columbia and when I want to come up. It's getting messy up there and I don't like it." He rested his hand on the table beside him, running a manicured fingernail up and down the outside of the empty glass. "I need you to tell Clark that I'm coming up in that first week of September to hunt in your territory, just like we talked about. What's out of season then?"

"Uh … what's out of …? Well, I don't have any quota for griz' this year," said Eastman, looking puzzled.

"That's perfect," said Castillo. "I want you to tell Clark that I'm coming up to get a big grizzly bear. And that I'm going to take it from that park in your territory. What's it called?"

"You mean the Purcell Wilderness Conservancy?"

"That's the one."

"You want me to tell him you're coming up to shoot somethin' that I don't have quota for, in another park?" said Eastman, still not understanding Castillo's intentions. His arms were crossed across his big chest. "What if he tells the conservation officers?"

"That's exactly what I want him to do," said Castillo, his gaze moving to the large window overlooking the casino. *One more hunt up there,* he thought. *It's the one I've dreamed about for years.* He could already see the head on his wall, could hear the admiration in the voices of his friends and family. He smiled a quick smile. And when that was done, it would be the last time he'd do business with these idiots from north of the border. Eastman would miss his money … and those stupid cops up there were going to be left empty-handed, again. Another quick smile, gone by the time he turned back to Eastman. "Please set up the hunt just as we talked about it."

"Okay, I'll do that," said Eastman, "but … because this next one is riskier and more complicated to pull off … with bigger expenses, I'll need … an extra ten grand on top of our normal fee."

Castillo took his time responding. *This guy has balls,* he thought, *to be asking for more money at a time when he really has no leverage at all.* But then again, he deeply desired this trophy. It was so unique and so rare that he'd be a member of a small and very exclusive club. And he liked that.

"I'll tell you what, Bernie," said Castillo, his eyes narrowing. "I'll pay you the fee we previously agreed on, plus five thousand more — when, *and only when*, the animal is in my possession in Spokane. But that's it."

Eastman was silent, apparently considering a counter-offer. But Castillo knew that the man was in no position to negotiate. "Fuck," said Eastman in resignation, "let's get it done."

"Good. I look forward to it," said Castillo. "And then, once you're sure that Clark told the game cops up there about what we're planning, I want you to make that problem go away. For good. Do you understand me?"

He saw Eastman's throat bob as he swallowed hard. "I understand," he said.

"Good. Now, what else did you want to talk to me about?"

Eastman wrung his hands and squirmed in the leather seat. "Have you got another beer?" he asked.

"No, I do not," replied Castillo, purposefully keeping the man on edge.

"It's about the production facility at my place," said Eastman, when he finally gained the courage to speak.

"What about it?"

"Well, I hate to say this, but Clark's bitch wife led some guys to it," said Eastman, looking down at the thick rug on the floor, "and they fuckin' ripped off all the plants and busted up all the equipment."

"I will assume that you are a smart enough man not to joke with me about something like this." Castillo now sat forward in his chair, his hands on his knees.

"This is no fuckin' joke," said Eastman. "I talked to some guys I know … and it looks like there's a bike gang workin' out of Calgary that's tryin' to take over all the business in the Kootenays. I'm sure it was them. I heard they did the same thing to a local meth lab two days after they hit my place."

"So you're telling me you let these guys walk in and take your product and destroy the equipment?"

"Jesus," said Eastman, "do you really think I'd let someone do that? It looks like the bitch tried to sell them some dope … and they musta forced her to take them to my place. I found her all beat up when I got back from camp."

"Where is she now?" asked Castillo.

"I made sure she won't be a problem for us again," said Eastman.

"Are you certain of that?" asked Castillo.

"I'm certain," replied Eastman. "She was near dead when I found her and she deserved what she got. She's been a pain in my ass since I first met her in Calgary. I guarantee the problem is buried." His look told Castillo that this was no metaphor.

Castillo was quiet, brooding, dangerous. He stared at Eastman with a look of white-hot anger.

"How are you going to fix this mess?" asked Castillo three uncomfortable minutes later.

"I need cash so I can get back into production as soon as possible," said Eastman. "I've been able to keep going since then by selling the stuff I had stored in another place on my property."

"Wait," said Castillo. "When did this happen?"

"Uh … back in early June," said Eastman.

Castillo slammed his fist down on the table beside him, knocking the crystal glass onto the rug. It did not break. Instead, it rolled in a lazy circle, bumping against a cabinet on the far wall.

"You idiot!" he shouted, rising to his feet. "You waited this long to tell me? Don't you realize that the guys who ripped you off will do that over and over again now they know what you're doing there? You can't start up again as if nothing happened. Not if they're still around. You're not thinking, Bernie. Don't you understand that by linking our business with that useless bitch, you've put my entire investment there at risk? And I've got buyers waiting for that product. It was supposed to be ready to move now!"

As Castillo stood glaring at Eastman, his hands opening and closing in rage, the door to the office opened. Billy Whitehead stepped into the room. "Is everything okay, Mr. Castillo?" he asked.

"Mr. Eastman just gave me some troubling news, Billy, so everything is not okay," said Castillo, still focused on Eastman. "Thank you for checking in. Please leave us for the moment."

After staring at Eastman for a few seconds, Whitehead left the room, pulling the door closed behind him.

"Hey," said Eastman, his hands open and wide, "none of this is my fault."

"Bernie, I hold you personally responsible for the two messes you brought me today," said Castillo. "There is no one else to blame. It is *all* your fault. The fact you don't understand makes me even angrier." He pondered his next move. He was not going to give Eastman any indication as to the state of his cash flow, how the loss of revenue from the grow op would affect that, or how angry his buyers would be when they heard he had nothing to sell them. He'd have to find other product somewhere else, fast, likely at a much higher cost. And he wasn't going to let Eastman off the hook for the imbeciles he'd hired around him. The fucker's incompetence had created this situation and he would make him pay, one way or another. But first, he needed a way out.

Castillo paced the room, his hands in the pockets of tan linen pants, his mind swirling. Focusing on his breathing as though he were about to shoot a rifle, he forced air in and out of his lungs, deep and slow.

"This puts my supply chain north of the border at significant risk," said Castillo. "Because of you and your trust in the wrong people, I've lost the ability to move any product south ... which puts me in a very difficult position."

"Whaddaya want me to do?" asked Eastman.

Castillo stood still for a moment, his hands on the corner of his desk now, his eyes piercing under thick, dark brows. He began to move his upper body up and down as though doing push-ups. "I need you to find out who's in this gang," he said. "How many are there? Who are they? Where do they live? Where do they work? Who are they selling to? Who do they hang out with, and where? I want to know everything about them, more than they know about themselves. There isn't room for two operations in that area, and I will not accept being on the outside looking in. Are you capable of doing that?"

"How am I gonna find out all that?"

"You're going to figure it out. Or do I need to find someone else to fix your mess?"

"No ... no, I can handle it," said Eastman.

"I will not accept failure on this, Bernie," said Castillo. He glowered at Eastman without blinking. "You've had a couple of major fuck-ups and I will not allow it to happen again. Do you hear what I am saying to you? Do you fully understand the implications of making another mistake?"

"I get it," said Eastman, again swallowing hard.

"I'm not sure you do," said Castillo. "Think about your wife and kids as a widow and orphans."

Eastman's earlier bravado was nearly gone. "When I find out who these guys are, what're you gonna do?"

"That is no longer any of your concern. Let me be clear. I need that information quickly. You have left me no choice but to take care of them myself, permanently. You deal with Clark and I'll deal with this. And before you go, I remind you that I need you to let me know when you've spoken to Clark. I will come across the border on September third, so you must talk to him soon."

With his emotions back under control, Castillo pushed a small button on the side of his desk. The outer door to the office opened quickly.

"Billy will ensure that you and your family have a few minutes to gather your things, check out of the hotel, and be on the road home," said Castillo. "It's unfortunate you couldn't stay longer to enjoy our hospitality. You have work to do and you don't have much time in which to do it." He dismissed Eastman by turning his back on him.

When Eastman left the office and the door clicked shut behind him, Castillo moved back to the window overlooking the casino. He looked down as Whitehead escorted Eastman across the floor of the casino toward the hotel entrance. The gambling patrons parted as the two big men moved through them, like supertankers through thin Arctic ice.

Just like earlier in the afternoon, Castillo's mind was not on the casino or the patrons feeding coins into his machines. He thought about Eastman, the man who'd just added another layer of problems to his world. Castillo rarely second-guessed his own decisions, but in the case of the outfitter, he recognized that doing anything more than hunting with the man had been a mistake. It was a mistake that needed fixing — and fast.

Castillo considered himself an optimist, but he was also a realist. He couldn't shake the feeling that he was slowly losing control of the world around him. For a man like him, that was the ultimate in failure.

CHAPTER 23

After his troubling meeting with Castillo in Bonners Ferry, Bernie Eastman arrived home, bad-tempered and thirsty. It wasn't enough that he'd been made to feel like a complete fuck-up, but his family's ejection from the hotel, only hours after checking in, had left them sullen and resentful. With two disappointed boys in the truck, Eastman would have preferred silence to their questions. "I don't understand why we had to leave, Daddy," the youngest kept saying. "Why did we have to get out of the pool so fast?" While he could deal with that, he knew that his wife would ask more questions when they got home, in her shrill, incredibly annoying voice. And she had.

It was at times like this that Eastman wondered why he always ended up around tiresome, unpleasant, yappy women. He despised them and yet, for most of his life, he'd been surrounded by them. Perhaps it was some kind of goddamn karma, he thought, for something he'd done in a past life. His mother had been a horrible nag until he left home, his older sister no better. Since they'd arrived home, his red-haired wife had asked the same dumb question again and again, so he'd tuned her out. She was clueless about their financial situation and would likely ignore any explanation he tried to offer, constantly reminding him that it was her money that bought the territory. As far as he knew, all she thought about was shopping and gambling. And not necessarily in that order, which was why he'd kept her away from the casino. Instead of listening to her, Eastman had pictured Wendy Clark in her hole in the ground, buried in a remote corner of his property. There was room for both women in there, he thought. They could complain and natter at each other forever, talking and never listening. But he was also sure that if there was a hell for him, that was what it would be, and that was where he'd end up. He shuddered at the thought.

Carrying their hastily packed bags, his sons had disappeared to their bedrooms as soon as the front door was opened. Eastman chose a chair in the small office from which he ran his business. His door closed, he placed an ice-cold Guinness on the desk in front of him, and then sat with a groan and a sigh. The swirling tans and dark browns in the tall glass matched the churning currents of his thoughts. He had contacts in the drug trade, some reliable, some less so, and he'd have to use every one of them to identify the guys who'd beat up Wendy Clark and then ripped him off. Of all the things Castillo had asked him to do since they'd first met, Eastman understood that the ultimatum he'd just been given had the most significant consequences. If he failed, his wife could spend the meager proceeds from his life insurance on whatever the hell she wanted. At that point, it wouldn't matter anymore.

An hour later, Eastman's cellphone rang, disturbing his random scribblings on a pad of paper. From the sound of the ringtone — a bad imitation of a bugling elk — he knew it was Charlie Clark. This was a surprise. He'd been trying to locate the guy for weeks.

"Charlie, where the hell've you been?" asked Eastman when he answered the phone. "I've been lookin' for you everywhere. You didn't return my calls."

"I know, I know, I've been lookin' for my wife," said Clark. "I haven't seen her for weeks. Any idea where she mighta gone?"

In the aftermath of his rage-fuelled assault on Wendy Clark, Eastman had given no thought to anyone missing her. Not even her husband. "Uh … I got no clue, Charlie. When and where did you last see her?"

"I haven't seen 'er since late May, I guess. I can't remember for sure. But this ain't like 'er," said Clark. "I think the last time I saw 'er she said she was headin' out your way."

"Jesus, Charlie, that was a long time ago. She was here to pick up somethin', but then I think she headed toward Kimberley," said Eastman, omitting a few key facts. "I'm sure she'll show up eventually."

The guy must be desperate for money, Eastman thought, and maybe for food and medication. But he knew he'd done Clark a favour. He was better off without her.

"Forget about her, Charlie, she'll show up," said Eastman. "What's important is that she told me you talked to the cops and COs about our hunts. How could you be so fuckin' stupid, Charlie? What did you tell 'em?"

"After they found the dope at our trailer," said Clark, his voice echoing that of his wife, "my lawyer told me I should meet with 'em 'cause he might be able to get the drug charges reduced. When we met with 'em, though, they already knew about your guarantee ... and they knew about Castillo, though they don't know his name yet. But they know he's an American and they knew he shot animals in the parks. I don't know how, but they knew everything! With all those uniforms and lawyers in one room, I got scared and confused. I didn't know what the hell was goin' on and I didn't understand the legal bullshit they threw at me. They tricked me into agreein' with what they said. It wasn't my fault! But I never told 'em Castillo's name. I never did."

In a disturbing shot of reality, Eastman heard himself saying the same thing to Castillo that very morning. It sounded as sad and empty coming from Clark now as it must have coming from him then. But if what Clark was saying was true, if he hadn't willingly ratted Eastman out, then how had the COs found out about his guarantee and about his client being an American? "Jesus Christ, Charlie," he said, "how could you do that to us? Castillo is gonna want our hides."

"I had no goddamn choice, Bernie, I'm sorry." He sounded completely defeated. "But ... but, like I said, they have no idea who he is. That's gotta be good, right?"

"That's the only thing you did good," said Eastman. "You are fuckin' lucky I didn't find you in person,

Charlie, because I woulda beat the shit out of you. I may do that, anyways. Are you still talking to the cops?"

"I got nothin' more to say to them," said Clark. "The lawyer's handlin' it. I tried to keep you out of it as much as I could, Bernie, I really did. You gotta believe me. But now, I know I'm goin' to jail. I just don't know for how long."

Even though his anger and anxiety were mounting by the second, Eastman remembered Castillo's precise instructions about the upcoming hunt. He didn't want to add to his already long list of screw-ups, and he could square things with Clark later. "Well, it's done now," he said. "We'll have to sit tight and see what happens. I guess I'll lose my fuckin' guide territory because of this — you and I are gonna square that up at some point." He paused before continuing. "But, Charlie, we've got one more hunt to do before that happens and I can pay you upfront for it."

"Say what?" asked Clark. "Who are we gonna hunt with?"

"Castillo. He's gonna come up one more time," said Eastman.

"Are ya sure?" asked Clark. "I can't believe it. The guy has got big brass balls. When's he comin' up and what's he goin' for?"

Eastman could tell that Clark was surprised by the news, but his question about when and what made it clear that he *was* going to tell the COs about the plans as soon as he could. But, whether it made any sense or not, that was what Castillo wanted. And after all that had happened so far, Eastman wasn't going to argue.

"He's comin' up to the territory in the first week of September to get a big male griz," he said.

"That goddamn Mexican doesn't give a shit about the COs or wardens, does he?" said Clark. "Are we really gonna risk shootin' somethin' else illegal?"

"At this point, Charlie, we got nothin' to lose," said Eastman. "This may be our last chance to make some money for a bit. So I need you to help guide. The base and satellite camps are ready to go. All I have to do is buy food, get the horses ready here, and hire a cook. I'll let you know when everythin's set. He's gonna arrive on September third, and we'll start the hunt on the fourth."

"What about the money?" asked Clark.

"I'll pay you two grand for this last one. I'll bring it over the next time I'm in town. Until then, try not to do anythin' else stupid." He hung up the phone. This was one guy he wasn't going to miss.

Finishing the last of his Guinness, which was now, like his current situation, warm and bitter, Eastman suddenly realized he had something on Castillo that he could use to his advantage, to help turn back the waves of legal and financial problems threatening to drown him. It was serious leverage, leverage that, if he chose to use it, had to be wielded carefully and at the right time. The COs and park wardens didn't know who Castillo was. And they didn't know all the activities the American had his dirty hand in. But Eastman did.

CHAPTER 24

JULY 23

The sun had abandoned the town of Banff for the day, but it still lit the west-facing slopes of Mount Rundle, the bare alpine glowing, trees below in shade. Jenny Willson stood at the window of the warden office, watching the line between light and dark creep up the mountain. In her hand was the final mug of Kick Ass poured from her thermos — a thermos hidden in her desk so she didn't have to share it. Steam from the coffee misted the window. With her right index finger, she traced a question mark in the condensation on the glass.

Since arriving in Banff from her Sandpoint meeting a month earlier, Willson had reviewed the case file, page by page, paying particular attention to her notes from the interview with Charlie Clark. Her focus was always on this case, even when doing other things. It distracted her during the day and dominated her dreams by night.

Throughout, she was looking for something, anything, that she could use to push, prod, or cajole Clark into saying more than he'd already told her. But so far, nothing.

She'd considered dropping in on Eastman, laying out the evidence they had against him, doing her best to persuade him to give up the American. Other than the quick meeting in a dark Banff parking lot, she still hadn't spoken to the guide, hadn't looked him in the eye, hadn't let him know that she was the one who was rocking his world, and not in a good way. And that left her dissatisfied, as though she was purposefully abstaining from the pleasure of seeing his face. But she wasn't delusional. She knew enough about the man to understand that unless she was there to arrest him, he'd probably laugh at her if she showed up at his door. There was no doubt that he knew about her, perhaps even had a vague recollection of her. She assumed that Clark had mentioned her name and her role in their troubles. But so far, it was probable that she was as much of a mystery to him as he was to her. Given that, perhaps it was best if she left him looking over his shoulder, wondering when she would come for him.

She walked back to her desk. "Not yet," she said to herself, "not yet. We'll get our chance to meet again, Bernie. You and I have lots to talk about."

Instead, she elected to call Clark, to tell him that she'd drop in to talk to him in person. She was confident that if she could get him alone, without his lawyer, she could persuade him to talk. The man was already uncertain, clearly on edge. She could push him over that edge, and once there, he might open up about the American hunter. But first, she'd tie a belay rope around his waist, at least figuratively. Clark's testimony in court would be critical, so she couldn't push him so far over a cliff, emotionally or legally, that he'd be useless to her. Willson found his phone number in her notes and dialled.

Clark answered on the third ring. "Yeah?"

"Charlie, this is Jenny Willson from the Banff warden office. I'm sure you'll remember that we met at your house and then again at the Cranbrook RCMP detachment."

"Yeah, I remember you. Whaddaya want?"

"I've got some information I want to share with you. I'd like to come down tomorrow to meet with you."

"New information?" asked Clark. "Is it about Wendy, my wife?"

"No," said Willson, suddenly curious. "What happened to your wife?"

"She's been missing for a while now — almost two months, I think — and I don't know what to do about it."

"You don't know how long she's been missing?"

"No, I … I don't remember for sure. They cops found her car in Kimberley. The door was open and it was out of gas. It was like she just walked away. But she knows how to get into our bank account and I don't. And now I've run out of money … and I can't get my pills … or any food. But I need those pills 'cause …"

Willson could tell that Clark was struggling. His speech was halting, slurred, and he was clearly anxious about his wife, or at least about the missing drugs and food. "Are you sick, Charlie?"

"Well, yeah," Clark said. "I got Parkinson's … and I need my meds."

"You mean Parkinson's disease, Charlie?"

"That what I said. I ... I need the money to buy my pills."

"Doesn't your B.C. health plan cover the cost?"

"Not all of it. And I need food ... and gas for the truck ... and I have to pay rent on the trailer."

"Geez, Charlie," said Willson, her voice rising. "Have you phoned the RCMP?"

"No, I'm not sure what to do ... or who to phone," Clark said, sounding scared and confused. "When they found her car, they called me so I could get it towed back here, but I didn't think she was missin' then. With all that's goin' on, I thought maybe she mighta gone off somewhere, maybe a holiday or to visit some of her family back east."

"You might be right. But two months is a long time. And to just abandon her car like that ..." Willson said. "Look, let me call the RCMP. One of them will want to talk to you and get more details about Wendy, just in case."

"Shit ... the last thing I need is more cops in my life," said Clark. "But yeah ... whatever."

"I'd still like to come down to talk to you. I need your help."

Clark coughed, as though he was having trouble breathing. "I'll help you out, but you gotta promise to help *me* out."

"I promise. I'll come down tomorrow. Is there anything else about Bernie's hunting plans that's changed since you and I last talked?"

"Yeah," said Clark. "You guys told me to tell you what Bernie's up to. You won't believe this, but Ca — I mean, that fuckin' American is comin' back up here to hunt again."

"Do you mean Bernie's American hunting client? The one we asked you about? Are you sure?" Willson had heard Clark almost say the hunter's name. Almost.

"Yeah, I just got off the phone with Bernie," Clark said. "He told me the guy was comin' up in the first week of … of September to get a grizzly in Bernie's territory. Bernie don't have quota, and it'll probably be in the park, so he shouldn't be doin' it. But he's gettin' things ready, so it looks like it's goin' ahead. I think it might be the guy's last hunt up here. He's supposed to arrive on September third."

"September third, eh? Does Bernie know you've talked to us?" asked Willson.

"Yeah, he knows … and he's really pissed off at me," said Clark. "I figure if he sees me in person, I'm gonna need a hospital bad."

"Come on, Charlie, this doesn't add up," she said. "Why would Bernie tell you about the hunt if he was angry with you, particularly since he knows you've told us what's going on? Why tell you the exact day the hunter's arriving? Are you bullshitting me?"

"No, no. I'm just tellin' ya what Bernie told me," said Clark. "It makes no fuckin' sense to me, either. But I guess Bernie thinks this is a chance for one last score before he loses his territory. He knows you guys are on to him, but I think he really needs the money … and he told me he needs my help. He's gonna phone me when things are set up. I assume you're gonna let me do this … that you haven't taken away my assistant guide licence."

"Leave this with me, Charlie," said Willson, "I need to think about it. We can talk again tomorrow. But no matter what, I want you to phone me when you hear any details about this hunt."

"Yeah, okay, I'll —"

"Wait a minute, Charlie, I thought of something else. You told us about you being there when the American shot the elk in Banff and when he shot that goat in Kootenay. And you said you knew that the same guy also shot the ram in Jasper, even though you weren't there. Right?"

"Yeah, you guys made me write all that stuff down at the cop shop," said Clark.

"When we talked to you, we assumed the hunter took the trophies into the United States himself. But you told us you didn't think he did. Without his name, we can't really check anything. So … how did he do it, Charlie? How did he get them out of the country?"

Clark went quiet. Willson assumed that his stress-addled brain was working overtime. *Must be painful,* she thought. "Charlie, you still there?"

"Yeah, I'm still here," he said. "I was tryin' to remember what I heard him and Bernie say."

"Think carefully, Charlie," said Willson. "This is important to our investigation."

"I was never there," said Clark, "but … I remember 'em talkin' about Bernie goin' to Elko, where he was gonna meet trucks."

"Trucks?"

"Yeah. It sounded like the client knew about trucks that were headin' from Calgary to the States, or somethin' like that. Bernie always had to meet them at Elko. I don't know if it was the American's trucks … or someone else's."

"Son of a bitch," said Willson. "That must be how he got the trophies across the border without the risk of doing it himself."

"Didn't you guys know that?" asked Clark. "I thought I told you that when you were interviewin' me at the cop shop that day."

"No, you didn't tell us that, Charlie," she said. "But maybe we didn't ask the right questions. What about the documents? Did they say anything about that?"

"If you're talkin' about papers to get them animals across the border into the U.S.," answered Clark, "I dunno nothin' about that."

"Fair enough. But if you remember anything, write it down and tell me tomorrow." Willson decided to give Clark something to sleep on. "A few moments ago, you almost told me the hunter's name, Charlie. I really need that name. There's not much I can offer you without going back to the federal prosecutor, but I want you to think long and hard about doing the right thing. I'm going to do all I can to help find your wife, and to help you get back on your meds. But I need you to do this for me. I can't tell you how important it is. If you do, I'll tell the prosecutor that you helped crack the case. That should help when your charges get to trial. And if you give us all the detail you can, maybe we can find enough evidence that your testimony becomes less important."

Willson could hear Clark's breathing. It was slow and irregular. He did not sound good.

"And one more thing," she said. "When we interviewed you at the RCMP detachment, you said Bernie kept the .308 in his gun cabinet in the garage. We still haven't found it. Are you sure he always kept it in the cabinet in the garage?"

"Yeah, the one in the basement. Down there with his other … Uh, never mind."

Willson quickly flipped through the file, looking for Forsyth's notes from their search of Eastman's property. Nothing. No mention of a basement. "There's a basement in the garage, Charlie?"

"Yep. That big metal building. I'm not surprised you didn't find it. Bernie doesn't like people goin' down there. It's hidden pretty good."

Shit. Willson now knew that Forsyth and Jenkins had missed a key part of the search. And Eastman could have moved the gun afterward. "Okay, Charlie, we'll talk about this tomorrow. But remember what I said. I need you to tell me who the hunter is. I *need* that name."

"I'm kinda upset and confused right now," he said in a voice that was strangely monotone. "I'll think about it."

"Thanks, Charlie, that's all I ask. I'll see you tomorrow. I should be at your place by mid-morning. We'll talk then."

When Willson disconnected, she made two calls. The first was to the head of the General Investigations Section at the RCMP detachment in Cranbrook. The sergeant there agreed to have one of his plainclothes officers talk to Clark about his missing wife.

The second call was to Tracy Brown of the U.S. Fish and Wildlife Service in Spokane. Brown didn't answer the phone, so Willson left a message. "Tracy, this is Jenny Willson from Banff," she said, trying hard to keep her voice from showing her excitement. "You'll remember our meeting about the American hunter who we believe has been poaching in our parks, and you'll remember our joint concern about not having any proof of him actually taking the poached animals into the U.S. I just talked to one of the guide-outfitter's employees and it seems the guide and maybe the American met trucks at Elko after his hunts. Elko is north of the Roosville border crossing into Montana. Can you possibly access the border databases to build a list of trucks that crossed the border southbound there — a day or two after each of the hunt dates I gave you? I know we don't have a name, and I know there could be hundreds of trucks, but at least it's a start. It's probably going to be commercial trucks, because private ones would be too small to hide the trophies. Maybe we can find a pattern. I'm going to head back to Cranbrook tomorrow to see if I can talk the guide's employee into giving me the name of the American hunter. I think I'm close. I'll give you a call when I get back to the office later in the week. Wish me luck."

Willson hung up and then sat back in her chair, sipped the last of the now-cold coffee, and thought of the American they were chasing. She had a half-formed picture of the man in her mind, a picture that she knew was probably an amalgam of bad guys from the many detective movies she'd watched over the years. In the absence of the real thing, the hazy image would have to do for now. "Whoever you are, we're circling in on you, you slimy bastard," she said with a smile.

CHAPTER 25

JULY 24

Crossing the Kootenay River north of Wasa on Highway 95, Jenny Willson drove directly toward the Rocky Mountains. They stretched as far as she could see to her left and to her right. The pyramid-shaped peak of Teepee Mountain was to the left, and Lakit Mountain, with its abandoned fire lookout glowing white, was to the right. Just visible beyond Lakit was the Matterhorn-like summit of Mount Fisher. She marvelled at how the mountain range soared dramatically and abruptly from grasslands and ponderosa-pine forests in the Rocky Mountain Trench to snowy peaks and rocky ridges over 2,700 metres high. She knew the vista before her was worthy of a postcard. But postcards always brought people, and — after working in Banff and experiencing its belching tour buses, crawling cars, and hordes of picture-taking, souvenir-buying tourists — she preferred places that were known to few. This place was heaven.

Tearing her eyes from the view, she pulled the nondescript Parks Canada car to the side of the highway, grabbed her cellphone from the seat beside her, and called Brad Jenkins.

"CO Service, Brad Jenkins."

Willson waited for the cardiac flutter in her chest, but — nothing. The thrill was gone. "Hey, Brad, it's Jenny."

"Jenny, long time, no hear. What're you up to? Any progress on the poaching case?"

"That's why I'm calling. I'm about twenty minutes out from Cranbrook as we speak, heading to talk to Charlie Clark."

"Why Clark?" asked Jenkins. "Have you got a new lead?"

"I don't, but I'm going to push Clark to give me one. I still don't have the name of Eastman's American client, and I'm hoping to persuade Clark to give it up."

"Interesting," said Jenkins. "Has something changed? Why do you think he'll talk now?"

"I spoke to him yesterday," she replied, "and it seems his wife's missing. It's hard to tell if he misses *her*, but he sure as hell misses having access to their bank account. I guess she controlled it. He told me he has Parkinson's and doesn't have enough money to get his meds and food and pay rent. So he's now a witness *and* potential informant who's more motivated than he was the last time I talked to him."

"Parkinson's. That sucks. But it explains why he often seems shaky and a bit goofy."

"Exactly," Willson said. "I'll come by to see you after I've talked to him ... but I've got a question for you. Have you guys taken any action yet to revoke Clark's assistant guide licence?"

"We're heading in that direction," said Jenkins. "But you know how the chain of command likes to be sure they're not breaking any rules or infringing on someone's Charter rights. So no, it hasn't happened yet."

"And what about Eastman's guide licence?"

"His is still in good standing because he hasn't been formally charged with anything ... yet. But it will likely follow the same route to cancellation. Why are you asking?"

"Clark told me yesterday that the American hunter is coming up again for what he describes as one last hunt. Eastman wants Clark to help him. And I want Clark to be part of it so he can keep us posted when the guy is actually here. I don't want him to lose his eligibility and be of no use to us."

"I can put the brakes on the cancellation process," said Jenkins, "at least until the hunt. But you said the American's coming into Canada again? He *must* know we're on to him, so that's pretty ballsy. When's it supposed to happen?"

"Clark told me the guy was coming up September third for a grizzly bear hunt in the Purcell Conservancy. He said it was out of season and that Eastman didn't have quota for a bear."

"He's right on both counts. So what's your plan?"

"I don't have a plan yet," she said, then told Jenkins about the Lacey Act and her need to follow the American back to the border with an illegally taken animal. "But I need the guy's name so we know who we're dealing with ...

so we can track him when he comes across the U.S.-Canada border. We'll have to covertly follow him from the border to the hunt and back to the border again, *with* the animal, if we want to bring the hammer down on both sides of the border."

"Jesus, Jenny, that's a long list of things that have to go right. That means there's a lot riding on your interview with Clark. Do you want me to come with you, either for moral support or to play good-cop, bad-cop?"

"Thanks, Brad, but no. I think it's best if I talk to him one-on-one. I'm not wearing my uniform today and I'm going to be as non-threatening and sympathetic as possible. I think he's close, and if I play my cards right, I can get him to name the guy. I might even have to pay for his prescription. Pharmaceuticals on a government expense claim. That'll raise some eyebrows at headquarters."

"If anyone can do it," said Jenkins with a chuckle, "you can. Good luck, Jenny. Give me a yell when you're done and I'll buy you a coffee."

"Sounds good. You hardly ever buy, so I'll be thirsty *and* hungry by then. Bring your wallet. Talk to you soon, Brad." Willson disconnected the call, again gazed at the mountains to her left, then pulled back on the highway toward Cranbrook.

Thirty minutes later, Willson turned into the short driveway beside the Clark trailer. The yard looked as bad as it had when she'd undertaken the search in April. If anything, it looked sadder in the light of day and in a different season. A small patch of lawn was more brown than green, and a truck and a car, both beaten and rusted and old, looked like they belonged in a wrecker's yard, a source of parts for vehicles that were, perhaps like their owners, in much better health.

Willson put the car in park, turned off the engine, and sat for a moment, breathing deeply to calm herself. With notebook and pen in hand, she climbed out of the car and walked up the pathway to the front porch, remembering when she'd banged on the same door in the darkness a few months ago, forever changing the lives of Charlie and Wendy Clark. This time, she'd returned not for physical evidence, but a name. A single name that would crack the case wide open. *No pressure,* she thought, *but this has to work.* Otherwise, she'd continue to chase her tail ... or be forced to accept the consolation prize, which was convictions against only Eastman and Clark.

Willson banged on the screen door, this time with less authority that she'd used in her last visit. *Remember,* she cautioned herself, *kinder, gentler.* Hearing nothing, she knocked on the door a second time, this time with more force. A yellowish grasshopper the size of her pinky finger leaped away from the screen, startling her. But still nothing from inside. No answer and no noise from within the trailer. She pulled the screen door open and knocked on the main door. When she did, the door moved a few inches away from its frame. It was unlocked and unlatched. With her senses on alert, Willson pushed the door open a few more inches.

"Charlie, are you here? It's Jenny. Jenny Willson." She again heard nothing, so she gently urged the door fully open, peering into the dark interior.

"Is anyone at home? Hello?" Her senses were tingling. Both vehicles were here. Why was no one answering? Where the hell were they? Her hand moved to her hip for her firearm — which was absent. Shit.

Willson entered the stale-smelling living room but saw and heard nothing. The adjacent kitchen was empty. Her eyes darting, she touched a kettle on the counter. It was warm. She again called out. "Hello. Anyone here?"

Growing more concerned with each silent second, Willson crept down the hallway, looking in the guest bedroom and in the bathroom. The floor creaked under her feet. Again no one. Pushing open the door to the master bedroom, she gasped when she saw Clark lying face down on the floor, a pool of blood under his head and neck. She moved quickly to check on him, kneeling down to feel for his carotid pulse. It was then she saw the massive hole in his skull, a crater-like opening from which all the blood in his wizened body had seeped onto the throw rug beneath him. In shock, she pulled back the fingers of her left hand, now smeared red with Clark's blood. She stared at them, not yet understanding the implications of what she'd just found. Without thinking, she reached for her cellphone.

She heard a noise behind her. Before she could turn, she felt a blow to the back of her head. Her vision clouded, darkened, and then she dropped to join Clark on the bloody floor.

A hand on her shoulder, gently shaking her. And then the voice. "Jenny, wake up. Jenny."

Willson looked into Brad Jenkins's eyes. Through a swirling haze, she saw eyes that were concerned and frightened, yet relieved. "Welcome back to the land of the living," he said quietly, smiling. "How do you feel?"

Willson put her hand to the back of her head. Pain. Movement made her dizzy. "Like shit. What the hell happened?"

"You tell me. When you didn't call me, I called your cell and got no response. Because I knew you wouldn't leave town without accepting my offer of coffee, I came up to see if you were here. And you were, unconscious and slumped over Clark's dead body. I slid you off him so I could check your injuries."

Willson worked hard to focus on her surroundings. She was still in Clark's master bedroom. But now she sat in a corner of the room, slumped against a closet door. She looked down and gulped, as much from the pain of movement as from the shock of seeing the front of her shirt covered in blood. Lots of blood.

Willson turned her head, slowly, and to one side of Jenkins, immediately to her left, she saw Clark's body, still dead and still bloody, her foot touching his leg. In an instant, her body and mind rebelled. She violently vomited to her right.

"Jesus," she said, feeling as bad as she'd ever felt. "Sorry, Brad." She wiped her mouth on her sleeve.

"It's okay, Jenny. I'm just glad you're okay. You probably have a concussion, so sit tight until the paramedics get here."

"What the hell happened?"

"I have no idea. I called 9-1-1 as soon as I found you. The ambulance and RCMP are on their way. Did you see who did this to you?"

"No. I … heard a noise behind me, then something or someone hit me. And then I saw you."

"Did you talk to Clark at all?"

Willson searched her scrambled brain for the answer. It was like trying to find a single piece of paper after a stack of file folders had been tossed in the air, their contents floating to the floor in a random jumble. "No … no. There was no answer when I knocked on the door. But the door was open. So I came in and found him on the floor. Dead. I saw no one else. And then nothing. And now you're here."

"Well, the RCMP member I spoke to on the phone told me they've had nine homicides in the past two days. This is the tenth. They think the nine are all drug-related, but who knows about this one? I'm sure the Serious Crimes guys are going to want to talk to you. They'll be here any second. You're damn lucky you weren't the eleventh body." His hand was still on her shoulder, comforting.

"Was … was there anybody here when you got here?"

"No. You were alone. Just you and Charlie, I mean."

Even through the haze and the pain, Willson could tell that something was not right. "What, Brad? What's wrong?"

"Uh … you had a pipe wrench in your hand when I found you. It dropped to the floor when I pulled you off his body. You and Charlie didn't have a fight, did you?"

"Jesus, Brad. I came here to talk to the guy … and I found him dead."

"It's okay, Jenny," Jenkins said, his hand still on her shoulder. "I had to ask. The Mounties are going to have many questions for you because your fingerprints are going to be on that wrench. I'm guessing it's the murder weapon."

Another wave of pain washed through Willson's head, this time supplemented by shock. She vomited again. Through tear-filled eyes, she looked up at Jenkins, slowly, comprehension infusing her still-hazy consciousness. "Shit, Brad, I didn't get to ask Clark who the American hunter is. I was *so* close. And now the one guy who might've told me is dead. And someone tried to make it look like *I* killed him. What a friggin' mess."

CHAPTER 26

SEPTEMBER 2

The old office chair creaked as Willson seated herself at the head of a boardroom table in the B.C. Environment office in Cranbrook, five weeks to the day since she'd been assaulted in Clark's trailer. Her recovery had been slow, and she'd gone batshit crazy with resting and sleeping, avoiding strenuous exercise, and being chauffeured by others. And the hours of interrogation by RCMP investigators hadn't helped her headaches. But with the blessing of her doctor and a confirmation that she wasn't a suspect in Clark's death, she was ready to go. In the not-too-distant back of her mind, Willson wondered whether she'd simply been at the wrong place at the wrong time, or if the attack on her had been just as personal as, but much less fatal than the murder of Clark. At this point, there was no answer.

To Willson's left was Kootenay Warden Peter MacDonald. Brad Jenkins smiled at her from his position at the table to her left, adding a thumbs-up. She smiled back, grateful he was here, grateful he'd been at her side, with regular visits from Kim Davidson, until she was released from the hospital in Cranbrook.

The conservation officers surrounding them stopped talking when their inspector walked in, taking his place at the opposite end of the table to Willson. Despite his youth, the officers clearly respected Tom Doyle for his common sense and his willingness to listen to men with more years of field experience than he had. "Let's get started," he said. "Lead away, Jenny. This is your show."

Willson had met with Doyle the day before to discuss the investigation. She'd laid out what she knew about the alleged plan for Eastman's American client to come north for another hunt. She knew that the chances of catching the American in the act were slim at best, particularly because they still didn't know who he was. And she couldn't shake the feeling they were being set up. But she'd chosen to play poker with the devil. The cards had been dealt and this was her last hand.

She'd anticipated that her request for a full-blown stakeout in such an uncertain situation — a plan that included local conservation officers and their Special Investigations Unit — would raise not only Doyle's blood pressure, but that of folks on the food chain above him. The B.C. government had invested an impressive amount of time and money in the investigation, and now she was asking for more. And at her urging, they'd held off their own charges against Eastman, charges that would likely see the man fined, jailed, and never allowed to hunt in B.C. again. But after three hours of describing her evidence on the poached elk, sheep, and goat, talking about legal implications and opportunities in both Canada and the U.S., and answering probing and thoughtful questions from Doyle, Willson saw the inspector agree by nodding once.

"We have no choice," he'd said without hesitation. "Let's do it. I'll ensure we have what we need to make this happen."

At that moment, Willson's assessment of the young inspector had risen. The fact that he wanted to be part of the surveillance not only meant that he believed in what Willson was doing, but also that he was willing to take responsibility for whatever happened.

"Okay, gentlemen," said Willson now, her gaze circling the table, "you know why we're here. I want us to design this surveillance until we've crossed every *t* and dotted every *i*. Based on statements made by Clark in what appears to be one of his last phone calls before his murder, we believe that, within the next twenty-four to forty-eight hours, an unnamed American hunter will come north to join Bernie Eastman in his territory in pursuit of a trophy grizzly. I'm sure all of you know Eastman."

Conservation officers in the room nodded their heads. Some rolled their eyes.

"Normally," said Willson, "we would send out a BOLF — that's 'Be On Lookout For' — on the American and his known vehicles to all Canadian enforcement agencies in the Kootenays, including the RCMP and Canada Border Services. But because we don't know who the guy is, that won't work. Instead, we'll key in on Eastman. By now, you've heard that we had hoped to have his assistant guide, Charlie Clark, as an inside informant. But his murder closed that door on us."

Over the next three hours, the group developed plans for placing surveillance teams at key locations on the way to and near Eastman's camp in Buhl Creek. Their sole focus was to observe the American shooting an animal out of season and then to follow him to the point where he crossed the border into the United States.

Willson divided the group into seven two-person surveillance teams and assigned key locations to each. Using maps and Google Earth images, she brainstormed a wide range of possible scenarios with the officers. They talked about what could go wrong and what they'd do as a result. They assumed that Eastman knew he was under suspicion, so they expected him to make it difficult for them. Key locations were given code names, with Eastman's camp designated as "Location Alpha." Even though they were using a scrambled tactical radio channel and cellphones, they chose not to take chances by sharing too much information over the air. Eastman was given the code name "Big Bear," while the client was designated as "Eagle." Then all the teams shared photographs of Eastman, along with several of Eastman's known employees and associates. Clark was no longer on that list.

"Brad," said Willson, "I want you to stake out Eastman's house — at a distance — because you were in on the original search. We can't afford to have him recognize you."

Willson pointed at the warden from Kootenay. "Peter and I are going to pose as ATVers, setting up our camp a few kilometres downstream from Eastman's camp.

Here" — she pointed to a spot on a large Google Earth image on the wall — "we'll watch for and record any vehicles that move up or down the Buhl Creek road near the camp." She grinned. "And I want to get a close look at this guy as he goes by. He doesn't know me yet ... but he soon will." The men in the room all laughed.

Willson opened her hand toward Tom Doyle. "Thanks to you, we have two teams from your Special Investigations Unit covertly watching the camp. Once Eastman and the client arrive, th teams willl follow them, wherever they're hunting," she said. "And the final teams, you guys —" she pointed at four COs to her right "— will sit in unmarked vehicles near the junction of Highways 95 and 95A, near Wasa. You'll confirm movement of the hunters heading north, but your main role will be to follow the client after the hunt, as he moves south toward the border, with you guys hopscotching down the highway to avoid being detected. I'll keep our U.S. colleagues in the loop as you get close to the border. All teams will be in radio or cellphone contact with each other, and Tom has agreed to coordinate from a location near the junction of Buhl and Skookumchuk Creek Roads. Any questions?"

Seeing none, Willson began to wrap up the meeting. "If we're able to get the client trying to cross the border with an animal," she said, "the plan is to arrest him at the U.S. border crossing. We'll then lay charges under our provincial and federal statutes, while our U.S. counterparts will initiate proceedings under the Lacey Act. I don't have to tell you that if we make this happen, it's going to be a very big deal — for all of us."

Willson looked at each individual in the room, one by one. "Before we adjourn, have we forgotten anything?"

"Yeah," said Jenkins. "What if your concern is correct that we're being played here? That our knowing the date of the guy's arrival in Canada seems too easy?"

"Thanks, Brad. Because I've raised it with some of you, I should get it out in the open. While we'll be lucky as hell if we catch the client crossing the border with the bear," she said, "this *does* seem too easy to me. Too straightforward. We've been told, over and over again, that this is a smart guy who thinks we're all idiots. So why would he broadcast what he's doing, using a loser like Clark, and then allow us to catch him in the act? I want to believe it … but it makes no sense. I don't trust anything we've been told. But this is our only hand left to play if we want to catch Eastman's client."

"What are you most worried about?" Inspector Doyle asked.

"Well," she replied, "every hunt the American has done with Eastman, at least the ones we know about, was in a national park. I know he might end up hunting in the Purcell Wilderness Conservancy this time, but why would he suddenly change his pattern? My bullshit detector is tingling here." Willson looked around the table for signs of support. "We could end up waiting for them to show up at the camp with our asses in the wind, while they go somewhere else, making us look like the bozos the American client apparently thinks we are."

"You have park wardens on alert in all the mountain parks, don't you, including Banff, Jasper, Kootenay, Yoho, and even Waterton?" asked one of the officers.

"I do," said Willson, "but those are huge parks and if we *are* being played, then Eastman and his client could be in and out of one of those places before we even know they're there. And from those parks, there are about six different border crossings the American could use going south."

"I hear your concerns, Jenny," said Doyle, jamming his fingers through his hair, "but I thought we sorted this out yesterday. We don't have unlimited resources. What do you suggest we do, beyond what we're already doing?"

Willson knew she had to be careful not to piss off the young inspector. He was already out on a limb on this. And she had to ensure that everyone in the room was confident about what they were doing, most of all herself.

"Look, the plan *is* the right one for what we know," she said. "I'm confident that the group around this table can pull it off. I'm proud to be working with each and every one of you. And I thank you for doing this."

The first hint of dawn silhouetted the peaks and ridges of the Rocky Mountains to the east as Brad Jenkins sat in an unmarked truck, watching Eastman's property through night-vision binoculars. Since 2:00 a.m., he'd been parked in a copse of ponderosa pines a kilometre away from the house. Just after he'd arrived, he'd slipped into the yard to place a GPS transmitter inside the bumper of Eastman's blue Dodge truck so they could follow it at a distance.

"Watcher One, this is Watcher Two," Jenkins said, after keying the microphone on his radio. "I've got two guys outside the house. They've loaded horses into the trailer and are now getting into the truck. One of them may be Big Bear, but I can't tell at this distance." He had no way of knowing if the second man was Eagle, the American hunter.

Jenkins heard the inspector's voice in reply. "Roger that, Watcher Two. All units, this is Watcher One. We may have Big Bear on the move. Watcher Three, advise if and when they pass your location. If you can get a visual on who's in the truck, let me know."

"Roger that," answered one of the teams sitting at the highway junction just to the north.

Jenkins watched Eastman's truck and trailer move slowly up the driveway and then turn right, heading north on Highway 95A.

"Watcher Three, this is Watcher Two. Vehicle is northbound toward your location. The GPS signal is strong and I'll continue to monitor." Jenkins smiled, knowing the two schmucks had no idea that Big Brother was watching their every move.

An hour later, the blue truck turned left at the junction of the Buhl and Skookumchuk roads. Inspector Doyle and a sergeant, watching the truck through binoculars from their position under a massive spruce tree, were the first to confirm that neither of the occupants was Eastman. Doyle immediately reported this to the other teams.

"All units, this is Watcher One. The suspect truck just passed our location heading toward Location Alpha and we have enough light to see. I can confirm that Big Bear is not in the vehicle," he said. "I repeat, Big Bear is not in the vehicle."

The officers listening to the radio transmission, most of all Jenny Willson, sensed the inspector's unease. While this was one of the scenarios they had discussed at their briefing, it was the possibility of greatest concern. They had assumed that Eastman would pick up the client, perhaps somewhere around Cranbrook, before driving him to his hunting camp. But the fact that someone else was driving Eastman's truck was a surprise. It meant they had no idea where the guide was. And no guide meant no client.

Eastman's hunting camp sat at the edge of a large meadow in the uppermost reaches of Buhl Creek, twenty kilometres upstream from Skookumchuk Creek. First built in the 1920s, it consisted of a main log cabin, three smaller sleeping cabins, an outhouse, and a corral. In the heart of the Purcell Mountains, the camp was located at 1,700 metres elevation and looked out at 2,500-metre-high peaks in all directions. Across the valley, light-green avalanche slopes sliced the dark of the Engelmann spruce and subalpine fir forests top to bottom, as if cut by a surgeon's scalpel. Immediately to the north, the boundary of the Purcell Wilderness Conservancy, a wilderness area of more than 200,000 hectares, beckoned to hikers and skiers. And it beckoned to hunters, as well, because it was one protected area in B.C. where hunting was allowed.

Willson and MacDonald, dressed in camouflage fleece, watched the blue truck pass the campsite they'd set up in an abandoned logging landing beside the road.

They waved at the men in a friendly way, like most did in that part of the country. The two men in the truck returned the wave, tooting their horn in greeting. When the truck rounded a corner beyond their campsite, Willson immediately keyed the radio to report that the truck would soon be at Eastman's camp.

By 2:00 p.m., the surveillance teams surrounding the camp reported in on what appeared to be a typical camp scene, quiet and well-organized. They confirmed that neither of the two men was Eastman, although, as they didn't work in the Kootenays, they couldn't say who they were. They watched and reported that the two men unloaded horses into the corral, then watered and fed them. A fire was burning in the cabin, white smoke drifting upward from the tall chimney built of river rocks and cement. Supplies — food, beer, and wine — had been unloaded from the truck, along with three rifles in leather scabbards. One man was splitting firewood, the other working on saddles. The man working with the axe was big, like Eastman. But he was not Eastman. Every one of the watchers, Willson most of all, wondered where their quarry was.

Moments after 3:00 p.m., the radios of the surveillance teams came to life with a call from Tom Doyle. "Watcher teams, this is Watcher One. Still no sign of Big Bear. Get comfortable — we might have a long wait."

CHAPTER 27

SEPTEMBER 3

Bernie Eastman watched Luis Castillo turn into the deserted parking lot of the Columbia Brewery in Creston, B.C. The windows of the black Lexus glinted in the late-afternoon sun when Castillo parked beside the bronze statue of the famed Sasquatch, mascot of Kokanee beer.

"How did things go at the border?" asked Eastman as he shook Castillo's hand.

"I expected more of a problem," said Castillo. "When the female agent scanned my passport, I thought I saw her raise her eyebrows. But then she asked me a couple of standard questions before letting me go. I guess no one up here knows my name yet."

"I sure as hell haven't told them, and I don't think Charlie did, either. What did the agent ask you?"

"The usual," said Castillo. "Where I was heading, did I have anything to declare, that kind of thing." He gave

Eastman a tight smile. "I assume you did a good job with Clark and they're now watching your camp?"

"Yeah, Charlie seemed pretty interested in your next hunt," said Eastman, "and I bet he told the COs what I told him. But now he's out of the picture. I don't know if they're watching or not, but I gotta think they are. I've got some of my guys up there getting the camp ready as though you're on your way."

"Excellent," said Castillo. "Whether he knew it or not, your Mr. Clark aided a worthy cause. Let's get on with it."

Eastman, driving a dark panel van he'd rented in Cranbrook two days earlier, led Castillo back to Highway 3. They headed west, passing the open hay-fields and cattle ranches in the broad valley bottom of the Kootenay River. Cottonwood trees framed the river in brilliant yellows, signalling an early start to another Kootenay autumn. The men passed the wetlands of the Creston Valley Wildlife Management area, now a tem-porary home to the first wave of southbound waterfowl. To the north was Kootenay Lake and dramatic views of the western side of the Purcell Mountains.

Thirty minutes later, the two vehicles arrived at the summit of the Salmo-Creston highway, a 1,774-metre-high pass through the craggy Selkirk Mountains and Stagleap Provincial Park. The ground cover under the Engelmann spruce and subalpine firs was a quilt of or-anges and reds, hinting at shorter and colder days ahead.

Eastman and Castillo pulled over beside Bridal Lake, a wind-free mirror of the ridge to the north. They both waited in the van with Castillo's car tucked in behind it so that the Washington State licence plates were hidden from passing traffic. As the last light of day faded to the west, the two men walked briskly across the highway and then climbed a rough access road to the south. Eastman knew where they were heading because he'd been there the day before, scouting, wanting to be as sure of success as possible. They both carried packs and Castillo had a rifle partly hidden under his coat, tucked against his leg.

About two kilometres up the road, they came to another small pass and began hiking toward the west, slowly and quietly, along a rocky, treed ridge. Large patches of arboreal lichens hung from the spruce and fir trees like ominous, black spiderwebs.

Within moments, Eastman saw the first signs of their quarry. With Castillo peering into the dark trees, the guide stooped to look at multiple sets of tracks in a patch of mud. "These are really fresh," he whispered, "and they're headed the same direction we are." He rose and then followed the tracks along the ridge.

The two men heard the animals before they saw them. It was the telltale clicking of tendons over bony protuberances in the animal's lower legs as they walked.

The men moved as silently as they could, stepping carefully over a piece of deadfall. They finally glimpsed a female on the other side of a copse of dark spruce. Beyond, a much larger male moved into a small clearing. His nose was blunt and square, his neck and mane a lighter brown than the rest of his body, his ears pointed and alert. Even though this was a week or two before the start of the rut, the male's focus had already shifted to females. Eastman saw him lower his head to sniff a fresh puddle of the female's urine, likely testing for the smell of estrus.

He slowly moved his arm to point at the target, but saw that Castillo was already raising his rifle. It was almost dark, but the rising sliver of moon was bright enough to allow the hunter to get a clear view of his target. Eastman watched as Castillo followed his normal practice of deep breathing. When it came, the shot was deafening.

In an opening of the ridgetop forest barely lit by the waning moon, a massive bull caribou dropped to the forest floor, its heart ripped open by a high-calibre bullet. It was a male in the prime of his years, one of the few remaining animals in an endangered herd of the mountain ecotype of the woodland caribou, a herd that moved back and forth across the border between British Columbia and Idaho. With one shot, Castillo had taken a healthy male from the shrinking population.

Castillo looked at Eastman and smiled, his white teeth the only feature visible in the dark. No words were spoken. The men pushed their way between two conical spruce trees and looked down at the fallen animal. The antlers were massive, pointing backward from the head and then expanding forward, like giant, palmated hands. While the antlers were impressive, it was the fact that this was a rare and valuable individual from an endangered species that made it so attractive to Castillo. As he would with the skin on a woman's inner thigh, he ran his fingertips slowly and lightly along the main oval-shaped beam onto one of the large brow tines, imagining the trophy on his wall in Spokane. He seemed lost in the moment, as his hand moved back and forth, back and forth, with a featherlight touch.

Eastman broke the silence. "We better get movin' in case someone heard the shot," he said. "Do you want a picture?"

Castillo handed his cellphone to Eastman, who took a single flash picture of the man kneeling beside the fallen bull.

Eastman then dropped his pack to the ground and slid a hunting knife and a butcher's saw out of side pockets. He pulled a headlamp onto his forehead, and with a click, its bright bulb illuminated the previously dark workspace. With deft strokes, Eastman first cut a jugular vein lengthwise, holding the bull's head above the ground while blood ran onto the mossy forest floor. Soon after, he separated the head from the rest of the body, wrapped it in a plastic tarp, and tied it to the outside of his pack. The body remained behind. It would be a multi-day meal for bears, wolves, and ravens.

With Eastman in the lead, his headlamp flashing alternately between the trees and the rough road, they descended the hill to a bend in the road only metres from the highway. The guide dropped the heavy pack, sliding it under a spruce. He turned off the headlamp and Castillo stepped into the shadows of the forest. Pulling the keys from his pocket, Eastman waited for a transport truck to pass by, hauling a load of wood chips to the pulp mill in Castlegar. He heard it engage its engine brakes, like the repeated, rapid hammering of a giant MRI machine, as it began its steep descent down the west side of the pass. And then he jogged across the highway to his van.

Eastman turned the key in the ignition, put the van in gear, and made a rapid U-turn across the two lanes of highway. The van was now parked facing northeast, sitting at the bottom of the dirt road. He turned off the lights, left the engine running, and made his way to where Castillo stood beside the hidden pack. In the darkness, the men shook hands.

"Well done," said Castillo. "I am pleased with the animal we got today. I will assume that all arrangements have been made. As we discussed, I expect to see this trophy in Spokane, soon. When that happens, you will be paid in full."

"I'll get it there," said Eastman. "You have my word."

"*Bueno*," said Castillo. "While we've had troubles along the way, you are a good guide, Señor Eastman. I have enjoyed the pursuit of many fine animals with you. You understand, I am sure, why I will not be coming to Canada to hunt with you again. Tonight was our last time together. And we will not speak again of what we have accomplished together, not to each other or to anyone else. As for our other business, I will wait to see if you can restart production now that I've removed your local competition."

"I understand," said Eastman. "Thanks, I guess." He looked at Castillo, his face partly illuminated by the distant lights of the highway compound to the east. At that moment, the man almost looked melancholy. But Eastman knew better; the man would sooner shoot him than hug him. And he felt the same. The American had been a reliable buyer of his products and services for the past two years. But now that this part of their relationship was ending, he wasn't going to miss the arrogance or the drop-whatever-you're-doing-whenever-I-call attitude. His mind wandered back to the meeting in the Bonners Ferry casino. It had been awkward and embarrassing and he was still furious at Castillo for the way he'd been treated. He didn't need this guy in his life. If things had been different, he would've laid a beating on him to teach him a lesson about arrogance. But it was time to move on. *Good fuckin' riddance.* Eastman knew he now had bigger things to worry about.

When the pass was clear of traffic, Castillo slid open the door of the van and stood aside as Eastman quickly loaded the tarp-covered pack and the rifle into the space behind the front seats. When the door slid closed, Castillo strode across the highway to his car without another word.

Eastman climbed into the driver's seat of the van, and before turning on the headlights, he looked across the highway to see Castillo's car leave the parking area, westbound. He knew that in about forty minutes, the man would re-enter the United States at the tiny Metaline Falls border station, moments before its midnight closure. From there, he'd drive south through the quiet Pend Oreille River valley, arriving home three hours later.

If all works out well at the border, thought Eastman, *that son of a bitch will have once again outwitted the jerks up here*. He had to give Castillo credit for that. While the cops and COs were probably sitting up in Buhl Creek waiting for them, Castillo had, right under their noses, snagged another trophy, this time from a provincial park. He knew it would seriously piss them off. Smiling, he imagined them up Buhl Creek, clueless. Castillo was no idiot.

After letting an eastbound truck pass his temporary parking spot, Eastman clicked on the van's headlights and headed downhill toward Creston, his mind on the big payday coming his way.

An hour later, he turned off Highway 3 into a narrow gravel driveway in Yahk, a small community on the Moyie River, a few minutes north of the Kingsgate border crossing. He beeped the horn, two short honks, as he pulled up to a dilapidated barn. He shut his headlights off, leaving on only the orange parking lights. As he did so, the door of the adjacent house opened, revealing the silhouette of a lone figure in the doorway. The door closed and a man with long, scraggly hair pulled on a coat as he crossed the yard to the barn.

Using both hands, the man pulled open a large door on the front of the old building, exposing the darkened interior. Eastman steered the van into the barn, stopping in the middle of the empty black space and shutting off the engine. The man pulled the door shut behind him and then flipped a wall switch, illuminating the van in the greenish glow of fluorescent bulbs. As it cooled, the van's engine ticked into silence.

Eastman breathed a deep sigh of relief, hands still on the steering wheel. He'd driven down from Kootenay Pass carefully, doing his best not to attract the attention of the local RCMP highway patrol. He knew that a large, strangely shaped item like the caribou head, wrapped in a tarp in the back of a solitary panel van on a lonely highway late at night, made a tempting target for a curious, well-trained Mountie with a flashlight. But he'd seen no police cars.

Sliding his bulk out of the van, Eastman shook his nephew's hand. With his long, thinning, reddish hair and his weathered skin a sickly greenish shade from the overhead lights, his nephew looked much older than his thirty years.

"How are you, Stevie-boy?" asked Eastman, continuing to vigorously pump the young man's hand.

"Good, Uncle Bernie. Have some luck tonight?" Barber asked.

"Yup, we did," Eastman responded. "Let's get it unloaded."

Eastman pulled back the door of the van and slid his pack onto the floor of the barn. Untying the ropes around the tarp, he revealed the head and antlers of the bull caribou. The edge of the neck, where it had been attached to the bull's powerful shoulders, was ragged and red, but the fur of the neck and mane were still a subtle, yet beautiful tan colour. The eyes were closed in death. The tongue hung out one side of the mouth.

The young man whistled in appreciation. "He's a beauty," he said, then reached down to stroke the antlers, repeating Castillo's motions of a few hours earlier.

"Fuckin' right," said Eastman. "My client is pleased. Now we have to get it down to him."

"Why aren't you using the trucks like the other times?"

"Because we can't hunt mountain caribou at all, and we can't risk the trucks being searched. And because there's so much money at stake and things are so hot for me that I can't risk usin' the same routes as before."

"Roger that," said Barber. "When do you need it done?"

"As soon as possible," Eastman said. He handed his nephew a piece of paper. "When you know your timin', phone this number and tell whoever answers when the package will arrive at the spot you and I talked about. Someone will meet you there."

"My plan is to do it tomorrow night, when there's a new moon," Barber said. "That way, there will be the fewest shadows. And with a clear sky forecast that night, there's less chance of lights reflecting against cloud cover. It will be as dark as it's ever going to get. I'll call you when I'm leaving here."

Eastman smiled. The young man had worked for him as a guide trainee for three autumns after high school, and he was pleased to see that he'd learned additional skills, useful skills, during his time in the infantry. "Good," said Eastman. "Let's put this away and then I better get movin'."

The two men carried the head across the barn, each holding one side of the antlers. They placed it behind a stack of cut and split firewood, loosely placing the tarp over it. In the darkness of a far corner of the barn, it would not be seen.

"You sure you don't want to stay for a beer ... or even a coffee?" asked Barber.

"Thanks, but I gotta get on the road," said Eastman. "It's been a long coupla days and I'm sure there'll be cops or COs waiting for me, if not tonight, then tomorrow morning."

The two men exchanged a quick hug. As Eastman climbed into the driver's seat with an audible groan, he spoke to Barber through the open door. "Good luck,

Stevie," he said. "Thanks for doing this for me." He paused before starting the engine. "This is a big deal. I know I can count on you."

"No problem, Uncle Bernie," the young man said with a wide, shit-eating grin. "Piece a' cake, piece a' cake."

Eastman backed the van out of the barn and drove into the darkness. His tail lights blinked once as he braked and turned left onto the highway.

Barber watched his uncle leave, the sound of the vehicle fading as it moved eastward. He was scared and excited for what was to come. With a jolt of recognition, he realized that the last time he'd felt this way was before his final tour outside the wall of the military compound near Kabul, in eastern Afghanistan. That was six months ago. It had not ended well. Now, as then, he accepted that even the most extensive training and planning didn't guarantee the success of a mission.

CHAPTER 28

Jenny Willson sat on a camp stool in front of a small fire, her hands wrapped around a mug of hot coffee. Steam rose in her face, swirling and mixing with woodsmoke in the frigid morning air. Even in her thick, down jacket, toque, and gloves, Willson felt cold and stiff. Having taken the 2:00 a.m. to 6:00 a.m. watch, she now waited impatiently for Peter MacDonald to climb out of the tent and join her. She envied him being there, snoring deep in a warm sleeping bag rather than sitting out here the way she was, freezing her butt off. She realized that she should've thought this through more carefully. It was warmer last night.

Clutching the mug below her chin, she inhaled the aroma and thought how this pursuit of a poacher resembled her love life — both were unsuccessful so far. She recalled her most recent date. After exchanging a series of promising emails through the meet-him.com website, and after learning he was a successful architect from Calgary, Willson had agreed to lunch at Earl's restaurant in Banff. She had enjoyed their light conversation, right up to the moment the man mentioned his wife. It quickly became obvious to Willson that this guy was looking for something on the side. And she was it.

"What's her name?" she'd asked him.

"Uh … Lori," he replied, noticeably squirming.

"Lori — nice name," she said. "Do you think Lori would be interested in a threesome?"

"Are … are you s-serious?" he'd stuttered, his eyes wide, his cheeks flushed.

"No, you dumb shit."

That was when, with a flick of her wrist, Willson sent a glass of ice water into his lap, signalling the end of another failed date.

As always, Willson wondered what she had done to deserve these losers. Did she give off weird vibrations? Was there something tattooed on her forehead that was visible only to the wrong guys? She understood that the very qualities that made her a good investigator, such as her doggedness, her attention to detail, and her ability to read people, gave her the appearance of a woman with a hard shell that was tough to crack. But she often speculated that it was more than that, that it had something to do with growing up without a father. Was she lacking the ability to trust, so that she unconsciously pushed men away or chose only the ones she couldn't have? Or was she always comparing them to the high standards set by her father?

When her mug was as empty as the list of answers she always seemed to be chasing for, Willson decided enough was enough. She stood, stretched, and made a noisy breakfast using a pot of hot water perched beside the fire. It took only a few banging pots and clanking spoons before she heard MacDonald stirring and groaning in the tent. As she blew a cooling breath on the first spoonful of thick oatmeal, sweet with maple syrup and plump raisins, she smirked at the sound of the lanky warden thrashing his way out of the tiny nylon shelter.

"Good morning, sunshine," she said. "It's about friggin' time you got up."

"Thanks for being so goddamn quiet," MacDonald said. He looked like his hair and a tornado had waged war during the night and the tornado had won.

Willson watched as he stood upright, slowly, working the kinks of out of his back with more groans. "You're looking good this morning, my dear," she said with a grin. "Sleep well?"

"Jesus," said MacDonald, "are you always this obnoxious first thing in the morning? Where's the coffee?"

Willson laughed and poured another cup of the strong brew, handing it to him as he sat on the other camp stool. She then refilled her own cup. She'd made the coffee, cowboy-style, from a bag of ground Kick Ass beans, dumping four tablespoons of coffee into boiling water, stirring, letting the grounds settle, pouring carefully to keep the grounds on the bottom. The two wardens sat in silence, staring into the flames and savouring the rich flavour. *Thank God for this find,* thought Willson. She reached down to place more wood on the fire. It crackled and popped and threw sparks into the air.

The quiet of the mountain morning broke when Willson's radio squawked to life. It was tucked into the pocket of her jacket and she jumped at the unexpected noise.

"Watchers Four, Five, and Six, this is Watcher One, do you copy?" It was Inspector Doyle at the junction of the Buhl and Skookumchuk Creek roads, calling his surveillance teams on the scrambled radio channel.

Willson clicked the microphone clipped to the collar of her jacket. "Go ahead, One, this is Four." She heard the other two teams responding.

"Five here," said one.

"Go for Six," said the other.

"I have an update for you," said Doyle. "Be advised that Big Bear was just seen returning to his residence, alone. We have no idea where he was for the last eighteen hours. But we'll continue watching to see what he does next, where he goes."

Willson could tell he was seriously pissed off — but no more so than she was.

"Roger that," she said, and then made a quick decision. "I need teams Five and Six to move into Location Alpha and immediately arrest both parties there. I'm assuming their presence was a diversion. We'll be right there and will then bring them to Cranbrook for interviews. I want to know what they know."

In sequence, the surveillance teams responded in the affirmative.

Willson stared at MacDonald. "Son of a bitch!" she yelled. "I knew something wasn't right."

As she and MacDonald broke camp, Willson immediately thought of Jenkins. Like her, he'd put so much time and energy into this investigation that the idea they had been purposefully misled would be, she knew, devastating for him. But that was what it looked like. She was just as devastated. And pissed off. And then her mind shifted to Eastman and his client. Had the guy come into Canada like he was supposed to? They'd had no calls from any border crossings telling them that someone had come north claiming to be hunting with Eastman, but that meant nothing. If the client had come north and if he and Eastman hadn't come to the Buhl Creek camp for a grizzly, then where the hell did they go? And what did they shoot, if anything? She saw her strategy unravelling, all the doubts she'd carried over the past few days coming alive. She now knew how unlikely it was that they'd catch the American heading back to the U.S. with a poached bear.

Sick with anger and doubt, Willson threw her duffle bag into the truck and poured the remaining coffee on the fire. It died with a hiss. "Just like our goddamn case," she said. "Fuck." She tossed the keys at MacDonald. "You drive, Peter. I'm so pissed off, I'll end up driving us into a tree."

By the time the two wardens reached Eastman's camp, after bouncing up the last three kilometres of logging road, the two surveillance teams had moved in from the trees to arrest the cook and the assistant guide. The two men sat shoeless on the front porch of the main cabin, in handcuffs and in shock. With one look, Willson was certain they had no idea what was going on and had, like the circle of six officers now standing around them, expected Eastman and a client to arrive at the camp the night before.

"What the hell's going on?" asked the camp cook when Willson pulled him to his feet.

"We'll give you a chance to tell us all you know when we get back to Cranbrook," she said, steering the man toward their idling crew cab.

With the two men seated in the truck, their hands cuffed behind them, Willson and MacDonald entered the main cabin, searching for evidence. Her gaze jumped to a trio of rifles leaning in one corner of the seating area. She brushed past MacDonald and picked them up one at a time. "Come on, .308. Come on, 308," she said as though rolling dice in a casino. But after studying the last weapon, she turned back to MacDonald, crestfallen. No .308. "Why can't we get a friggin' break?" she asked.

Leaning against the dining table, MacDonald flipped the pages of a notebook. "I don't know, Jenny," he said. "The calendar here shows that Eastman and a client were supposed to arrive yesterday for a seven-day hunt starting today. These guys seemed to believe it. Either Eastman changed his mind at the last minute ... or he's trying to mess with our heads."

Frustrated, Willson walked outside and stood alone on the front porch of the cabin. She looked at Eastman's GPS-tagged truck parked near the corral, its windows opaque with frost. "You're one tricky son of a bitch and you've outmanoeuvred us again," Willson said, shaking her head, her accusation directed more at Eastman's mysterious client than Eastman himself. "Where the hell are you?"

Three hours later, the entire enforcement team of conservation officers and wardens again sat in the boardroom at the B.C. Environment office in Cranbrook. Down the hall, the camp cook was in one interview room, the assistant guide in another.

Willson spoke first. "Gentlemen, before we interview our two guys, let's take a moment. While I appreciate your efforts, you now know that my suspicions were, unfortunately, right. It appears that Eastman set this whole thing up. He wanted us to believe that he and his client were heading into camp. But now we know different. What we don't know is where the hell he *did* go while we were freezing our asses near his camp." She slammed her open hand on the table, startling everyone. "And I still don't know who his American client is! We don't even know if they were together. After all this, we've got squat."

Willson looked around the table. She knew everyone felt as dismayed as she did. "I'm open to ideas."

MacDonald's grim smile was an attempt to offer hope. "We *could* push Eastman's two guys hard," he said, "but I don't believe they knew what was going on. They appeared to be in shock when we showed up. And all the way here, they kept asking why they'd been arrested. I think they were pawns in Eastman's chess game."

"I agree," said one of the COs from the Special Investigations Unit who'd been watching the Buhl Creek camp while lying on the forest floor a hundred metres away. "From what we could see, they appeared to be getting the camp ready for hunters. And I thought they'd shit themselves when they opened the cabin door to *us* this morning."

"Jesus," said Willson with a sigh, "what a friggin' mess. I really should've listened to my gut on this."

"She's right," said an older CO who was on the verge of retirement and overtly resentful of Inspector Doyle. "Why *did* we put all our eggs in this one basket? We could've —"

The inspector stared the man into silence. "Could've what, Dennis? If you had all the answers, why the hell didn't you speak up earlier?"

"Hey," Dennis said snidely, "you acted like you and the lady warden had all the answers. Now it looks like you maybe didn't."

"Shut the hell up," said Doyle. "I'll see you in my office as soon as we're done here." He turned his attention back to the group. "We can sit around here all afternoon and navel-gaze and lay blame, or we can deal with the steaming pile of shit we've been handed. Jenny and I will do the interviews in a few minutes, so why doesn't everyone take a break and grab some coffee. We got lots of work ahead of us." He rose quickly, glared again at the older CO, threw open the door to the boardroom, and stalked off down the hallway.

The room emptied, with Willson, Jenkins, and MacDonald staying behind.

"Sorry you had to witness the internal pissing match, Jenny," said Jenkins, looking across the table at the two wardens while he leaned as far back as his chair would allow. They all appeared equally exhausted and deflated. "I really thought we were going to nail Eastman and his guy this time. Based on what we know, it's possible they were somewhere else, doing God knows what, while we were waiting in Buhl Creek. But we don't know. And if the American did come across the border into Canada, then the prick is probably home and out of our hands again. You were right to think it was a set-up. The fucker outwitted us. Whoever he is, he must be laughing his ass off at us right now."

"I don't know what to say, Brad," said Willson. "Based on what Clark told us before he was killed, there was a good chance the hunt was going down from the camp. But there was that little voice in my head telling me things weren't as they appeared. It seemed too easy. If what we now suspect is right, Eastman and his client must've used Clark to set this up ... and then took him out of the picture so he wouldn't talk. There's no way in hell we could have known or suspected *that*."

"I don't know, Jenny," said Jenkins. "Going from poaching to homicide is a hell of a big leap. What the hell were they doing to make this worthwhile?" he asked, not expecting an answer.

"Whatever it was," said Willson, "this just became a lot more personal."

"What's next, Jenny?" asked MacDonald.

"What's next? We're going to arrest Eastman, and I'm going to get another search warrant for his place. I'm done playing games with that fucker. It's time for us to meet again, face to face, with him in handcuffs and me asking the questions."

Later that same day, Steve Barber backed his pickup into his barn in Yahk. The bed of the truck was capped with a fibreglass canopy, its windows blackened. He flipped up the door of the canopy, making the hinges squeak, and lowered the tailgate with a thump.

For the fifth time that day, he mentally reviewed, step-by-step, what he needed to accomplish that night. It was his military experience that made him plan and train, and plan and train again. After phoning his contact across the border the day before, he'd left a message on his uncle Bernie's cellphone, confirming that tonight was the night.

Barber loaded the truck in reverse sequence so the items he needed first would be closest to the tailgate. First in went the bull caribou head, covered with a dark canvas tarp and wrapped securely with black electrical tape. Next, he slid in a small black two-man raft, not quite fully inflated. He'd bought it at a U.S. surplus store after he left the army, thinking it would be ideal for fishing in remote lakes. But he'd never imagined that it would be used for something like this, something that would make him money. Finally, he added a nylon duffle bag filled with gear.

When the sky was hours beyond sunset, filled with bands of stars from horizon to mountain-topped horizon, Barber drove out of his garage and turned right onto the highway. Ten minutes later, he shut off his headlights as he turned right onto the Shorty Creek Forest Service Road.

Driving slowly on the gravel so as not to awaken the residents of a house a few hundred metres to the west, he crossed the Moyie River on a log bridge. He turned left into a private driveway and immediately pulled into a small clearing between the driveway and the river. He shut off the truck, punched the button on his watch, and read the time on the illuminated dial. Thirty minutes past midnight. From thoroughly scouting the location previously, Barber knew that in a few moments, a southbound train would pass this spot, slowing as it approached the U.S. border, obliterating all other sound for three loud minutes.

Barber emerged from his truck, shutting the driver's door carefully and quietly. Doing the same with the canopy door and tailgate, he unzipped the duffle bag and began to pull on a black neoprene wetsuit. He stuck his B.C. driver's licence in a waterproof sleeve down the zippered front. He thought about his old dog tags hanging from his bathroom mirror. This was his first mission without them. He pulled the neoprene hood over his head, forced his feet into black booties with rubber soles, and as a last step, worked his hands into thick, black, neoprene gloves. He strapped a diver's watch on his left arm and drew a mask, snorkel, and fins from the bottom of the duffle bag. Two warm beers sat on the seat in the truck, and although he knew that if he pounded them both back now they would add credibility to the story he'd no doubt have to tell later on, Barber left them. Drinking before a mission, a mission that involved swimming in an icy river, was a dumb idea.

Barber heard the rumble of the approaching train and felt an injection of adrenalin into his bloodstream.

Moving to the opposite side of the truck from the tracks, he waited until the twin engines passed where he stood, a bright cyclops-like headlight illuminating the steel tracks ahead in twin bands of white.

In a first quick trip, he dragged the raft, his fins, snorkel, and mask to the edge of the Moyie River. In a second trip, he wrestled the wrapped caribou head to the waiting raft, lashing it securely against the middle inflated thwart using black garden twine. It was a difficult task wearing neoprene gloves, but he'd practised it many times in preparation for that moment. As the last train car rattled by, a small electronic conductor box blinking on the back, Barber slipped into the river, sliding the loaded raft in behind him. Time to rock and roll.

The shock of the cold water hitting his exposed cheeks, chin, and forehead made him gasp. *Suck it up,* he thought. Night patrols outside their Kandahar base had been worse than this. The current caught him and pulled him through a wide left-hand curve south and east toward the Kingsgate border crossing. As best he could, Barber stayed tight against the west bank where the current was deepest. Twice, he was forced to paddle aggressively to avoid log-jams.

When he saw the bright lights of the new Canadian border station with the U.S. crossing behind it, Barber submerged on the side of the raft away from the buildings, began breathing through the upright snorkel, and let the current carry him onward. He remained still, hanging on to a rope on the bottom of the raft, hoping the raft's low profile would not trigger the infrared beams he assumed were pointing across the river.

He made it beyond the border and floated motionlessly down the Moyie River into northern Idaho. Scanning the banks, his mask just above the waterline, he saw no signs of movement and heard no wailing sirens or racing vehicles amidst the sounds of moving water gurgling in his neoprene-covered ears. He tried to smile, but his frozen face wouldn't obey the commands from his brain. He knew that his destination, a bridge on Moyie River Road, was still another five kilometres downstream, yet he was confident of success. However, like the ex-soldier he was, he also knew that it wasn't over until it was over.

CHAPTER 29

The Moyie River carved a series of sinuous curves as it flowed south through Idaho. At the last major bend before the bridge on Moyie River Road, Barber crawled out of the water on the west side, his arms and legs wobbly from cold and exhaustion. He pulled himself and the raft up the rocky shoreline and into the trees. As he was asked to do, he untied the caribou head from the raft and tucked the trophy against the north side of a large veteran cottonwood, its leaves on the ground crisp and dry. Because the head was wrapped in black, Barber knew it would be difficult to detect, even in daylight. It was a black shadow, one of many amongst the tall cottonwoods. The raft was no longer of value to him, so he punctured the main tubes with his knife, pushed as much air out of it as he could, and heaved the pieces into the main current of the river. He wrapped himself in an emergency blanket and sat down to wait.

Thirty minutes later, Barber heard the sound of a truck rolling down Moyie River Road from the west. When the vehicle squealed to a stop and the engine fell silent, he raised two fingers to his mouth and produced a high-pitched whistle. Once, twice. He watched a flashlight beam bouncing toward him through the shoreline trees and heard two men approaching, their footsteps crunching in the carpet of fallen leaves. Concerned that it might be the Border Patrol or a local sheriff, Barber stood motionless behind a second cottonwood.

One of the two men whispered the only words spoken between them that night. "Hey, it's us. Have you got the package?" he asked, his voice thick with nerves.

Barber stepped out from behind the tree, startling the men. Without responding, he simply pointed to the wrapped head leaning against the tree. The men picked it up and moved away quickly.

When the truck was gone and all was again quiet, Barber took a deep breath, girding himself for the next stage. He was tired and cold. His energy reserves were nearly gone, but he had to finish the mission if he was to collect payment from his uncle.

After cutting the blanket into pieces, Barber tossed them and the knife into the water. He then slipped back into the river and let the current again carry him downstream. When he reached the bridge, he escaped the river's pull and scrambled up a gravel slope on the east bank, reaching the road moments later. The snorkel, mask, and fins joined the raft, knife, and shredded blanket in the water.

Leaving behind the sound of the river, Barber staggered toward the lights of a distant house. Out of the cold water and moving on dry land, his extremities came to life again. He swung his arms in circles as he walked, moving warm blood into his frozen hands. His legs began to work as they should, but it was painful to walk on the frozen ground, his feet covered only in the thin layer of neoprene. As he approached the house, he saw the first signs of sunrise in the eastern sky.

Here we go, he thought. These folks are going to come out to see why their dog is barking, and they'll see a man dressed in black opening the gate to their yard. This is the most dangerous part of the mission. Because this was northern Idaho, Barber wasn't surprised when he saw the homeowner open the door, shotgun in hand.

"Who the hell are you and why're you on my property?" the man asked, while sighting down the barrel toward Barber.

Barber was ready for this, his hands already in the air. He stopped walking.

"I ... I ... need help and I don't know where I am," he said to the man, trying his best to sound tired and confused. After what he'd just done, the tired part was easy.

"What the hell are you doing here?" said the man, the shotgun still pointed at Barber's chest.

"Am I ... still in Canada?"

"No, you're not in Canada. You're in Idaho, in the United States of America," said the man. "Here, we shoot trespassers first and ask questions later."

"Oh shit," said Barber. "Then I need your help, please. My buddies and I were having a few cold pops up in

B.C. and they dared me to cross the border in the river." He took some deep breaths. "I'm *so* screwed. I guess I bumped my head on a rock and ended up on the shore over there. I have no idea where I am."

When it came to having a gun pointed at him, Barber's fear was real. In fact, he had to work very hard to control a growing sense of panic and an intense desire to run, both of which were symptoms of his time in Afghanistan.

The armed man slid a cellphone from his pocket and punched in a number with the thumb of one hand, his shotgun still pointing at Barber. "Stay there and keep your hands in the air," he said. "I'll let the border patrol decide if your story makes sense or not."

A few moments later, two U.S. border patrol vehicles raced down Moyie River Road toward the house, their emergency lights flashing. When they reached the edge of the property, their headlights illuminated Barber's back, his hands in the air, and the property owner standing on his front porch with his shotgun. A commanding voice came over a loudspeaker: "Man on the porch, put the gun down!"

When the weapon was no longer a threat, three border patrol officers jumped out of the vehicles. Two of them immediately handcuffed Barber, thoroughly searching him for weapons. In the process, they found his driver's licence. They immediately put him in the back seat of one of the vehicles. The other officer moved toward the front porch, asking the man there if he'd made the phone call.

"Yes, I did," said the man. "The guy tried to feed me a bullshit story about floating down here from Canada."

Barber had expected that the American officials would be suspicious of his story, and later, in a concrete holding cell at the border station, he was proven right. The officials aggressively interrogated him. They challenged his story, accusing him of drug smuggling. They threatened him with a lengthy jail sentence and forced him to undergo a full body-cavity search.

"Come on, Mr. Barber," said one agent. "We see B.C.-grown marijuana moving south across our border in a never-ending list of increasingly creative ways. Drugs moved in secret tunnels, hidden in commercial transport trucks, inside the wheel wells of cars, in diaper bags, musical instruments, and loads of lumber. You're the first one trying to do it in the river. We've got teams of agents, with dogs, scouring both banks of the river upstream of the bridge. They're going to find what you dropped there. So why don't you just come clean and tell us where you hid the stuff?"

"Honestly," said Barber, "I'm telling you the truth. I wasn't smuggling drugs."

"Why'd you have your driver's licence with you," asked a second officer, "when you say this was a spur-of-the-moment, drunken stunt?"

"I always carry it with me when I go out with the boys," said Barber.

"And why was there no alcohol in your blood when we tested you?"

"I have no idea. I had a couple of beers but maybe they wore off in the cold water?"

"While you were down here, did you have contact with any U.S. citizens other than the homeowner who nearly shot you?" asked the first officer.

"No," replied Barber, "and I'm sorry about that. I guess I'm pretty lucky that guy didn't shoot me."

"You got that right," said one officer.

"Look," said Barber, "phone my buddies in Yahk and they'll confirm my story." He recited two phone numbers.

Both friends backed up his story of the drunken dare. They'd been sleeping off a bender, they told the officers, and were going to phone the RCMP later that day if Barber didn't show up. They both expressed gratitude that he'd been found.

Through it all, Barber repeated the same story. "Guys," he said, "I am very, very sorry about this. I just want to go home and forget that this whole stupid thing ever happened."

Late the next day, after a meeting with an immigration judge in Sandpoint, two U.S. border patrol agents walked Barber across the forty-ninth line of latitude past a white concrete marker. Beneath a large maple-leaf flag moving slowly in a slight breeze, they handed Barber to a Canadian Border Services officer. In Barber's hand was an expedited exclusion order, issued by the U.S. judge. It required him to leave the country immediately and barred him from re-entry for five years.

After a long, cold swim in the river, the adrenalin rush of facing a loaded shotgun, hours of interrogation in a windowless interview room, and drives back and forth to Sandpoint chained to the floor of a van, Barber was drained as he walked north from the border. The only thing keeping him going was elation. He'd done what he told his uncle he would do. Unless something had gone seriously wrong, he knew that the package he'd given to the men in the truck was safely at its destination. Barber smiled. He admired his uncle and looked forward to a congratulatory hug from the man. Payment was almost an afterthought. Almost.

Barber stuck out the thumb of his left hand as he trudged north on Highway 95, still dressed in the black neoprene wetsuit. Two vehicles passed him without slowing down. The third, a car containing three young men, pulled over to the shoulder ahead of him. He walked as fast as he could to catch up. He quickly realized that of the three, only the driver was sober. He sat in the back seat, fending off drunken questions about why he was walking on a highway in a wetsuit. The men were surprised when Barber asked them to let him out only three kilometres up the road.

The car drove off, sending a shower of stones back at him. He walked down the gravel road to his truck and found his keys tucked safely under sandbags in the back. Once inside, he turned on the ignition and cranked the heater on full-blast. He again looked at the two beers. Still not a good idea. Knowing he would fall asleep if he stayed in the warming cab, he called his uncle's number.

"Uncle Bernie, this is Steve," he said, his voice slow with exhaustion as he left a message. "It's done. I'm heading home now."

Disconnecting, Barber drove northward, first on the gravel road and then on the highway. He barely made it to his house in Yahk before exhaustion overtook him. He peeled the rank rubber suit from his body, took a hot shower, and crawled into bed. He slept for fourteen hours, visions of cold, flowing water filling his dreams.

CHAPTER 30

The day after Barber made his delivery, Jenny Willson smiled grimly as she, Brad Jenkins, and two burly colleagues walked Bernie Eastman, his hands cuffed in front of him, across the parking lot from her truck to the B.C. Environment office in Cranbrook. Every window on the west and north sides of the one-storey building was lined with faces of staff, all anxious to see the much reviled guide-outfitter in custody. It was, thought Willson, the East Kootenay version of the "perp walk" the FBI used when arresting high-profile financial offenders. With a lone *Daily Townsman* photographer shooting pictures, Eastman's walk of shame wouldn't be on the front page of the *New York Times*. But for Willson, it was equally satisfying.

Inside, she escorted Eastman down a hallway. More faces peered from doorways. "Have a seat, Bernie," she said when they reached a sparse interview room. "You and I are going to talk." She gestured at the burly colleague accompanying her. "This officer will babysit you until I'm ready to begin."

Eastman sneered at Willson as he eased his big body into a small chair in the corner. "Hey, Warden, how's your head?"

"Why do you ask?" she said, stopping in the doorway.

"You seem sure of yourself when you're surrounded by men in uniform, but I hear you got beat up when you didn't have 'em around to protect you."

"Where'd you hear that?"

"Oh, you know. Around. Lots of folks are talkin' about it."

Willson knew that Eastman, arrogant bully that he was, would try to push her buttons, get her to lose her cool. But she understood that to get what she needed from the outfitter, she'd have to control her emotions, ignore his baiting, as tough as that might be. "Thanks for your concern, Bernie, I appreciate it."

Eastman's sneer evolved into a smirk, a subtle shift that made Willson want to drive the heel of her hand into his nose. Instead, she clenched her fists behind her back.

"I heard you got beat up by someone who didn't like your attitude," he said, "someone who didn't like you poking your nose into things that maybe aren't any of your business."

Willson stared at Eastman for a moment, wondering how much he knew, how much he'd been involved in the violence at Clark's trailer.

"It was nothing," she said, "just a knock on the head. No big deal. If the coward who did it was trying to hurt me, he didn't succeed. I don't know … maybe he's proud that he murdered an old man with Parkinson's, an old man who could barely defend himself. And then jumped me from behind. That's pretty brave, eh? If anything, my experience there made me *more* curious to find answers to questions that are *very much* my business. And that's why you're here today, Bernie. You're going to help me with those answers before you spend time behind bars. And maybe, just maybe, we'll have more things to talk about once my colleagues finish their search at your place." She looked at him, without expression, and left the room.

By the time Willson reached Jenkins's office, she was wringing her hands with anticipation. "Brad, I am *so* going to enjoy this. It feels good to get that smug asshole where I want him. Not getting him *and* his client is like finishing second in a race, but *damn*, this still feels good." She laughed at herself, at her own elation. "Maybe I should've done this sooner like my bosses wanted me to."

Jenkins smiled with her. "I still think you made the right call, Jenny," he said, "despite the pressure from above to get a conviction … any conviction. We knew you had almost everything you needed on Eastman, so waiting to see if you could get the client didn't put you in a worse position. For what it's worth, I was with you one hundred percent. Still am."

"Thanks, Brad," said Willson warmly, her eyes bright. "I appreciate that more than you know. I haven't given up. Now's my chance to work my interrogation magic on Eastman. Who knows what I can talk him into?" She placed her Stetson hat on the desk, crown down. "Hey, Rocky, watch me pull a rabbit out of my hat."

As she jokingly reached for the inside of her hat, she felt her cellphone buzz in her breast pocket. She unbuttoned her pocket and slid out the phone. "Willson here."

"I told you I'd phone you back … and now I have," said a male voice.

"Who's this?"

"You don't recognize me? I'm hurt. It's Sprague."

Willson's eyebrows shot up. She motioned to Jenkins for a piece of paper and a pen. She scribbled "informant" and pushed the paper back at him.

"Sprague," said Willson, trying to hide the excitement in her voice. "Long time, no hear. Let me put you on speaker so my colleague can hear you."

"Wait," said her caller. "Who's your colleague?"

"Don't worry. He's a B.C. conservation officer who's working with me on the poaching case that you and I talked about in early summer. Remember, we don't know who you are, so there's nothing to worry about if he listens in. His name's Brad and he's going to take notes so I don't miss anything you say. And I'm not tracing the call. Have you got something for me?"

"Well, I heard you didn't catch my guy when he was up there," said the informant, a chuckle punctuating his observation. "You folks must be seriously pissed off."

"How do you know that?" asked Willson, looking across the desk at Jenkins, her eyebrows still raised.

"I talked to him this morning," said the man, "and he boasted about making you guys look like incompetents … *again*."

Willson ignored the cheap shot. "So he was up here recently?"

"Yeah, I met him this morning. He told me he was there in the last couple of days."

"We thought so," said Willson, "and you're right. I'm disappointed that I didn't get to talk to him while he was in Canada. Did he, by any chance, tell you why he was here?"

"You mean, besides shooting a caribou with that outfitter?" the man said mockingly.

Willson couldn't hide her surprise and anger. "He did what?"

"He shot a caribou," said the man. "It was all the little fucker could talk about."

"Did he say where and when he shot it?" she asked.

"Nope," said the man, "I can't help you there. All I know is it was north of the border and a day or two ago."

"Are you sure he got it across the border?"

"Oh, yeah," said the man, "there's no doubt. He said the thing was already at his taxidermist. He can't wait to show it off when it's done. He's extra-excited that it's an endangered species."

Willson could barely contain the excitement and despair that were fighting for control of her thoughts. "Interesting. Did he tell you how he got it across the border?"

"I can't help you there, either," said the man. "All I know is he's damned proud of himself for shooting it at the same time you guys were looking for him. If you ask me how I *think* he did it, I'd bet one of his trucks was involved." The man paused and then spoke again. "You should see the picture. He got a real beauty."

"He showed a picture to you?" asked Willson, incredulous at the poacher's arrogance. Either his ego had completely overwhelmed his common sense, she thought, or he had something so significant on the informant that he believed the man wouldn't talk to law enforcement.

"Yup. He showed it to me on his cellphone. All I could see in the background was trees, like pine trees or something. It was dark. And it was just him and a really big bull caribou. Dead. That's all I know."

Jenkins wrote furiously on the same piece of paper and slid it at Willson. It read, "Salmo-Creston. Mountain caribou."

"Sprague, this is information we weren't aware of," said Willson, again focusing on the caller. "It's a major step forward in our investigation. I've got two questions for you. First, you said something about 'his trucks.' What did you mean?"

"Well, do you know that he owns a trucking company?"

"No. We wondered about that though," said Willson. "But because we don't know who he is, that doesn't help us at all. Do you know anything about it?"

"If I tell you more, you'll figure out his name," replied the man. "Let's just say it's a subsidiary of a subsidiary. And he owns a bunch of warehouses, too. Some of them buildings might fall down one day," he said, laughing at a joke only he understood.

"You haven't given me much to go on," said Willson.

"Look, I gotta go," said the man impatiently. "What else did you want to ask me?"

"If what you've told us is true, are you willing to make a formal statement about your guy shooting the caribou, exactly what he said to you?" she asked.

"First," said the man on the phone, "what I told you *is* true, and as I said, he showed me a picture of the caribou. He was kneeling beside it. And second, we're dealing with a guy who scares me. I'm in deep with him on stuff that would be a problem for me if it ever came out."

Willson and Jenkins could hear the man breathing over the speaker. It was a long time before he spoke again.

"I don't want to testify against him in court," said the man. "If he finds out I talked, I'm a dead man."

Unlike Jenkins, Willson had worked with confidential informants in the past. She fully understood their reticence. But she'd never had an informant claim he would be killed if he talked.

"Look, Sprague," she said, "I understand. We're probably never going to see your friend up here again, so my goal now is to convict him in a U.S. court. I can talk to my contacts in the U.S. Fish and Wildlife Service about you becoming a confidential informant for them. No guarantees. But I bet if they find other evidence to corroborate what you've told me, I don't believe you'd have to testify. Are you willing to do that?"

"Can I keep my other business with him out of this?"

"I can't speak for the U.S. feds," said Jenkins. "But if it's anything like here, all they'll want to know is details about his poaching up here and bringing the animals into the U.S."

Willson waited through another long pause. She could almost hear the man thinking.

"Jesus, I'm scared shitless," said the man. "But at the same time, I hate that little fucker more than I can tell you. Give me a day to think about it."

"Can I call you as soon as I've talked to our colleagues at U.S. Fish and Wildlife?" asked Jenkins.

The man laughed. "Nice try. I'll call *you* at the same time tomorrow," he said. "Make sure you've got a solid offer. And if there's a bit of cash in it for me, even better." The phone line went dead.

Willson and Jenkins looked at each other in silence for long seconds.

"Holy shit," said Willson at last. "I'm not sure if my system can take more of this. Yesterday, I was feeling about as shitty as I could possibly feel. It looked like the American had fucked us up again. But things have changed. Now we know the guy was in and out of Canada in a very short window of time."

"How's that going to help?" asked Jenkins.

"Remember that list of twenty-seven names that you worked on with Bill Forsyth? The names of Eastman's American clients?"

"Yeah."

"Well, Brad, you're going to get on the phone with Canada Border Services and cross-reference our list with the names of U.S. citizens who came north over the past three days. At some point, we're going to find the same name on both lists. And that, my friend, will be our guy."

Willson watched Jenkins's face move from confusion to understanding. "That," he said, grinning, "is fucking brilliant."

"And once we've got the name, we can ask Canada Border Services to contact their U.S. counterparts and confirm when he returned to the U.S. That will give us the timing for his visit to Canada. And if we can connect that with what we just heard from our informant, then maybe the U.S. agents will have enough to pursue a charge under their Lacey Act."

"I love it," said Jenkins. "I'll get on the phone now. Because there's no caribou east of here, I'll start with the Rykerts and Kingsgate border crossings and see what comes up."

"Excellent. And while you do that, I'm going to talk to our friend Bernie. Now that I know something he doesn't know I know, maybe I can wipe that smug smile off his ugly face."

CHAPTER 31

Willson placed a thick and well-worn file folder on the interview room table and then sat across from Bernie Eastman. Like Charlie Clark had done months before, she saw Eastman's eyes flick to the file quickly, furtively, and then back to her.

"So, Bernie," she said, "I'm sure you've been looking forward to this as much as I have. Before we get started, do you want your lawyer here while we talk?"

"Ha," said Eastman, again sneering at her, "you give yourself too much credit. I don't need no lawyer."

"Fair enough. I have to give you that opportunity, even if you don't feel you need it."

"What the hell do you want? You got nothin' on me."

Willson watched him sit back in the chair, only the back legs on the floor, his cuffed hands behind his head like he was enjoying himself. *Time to go for it.*

"Was your client happy with his caribou, Bernie?" Her pen was poised over a blank pad of paper as if to record his every word.

Eastman slammed forward in his chair, his confined fists coming over his head and banging on the table like two beef roasts, the look on his face making Willson's day. And she was barely getting started.

"What did you say?" he asked.

It was Willson's turn to smirk. "I didn't realize you were deaf. My apologies, Bernie. Maybe it's from all that illegal shooting you've been doing. I'll speak louder and slower. I asked if your client … was happy …with the caribou … that *you* found for him?"

"Why are you askin' me *that*?"

"Because he's already telling everybody about it back home, showing a photo."

Suddenly Eastman looked much less comfortable, less cocky. "I had nothing to do with shootin' any caribou."

"That's not what your guy is saying. He's telling everyone you led him to it. It was up on the Salmo-Creston, wasn't it?" She tried hard to keep her face neutral; she hoped the outfitter was too surprised to notice how much she was enjoying the moment.

"You keep sayin' 'he.' Do you even have a name for the guy I allegedly helped shoot a caribou? Or is this more of your bullshit?"

Willson lifted her eyebrows and tilted her head to one side. "Maybe I do, and maybe I don't. Do you want to take the chance that I'm talking to him and not to you?"

"Oh, fuck off. You got nothin'."

"If I had nothing, Bernie, how would I know about the mountain caribou bull your client shot? How would I know where you got it … and that you took his picture kneeling beside it? How would I know all *that*?" She watched waves of surprise, anger, and incredulity wash over Eastman's face.

"Who … who've you been talkin' to?" he asked.

"That doesn't matter, does it? The important thing is that the situation's beginning to unravel, Bernie. And it's all coming down on *you*. All the evidence is pointing at *you*. So, you have decisions to make. You can talk to me now and get out ahead of this or —" she paused for effect "— you can sit there and drown in the tsunami of shit that's coming at you. It's your call."

"I think I want my lawyer now," Eastman said, bringing his shackled hands to his chest as if praying. "I'm done talkin.'"

"That's your call, too. Are you using Samuel Lindsay, the same guy who represented Clark?"

"Fuckin' right. I want him here now."

"Not a problem, Bernie. I'll call him now, tell him you've asked him to come here to speak with you. I guess we're done for now. When your lawyer gets here, I'll have more questions for you. Until he does, I'll change your babysitter so no one has to sit here and look at your ugly face all day."

Willson rose, gathered the file folder and notepad, and left the room. She saw Jenkins coming toward her in the hallway. She held up one finger while she called Lindsay's law office.

She got his secretary. "This is Jenny Willson, park warden. Please tell Mr. Lindsay that his client Bernie Eastman is under arrest and being held for questioning at the B.C. Environment office in Cranbrook." She thought about her first encounter with the elderly lawyer. "He may not remember me, but I'm sure he'll want to get here as soon as he can. I won't be speaking to his client again until he arrives."

When she disconnected the call, she turned to Jenkins. "Let's go outside. I need some fresh air."

When they were standing amongst the wild roses and kinnikinnick in the front yard of the office, with Fisher Peak and the Steeples Range of the Rockies their backdrop, Willson breathed in the warm mountain air.

"How did it go in there?" asked Jenkins.

"Good. Real good," said Willson, running her fingers through her hair. "I jumped right in with the caribou and it rattled him. He thinks we know more than we actually do, but he asked for his lawyer. While we're waiting, tell me what you found. I need something new so I can keep him off balance."

"Well, Jenny, this day just keeps getting better and better for you. First the call from your informant and now some fascinating news. The boys searching Eastman's place called me a few moments ago. Guess what they found? They found a hidden basement in a Quonset hut and they think it was being used as a grow op. It was full of lights and piping — and hundreds of young marijuana plants."

"What? Are you shitting me?"

"Nope. It's a huge space. And in the midst of that grow op is a gun cabinet. And in that gun cabinet, along with a bunch of other rifles, they found a .308. It's on its way to the crime lab as we speak."

"Un-friggin'-believable!" Willson said, her arms and clenched fists high in the air, triumphant. In an instant, she'd moved from a second-place finish into a healthy lead.

"Yup," said Jenkins. "The drug squad is waiting in Eastman's driveway for their own warrant."

Willson smiled a confident smile.

"But wait, there's more," said Jenkins, grinning.

"This is like Christmas in September! Tell me, Brad."

"I'm waiting for confirmation from the U.S. border folks, but it appears that Eastman's client is a guy by the name of Luis José Castillo, from Spokane, Washington. He's on the list of American clients from Eastman's past guide declarations, and he came into Canada on September third via the Rykerts border crossing near Creston. That matches with my guess that they shot the caribou somewhere on the Salmo-Creston. His is the only name on both lists. He *must* be our guy."

Willson stared at the Rocky Mountains to the east, trying to process the avalanche of information that had swept over her through the course of the day. Her mind raced like a Ping-Pong ball thrown into an empty room, bouncing off one wall to the next, each time at a different angle.

When Willson returned to the interview room an hour later at the request of Eastman's lawyer, it was hard not to feel giddy with excitement.

Lindsay spoke first. "Ms. Willson, I presume? My secretary said that we've met, but I don't recall. My client tells me that you arrested him on federal and provincial wildlife charges and that you tried to question him about his alleged involvement in the alleged shooting of a caribou?"

"That's correct," said Willson. "And now, here we are. We can talk about the poached mountain caribou … *or* we can talk about a .308 rifle that we seized at your client's residence, a rifle that was probably used in the commission of a number of serious offences ... *or* we can talk about the grow op we found there, a grow op that the RCMP drug squad is searching as we speak. *Or*, if none of that's of interest, perhaps we can talk about ... Luis José Castillo." She stared hard at the outfitter, whose wide eyes revealed his surprise. "Where would you like to start, Bernie?"

CHAPTER 32

SEPTEMBER 8

Jenny Willson left I-90 at Exit 289, grateful to be off the busy interstate freeway. She was in the Spokane Valley, east of downtown Spokane, in a featureless mix of commercial and industrial buildings. Always distrustful of GPS units and their insistent voices, she had an old-school street map spread across her lap below the steering wheel, her finger tracing the route. Shining in the rear-view mirror was one of the wheels from her road bike, spinning in the morning sun. Willson had locked the bicycle in the back of the Parks Canada truck in the hope that she'd have some free time to ride the trails along the Spokane River.

After two wrong turns, she found East Mansfield Avenue, negotiated a roundabout, and then saw the offices of the U.S. Fish and Wildlife Service on East Montgomery Drive. The offices were in a squat two-storey commercial building with plenty of glass, not unlike thousands of similar buildings scattered across North America.

Entering the double front doors, Willson found the building directory, ran her finger down the list of tenants, and saw what she was looking for. She walked up the stairs to unit two, where she was met by a smiling Tracy Brown, Special Agent in charge of the Spokane office.

Brown shook Willson's hand vigorously, her other hand on Willson's shoulder. "Good morning, Jenny. It's great to see you again," she said. "Welcome to Spokane."

As the two women walked down a narrow hallway toward a conference room, Brown looked over her shoulder at Willson. "You've been busy since we met in Sandpoint," she said with a grin.

"It's been an interesting few months," said Willson, "but I gotta say I'm pleased to be here. I can't thank you enough for what you've done at your end."

"We're as happy as you are that we can finally move on this," said Brown. "Come in to meet the team."

When they reached the large windowless room, Brown introduced Willson to her three USFW colleagues, along with a federal prosecutor, six members of the Spokane Police Department, and four deputies from the Spokane County Sheriff's Office. Amidst coffee cups and partly eaten muffins, Willson saw files, maps, and air photos spread across a rectangular table in the centre of the room.

When everyone was seated, Tracy Brown kicked off the meeting.

"Thank you all for being here this morning," she said. "Not all of you know all the details of the situation that's brought us together today, so this morning's session will be part briefing, part tactical planning for execution of search warrants. Before we get into it, I want to express a special thanks to our Canadian colleague for her investigative diligence and her willingness to share her work with us." All eyes momentarily shifted to Willson.

"I'm going to turn things over to Assistant District Attorney Roger Hancock, who works with us on poaching cases," said Brown. "But first, I want to say how pleased I am that we've persuaded a judge to give us warrants, under the Lacey Act, to search a South Hill residence, a downtown office, and a series of warehouses east of here."

Brown paused for a moment. "And second, all of you now know that our person of interest today is a Luis José Castillo," she said. "In front of you are full dossiers on Castillo. As you can see, he's a forty-two-year-old, prominent local businessman, a U.S. citizen born in Mexico. He operates a group of construction, trucking, and warehousing businesses throughout the Pacific Northwest, all headquartered here in Spokane."

The sound of rustling paper filled the room as the officers reviewed the files on Castillo. The officers paused to stare at the picture of their quarry, memorizing his facial features.

"Depending on what we find during the searches," said Brown, "we may or may not arrest Castillo today under the Lacey Act. However, you can be sure that he's ultimately facing a large number of Canadian and American wildlife-related offences."

Brown continued. "Before I turn this meeting over to Roger, I also want to take a moment to let Jenny

Willson tell us how she and her Canadian colleagues broke this case open two days ago."

"Thanks, Tracy," said Willson. She passed a series of images around the table, waiting until each person had a full set. They were Jim Canon's photos of the massive bighorn sheep in Wilcox Pass. Willson heard a few whistles of admiration as the officers studied the images. Some were head on, some were in profile, and a few were close-ups of the full curl horns. "This all began with the shooting of a bull elk in Banff National Park, and then shortly after, this bighorn sheep ram was shot with a handgun in Jasper National Park. We also lost a mountain goat to the same guys. We've been chasing these perps — the B.C. guide-outfitter who's been offering guaranteed hunts, a guy by the name of Bernie Eastman, and his American client — for nearly a year now. Each time we got close to catching them in the act, they found a way to avoid us. One example is when we recently undertook a major backcountry surveillance based on information received from an assistant guide who was subsequently murdered. Neither the outfitter nor the client showed up when and where we thought they would. Based on intel from a confidential informant down here, we learned that the client shot an endangered mountain caribou just north of your Idaho border at the same time we were cooling our butts in the Purcell Mountains well to the north. To say we were pissed off is an understatement." Officers around the table chuckled. "But we were able to identify Castillo from that one call from the informant because he was the only U.S. citizen who crossed the border around that time who was also on Eastman's list of past clients."

"Two days ago," Willson continued, "I went back at Eastman and I went back hard. The guy is a classic bully, so he started out smug, not willing to say a word. You've all seen it dozens of times. His lawyer is an old guy who was completely unprepared for my interview or my accusations, which worked in my favour. By then, we'd executed another search of Eastman's property and found the rifle I was looking for. With all that in hand, I laid out the charges he was facing, I told him we had a signed statement from an informant about the caribou hunt, and I told him how much time he'd spend in jail and the huge fines he'd pay as a result. After I finished, his face had changed from a ruddy red to a scared-shitless white. He decided that rolling over on Castillo made a lot of sense."

She paused to look around the room. "But wait," she said with a grin, "there's more. Seems there's an interesting drug angle to all this. When my colleagues searched Eastman's place the second time, they also found a marijuana grow op hidden in the basement of one of his buildings. It was actually quite clever. When Eastman realized that he was facing even more serious federal charges, he rolled over so far on Castillo that he almost ended up back where he started. Seems that Castillo was his main buyer. Based on what Eastman told me, our RCMP are now trying to find proof that Castillo was involved in, or even ordered, the murder of nine competing drug dealers. It appears they may have hit Eastman's facility back in June, and Castillo told Eastman he had taken care of them, made them disappear permanently, once he found out who they were. Because the Canada

International Extradition Treaty with the United States comes into play on a murder charge, the Mounties are leaving no stone unturned in their investigation."

"Holy crap," said Brown. "Talk about peeling back the layers on this, Jenny. Nice job. I think we'll be using this case for future training."

"Thanks, Tracy," Willson said with a smile and a slight flush in her cheeks. "It was hard work and a lot of luck. But eventually, I got Eastman to admit to guiding Castillo to the caribou in Kootenay Pass and seeing him shoot it. He gave me a full statement on how they used the assistant guide to create a diversion so they could pull it off. But that was only after I promised he wouldn't be charged with that offence. Our B.C. conservation officer colleagues found the caribou carcass where the outfitter said it would be, so we have a solid DNA sample to compare to anything we might seize down here. But no matter what persuasive tools I used, Eastman refused to tell me how he got the caribou head across the border into the U.S. Unfortunately, we may never find out for sure."

Willson checked her notes to ensure she hadn't neglected anything important. "So, here I am," she said, "happy as hell to be hitting Castillo right where he lives and works."

"Thanks, Jenny," said Brown. "We love persistence down here and you're an example of that in action. Well done." She then pointed toward the assistant district attorney. "Take it away, Roger," she said.

Hancock, a lanky lawyer who'd been a power forward on the Gonzaga University Bulldogs basketball team, led the assembled officers through the warrants, carefully describing the locations they were authorized to search and what they could seize. Because of the work done by Willson, and because Hancock had appeared before a sympathetic judge, the list was extensive, their latitude for search and seizure broad. When he finished, Hancock gave the officers his cellphone number. He told them he would stand by while they undertook the searches, ready to answer questions during the day.

When Hancock sat down, Willson again took over the meeting, leading the officers through detailed planning to execute the warrants.

"We've got four locations to hit this morning," she said. "Castillo's home, his office, and two warehouses out in the valley, not far from here. You'll see those outlined on the maps in front of you. Tracy and I have assigned teams of at least one U.S. Fish and Wildlife agent, one city police officer, and one sheriff to each location. We've got additional officers ready to back you up on the scene; they're only a radio call away. You won't be surprised to hear that Tracy and I will visit Señor Castillo. In my humble opinion, I deserve nothing less than the satisfaction of showing up at his front door."

"We're done here," she said, as the officers began to rise, "so unless there are any final questions, let's synchronize our watches so we arrive at each location at exactly the same time. I want no screw-ups."

CHAPTER 33

Parked in an unmarked Police Interceptor SUV down the curved block from Castillo's house, Willson sat nervously while Brown, behind the wheel, watched the house through binoculars. The front steps, porch, and front columns were built of river rock, the house soared into gables and dormers above, and the yard was immaculate.

Willson checked her watch for the fourth time in the past five minutes. "I never thought this day would come," she said. "I hope the *señor* is in his *casa*, because I want to personally see the look in his eyes when we walk through his front door."

When their watches beeped 11:00 a.m., Brown floored the SUV and then screeched to a halt in front of Castillo's house. A Spokane Police Department car arrived at the same time from the opposite direction, the two vehicles parking nose to nose against the curb. A deputy sheriff's truck pulled in behind the police car.

The occupants of the three vehicles strode up the shrub-lined walkway and climbed the rock steps to the porch. Warrant in hand, Willson pounded on the heavy wooden door. The officers heard the sound of movement inside. The door opened to reveal a Latino woman in her late fifties, her greying hair in a severe bun. Her eyes widened when she saw six uniformed officers on the porch.

"Yes … can I help you?" she asked.

"I am National Park Warden Jenny Willson and with me is Special Agent Tracy Brown from the U.S. Fish and Wildlife Service. I have a warrant to search these premises and we now intend to do that."

"Uh … I am only the housekeeper here," said the woman, her voice shaky. "I must let Señor Castillo know you are here." She moved to close the door, but Willson pushed her way into the front foyer, the others following. The door remained open behind them.

The officers heard a voice from the far end of the hallway. "Who is it, Juanita?"

Willson, standing to the left of Brown, saw a head poke around the corner of a far right-hand doorway. Having stared at his picture many times over the last few days so that his image had begun to appear in her dreams, Willson immediately recognized Luis Castillo. Instead of a monster or an ogre, he was just a man, a man who looked small and alone. But his eyes were dark, calculating, evil. Filled with a sense of triumph, she smiled at him.

"Señor Castillo, it's a pleasure to finally meet you," she said. "I've been looking forward to this moment for a long time."

Castillo did not move. He stared at Willson and her colleagues, his eyes wide in overt surprise. A clock ticked in the hallway, measuring the silence. Then, as if he recognized that he had to act, Castillo strode down the hall toward them.

"What is the meaning of this intrusion into my home?" he asked as he approached Willson.

"Señor Castillo, these officers say they have a warrant to search the house," said the housekeeper, wringing her hands.

"A warrant?" asked Castillo. "What is this all about?" He looked at each of the officers in turn. He paused, visibly stiffening when he saw the Parks Canada crest on the shoulder of Willson's uniform jacket.

Willson aggressively pushed a copy of the warrant, rolled into a cylinder, hard into Castillo's chest. The man automatically reached up to grab the document.

"Luis José Castillo," said Willson, her voice strong and confident, "that is your copy of a warrant signed by a federal court judge under the authority of the Lacey Act. It gives us the legal right to search this residence and all associated outbuildings."

"You have no right to do this," said Castillo. "You stay there. I want to call my lawyer."

"Feel free to call your lawyer," said Willson, moving a step closer to Castillo, "but I can tell you that we will begin an immediate search of this residence. If you hamper our efforts in any way, one of these police officers will arrest you for obstruction. Do you understand?"

The officers watched Castillo's facial expression shift through a range of emotions. They all knew that a woman taking control of the situation as Willson had would boil the man's blood. They were on edge, waiting for Castillo's reaction.

To their surprise, Castillo simply smiled. "Very well," he said, "but I am going to phone my lawyer so he can deal with this charade." He turned and walked quickly down the hall toward the back of the house. The housekeeper stood unmoving, her eyes darting between Castillo and the officers in the front foyer.

Willson turned to one of the deputies. "Please stay with Mr. Castillo to ensure he doesn't do anything stupid," she said firmly. With a high likelihood of weapons in the house, she didn't want to take chances.

The deputy nodded and strode down the hall, following Castillo.

Willson faced the remaining officers and reminded them of their assignments. At that moment, they heard a door slam somewhere in the back of the house.

"He's running!" the deputy shouted. They heard pounding footsteps and then the deputy sprinted back through the same doorway where they'd first seen Castillo. "He grabbed keys," the man said as he rushed by them, "and was already in his car when I got to the door." They heard the sound of squealing tires and turned to see a black Lexus pass them on Park Drive. Castillo was gone.

Willson made a snap decision. "You follow him," she yelled at the deputy as he went out the front door toward his truck. "We'll be right behind you."

To the remaining officers, Willson's order was curt. "Stay here, secure the residence, do not allow anyone inside, and wait for us to get back."

Brown stood wide-eyed, apparently shocked at how quickly the situation had changed.

As Willson moved quickly out the front door, she yelled over her shoulder at her American colleague, "Are you coming or what? The fun's just begun!"

With Brown driving, they pursued Castillo through the streets of Spokane, wailing sirens and flashing lights clearing a path through the midday traffic. They roared down South Grand Boulevard and followed Fourteenth Avenue west to Monroe, blowing red lights and passing gaping motorists. They watched as Castillo narrowly missed a municipal garbage truck, averting a crash by centimetres. They then followed him northbound on Monroe and then Lincoln, passing under I-90. Willson looked at the speedometer. Sixty miles an hour. She couldn't remember what that was in kilometres an hour, but it was fast, particularly in the middle of a city.

"I bet he's heading to his office!" yelled Brown as she worked to stay in sight of the speeding sheriff's vehicle ahead of them. "There must be something there he doesn't want us to find."

Willson didn't answer; she was too busy hanging on, astonished at how quickly the day had changed.

With one hand on the steering wheel, Brown grabbed the microphone from the dash, calling her USFW colleague at Castillo's office. "We're northbound on Lincoln in downtown," she said, "and the suspect's heading in your direction."

Willson heard the response. "We're at his office now, so we'll say hello when he gets here."

As they turned left onto Main Street, heading toward a turn north on Monroe again, the radio crackled to life. The voice of the deputy ahead of them was surprisingly calm.

"Agent Brown, the suspect apparently saw police vehicles at his office," he said, "so he pulled a U-turn and is heading back in our direction southbound on Monroe."

By now, Brown's vehicle had reached the four-lane bridge where Monroe Street passed over the Spokane River. They could see Castillo's car speeding directly toward them in the inside lane, down the hill on Monroe, the deputy behind him, his red and blue lights flashing. He ignored them as he went by.

Brown tried to turn to follow him. As she did so, she clipped the back corner of a southbound Spokane Transit bus in the outside lane. The SUV spun twice, coming to a sudden stop against the railing on the east side of the bridge, the front air bags deployed. Brown's vehicle blocked the two northbound lanes, the stalled bus the two southbound lanes. Castillo was gone.

While Willson sat in shock, the fine white powder from the air bags filling the air, Brown was immediately back on the radio after wrestling the deflated fabric out of her way.

"Suspect is headed south on Monroe," said Brown, "and we've been involved in an MVA that's blocked all lanes on the bridge."

Brown and Willson heard the deputy speaking into his shoulder-mounted microphone, his head tilted to the left as he sprinted toward them from his vehicle, now pulled to a stop on the north side of the accident. "We need other units here to deal with the MVA and to divert traffic at both ends of the bridge," he said, "and we may need an ambulance. Stand by and I'll advise."

The deputy peered in the window of Brown's vehicle. "Are you all okay in here?" he asked.

"Yeah, we're okay," said Brown. "Go help the bus passengers."

Willson slammed her hands down on the dashboard. "Shit!" she exclaimed in frustration. "That lucky fucker got away from me … again!"

CHAPTER 34

It was nearly an hour before the downtown accident scene was cleared, written statements taken by traffic officers, and Willson and Brown transported to Castillo's business offices on the north side of the river. By then, their suspect had disappeared into downtown Spokane traffic, despite the fact that a BOLO (Be On Look Out) had gone out to all police officers and sheriff's deputies in the area. If he was seen or stopped for a traffic violation, or if he showed up at a border crossing or airport, they would know it.

When Willson and Brown arrived at the offices, the search was winding down. "The bad news," said the lead Fish and Wildlife officer on the scene, "is that the only evidence we found that might relate to poaching is a single photograph hanging on the wall of Castillo's private office." He handed a framed eight-by-ten print in a clear plastic evidence envelope to Willson.

She saw an image of Castillo kneeling beside a dead mountain goat. "There's no way to tell where this was taken or when, but let's seize it regardless," said Willson.

"Yes, we've done that," said the officer. "We've also interviewed the twelve employees who were here today and they all say they knew their boss liked hunting."

"Okay," said Willson, "you said that was the bad news. What's the good news?"

"Come with me," said the man. He led Willson and Brown down a carpeted hall to a spot where they could look through the floor-to-ceiling glass window of a small conference room. On the far side of a table, they saw a thin, hawk-like man dotting his face with tissues. One eye twitched nervously when the man saw the officers at the window. An African-American woman sat across the table from him, a pad of lined paper by her right hand.

"Who is this?" asked Willson.

"Meet Luis Castillo's chief financial officer," said the officer. "James Whistler. When we searched Mr. Whistler's office, we found a large bag of fentanyl tablets hidden in a file cabinet in his office. He claims they're not his. That's a Spokane detective interviewing him now."

"Are you kidding me?" Willson asked. "Can we seize the drugs and link them to Castillo?"

"Normally, we couldn't because the search warrant doesn't cover it. But today, we don't have to. It seems that Mr. Whistler has agreed to give us a full statement — without his lawyer present — about the drugs *and* about Mr. Castillo's business affairs."

"Does he realize he's not compelled to say anything and that because drugs weren't in our search warrant, he probably can't be charged without a confession?"

asked Brown. At that moment, her cellphone rang, so she moved away to answer it.

The officer smiled at the question. "He does. We were clear with him, and we read him his rights. It appears he wants to get things off his chest. From what he's told us so far, he joined the company believing it was a legit business. When he discovered that some of it was and some of it wasn't, he started asking questions, as any good financial professional would do. When Castillo heard about his inquiries, he sent two of his so-called security staff to visit Whistler at his condo. They strongly encouraged him not to tell anyone about his suspicions. And they suggested that resigning wasn't an option for him. It seems the last CFO disappeared soon after he threatened to call the police. At that point, Whistler knew he was in over his head and it was too late to back out. It's almost like he's happy to see us. I've never seen such a willing witness in all my years on the job."

"Wow. Do we know what he's going to talk about?" asked Willson.

"Oh, yeah," said the officer, "he's already told us stories of bribing government officials for construction contracts, having city staff on their payroll, and inexplicable injections of cash in and out of Castillo's businesses. We found the official financial statements ourselves, and Mr. Whistler just showed us where the shadow books are kept. He told me about interstate and inter-country transportation of illicit goods — weapons, counterfeit money, drugs. To me, it looks like there's money laundering going on, too, and that means links to organized crime."

As they peered at the man through the window, Brown moved back toward them, her face dark. "I've got bad news," she said. "At one of Castillo's two warehouses in the valley, our officers walked in on a group of armed men. They were loading bundles of counterfeit money and weapons into the false floor of a semi-trailer truck. There was a shootout. One of the sheriff's deputies was badly wounded. He's going to make it, but the Drug Enforcement Administration, the Bureau of Alcohol, Tobacco, Firearms and Explosives, and even the Secret Service are now involved, and it looks like this has gone far beyond wildlife poaching."

"This thing gets more and more interesting by the moment," said Willson, shaking her head in amazement. "This is great work. There's not much more we can do here. You have it under control. Tracy, can we get a ride back to Castillo's residence? I'm itching to see what we find there."

Back in South Hill again, Willson and Brown were met by a Spokane police officer on the front porch of Castillo's house.

"Anything interesting happen while we were gone?" asked Willson.

"Nothing like your experience," said the officer. "Are you guys okay? I heard what was going down on the radio."

"Other than being seriously pissed off about losing Castillo, we're fine," said Willson.

"His lawyer showed up about twenty minutes after you left," said the officer. "He read the warrant, tried to push his way into the house, and nearly got his ass arrested. By the time he left, he was threatening to sue everyone involved. Other than that, it's been quiet, with no sign of Castillo."

Like Willson, Brown was anxious to start the search, so they pushed open the front door. Using the same approach they'd planned two hours earlier, they started their methodical examination of the house, floor by floor, room by room.

Willson was the first to enter Castillo's trophy room on the main floor, to the right of the sweeping staircase. She turned on the lights, took a single step into the room, and stood still. The soaring walls were covered with trophies of animals from across the globe. Once alive and watchful, their glassy eyes now stared into eternity. She saw species from Africa, South America, North America, and Eurasia. Many were ungulates, some carnivores. Willson, used to seeing wildlife alive in their natural habitats in the parks, was sickened by the gallery of human greed. Her guts churned, her heart pounded, and her vision blurred with unshed tears. For her, it was everything that was wrong with trophy hunting, all in one place.

Willson felt Brown put a comforting hand on her shoulder. They stood in silence.

"After all that's happened, is that what you've come for, Jenny?" asked the American agent quietly, pointing to a bull elk and a mountain goat billy on one wall, and a bighorn sheep ram on the next wall to the right.

Without a word, Willson pulled from her briefcase the full series of Jim Canon's images of the Jasper bighorn ram, and the professional photographer's images of the Banff elk a few days before it was murdered. She walked across the room toward the massive head, a deep pile carpet dampening the sounds of her footsteps. She studied the head, looking at it from the front and then from both sides. When compared to the images in her hand, Willson knew it was the missing sheep head. The horns were the same shape and length, the growth rings a perfect match to those in the photographs. After doing the same with the elk, she looked toward Brown with great sadness, nodding once in the affirmative.

By late that evening, the officers had peered into every corner of the massive house. Castillo's housekeeper followed them, still wringing her hands but saying nothing. They not only seized the three trophies of interest to Willson — the elk, the sheep, and the goat — but they also took a black rhino and a polar bear, likely shot illegally elsewhere. They gathered two boxes of documents, one of which contained a receipt from a local taxidermist for a caribou head. It was dated a day or two after Castillo had last entered Canada. While it was possible to hunt barren-ground caribou legally in some parts of Canada, one of Brown's colleagues was immediately dispatched to seize the head on the assumption it was the endangered mountain caribou taken in British Columbia. They also found rifles and handguns, all of which were seized as evidence.

While working her way through one of the three upstairs guest bedrooms, Willson discovered a tablet hidden in a gym bag at the back of a closet. With Brown looking over her shoulder, she crossed her fingers that a password wasn't necessary. It wasn't. Scrolling through the picture gallery, Willson found a folder of colour images under "travels." She clicked through them, and it was immediately obvious that they were all from Castillo's many hunting trips. Willson and Brown smiled and shared vigorous high-fives. Over and over again, on image after image, they saw Castillo kneeling beside dead animals. There were no landscapes, no people. Every image was of Castillo with a trophy. It was unlike anything Willson had ever seen. Sometimes Castillo was smiling, but more often his face showed no emotion at all. In every image, the man had one hand on his rifle, the other on the animal's shoulder or head as though it had, in death, become his possession. One of the last images in the folder showed Castillo, framed against a dark sky, beside a dead caribou bull.

Willson knew that significant forensic work would have to be done to match the pictures with the poached animals, at least to a degree that would persuade a judge to convict. But with all the evidence she now had, she was confident she'd hit the jackpot.

It was after midnight when Willson and Brown left Castillo's now silent house. A single overhead light illuminated the kitchen counter. On it: a multi-page list of items seized during the search. The list was long and, added to the events of the past few days, it signalled the end of Castillo's career as a hunter … as an entrepreneur … and as a free man. But first, Willson had to find him.

CHAPTER 35

SEPTEMBER 10

It was five o'clock in the afternoon as Luis Castillo watched his wife walk toward him, a bottle of water in her left hand. Her long, dark hair, tied in a ponytail for travelling, trailed behind her. Adelina Castillo wore a blue silk blouse that clung to her like water, matched with a pair of black leggings and black stilettos. As she moved, Castillo saw other men in the lounge area watching her, lust and longing in their eyes. It was not the first time. Wives and girlfriends watched her, too, but theirs were looks of envy.

"I assume that our sudden pending departure is connected to your business?" Adelina asked, sitting beside him in a plush leather chair. "You haven't put us at risk, have you? I've had to reschedule the charity gala and that's going to cost us."

"Nothing to worry about, my dear," he said, placing a hand on her toned arm. "It will only be for a while.

Just until some legal issues are resolved. I appreciate your patience. You seemed to enjoy our two nights at our friend's house on Puget Sound."

She pushed his hand away. "That was, at best, an inconvenience. Does this have anything to do with your trucking company, Luis," she asked, "and the items you move for others? I expect those people are very dangerous, in a very dangerous business."

Castillo's eyes flashed at her. He knew his wife had suspicions about his business affairs, but had assumed that because of the lifestyle he provided her she didn't want to know too much. He now realized he'd severely underestimated her, and she might know more than he'd ever thought she did. If that was the case, and if she was angry with him, she could be dangerous. That was not good.

"It has nothing to do with them," he said. "The U.S. government is poking its nose into my business affairs and my lawyers have suggested I go overseas until the matter is resolved."

"What about our daughters?" asked Adelina. "Do they know what's going on?"

"I phoned them yesterday," Castillo replied, "to tell them that you and I are going on a holiday. I have someone watching them, so I'm certain that they will be fine."

"I will be very unhappy with you if they're not," said his wife before turning away. "It would change *everything*."

Castillo looked out of the floor-to-ceiling windows of the lounge, watching the September rain fall in waves. His wife stared at a television set hanging from the ceiling. Seattle news and weather ran in a continuous loop, as much to distract guests as inform them. Out of the corner of his eye, he saw signs of his wife's anger — the thin mouth, the flushed cheeks, the rapid blinking — so he chose not to engage her further. He was certain that when they reached their final destination, one flight beyond London, she would be better company. But perhaps not. Her disclosure of her understanding of his business affairs had shifted both the foundation and the power balance of their relationship dramatically.

An hour later, Castillo and his wife were finishing last sips of wine and last nibbles from a cheese plate when they heard a call over the public-address system.

"British Airways Flight number forty-eight to London Heathrow is ready for boarding at Gate S4. We invite all business-class passengers to come forward."

Gathering their carry-ons, his wife's large purse and Castillo's bulging leather briefcase, the two made their way to the gate and lined up behind other business passengers, waiting to show their boarding passes. Only two passengers were ahead of them in the line when Castillo felt a hand on his shoulder. He turned to see two men in suits and a pair of uniformed Seattle police officers standing in a semicircle behind him.

"Luis José Castillo?" asked one of the men in suits.

"Yes," said Castillo, turning. "What is the meaning of this? We're about to board the plane."

A uniformed officer stepped forward, grabbing Castillo firmly by the right elbow. "You'll have to come with us, sir," he said. "You won't be flying today. Instead, you've won a free trip to Spokane chained to a bench in our van."

Castillo began to protest, but his hands were pulled behind his back. He felt the cold metal of handcuffs and heard the ratcheting sound as they closed around his wrists.

One of the suits took Castillo's briefcase, still clutched awkwardly in his hand. "Luis José Castillo," he said, "you're under arrest for violations of the Lacey Act." Reading from a plasticized card in his hand, the man continued. "You have the right to remain silent. Anything you say can and will be used against you in a court of law. You have the right to an attorney. If you cannot afford an attorney, one will be provided for you. Do you understand the rights I have read to you?"

Castillo nodded and muttered, "Yes."

In obvious shock, Adelina Castillo dropped her purse and, open-mouthed, watched the four officers escort her handcuffed husband away from the gate. The wide, wondering eyes of waiting passengers followed them.

As Castillo was led down the length of the building toward the British Airways lounge and escalators leading to underground transit, he twisted to look at his wife. His eyes met hers for a moment. He saw that her face had shifted from surprise to rage. He watched her lift her purse from the floor, turn, and walk down the ramp to the waiting airplane. She did not look back.

CHAPTER 36

AUGUST 28, THE FOLLOWING YEAR

Led by a burly guard, Luis Castillo walked down a long concrete hallway toward a steel door. His plastic sandals scuffed along the floor, echoing in the corridor. His orange coveralls were two sizes too big for his thin frame. When they reached the door, the guard waved a plastic card at a wall-mounted sensor. The steel door swung open to reveal a cafeteria-sized visiting area. Saying nothing, the guard waved Castillo through to the large room beyond.

Castillo paused and then shuffled toward a lone woman seated at a table. A file folder was on the steel surface in front of her, a digital recorder to one side, a nylon briefcase on the floor at her feet. As he moved across the room, Castillo passed mothers and sisters and wives and girlfriends meeting with other prisoners. He heard bits of conversations. Some were pointed and accusatory, others quiet and tear-filled.

Castillo sat on a floor-mounted metal stool and looked across the table at Jenny Willson. He had only met the woman once, very quickly, when she'd barged into his home with a search warrant. For a silent moment, he studied her as carefully as she appeared to study him.

"We meet again," said Willson. "Are they treating you well in here, Luis?"

"I'm sure you don't care if they are treating me well … or mistreating me," said Castillo. "It's clearly not the Four Seasons in here, so I'm very much looking forward to getting out."

"I'm no lawyer," said Willson, "but I can't imagine that you'll be getting out of here anytime soon."

"Why do you say that?"

"Because our cases against you are so strong and because they arrested you in the act of trying to leave the country, the judge chose not to grant bail and he seized your passport. In my experience, that means that this will likely be your home for many years to come."

Castillo resented the woman's confidence but chose not to play her game. "We can engage in this interesting conversation for hours, Ms. Willson, but I have better things to do with my time. Tell me why you're here today. To what do I owe the pleasure of your company?"

"I understand that you were extremely lucky in court last week," said Willson.

"Lucky?" said Castillo. "I was sentenced to ten years for bringing animals into the U.S. that were allegedly illegally shot elsewhere and you say I'm lucky?" The woman was getting under his skin and he could feel his blood pressure rising. He breathed in deeply and then smiled.

"The reason I suggested you were lucky," said Willson, returning his smile, "is that, along with the significant financial penalties you now have to pay, the district court judge could have given you five years for *each* of the Lacey Act offences for which you were charged. You could've ended up with a twenty-five-year sentence. Quite frankly, the fact that you didn't get that longer sentence is a disappointment for me. But I'll get over that disappointment knowing that that's just the start of your legal troubles."

"What do you mean?" he asked.

"Because of what happened at your Spokane Valley warehouse while we were chasing you through Spokane, because of what they found there after the shooting," said Willson, "*and* because your chief financial officer negotiated a plea bargain with the feds down here, I'm hearing rumours that you've now got the DEA, the FBI, and the Secret Service looking into every corner of every business you own. Apparently, they'll be charging you under the U.S. Controlled Substances Act. You'll also face charges for conspiracy, money laundering, and tax evasion. And they'll probably go after you under the RICO Act — that's the Racketeer Influenced and Corrupt Organizations Act — because in their eyes, some of your businesses look like ongoing criminal organizations. If you're convicted of those offences, we're talking one hell of a lot of jail time, and it will mean seizures of most, if not all of your assets, both personal and business. You may not get out of prison at all, and if you *ever* do, there won't be much left for you."

Castillo stared at Willson, his eyes like laser beams. "You could have mailed me a newspaper instead of wasting my time by coming here to share this gossip with me."

"You're right," said Willson. "I could have done that. But then I wouldn't have had the chance to tell you to your face that I know what you did in our parks and that I consider you to be a low-life scumbag who deserves the same friggin' fate as those animals. But I'm certain you don't care what I think. And —" she paused "— I wouldn't have been able to tell you in person that you're under investigation for murder in Canada."

"What?"

"Murder. In Canada. Your friend Bernie told us all about how you took care of those nine guys who attacked his grow op, how you boasted about making them disappear permanently. They must have *seriously* pissed you off. But I'll give you credit where credit is due, Luis. Nice job there. Until Bernie told me what you did, they were nine unsolved homicides with few leads. Now the RCMP is pursuing a whole new avenue of investigation, and you're the one in their crosshairs."

Castillo turned to stare out the barred window, his focus on the barren wheatfields far to the north of the prison. Below the table, his hands clenched into fists, his knuckles white. "That fucking Eastman told you that, did he?"

"He did … and I hear that the RCMP have found evidence that confirms his story, although I don't know what that is."

A bank of fluorescent lights above them buzzed and then blinked on and off. Looking back at Willson, at the smug smile he wanted to wipe from her face with the back of his hand, Castillo knew he was being played in an age-old game of pitting co-accused against each other. But the thought of Eastman making a fool of him drove an anger deep inside him. Willson's face shimmied and blurred as though he was looking at her through the wrong end of a pair of binoculars. Despite the red haze of his anger, he realized that he was only getting in deeper and had nothing left to lose. He had no power, no control. Nor did he have any remaining reason to protect the treacherous bastard who'd taken his money and then ratted him out. All he had left now was information.

"Did Eastman tell you about the Clarks?" asked Castillo. He saw Willson move forward on her metal stool, her eyes widening.

"What do you mean, Luis? What should he have told us about the Clarks?"

Castillo again smiled. He clearly had the female warden's attention. His anger cooled slightly, allowing his conscious mind to regain control, if only for a moment. A small sliver of his old mastery was back. "Why should I share anything with you?" he asked. "What's in it for me?"

He watched Willson slide back on the stool. "You're in this *so* deep, Luis, that there's very little I can offer. I'm not going to bullshit you. But here's something for you to consider when you have some free time. I'm guessing that your business partners — and yes, we know who most of them are — are extremely nervous about what you might say if and when the additional charges come to trial. In fact, I bet they'd rather not have any trials at all so their business dealings in the U.S. and Canada, legal or otherwise, aren't exposed to the light of day."

"Perhaps you're right," said Castillo, "perhaps not. So what's your point?"

"I believe I *am* right. My point is that through my contacts in law enforcement here, those partners can either hear confirmation that you're pleading guilty to all charges … *or* they can hear that you're talking to us, singing like the proverbial canary. The choices you make today will lead to one of two very different outcomes for you. Am I right, Luis?"

Castillo slammed his open palms down on the table with a bang, startling everyone in the room. From a far corner, a prison guard moved quickly toward them. Willson waved him off.

"Fuck you and fuck them," said Castillo, spittle flying across the table, his hands spread on the table like he was bracing himself against a strong wind. "I will not spend the rest of my life in jail so those fuckers can sit on their fat asses on top of the piles of cash I made for them. The same goes for that goddamn Eastman. I won't do it." He saw Willson staring at him, calm, expressionless. Despite his earlier attempts at dominating the young officer, he knew that the woman had triumphed. Game, set, and match. And he'd let it happen. He slumped back on the stool, defeated.

"Luis, tell me what you know about Bernie Eastman and Charlie and Wendy Clark," she said. "That's the missing piece for me — and for the RCMP."

Later, when they'd finished talking, after he'd told Willson all she wanted to know, after he'd answered every question she'd asked him, Castillo stood and looked at the Canadian park warden. He was confused by what had just happened, by what she'd done to him, and about what was to come for him. He had never let a woman get the best of him like that. This confusion was a strange sensation for Castillo, something for which he had no frame of reference. It left him numb, disoriented. He opened his mouth to speak but quickly realized that there was nothing left to say. As if knowing what he was thinking, he watched her slowly close the case file and turn off the recorder. He turned and walked purposefully toward the door leading back to his cell, leaving Willson sitting alone at the steel table. His decision was made, his information shared, his future firmly in the hands of others. He was an empty shell. He looked back once to see her smiling.

When Willson was sitting in her truck again, the Walla Walla State Penitentiary sign standing prominently to her left at the edge of the parking lot, she powered up her cellphone to see that while she was in the prison with Castillo, she had received two calls from a blocked number. As she looked down at the screen, it buzzed in her hand, startling her.

"Willson here."

A man's voice. "Is it true?"

"Who is this?" she asked, recognizing the voice but not placing it.

"Once again, you don't recognize me. I'm beginning to get a complex. It's Sprague."

"Sprague. Is what true?"

"Is it true that Castillo is done? In jail for the rest of his life? Did that arrogant son of a bitch finally get what he deserved?"

"Yes. It seems to be true. You must be very pleased."

"You have *no* fucking idea how happy I am. My life just got a whole lot easier."

Willson could hear the elation in the man's voice, as though he was smiling right through the phone. "Well, you played a key part in what happened to him, Sprague. I appreciate that. And that must make you feel even better. Are you ready to tell me who you are now? I'm less than three hours from Spokane, so I could meet you somewhere in town if you'd like to talk."

The man chuckled. "I don't think so," he said. "With that fucker behind bars now and none of our transactions coming to light so far, there's no reason for me to come out of the shadows."

"Are you sure?" asked Willson. "I'd like to meet you, tie up some loose ends, thank you in person ..." While she still didn't know the man's name, she guessed that he might yet get a visit from the authorities if his name was in the material the U.S. feds had seized from Castillo's downtown office. She ignored the urge to ruin his day.

"Nothing personal, Warden, but no thanks. You saved my ass. Now we're done."

Willson heard a dial tone, stared at the phone for a moment, and then dropped it on the bench seat beside her. She turned and looked at the prison as though she could, through the thick concrete walls, give Castillo one final message. "I got you, you bastard. You tangled with a Willson — and you lost big time."

She steered her car out of the parking lot, headed south into Walla Walla, and then turned right onto Highway 12. It would be a long drive back to Banff via Spokane. But she'd enjoy every moment of it.

CHAPTER 37

She was late. Willson ran down the hallway, nearly colliding with a janitor as she rounded a corner. Her nervous eyes shifted from door to door, searching for room 208. After getting lost in downtown Calgary and then struggling to find parking, she was sweating and fifteen minutes behind schedule.

When Willson reached the conference room on the second floor of the Harry Hays Building, she saw Brad Jenkins and Peter MacDonald waiting outside the door. They were in full dress uniform and smiling at her. Bill Forsyth stood beside them in an ill-fitting suit.

"Glad you could join us, Jenny," said MacDonald. "They're a half-hour behind so you can relax."

"Excellent," said Willson. "I'm a friggin' sweaty mess. Did I tell you I hate big cities?"

"Love the traffic, eh?" Jenkins said with a grin. "There's a washroom to your left. Take a few moments to clean up."

She walked down the hall, pushed open the door, and then washed her face and neck with paper towels soaked in cold water. Peering at herself in the grimy mirror, she straightened the tie on her dress uniform. "Good enough for the guys I go out with," she said to herself.

When Willson found her way back to her three colleagues, she saw they'd been joined by a severe-looking woman who introduced herself as the administrative assistant for Parks Canada's western regional director. "We're ready for you," she said. "Please come in."

As the door opened, Willson was surprised by the scene in front of her. On one side, a bank of tripod-mounted TV cameras pointed across rows of metal chairs, toward a raised stage with a podium at its centre. The chairs were filled with people she didn't recognize, while a row of smiling dignitaries sat on the stage. Willson saw Chief Park Warden Frank Speer there, along with the regional director, three members of Parliament, and the federal deputy environment minister. The four officers were led to empty chairs in the front row.

Over the next forty minutes, Willson listened to a chain of speeches from the dignitaries, each more passionate and self-congratulatory than the one before. And each equally as nauseating. Repeatedly, she heard a message that must have come direct from the communications staff in the prime minister's office: "This government continues to be committed to the sanctity of our national parks ..." In one windy ramble, she heard the regional director take credit for encouraging the investigation and for pushing the officers to keep digging. When he finally wound down, Willson turned to Jenkins.

"Jesus Christ, I'm going to vomit," she whispered in his ear. "I'd rather be at the fucking dentist getting drilled than listen to this shit."

"Grin and bear it, Jenny," said Jenkins. "It'll be over soon."

It was then that the regional director asked the four enforcement officers to join him on stage. Willson, Jenkins, Forsyth, and MacDonald stepped up and stood in a line, Jenkins's black CO uniform a dramatic contrast to the green-and-brown warden uniforms of Willson and MacDonald. Forsyth's suit was like an awkward punctuation at the end of a sentence. One at a time, the director presented each of them with a framed certificate of appreciation. As he did so, he shook hands, smiled, and then turned robotically toward the official Parks Canada photographer, who captured the moment. The four officers then ran the gauntlet of handshaking dignitaries.

Unbeknownst to anyone, Willson had prepared a short speech for the occasion. After she had her certificate in hand, she moved toward the microphone on the podium, pulling a sweaty piece of paper from her breast pocket. She felt a firm hand on her elbow. It was the regional director, urging her back to her seat with a subtle shake of his head. "I don't think so," he whispered.

Just as well, Willson thought with a smile. She knew it would've been her last day as a warden and she would have missed the opportunity to tranquilize someone in the ass — although the desire was now greater than ever.

When the ceremony and the carefully managed media interviews were over, and when they'd shaken all the hands there were to shake and had their pictures taken with every dignitary and wannabe in the room, Willson sidled up beside the official government photographer.

"Would you take a special picture for me?" she asked the woman.

"Sure," said the photographer. "It's your day."

Willson led her across the room toward the little bureaucrat with whom she'd tangled in the Banff boardroom, more than a year earlier. She'd noticed him when she was on stage. His head was down, focused on his BlackBerry. *Jesus*, she thought, *does he read that goddamn thing when he's sitting on the can?*

With her certificate in her right hand, proudly in front of her, Willson quickly grabbed the man's left shoulder with her free hand and gave it a vigorous squeeze. The camera flash illuminated the two of them in that pose. The resulting picture would always act as a reminder for Willson, not only of that moment but of the entire challenging investigation: Willson with a grin on her face, the little bureaucrat with a look of surprise and pain on his.

"Thanks for your help," said Willson. "I appreciated it." She walked away from the bureaucrat, not looking back and not waiting for a reply. She saw Frank Speer smirk and give her a thumb's-up from across the room.

When Willson and her colleagues reached the hallway outside the large conference room, they burst out laughing.

"That was the funniest thing I've seen in a long time," said Jenkins, his arm across Willson's shoulders. "That made listening to the crap from the podium worth the price of admission. You deserve a drink, Jenny."

"Yes, I do," said Willson, "that made me feel exceptionally good."

An hour later, the four sat at a table near the back of the Anejo Restaurant, on the southern edge of downtown Calgary. They were into their second mojitos when the restaurant's skull-emblazoned door flew open. They saw Jim Canon, Sue Browning, and Jenkins's fiancée, Kim Davidson, come through the door in a boisterous bunch. Making their way to the table, their friends noisily pulled chairs from adjacent tables and asked the waitress to bring a fresh pitcher of mojitos and three more glasses.

When the sweating pitcher of drinks arrived and all were served, Brad Jenkins took the lead, raising his glass in the air, pointing it toward Willson.

"A toast and a gift," he said. "Here's to the best investigator in Western Canada!" Glasses were raised and clinked around the table.

Jenkins then handed Willson a gift-wrapped cylinder. She opened it and lifted up a grey T-shirt. Emblazoned across the chest were the words *Where there's a Willson, there's a way!* The group broke into raucous applause.

"Hey, you guys, this means a lot to me," said Willson, a grin on her face, the T-shirt held against her chest. "I thought we should meet in one of Calgary's best Mexican restaurants to celebrate the fact that Luis Castillo will be in jail for a long time."

"*Salud!*" everyone in the group toasted, as glasses were raised again.

Willson grinned and said, "Most of you played a part in this, so my sincere thanks. I know we're all pleased that Castillo got what he deserved. Believe it or not, dinner is on me!"

This time, the responding toast was even more enthusiastic. The dark-haired waitress waited for the toasts to finish and then took their dinner orders. The celebration was on. Plates filled with tacos, chili rellennos, and red mole chicken were shared amongst the friends, washed down with sweet mojitos.

When they had finished the meal, Canon couldn't hold his curiosity any longer. "You've been keeping secrets, Jenny. It's finally time you told us how everything ended up in court!" he declared.

Willson, her cheeks glowing with the warmth of success, friends, and alcohol, laid out the story. "We got convictions in federal court against Eastman for the park hunts," she said. "We got him for the Banff elk, the Jasper sheep, and the Kootenay goat. The rifle we seized at his residence in the *second* search," she said, looking at Forsyth, "matched the elk and the goat."

"Did he get jail time?" asked Canon.

"Oh, yeah," said Willson, "the judge wasn't impressed with him. Eastman got fifteen years in federal prison, five for each of the three offences in the parks. And then there's the $500,000 fine. I understand he's had to sell his Ta Ta Creek property to pay that."

"Well," said Canon, "I don't feel sorry for the guy. He got what he deserved."

"And it was your picture of the sheep that finally tied up some of the loose ends, Jim," Willson said, raising her nearly empty glass. "So here's to the best wildlife photographer in all of Western Canada."

"Hey, why only Western Canada?" asked Canon with a smile. "But enough about me. What about on the B.C. side?"

"I'll let Brad tell you about that," said Willson.

"After he was thrashed by the feds," began Jenkins, "we almost felt sorry for Eastman. But not so sorry that we didn't throw the book at him, too." Jenkins explained that after plea bargaining, the guide ended up with an additional $100,000 fine and a ban from hunting in B.C. for ten years. He also lost his guiding territory. "And that's only after he gave us detailed statements outlining every hunt he was on with Castillo," Jenkins added.

He paused for dramatic effect. "Oh … and remember that massive grow op we found in the basement of Eastman's garage when our guys went back a second time?"

"Yeah," said Canon, "you told us about that."

"That was a surprise for all of us," said Willson, jumping in. "We had no idea Eastman was in *that* business, and then to find the rifle down there was icing on the cake." She paused to finish a mojito. "But that's another part of the story with Castillo. Turns out that Eastman was sending his pot south via the American's trucking company. Eastman finally admitted that was how they moved the elk and sheep trophies across the border. The drug charges against Eastman are working their way through the courts. But after all that, after all the crimes we've solved, we still don't know how they got the caribou head across the border."

"You guys are killing me here!" said Canon. "Do I have to drag it out of you, one bad guy at a time? What about the reason we're here tonight? Señor Castillo …?"

By this time, Willson had enough alcohol in her bloodstream that parts of the restaurant began to shimmy. "All I can shay … say," said Willson, "is that he's been charged or convicted of so many things that I've lost track. Illegal hunting, illegal transport of wildlife, illegal importing of wildlife into the U.S., drug trafficking, money laundering, illegal transport of firearms and counterfeit money, conspiracy…. The guy is screwed. And oh, yeah, money laundering. Or did I already say that? Whatever. We'll never see him up here again to face our charges. But who cares? I hope he rots in some hellhole of a U.S. prison."

"Did you figure out what happened to Charlie Clark?" asked Canon.

"That poor son of a bitch," Willson said. "I interviewed Eastman and Castillo a few times, and once they realized how much we had on them, the rats jumped from the sinking ship. Castillo told me that it was Eastman's nephew, a young guy named Steve Barber, who killed Charlie Clark. I assume he was the same guy who assaulted me that same day. Once they had the name, the RCMP matched some DNA found at Clark's trailer to the nephew, so he'll probably go to prison for that murder. And Castillo told me it was Eastman himself who killed Wendy Clark. Using cadaver dogs, police found her body buried on Eastman's property. Not smart at all. And in turn, Eastman told us that it was Castillo who ordered a hit on nine guys in a competing drug gang. The RCMP homicide investigators are still trying to sort that one out; they may request rendition. I mean extradition. So both Eastman and Castillo will likely be charged with murder, as if killing animals wasn't enough fucking fun for them."

Kim Davidson placed her arm around Willson's increasingly slumped form. "Celebration is over, princess," she said. "Time for bed. I'll call you a taxi."

CHAPTER 38

OCTOBER 8

Two weeks later, Jenny Willson cycled along the paved road on the west side of Lake Minnewanka. Despite the burning in her thighs from the aggressive climb up from Banff on the Minnewanka Loop Road, her mind still wandered, as it did every day, to the poaching case and to Eastman, Castillo, and the Clarks. When her cellphone rang, she pulled off the road to answer the call.

"Willson here."

"Jenny, it's Tracy Brown from Spokane. You're breathing hard. Did I catch you in the middle of someone?"

Willson laughed. "I wish. No, I'm on a bike ride. Had to get off my ass and out of the office for a while."

"I know what you mean. How's everything?"

"Good," said Willson, "although it's boring now that our case's done. What about you?"

"We went from that case to another so I've had no time to take that holiday you and I talked about. It'll happen. But hey, I wanted to call you with two pieces of news."

"What's up?" asked Willson.

"First," said Brown, "I found an opportunity for us. Do you want to go to Namibia?"

"Namibia?" said Willson. "What's in Namibia?"

"The Namibian government is looking for two wildlife officers from North America to train their anti-poaching squads on investigative techniques. It would be a temporary assignment, about six months. They're losing rhinos and elephants and other animals, and they don't have the capacity to successfully investigate after the fact. They're willing to pay the whole shot for us to come over. I thought about you and me right away. Interested?"

"Hell, yeah," said Willson. "Count me in. What do we need to do?"

"Well, it's a long application process and we have to get our bosses' support. I'll send you the details. But I wanted to first see if you were interested. We would have fun working together. I'll let them know that we'll get back to them."

"Thanks, Tracy," said Willson, smiling, "that would be great! I've always wanted to go to Africa, and what a way to do it. So what's the other piece of news?"

"Well, I also phoned to tell you that your friend Luis Castillo won't be spending any more time in prison."

"What! Did he make bail … or did he escape?"

"Neither," answered Brown. "He was killed yesterday. Whoever did it tried to make it look like a suicide."

"Wow." Willson was stunned. "So what happened?"

"In the midst of a disturbance in the cellblock, they found him hanging from a second-floor railing, a bedsheet around his neck. The guards are saying they tried to revive him but he was already gone. From the reports I've seen, there's no way in hell he could've done it himself."

"Holy shit," said Willson, "That's a friggin' surprise. Do they know who did it?"

"They don't yet," Brown said. "But he pissed off so many people that it could've been anyone. Whoever's responsible likely didn't want him spilling his guts during a trial, and now they've got their wish."

"Wow," said Willson again, pulling her helmet off her head to run her fingers through her sweat-dampened hair. "I don't know how to feel about this. On the one hand, it's almost a shame he was killed. Once I saw him in prison, saw how out of place and defeated and completely bewildered he was, I loved the fact that he'd have to spend the rest of his sad life in there. But on the other, maybe the arrogant prick got what was coming to him. Thanks, Tracy."

"No problem," said Brown, "I thought you should know. We'll talk soon." She disconnected the call.

Willson stood astride her bike, her helmet looped over the handlebar, the news of Castillo's murder bouncing in her brain. The American had been at the centre of her waking hours, of her dreams, for nearly two years. Now he was gone. There was a long list of things she'd hated about him. His arrogance, his disrespect for the law and for protected areas, his contempt for her and her colleagues, his belief that wild animals were nothing but trophies, his involvement in businesses on the wrong side of the law. She'd despised the man and everything he represented and she'd wanted him to spend his life rotting in a tiny cell.

She remembered her first view of the animal heads in his trophy room in Spokane — the elk, the sheep, the mountain goat, and others, their glassy, lifeless eyes staring at nothing. And then she thought of Castillo, hanging in the prison, on graphic display. A trophy of the worst kind. Disgraced. Humiliated on his last day on earth. For a fleeting moment, Willson toyed with an image of Castillo's head, prepared by a taxidermist, on the wall of the Banff warden office. A cautionary symbol, a warning to future park poachers. *Nope,* she thought, *there's probably some friggin' rule somewhere against that kind of thing.* Too bad. It would send a hell of a message.

Willson looked at the layers of tape on her handlebar, the ridges mirroring the growth rings on the sheep horns she'd seen hanging on Castillo's wall months earlier. *After all I've been through with this case,* she thought, *all the ups and downs and dead ends, all the distractions and deceit, maybe this is what real justice looks like. Maybe.*

Willson's cellphone rang again, breaking her internal debate. "Willson here."

"Jenny, it's Marilyn at the office. The chief wants to talk to you about a ski area. Can you get there right away?"

"I'm out for a bike ride," said Willson. "I'll be in right after lunch if that works for him. What's a ski area got to do with me?"

"I have no idea. I guess you'll find out when you get there. I'll tell him you'll be in." The dispatcher disconnected.

Willson raised her head to look at Mount Rundle, high above Banff. The patches of snow on the north side that had survived the long summer were grey and sad. A brisk wind pushed tails of clouds off the top ridge. Sensing movement out of the corner of her eye, her gaze shifted to a rocky bluff above the road. There, peering down at her, was a lone bighorn ram, its horns full curl. The animal lifted its nose to sniff the wind. Clouds of vapour drifted upward from its exhalations. Turning, it climbed higher up the bank and disappeared behind the bluff.

"You're welcome," said Willson, smiling.

ACKNOWLEDGEMENTS

From idea to published novel, *Full Curl*'s gestation can be measured in years, if not decades. Many people played a part in that process.

First, I want to acknowledge and thank Mike Gibeau, who, at one stop on his inspiring evolution from bull rider to Ph.D.-carrying conservation scientist, was my warden partner in Banff National Park. This is a work of fiction, but Mike will recognize the seeds of the story.

Angie Abdou, celebrated novelist and creative writing professor, persuaded me to dust off an abandoned manuscript, and with wise counsel and constant encouragement, helped me transform it into something worth sharing with readers. My sincere gratitude, Angie.

Thanks to those who read and commented on early versions of *Full Curl*: Karolina Ekman, Ingrid Dilschneider, ER Brown, my incredibly patient wife, Heather, and Dinah Forbes, the "doyen of Canadian crime fiction." And thanks to the many close friends and family (this means Court, Curt, Christy, Barrie, and my writer brother Bruce) who seemed excited about my writing and urged me to keep going.

The team at Dundurn Press has been a joy to work with. From my first contact with Carrie Gleason and Sheila Douglas, to Margaret Bryant, Michelle Melski, Maryan Gibson (a superb editor!), Cheryl Hawley, and Laura Boyle, they've all made my first foray into the mysterious world of publishing fiction an easier journey. And for their constant encouragement, a special thanks to Erin and the team at Lotus Books in Cranbrook, B.C.

My technical advisors for *Full Curl* were RCMP Sergeant Chris Newel and B.C. Conservation Officer Service Inspector Joe Caravetta, along with unnamed Canadian and American border officers who answered my strange questions despite, I'm sure, wondering what my *real* agenda was in asking. Despite their excellent advice, any errors in law or procedure are mine.

A special note of appreciation to award-wining writer Ian Hamilton (and to author Deryn Collier, for introducing us). Over a glass or two of Forty Creek whisky in a Toronto bar, Ian kindly offered advice that dramatically changed my perspective on this book. "Let your wife read it," he said, "… and why don't you write a series?" Both worked out very well.

Finally, I dedicate *Full Curl* to my father, Rod, and to my grandson Mason, my generational bookends who are in my thoughts every day. This one is for you.

🌐 dundurn.com   📷 dundurnpress

🐦 @dundurnpress   📌 dundurnpress

📘 dundurnpress   ✉️ info@dundurn.com

FIND US ON NETGALLEY & GOODREADS TOO!

🏛 DUNDURN

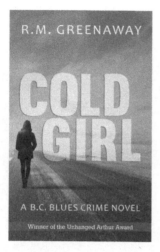

Cold Girl
R.M. Greenaway

*2014 Unhanged Arthur Award
for Best Unpublished First Crime
Novel — Winner*

It's too cold to go missing in northern B.C., as a mismatched team of investigators battle the clock while the disappearances add up.

A popular rockabilly singer has vanished in the snowbound Hazeltons of northern B.C. Lead RCMP investigator David Leith and his team work through the possibilities: has she been snatched by the so-called Pickup Killer, or does the answer lie here in the community, somewhere among her reticent fans and friends?

Leith has much to contend with: rough terrain and punishing weather, motel-living and wily witnesses. The local police force is tiny but headstrong, and one young constable seems more hindrance than help — until he wanders straight into the heart of the matter.

The urgency ramps up as one missing woman becomes two, the second barely a ghost passing through. Suspects multiply, but only at the bitter end does Leith discover who is the coldest girl of all.

Strange Things Done
Elle Wild

2015 Unhanged Arthur Award for Best Unpublished First Crime Novel — Winner
2014 Telegraph/Harvill Secker Crime Competition — Shortlisted
2014 Southwest Writers Annual Novel Writing Contest — Silver Winner
2014 Criminal Lines Crime-Writing Competition — Shortlisted
2014 Amazon Breakthrough Novel Award — Longlisted

A dark and suspenseful noir thriller, set in the Yukon.
As winter closes in and the roads snow over in Dawson City, Yukon, newly arrived journalist Jo Silver investigates the dubious suicide of a local politician and quickly discovers that not everything in the sleepy tourist town is what it seems. Before long, law enforcement begins treating the death as a possible murder and Jo is the prime suspect.

Strange Things Done is a top-notch thriller — a tense and stylish crime novel that explores the double themes of trust and betrayal.